Broken Together

k.s. ruff

BOOK FIVE IN THE BROKEN SERIES

Discover other titles by K.S. Ruff at ksruff.com

To my daughters,
Lexie and Madison,
Dream big, follow your hearts, and trust in God

Table of Contents

Acknowledgments

This book proved difficult to write, in part because of the competing demands on my time and in part because I didn't want this story to end. There were several people who saw me through, who served as my inspiration, and helped me finish this book.

I couldn't possibly thank my husband, Tobin, enough. He's put up with a considerable amount of neglect while I worked on this book, and he hasn't complained, not once. He's been invaluable as a military, security, and martial arts advisor. And there's a reason he served as my inspiration for Kadyn. He is truly that supportive and kind.

I want to thank my daughters, Lexie and Madison, for coaxing me off my computer so life didn't pass me by. I'd also like to thank my parents for their love and support. They are the ones who taught me to dream big, to follow my heart, and to trust in God, a central theme in my books.

I'd really like to thank those friends who inspired the characters in this book, those who are mentioned by name and those who preferred aliases. They have seen me through so many difficult experiences, some of which have been touched on in this and previous books. This world would be a far better place if everyone had friends like you.

I also want to thank my dear friend, Kari Kunkel-Anderson, for photographing and designing my book covers. I loved exploring Portugal with you!

I'd also like to thank my reviewers; Amy Goodyear, Erica Allder, Gloria Berini, Faddwa Brubaker, Christina Kaplan, and Cenia Miller. Thanks for all your wonderful advice. A special thanks to my phenomenal editors, Heidi Lieu and Shira Ben-Zion, for helping me improve the book.

I'd like to thank my friend, TJ Crane, for his copyright advice. A huge thanks to Phil Hagen for guiding me through the process of getting a small business up and running. I'd also like to thank Dave Burris for designing a website that still takes my breath away!

I'd also like to thank those fans who have regularly inquired about my progress on this book. Truly, you kept me motivated!

Finally, I'd like to give a shout out to my dogs, Khiyara and Kovu, for reminding me that Kri's life wouldn't be complete without another Shih Tzu. Kovu, you took a piece of me with you when you were called home earlier this week. I will always picture you with that racquetball in your mouth. Thank you for loving me so unconditionally.

Chapter 1 – Riptide

Sunlight spilled across my face. I stretched my arms over my head. Bracing my palms against the headboard, I lengthened my torso in a long, luxurious stretch that would have made even the most self-indulgent cat jealous. *Saturday,* I thought with a deeply contented smile. *How I adore Saturdays.* Finals were over. *Three semesters down. One to go.* My heart and head were doing the happy dance.

I reached for Rafael. My eyes popped open when I felt the cold mattress. Sitting up, I raked my hand through my hair and craned my ears. The house was quiet; no shower running, no dishes clanging, and no coffee percolating. I frowned. "Rafael?"

The silence was deafening. I flung the covers aside and stepped out of bed before spotting the envelope propped against Rafael's pillow. *Kristine* was scrawled across the envelope in Rafael's elegantly slanted script. I wracked my brain trying to discern whether I'd missed some important anniversary or holiday. A big, fat nothing came to mind.

"Huh."

I climbed back onto the bed, grabbed the envelope, and gently loosened the seal. I coaxed a charcoal gray notecard from the envelope. *Love* was embossed in lowercase letters across the bottom right hand corner in a dark red cursive font. Smiling, I opened the card.

> *It seems only fitting that this adventure would begin in the place we first made love. Because the future is spun from the past, look for me in the place we made love…last.*

I stared dumbfounded at the note. "What are you up to?" I whispered. The last place we'd made love was on the desk in the library. Rafael had been prowling around the library while waiting for me to finish my final paper. He swept everything but the laptop aside. He set the laptop on the chair before taking me ten ways to heaven on the desk.

I tucked the notecard back inside the envelope and carted it off to the bathroom so I could brush my teeth and comb my hair before meeting Rafael in the library. The house was still eerily quiet, but Rafael could move like a ninja when he was trying to be stealthy. He'd crept up behind me without making a sound more times than I cared to count.

I traded my silk sleep shorts for a pair of sweats, tugged a pair of socks on, and pulled a hoodie over my camisole before heading downstairs. The townhouse felt empty and cold, which wasn't terribly surprising since we were expecting snow.

I crept down the stairs, intending to prove just how quiet *I* could move, but the effort proved futile. Rafael wasn't in the library. Another envelope bearing my name was propped against my laptop. I stared at the desk. When did he clean up and replace everything on the desk? I tapped the spacebar and glanced at the clock on the laptop. It was only eight o'clock.

I plucked the envelope off the computer. The same charcoal gray notecard, displaying the word "love," was tucked inside. I quickly read the note.

> *I'm afraid you have a longer journey in store. Look in the place we first professed our love. You'll find that and so much more.*

I took a step toward the door, then paused. Where were we when we first confessed our love? I sifted through several intimate moments, each one brimming with heartfelt words. "Yes, but when was the *first* time?" I asked aloud. My eyes suddenly widened. Rafael had professed his love in the sunroom the morning after we first made love. When I awoke that morning, Rafael was in the kitchen cooking breakfast for me. We ate in the sunroom. He told me he loved me and asked for a chance to prove it. He'd proven it every minute of every day over the past nine months.

I started walking, then stopped again. Where were we when I first professed my love? My laughter echoed in the foyer when it struck me. I first professed my love in the sunroom after baking scones for Rafael. I'd deemed him my dark angel before inadvertently confessing my love. I shook my head in disbelief. I hadn't realized that we'd taken that monumental step at two different points in time but in the very same location. I hurried toward the sunroom.

I smiled when I found another envelope propped against a travel mug filled with coffee. A chocolate croissant lay nestled inside a white pastry bag next to the coffee on the wrought iron table. I sampled the croissant and the coffee before sinking into one of the chairs. I was fairly certain Rafael wasn't inside the house. If he'd been inside the townhouse, he would have poured the coffee into a coffee cup, not a travel mug. He'd poured it into a travel mug so it would stay hot for a longer period of time. There was no telling how long he'd been gone, where he'd gone, or what he was up to.

I took another bite out of the croissant before opening the envelope.

> *Without further ado, linger in the place where my hands linger over you.*

Desire spun through me the second I read the note. I gathered up the notecards, the travel mug, and the croissant and headed back upstairs. Rafael's hands linger over my body in the shower, and he prefers my shower over his because it has a marble bench which allows him to get creative when we make love under those twelve pulsing jets.

I polished off the croissant, took a few sips of coffee, and walked into the bathroom. Rafael told me to linger in the shower. Why? "Am I supposed to take a shower?"

Silence was my only answer.

I set the coffee down, removed the envelope from the bench inside the shower, and peeled my clothes off before turning all twelve jets on. This little jaunt down memory lane had left me longing for Rafael in the worst possible way. I suspected that was the whole point of this exercise. I'd linger just long enough to look and feel presentable for whatever he had in store for me.

I didn't open the fourth envelope until I had showered, dressed, dried my hair, and applied a bit of makeup. I was wearing fitted jeans, a long black sweater, and black boots. My body was humming from the chocolate and the coffee by the time I sat on the bed to open the envelope.

I chose you long before you chose me. Where were we when you finally chose me?

I chuckled softly. I'd never forget the look on Rafael's face when I arrived at his house and announced I was no longer dating Kadyn. Rafael had wadded up a half-eaten piece of pizza, thrown it toward the garbage can, and missed. I laughed until I got a good look at him. He looked every bit the predator when he closed the distance between us. "This changes everything," he growled huskily. He pulled me against his chest. Hard. "No more holding back, Kristine. I want *everything*... every single part of you."

My pulse quickened, both then and now. "I want you to own every part of me," I'd answered recklessly. A delicious shiver slid down my spine. "I still do," I whispered. I grabbed my keys and walked next door to Rafael's townhouse.

Sure enough, there was another envelope propped against the banister in the foyer. I broke the seal.

Always one to surprise, search the place where I discovered your fantasies rival even mine.

I bounded up the stairs. Rafael had to be referring to his weight room. While training me in self-defense, he'd pinned me against the mirrored wall and advised me to do the unexpected if I couldn't hit my assailant's shin, groin, neck, or eyes. I'd grabbed him by the shirt, kissed him long and hard, and confessed I'd been fantasizing about having sex against the mirrored wall. Rafael was so shocked, he released me. I ran, hell bent on escaping. Rafael tackled me to the floor, peeled our clothes off in the hallway, and then hauled me back to the weight room where we proceeded to have sex against that very same wall.

I was out of breath by the time I reached the weight room. "*Yes!*" I snatched the envelope he'd taped against the mirrored wall.

Well played, my love. Now the place where I would hold and keep you for all eternity.

I snorted softly. "Either I know you too well or you're purposely making this easy for me." I walked to Rafael's bedroom. He'd threatened to chain me to his bed for all eternity countless times. I loved the look on his face when he tossed me onto his bed. His expression suggested he'd won a much coveted prize, as if it were unfathomable that I was lying in *his* bed, and he looked fiercely determined to keep me there. That look did unspeakable things to me. There was just something about a man, his woman, and his bed.

I kicked my boots off, crawled onto Rafael's bed, grabbed the envelope, and burrowed beneath the duvet. I loved Rafael's bed, and it wasn't just the cedar and clove scented cologne lingering on his bed linens. There was nothing floral or feminine about this bed. The mattress, the bedding, the colors, and the smell were all inherently male. Rafael's bed was one of my favorite places to be. I could easily remain here for all eternity.

I set the other cards aside so I could open the envelope. The envelope held the same charcoal gray notecard with "love" embossed in a crimson font across the bottom right hand side. I could end this game, remain in his bed, and he'd find me eventually. The idea was tempting until I opened the card.

Courage and strength, my dear. Seek the place where I made my intentions clear.

I bolted upright. My heart beat so frantically I could hear nothing beyond my thunderous pulse. Suddenly, I knew what he was up to. "No," I whispered. I fell abruptly from the bed. Somehow the duvet had gotten tangled around my legs. I jumped to my feet after wrestling with the duvet. *"Marriage,"* I gasped.

Rafael's voice echoed in my mind. *"I'm not dating you to pass the time. I have every intention of marrying you, Kristine."*

I swallowed forcefully. "This is…" Tears pricked my eyes. "Rafael's *proposing.*" I paced blindly across his bedroom. "Oh my God. He's proposing."

I sank to my knees when the room tilted. "I can… *we can*…" I forced myself to breathe. "We're really going to do this." I pressed my hands against my chest. My heart was beating wildly, as if demanding… *him.*

I stumbled toward the bed, straightened the duvet, pulled my boots back on, and gathered up the cards. Each was tucked securely in its own envelope. I took a deep breath… then another… and another. "I want this," I confessed to the empty room. "I want to marry Rafael."

I glanced uncertainly at the envelopes. Rafael had made his intentions clear in nearly every room of both our townhomes… at Reagan National Airport… in Delaware… in Saint Tropez… in Montana… in New York… in

Mexico… and in Texas. He'd made his intentions clear at every possible turn. So, where was I supposed to go?

I sat on the edge of his bed for the longest time, mulling over the possibilities. Suddenly, it struck me. Rafael had never been more emphatic about his intentions than when I drove to Harper's Ferry. I'd felt the determination behind those words so forcefully I'd genuinely feared I was going to wreck his car. "The Enzo."

I ran to the kitchen, grabbed his keys from the hook, and bolted down the staircase leading into his garage. The envelope was sitting inside the Enzo. I quickly scanned the note.

You know how I long to see you pregnant with my child, but do you recall where we first spoke of having children?

I lowered the door to the Enzo. Fear, desire, and an exquisite yet painful yearning were now spiraling within me. I could barely breathe. I returned his keys to the hook and locked the front door when I stepped outside.

I walked down the front steps, cut across the trail, and strode across the grass. A large rock had been strategically placed in the spot where Rafael and I played twenty questions while enjoying a picnic dinner and wine along the Potomac River. He didn't play that game fairly. He asked only the most important questions, even after I insisted he work up to the more difficult ones. That shouldn't have surprised me. Rafael warned me he wouldn't play fair once I gave him a chance to win my heart.

I dropped onto my knees and stared at the stone. "*I won't play fair, Kristine. Once I'm in, I'm all in. You give me this chance, and*

I won't walk away... not ever," Rafael warned. My hand trembled as I reached for the stone. I thought about everything we'd been through since Rafael had spoken those words... my fraternizing with the Russian mafia, being held captive by the SVR, Michael's death, my unspoken desire to join him in death, the shoot-out between the drug cartels, Kadyn's abduction, and the favor I now owed Maxim. Rafael hadn't wavered from that position... although he was certainly justified in doing so. He'd remained fiercely devoted, despite all of the seemingly insurmountable obstacles. I lifted the stone and freed the envelope.

I hugged my knees to my chest and peered at the Potomac River before reading the note.

> *You know how much I love you, but do you know where I last spoke those three most coveted words?*

"In the kitchen, when we were cooking dinner." I pushed back onto my feet and walked the short distance to my house. There was an envelope lying on the counter next to the stove.

> *Grab your coat, keys, and purse, and seek the place where you last spoke those very same words.*

I grabbed my heavy winter coat, pocketed my keys, and retrieved my purse. I shoved all the envelopes I'd acquired thus far into my purse before tromping down the stairs to my garage. I told Rafael I loved him just before climbing into my Jeep yesterday morning. We were saying our goodbyes before driving to work.

The envelope was sitting on the driver's seat. I shoved the key into the ignition and tapped the garage door opener so I could warm the Jeep while reading the note. Between the coat, the keys, and purse, I was certain this note would lead me away from the house.

If you want me, you'll ask for me in the place where we enjoyed our last date.

I slid the card back inside the envelope, shoved it inside my purse, fastened my seatbelt, and eased out of the garage. Within minutes, I was pulling into a parking garage just down the street from La Madeleine, the French café where we ate breakfast Sunday morning. I walked the short distance to the restaurant. The place was packed. I squeezed through the crowd and scanned the tables, but I didn't see Rafael.

The gentleman standing behind the pastry counter waved me over. "Are you Ms. Stone?"

"Yes," I replied uncertainly. I wasn't sure how he knew me.

"This is for you." He handed me an envelope, a pastry bag, and an eco-friendly cup.

"What's in the cup?" He'd obviously just made the drink. Steam was shimmying out of a small hole in the lid. I scanned the crowd again. The man couldn't have timed that drink more perfectly. Was Rafael watching me?

"A double shot café latte with cinnamon on top." His eyes sparkled, like he knew some tantalizing piece of information.

I peeked inside the bag. "Another chocolate croissant?" I laughed. "I never could eat just one." I set the coffee and pastry bag on the counter so I could retrieve my wallet.

"That's already been paid for." He smiled. "Aren't you going to read the card?"

"Oh!" One decadent cup of coffee would cause me to forget all about the note. I peeled open the envelope.

You're nearly there, love. Enjoy the coffee and croissant, then ask for me in the restaurant where we enjoyed our first date... in the United States.

I laughed. Rafael had long insisted our first date was at a café on the Champs-Élysées in Paris, before I committed myself to Michael. Hence, the clarification "in the United States."

"Where are you off to next?" the man asked.

"Komi." I stashed the envelope inside my purse before grabbing the coffee and croissant. "Thank you."

"You must return and tell me the whole story," he insisted, "on a slow day!"

"Will do." I squeezed outside and hurried toward the garage.

Thirty minutes later, I was idling in front of Komi while weighing my options. I was fairly certain the restaurant wasn't open at ten-thirty in the morning. With my bottom lip caught securely between my teeth, I turned the hazard lights on and hopped out of the Jeep. The door to the restaurant opened before I reached the top of the stairs. "Ms. Stone?"

I smiled sheepishly. "Yes."

The man bowed as he presented the envelope. "Mr. Garcia left this for you. Please come back and visit us again soon."

My cheeks heated. "Thank you. I'm sure we'll see you soon." I loved Komi with their synchronized waiters, top secret tasting menu, and decadent desserts. I clambered back down the stairs and climbed into my Jeep. There were some signs indicating that I should not be idling there, so I broke the seal on the envelope and quickly read Rafael's note.

Take a chance... and journey to the place where we first danced.

"Jaleo's," I recalled with a smile. "We danced at my thirtieth birthday party." I downed the remaining dregs of coffee before easing into traffic. Rafael had thrown me a surprise birthday party. He'd invited several colleagues and friends, but Kadyn and my cousin, Lexie, topped the list. Rafael's efforts to secure their presence brought tears to my eyes. Hands down, that was the best birthday present anyone had ever given me.

Although I couldn't for the life of me picture Rafael proposing at Jaleo's, I was praying it was my final destination. My breath caught when my assumptions caught up with me. I slammed on the brakes. Maybe this wasn't a proposal. Maybe this was simply a trip down memory lane... a fun and romantic way to spend the day. "Well, if you don't propose, then I will," I announced decidedly.

The car behind me honked. I resumed driving, but I was trembling violently. Should I stop and buy a ring? I twisted and craned my neck as I began searching for jewelry stores. My heart skipped a few more beats. I couldn't just run into the nearest jewelry store and purchase a ring. It would take days maybe even weeks of prowling through stores to find the perfect ring.

I was thoroughly wrecked by the time I walked into Jaleo's. I felt anxious and jittery... nervous, scared, excited, hopeful, vulnerable, and eager all at once. I hadn't a clue how you could pack so many emotions into a single moment, but I felt every single one, along with a few I couldn't even begin to identify.

"Ms. Stone?" a young woman asked.

I shook my head while attempting to clear my thoughts. Belatedly, I realized my mistake. "I'm sorry. I didn't mean to shake my head 'no.' I mean 'yes,' I'm Kristine Stone."

The woman eyed me worriedly. "Would you like to sit down? You look a little shaky."

Gratefully, I collapsed onto the nearest chair. "May I have a drink of water?" I bolted out of the chair when she turned to retrieve the drink. "No. Wait. Is Rafael Garcia here?"

She smiled. She had a beautiful smile that reached all the way into her eyes. "No, but he asked me to give this to you." She pulled an envelope from the black apron she had tied around her slender waist.

The woman and the envelope glistened through my tears.

"Are you okay?" She helped me back onto the chair. A second employee handed me a glass of water.

"I'm just feeling emotional." I drank the entire glass of water before opening the envelope.

> *One final request, love. Help me roll back time. Return to the place I first made you smile, so I may reveal myself... this time.*

A strangled sob escaped my chest. I slid the card back inside the envelope and tucked it alongside the other envelopes inside my purse. "Thank you for the water." I pressed a wad of money into the woman's hand before walking out the door. I knew exactly where I had to go.

I parked the Jeep inside Union Station and walked to the park in front of the Senate Hart Building. I stopped just short of the park bench I'd been seeking. Another envelope was sitting on the bench. "No," I groaned. I turned in a circle as I surveyed the park. I'd been expecting Rafael.

There weren't many people lingering in the park, but quite a few staffers were walking toward Union Station for lunch. I picked up the envelope before sinking onto the bench. "I should know where I'm going before I indulge in a good cry," I lamented under my breath.

I opened the envelope. I stared at the inside of the card. "It's blank," I objected. "Why would it be blank?"

I pondered that question for quite some time. When no easy answers came to mind, I sifted through my memories until I reached the day Rafael saw me crying on the park bench. I'd walked outside to eat lunch, so I could escape the noise and the insanity surrounding the Senate. It was a crisp fall day... a day that pre-dated Kadyn, Justin's abduction, Michael whisking me off to Paris, Maxim, and Ukraine. At that time, there was only me... and Cade... and the Senate. I was on the verge of meeting Kadyn, I didn't know that Michael asked Rafael to watch over me, and I was terribly homesick.

I pulled my knees to my chest. The twists and turns that carved my life were filled with heartache and pain, and yet I questioned whether I would change a single moment. Part of me longed to roll back time to this very moment in time, when Rafael discovered me crying on this park bench. The other part of me insisted on cherishing the good that grew from every difficult experience transpiring *after* that moment in time.

I brushed away my tears so I could study the card. I ran

my finger along the heavily embossed crimson font that formed the word "love" on the front of the note card. I opened the card and studied the inside. Was the blank interior supposed to symbolize something? Rafael was poetic. Maybe this was meant to symbolize a blank page at the end of an unfinished book, a page where the author could take the story in a thousand different directions, add a plot twist, or change the ending.

The card slipped from my fingers. I knelt to pick it up, then froze. There was a question mark penned on the back of the card. An icy breeze ruffled my hair. I grabbed the card before it could blow away.

I sat on the ground while staring at the question mark. A million questions danced along the outskirts of my mind. I reached for the stack of envelopes I'd stashed inside my purse. I removed one of the cards and slowly turned it over. There was an "M" written in cursive on the back. My heart leapt. I scrambled onto my knees and tore through another envelope... then another... and another... until the back of every single card lay facing me on the ground. The back of each card held a single letter. In addition to the question mark, there were two M's, two L's, two R's, two Y's, a W, A, E, I, O, and U.

A shadow fell over me when I began rearranging the cards.

My eyes snagged on a pair of black boots... traveled up black jeans... skimmed a black coat hiding broad shoulders and a trim waist... then locked on Rafael's devastatingly handsome face. At six foot three, with long dark hair, and a body carved from stone; "Dark Angel" was the only term that could possibly describe him.

Rafael drew me to my feet. Without speaking a single

word, he sat me on the park bench. He handed me a long-stemmed rose, then knelt at my feet.

I couldn't speak.

Grasping my hands in his, Rafael began to sing Adele's "Make You Feel My Love," the same song he'd asked the young man to sing two years ago when he saw me crying on the park bench.

Rafael's rich, velvety tone both soothed and shredded my heart. Tears warmed my cheeks. His raw and unaccompanied rendition of the song would have made even the bitterest soul weep.

Rafael's feelings were so in tune with the lyrics that his voice broke on the very last word... *love*.

Heaven and earth remained spellbound while that word lay claim to the universe.

Finally, Rafael spoke. "Kristine, you unknowingly claimed my heart the day you wept in this park. I have longed for your heart ever since. Out of respect for my brother, I tried not to love you, but my heart would not be swayed. I loved you more with each passing day. By the time I pulled you into that safe room, it was too late. Right or wrong, I fell hopelessly in love with you."

Rafael took a deep breath. "I cannot promise you an easy or carefree life, but I can promise you that I will love and cherish you every second of every day that there is blood coursing through my veins. I give you my heart, asking only that you do the same." He paused briefly to arrange the cards at my feet.

WILL YOU MARRY ME?

Rafael removed a black velvet box from his coat pocket.

He opened the lid before peering up at me. "Kristine Annabelle Stone, will you marry me?"

Tears streamed down my face. "Yes. Yes, Rafael, I will marry you!" I threw my arms around his neck and kissed him with everything I had. He snapped the box shut and cushioned the blow as we tumbled to the ground. Rafael tucked me beneath him and resumed kissing me despite the applause and laughter that surrounded us. He continued kissing me until everyone walked away.

* * * * *

We lie; hands clasped, eyes sparkling, and cheeks flushed; facing one another in the crisp, cold grass. I hadn't a clue how much time had passed. "Will you run away with me?" Rafael finally asked.

My eyes widened. "Run away? Where?"

He studied my expression closely. "Does the 'where' matter?"

My heart skipped a few beats. "No," I conceded. "How long will we be gone?" I was thinking of work.

A single eyebrow rose. "Does *that* matter?"

A nervous giggle escaped my lips. "Evidently not."

"Will you run away with me?" he repeated.

I grinned. "I told you some time ago… you're the only dream that matters. So, yes. Where you go, I go. If need be, I'll follow you to the ends of the earth, to heaven, and hell, and back."

A look of complete and utter satisfaction lay claim to his face. He stood and pulled me onto the bench. "There is this small matter of the ring."

I fidgeted nervously. It wasn't so much the ring. It was

what that ring symbolized. Rafael's proposal and our engagement were about to become undeniably real.

Rafael lifted my right hand. His eyes darkened when they settled on Maxim's ring. "As is true for the people of Ukraine, the Portuguese place their engagement rings on the right hand."

I sucked in a sharp breath. "Rafael, I didn't know. When Maxim placed this ring on my finger, I didn't know that." I thought it was okay, that somehow it symbolized less, if the ring was on my right hand. I swallowed nervously. "Americans wear engagement rings on their left hands." I was now thoroughly regretting my decision to accept Maxim's ring. He had deemed it a promise ring, not an engagement ring. He'd released me from that promise, but I continued to wear the ring because it reminded me of all I'd endured and lost in Ukraine.

Rafael's eyes met mine. "Regardless, my wife will not wear another man's ring." His eyes remained locked on mine while he removed Maxim's ring.

I couldn't possibly object. Maxim had rubbed that ring in Rafael's face at Cenia's wedding reception. Clearly, there was a great deal of symbolism involved for Rafael and for Maxim. I forced myself to breathe when Rafael pocketed Maxim's ring.

Rafael opened the black velvet box. A diamond ring glittered brilliantly against the black backdrop.

My breath caught. Rafael was presenting me with the most exquisite ring I'd ever seen. The platinum and diamond ring had been sculpted in such a way that the center stone appeared to be unfolding like a rose. Two smaller stones flanked the center stone, like leaves. Diamond braids formed the band along the top of the ring. Still more diamonds were secreted into a breathtaking scroll-like display along either side of the ring. The center stone was quite large, and there were more accent diamonds in the melee than I could possibly count. It was as if I'd stumbled upon an elegant diamond encrusted garden. "It's beautiful," I breathed.

Rafael held the ring over the tip of my right ring finger. "I'm going to repeat the question, Kristine. Will you accept me as your husband? Choose me above all others? Marry me and become my wife?"

I gazed deep into his eyes. "Yes, Rafael. I will marry you... honor, love, and cherish you every minute of every day for the rest of my life."

The ring slid securely into place.

Chapter 2 – Believe

I gaped at the sleek white jet. "You bought this?"

Rafael laughed. "At your request."

I turned sharply. "What?"

He placed his hand on the small of my back as we neared the metal stairs leading into the aircraft. "At Reagan National Airport, you said, and I quote, '*Win the property owners over, purchase the jet, and meet me in McAllen.*'"

I stared at him incredulously. "I was joking."

He shrugged. "It seemed like a good idea at the time."

I carefully climbed the stairs. "Did you buy this in Paris?" Rafael hadn't breathed a word about the jet when he joined me in Mexico or during the six weeks that had passed since Cenia's wedding.

Rafael smiled. "I purchased the jet while I was in Paris, ordered a few modifications, and had it delivered here." He was climbing the stairs directly behind me.

"Ms. Stone, Mr. Garcia," the flight attendant greeted warmly. "Welcome aboard."

The pilot stepped out of the cockpit. "Mr. Garcia. It's a

pleasure to meet you. I'd like you to meet my co-pilot, Robin Tatman. We just completed the pre-flight inspection and checked the weather. You picked a perfect day to fly. We may hit a few bumps during the climb out, but it should be smooth en route. We'll have about a hundred knot tail wind, which should shorten the time." He glanced adoringly at the flight attendant. "If there is anything we can do to make the flight more comfortable, please let me or my wife, Kari, know."

Rafael shook the pilot's hand. "Captain Anderson, you and your wife came highly recommended." He shook Kari's hand before greeting the co-pilot. "Ms. Tatman, it's a pleasure to meet you. Thanks for assisting Captain Anderson."

I tried to exchange pleasantries with the flight crew, but I was rendered speechless by the décor inside the jet. A sleek leather U-shaped couch cradled a deep mahogany table with an inlaid chess board. Three plush leather chairs flanked each table on either side of the couch. The furniture had a contemporary feel. The upholstery was white with dark brown trim. Recessed lighting glowed softly along white walls, just above the windows and from within the tray ceiling. As if that wasn't impressive enough, the couch faced a large contemporary gas fireplace, framed on all four sides with the same dark mahogany wood. The fire was already lit and glowing brightly from within. "There's... there's..."

"A fireplace?" Rafael finished as he stepped behind me. He pulled me flush against his chest. His chin rested briefly on top of my head, but he shifted so he could press his lips to my ear. "That fireplace extends into the room on the other side of that wall. Would you like to see it?"

My breath rushed out all at once. "You didn't."

A laugh rumbled from deep within his chest. The

vibration tickled my spine, which was still pressed to his chest. "Didn't what?"

I spun in his arms. "You did *not* buy a jet with a private bedroom."

Rafael locked his arms around me as he stepped forward, forcing me to walk backwards while he made his way toward the back of the jet. He snagged a bottle of wine, a corkscrew, and two wine glasses from the table when we walked by, pressing them all against my back. "Why don't you see for yourself?"

"We'll be departing in twenty minutes," Kari warned. She coughed, trying to stifle a laugh.

"We'll be seated by then," Rafael replied.

My legs nearly buckled when I caught sight of the bedroom. A queen sized bed dominated the room. A dresser sat beneath the windows on the left, but there was still enough room to walk around the bed. The dresser and the bed were carved from the same dark mahogany wood that framed the fireplace, which was, as Rafael promised, visible from the bed. Glass shelves and lights were tucked inside the headboard. A white suede duvet covered the bed. White and brown pillows lined the headboard, and a plush, dark chocolate blanket lay at the foot of the bed. "This bedroom is... incredible."

"I'm glad you like it." Rafael pulled the cork out of the Chianti and handed me a glass of wine. "Would you like to see the bathroom before we depart?"

I took a sip of wine while running my fingers along the soft duvet. "Yes, please."

Rafael opened a door to the right of the bed. The white door blended in with the wall, so I was surprised to see him open it. He waved me inside.

Had the lid been open, my jaw would have fallen inside the toilet. The bathroom held a mahogany vanity with a dark brown, black, and bronze marble countertop. A brushed bronze faucet and clear glass bowl rested beneath a mahogany mirror. A brown hatbox toilet sat beside the vanity. Both faced a good-sized shower, tiled in the same marble as the floor and the vanity. The shower boasted six jets and a rainfall showerhead.

Rafael stepped inside the bathroom. "Do you think we'll both fit in that shower?"

"I think we can make it work," I replied with a wry smile. I slowly turned around. "This aircraft is beautiful... beyond beautiful."

He set our wine glasses on the vanity before pulling me into his arms. "I'm so glad you like it. I was worried it was a little over the top."

I practically snorted. "Oh, it's over the top... but it's also elegant and quietly understated... like you."

"I'm elegant?" Rafael chuckled.

I pulled the leather band from his hair, slipped it over my wrist and buried my hands in the dark, silky strands. "We're going to have so much fun making love on this airplane."

He grinned. "So it doesn't matter where we're going."

I pressed my body against his. "This jet could circle DC or sit on the tarmac for all I care."

Rafael's arms tightened around me. He lowered his head and brushed his lips slowly... softly... teasingly... against mine. His hand wound through my hair, tugging my head back as his lips captured my mouth in a dominating kiss. His tongue delved deep inside, stroking... demanding... branding me from the inside out. My nipples hardened, pleading for his attention, while heat pooled between my legs.

We both groaned when Captain Anderson's voice sounded over the intercom. "Cabin crew, please prepare for departure."

"Soon," Rafael promised. His husky tone promised sinful things. We grabbed the wine and returned to the main cabin.

Two bottles of sparkling mineral water and a platter filled with grapes, sliced pears, sliced baguette, and a variety of meats and cheeses were sitting on the table. Neither of us had eaten lunch, so I dropped into one of the plush leather chairs flanking the table. "Oh! This seat is comfortable."

Rafael fastened my seatbelt. He dropped a quick kiss on my lips before taking his seat. "Good. We've a long flight ahead."

The flight attendant stepped out of the galley and approached the table. "I have to remain in my seat until we reach cruising altitude. After that, I'll be available for anything you might need. I'm sure you would prefer some privacy, so I'll remain in the galley while you're in the main cabin. I'll check on you periodically, but please don't hesitate to call me if you need anything."

Rafael nodded. "Thanks, Kari."

She topped off our wine and set the bottle inside a wine bucket that was built into the wall next to the table. She waved toward the food. "This should tide you over until we level off. When would you prefer the remaining courses?"

Rafael glanced at me.

"Two maybe three hours?" Frankly, I was more interested in the bed.

Rafael smiled, as if reading my mind. "We plan to retire to the bedroom once the plane has leveled off. May I call you when we're ready for dinner?"

"Of course. There's a call button next to the bed." The plane began to back away from the terminal. Kari walked to the front of the jet. "Enjoy the flight." She disappeared into the galley.

Rafael raised his wine glass. "To my future wife."

I tapped my glass against his. "To my future husband." I studied him over the top of my wine glass. He had refused to tell me where we were going, claimed we didn't need luggage, and drove straight to the airport in his SUV. He asked Jase to drive my Jeep back home. He also cleared my absence with Paul. Seeds for Peace was closed between Christmas Eve and New Year's Day, so we could be gone for two weeks and I'd only miss five days of work. As far as my schedule went, he couldn't have timed this trip more perfectly.

The jet picked up speed. I took another sip of wine as the nose of the aircraft lifted. Where to begin with my inquiry? "How long is our flight?"

Rafael stacked meat and cheese on top of a slice of bread. "Twelve and a half hours, which includes a two hour layover while we refuel the jet." He popped the sandwich into his mouth.

My eyes widened. "Twelve and a half hours? Clearly, we're sleeping on the plane."

He nodded. "We should arrive at our final destination around seven-thirty tomorrow morning… their time, not ours."

I paired a piece of bread with some cheese. I still couldn't believe Rafael sang to me. "You have such a beautiful voice. How is it I've never heard you sing?"

"'Make you Feel My Love' is the only song I can sing. I was going to search for the man who sang that song to you the first time, but I didn't want you gazing into his eyes while

I was proposing. I decided to take singing lessons. I started about three months ago, so I could sing the song myself." A boyish grin lit his handsome face.

I shook my head in disbelief. "You have got to be the most romantic man to have ever walked the planet." I tasted the pear and another piece of cheese.

"I'm glad you think so." Rafael smiled. "Shall we set a wedding date?"

"Sure." I glanced out the window. The jet was already beginning to level off. "When would you like to be married?"

"Tomorrow." He looked... serious.

My eyebrows shot up. "Tomorrow? Is that even possible?"

He laughed. "Anything is possible."

My curiosity piqued. "What type of wedding would you like to have? Aren't there people you'd like to invite?"

Rafael looked thoughtful. "Honestly? No."

The man had a point. Aside from the minister or priest and the two requisite witnesses, we were the only two people who really had to be there. Large wedding ceremonies could be stressful. They seldom focused on the bride and groom. Besides, I had a good-sized family to include, while Rafael had no family to speak of. Having my family present could make Rafael feel the absence of his parents and brother even more. I reached for his hand. "I have to admit, the thought that our wedding would be focused solely on our vows, our relationship, and our marriage is appealing." I truly didn't feel the need for a large wedding.

His eyes softened.

A soft "ding" sounded before the captain made his announcement. "We've reached cruising altitude. The flight attendant and passengers are now free to move about the cabin."

We exchanged smiles.

"The bedroom?" I bit my bottom lip.

Rafael unfastened his seatbelt and mine. He grabbed the food and bottled water while I finished my wine.

"About that date," I murmured. "Can we wait until after I graduate in May? Even if we have a small, intimate wedding, I'd rather not juggle all the last minute preparations against work and school."

Rafael offered me his elbow since his hands were full. "If we were married tomorrow, there would be no juggling."

"I hate to be the bearer of bad news, but there's paperwork involved." We walked back to the bedroom.

Rafael set the appetizers and bottled water on top of the dresser. "Paperwork? What kind of paperwork?" He began to undress.

I fidgeted nervously. "Well, if I remember correctly, we'll need our birth certificates. I'll probably need to provide my divorce decree. We'll need baptismal records and my annulment paperwork if you want to be married by a priest." Suddenly, I felt like damaged goods. I took a deep breath and continued. "The Catholic Church requires engaged couples to attend a marriage preparation course in advance of the wedding. Some states require blood tests, and we have to fill out an application for a marriage license."

Rafael looked thoughtful. "Are you Catholic?"

I shook my head. "Lutheran."

He pulled the sweater over my head. "But you were married in the Catholic Church when you were married to your first husband?"

My cheeks heated. "Yes."

Rafael fingered my bra before unbuttoning my jeans.

"And you'd be willing to go through all that again for me?"

"Yes," I breathed. "I... I presume you're Catholic?" I couldn't believe we hadn't discussed our religious affiliations before now. I'd presumed Rafael was Catholic simply because Michael was. I stepped out of my jeans when they slid to the floor.

Rafael nodded. He looked... conflicted.

I wrapped my arms around his neck so I could feel him and not my tainted past. "I would prefer our marriage was blessed."

His eyes locked on mine. "Me too."

I ran my fingers along the chiseled planes that shaped his broad shoulders as he backed me toward the bed. "Then perhaps we should set a wedding date in June or July and meet with a priest when we return home."

Rafael shook his head. "I'd prefer not to wait that long."

"That's only six months away," I protested.

His eyes darkened.

"Why..." My question ended abruptly. "Are you trying to expedite our wedding because of Maxim?"

His jaw clenched.

I sighed softly. An earlier date would require me to juggle wedding preparations while I was still in school. "What about the third weekend in May? The weekend after I graduate?"

Rafael released the clasp on my bra, eased the straps down my arms, and dropped it on the floor. "What about spring break?" He knelt and drew each nipple deep inside his mouth.

My eyes slid closed. I was finding it increasingly difficult to argue my point. "I'm going to be in Rwanda over spring break. Remember?"

He hooked his thumbs in my thong and tugged it toward

the floor. "May, then."

I nodded my consent.

Rafael lowered me onto the bed. "I can't believe there's a class."

I tugged the leather band from his hair. "It's really not that bad. The class helps ensure we're on the same page about our finances, marital roles, and children."

"About those children…" He nudged my knees apart as he pressed his body to mine. "I think we should work on that requirement now."

"Mmmm," was my only reply. I wrapped my legs around his waist and pulled his hips to mine.

In one long, decadent stroke he filled me. "Mine," he sighed.

"Yours," I conceded. I linked my hands with his.

We fell into a sweetly seductive kiss. Rafael thrust harder, knitting us together again and again.

Tension coiled deep and low. "Rafael," I panted. Pleasure sparked. I was so close… too close. More than anything, I wanted to prolong this moment.

Rafael slowed. His hands clenched mine as he gazed into my eyes. He moved deep and slow.

I fought for control even as my body demanded more.

Rafael grasped my shoulders. He held me tight and thrust. "You. Are. Mine." His muscles clenched. With a final thrust he owned me.

My back arched as he pulsed inside of me. We unraveled in the searing heat.

Rafael rolled his hips against mine, prolonging the pleasure, wringing even more desire from my deeply sated body. Slowly, he began to thrust.

Still quivering, I relinquished control. "Yes," I moaned. "More."

* * * * *

The bedroom was bathed in a soft flickering light. I shifted slightly so I could watch the flames dance in the fireplace. I was surprised to find the fireplace was radiating heat. The room felt cozy and warm. Rafael's arms and legs were locked around mine, and we were both tangled in the sheets. My eyes widened when the plane lurched unexpectedly.

"Turbulence," Rafael grumbled. He opened his eyes when my stomach growled. "Hungry?"

"Very." I briefly considered searching for my phone so I could see what time it was. I hadn't a clue how much time had passed since the flight began.

Rafael leaned over me to press the call button next to the bed. "Hi, Kari. We're ready for the remaining courses."

"Will you be eating in the main cabin, or would you prefer I bring your trays back to the bedroom?"

He grinned. "The bedroom, please."

"But we're not even dressed!" I ducked under his arm and dove for my thong. Like that would cover me.

A well-muscled arm wrapped around my waist. Rafael picked me up and tossed me back in bed. "There are bathrobes in the closet." He strode to the other side of the bed and opened a white door that was built into the wall, just like the door to the bathroom.

"There's a closet?" I crawled back out of bed so I could peek over his shoulder. "You... there's... everything!" Rafael had stocked the closet with bathrobes, slippers, shoes, coats, and at least three changes of clothes for each of us.

He tugged a black fleece bathrobe over his shoulders before sliding a slightly smaller version over my arms. "The dresser contains additional bed linens and clothes. The bathroom is stocked with towels, washcloths, and of all the same products we use at home."

I pulled the bathrobe closed and tied the belt. "Wow." I shook my head and wrapped my arms around his neck. "Clearly, you've thought of everything."

Rafael beamed. His hands settled against the small of my back. "The place we'll be staying is similarly stocked."

I pulled him down for a kiss. "Now I get why I didn't need luggage."

A light knock sounded at the door.

Rafael deposited me on the bed before opening the door. "Thanks."

"Ring me when you're ready for the main course," Kari encouraged softly.

"Will do." Rafael returned with two trays. The top tray held two Caesar salads, an assortment of bread, small salt and pepper grinders, herb butter, sparkling water, a cork screw, and a bottle of Apothic Red.

Rafael set the bottom tray on my lap before distributing the food. He handed me a glass of wine before joining me in bed.

I took a sip. A heady mix of rhubarb, black cherry, mocha, and vanilla notes slid soft as silk down my throat. I hummed my appreciation. "We should stock this wine at home."

He tried the wine. "Not bad for a California blend." He speared some lettuce against a rather large crouton. "Has Oni firmed up her plane ticket?"

I slathered the butter over a warm slice of French bread, tore a small piece off, and popped it into my mouth. "Yes. She's flying in on January 10th. Can she stay with us for a week? The dorms don't open until January 17th."

Rafael shrugged. "A week is fine with me. When does spring semester begin?"

"January 20th." I dug into the salad.

"Is she excited about the move?" He buttered a piece of bread.

My fork stalled. "Oni's excited about graduate school, but she's not looking forward to being separated from her family, especially given the instability in Ukraine."

He finished his salad. "That's certainly understandable. How's her English? Do you think she'll get along okay?"

"Her English is impeccable. I can't wait for you to meet her. You're really going to like Oni."

Rafael hit the call button before setting his tray on the dresser. "Hi, Kari. We're ready for the main course." He snagged another piece of bread before climbing back into bed. "I look forward to meeting her. Has Maxim revealed what he's going to ask of you?"

"No." I pushed the last of my salad aside. In a moment of sheer desperation, I'd panicked and promised Maxim anything... well, anything but sex... in order to secure his assistance in finding and freeing Kadyn, who'd been taken hostage during a shootout between the drug cartels outside San Fernando, Mexico. Maxim asked the Russian Mafia to secure Kadyn's release from the Gulf Cartel just last month. I owed Maxim, big time, but Maxim had yet to reveal what he was going to ask of me. The not knowing was killing me. I was terrified Maxim was going to ask something that would cost me my relationship with Rafael.

Rafael twirled the glittering engagement ring around my finger. "Maybe this will help Maxim adjust his expectations."

I blew out a breath. "Knowing Maxim, he'll see I've replaced his ring with yours, raise the stakes, and demand even more."

A soft knock sounded at the door.

Rafael scowled. He gathered the trays and answered the door. "Thanks, Kari. Why don't we plan for dessert in a half hour or so?"

"Sure."

"Let's not talk about Maxim," I pleaded.

"Agreed." Rafael separated the trays before doling out the plates.

The peppercorn cream sauce tickled my nose. "Wow. Steak, steamed broccoli, and a baked potato loaded with butter, bacon, shredded cheese, and sour cream? I've gained ten pounds just looking at this."

Rafael settled in next to me with his tray. "No worries. I'll burn every single calorie off you over the next few hours."

My entire body clenched. I set my tray and his on the bed so I could straddle his lap. "Maybe I should feed you, so you can conserve your energy."

Rafael's eyes heated. He pulled our hips flush so that his body pressed intimately against mine. "I think that's a brilliant idea."

I cut a piece of steak and traced his lips with the peppery cream sauce before leaning in for a kiss. We both moaned when we tasted the sauce. I pulled the steak off the fork and slid it in his mouth. Rafael captured my hand and sucked my fingers clean before savoring the meat. I tried the steak while Rafael finished his piece.

I offered him the loaded baked potato. He drew me in

for a sour cream infused kiss. Every bite was interspersed with a kiss. Each kiss grew more heated until we finally abandoned the meal.

I layered open mouthed kisses along his jaw... down his neck, shoulders, and chest. I peeked up at him before capturing his nipple between my teeth. Gently, I bit.

With an ominous growl, he lifted my hips and drove. Hard.

My chest thrust forward. My back arched. "Oh, God!"

Rafael drew my breast inside his mouth... bit down... and rolled my hips.

Softly, I moaned. My eyes slid closed when he began to thrust.

Rafael licked and kissed his way to my other breast before drawing it deep inside his mouth. My toes curled when he sucked. He scraped his teeth against my breast, clamped his lips around the nipple, and pulled.

Pleasure rolled all the way from my head to my toes. My hands clenched in his hair. "Don't stop," I pleaded. The most exquisite pain pulsed between my legs.

Slowly, he lifted me. Swiftly, he slammed right where I needed him most. He repeated the move, using a bit more force with every stroke.

Rafael captured my lips as I curled around him. His tongue thrust deep inside my mouth, claiming yet another part of me. He coaxed me to that place where pleasure bordered pain. He pushed me over the cliff, following me when I finally screamed his name.

Rafael kissed me tenderly when our bodies finally quieted. "I love making love to you."

"The feeling's mutual." A few seconds passed. "What's for dessert?"

He smiled. "Spiced chocolate molten lava cake with vanilla ice cream."

"The ice cream sounds promising." I nuzzled his neck. I was looking forward to lapping the ice cream off his chest.

The serving trays bounced against the bed as Rafael shifted his weight. He tucked me beneath him. "Dessert can wait."

My thighs clamped around his waist. "Yes," I breathed. "A thousand times 'yes.'"

Rafael took me two more times... once with the ice cream... before we crashed headlong into sleep.

Kari coaxed us out of bed with coffee. We stumbled into the main cabin sometime around three o'clock in the morning so the pilot could land the plane... in England, evidently.

We decided to take a shower while the ground crew fueled the jet. The shower was about half the size of the one we had at home but still plenty big for what Rafael had in mind. I was pretty certain I'd been screwed senseless by the time the plane took off again. We both collapsed onto the bed once we reached cruising altitude, only this time we slept like the dead.

* * * * *

"Portugal?" I gasped. "We're in Portugal?" As soon as the wheels touched down, the pilot welcomed us to Lisbon, Portugal. I peered out the window. Hopefully, the soft gray sweater, faded blue jeans, and gray suede boots I was wearing were appropriate for the weather. Rafael was wearing black jeans, a gray long-sleeved shirt, and a black leather jacket.

"I want you to see where I'm from." Suddenly, he looked worried. The jet slowed. The pilot turned toward the terminal.

My heart clenched. Rafael surprised me with a trip to Montana three and a half months ago. He thought the trip would help me heal from Michael's death. Would Portugal offer Rafael the same opportunity or trigger painful memories? I reached over and squeezed his hand. "Will this be difficult for you?"

Rafael shook his head before peering out the window. I wondered whether he was diverting his eyes intentionally. Rafael's parents were murdered when he was seventeen. His family was extremely wealthy. Some thugs raped his mother and shot his father after breaking into their house to rob them. His father was dead by the time Rafael arrived home from an outing with his friends. His mother died a few days later in the hospital. Rafael pursued a career with the Portuguese Police Special Operations Group because of that horrific experience. He served in the counter-terrorism unit before working in VIP protection. He'd been protecting people ever since.

I traced a heart in the palm of his hand. "Do you still have a lot of friends here?"

He glanced at his hand before searching my eyes. "A few. Most of my friends serve on the police force."

The airplane rolled to a stop. The ground crew rolled metal stairs toward the front of the aircraft. I glanced toward the front of the jet. "How long did you serve on the police force?"

Rafael unhooked his seatbelt. "Ten years."

"You should try to catch up with your friends while we're here." I gave him a hug when he drew me to my feet.

"There are a few people I'd like you to meet." He coaxed my lips into a slow, tender kiss. With a low growl, he grasped my jaw, angled his head, and delved deep inside my mouth. He took his time seducing... teasing... tempting me to surrender everything.

Either he was unaware of the fact the flight and ground crew were waiting for us to disembark or he simply didn't care. It wasn't until my nipples hardened, until I shifted so that his erection slid securely between my legs, that he finally released me. "Soon," he promised. "As soon as we get home."

"Home?" I inquired a bit dazedly. Rafael's already high sex drive seemed to be in overdrive ever since he slipped that ring on my finger. I sincerely hoped he wasn't referring to Virginia, because the need he'd just wrung from me required more immediate attention.

"My flat in Lisbon." He linked his hand in mine and tugged me toward the door.

"You have a home here?" *Why didn't I know that?*

Kari smiled as we neared the front of the aircraft. "I hope you enjoy your stay in Lisbon." The pilot and co-pilot joined her outside the cockpit.

A smile tugged at my lips. "Thanks for the wonderful flight."

Rafael shook their hands. "Will you be joining us for the return flight?"

The two pilots exchanged glances. "Definitely."

"You're aware of the date?" Rafael was determined to keep me in the dark about when that might be.

They nodded.

"We'll see you then." Rafael led me down the stairs. He stopped to speak with the ground crew when we reached the bottom of the stairs.

My eyes widened when I realized he was speaking in

Portuguese. I made a mental note to study his native language.

He pulled me close when we resumed walking. "Just making sure the jet will be well cared for."

My feet stalled when we entered the main terminal. The building was constructed of metal and glass. Crisp, clean lines, metal beams, and highly polished floors reflected the light pouring in through the glass ceiling and walls. "I wasn't expecting such a contemporary looking airport."

"You'll find that Lisbon offers a nice blend of contemporary and historic buildings, a lot like DC." He led me away from the other travelers. "We don't need to go through customs. I made sure we were pre-cleared."

I gaped at him. "Seriously? I didn't know you could do that." We crossed through a section of the airport that looked more like a shopping mall than a transportation hub. The place was packed.

Rafael pulled me closer. "This way. My car is parked in the parking garage."

"You have a car here?" I shook my head. Rafael had a life I knew nothing about. The man I'd just agreed to marry had suddenly become a complete mystery to me.

"Yes. A 2007 Porsche 911 Turbo. I hope the thing still runs." We stepped through the automatic doors and walked toward the garage. The sky was overcast. The temperature was cool but not cold.

I snorted more than laughed. "As if you'd own a car that doesn't run."

Rafael chuckled. "My attorney took the car to be serviced last week, so it should be fine. He left the car here earlier this morning."

My jaw fell slack. "Why would you task your attorney

with that?"

Rafael laughed. "Well, he's more friend than attorney. He manages housekeeping and utilities for the flat and services the car. In exchange, I let him drive the Porsche and loan the flat to some international clients." He pressed the car shaped key fob dangling from his other hand.

The lights flashed on a sexy metallic silver Porsche. Rafael opened the passenger door. He held my hand as I sank into the luxurious leather seat. "This car is gorgeous."

He folded himself into the driver's seat. "And really fun to drive." He backed out of the parking space and idled at the entrance to the garage. Several cars drove by before Rafael merged into traffic. Once we exited the airport, he hit the accelerator and shifted. Hard.

My breath caught when the sudden speed slammed me back into the seat. "What are you doing?" I clutched both sides of the seat.

Rafael shifted again. "Don't worry, everyone drives like a madman in Lisbon."

I glanced at the speedometer. He was pushing one hundred forty-five kilometers per hour. My chest was pounding. Hard. "We're going to die."

Rafael laughed. "We're not going to die. Do you want to eat breakfast, sleep for a while, or go sightseeing?"

"Must. Have. Food," I panted dramatically. "You burned far too many calories off of me."

He grinned. "Food it is then."

I peered out the window, trying to absorb the city. The buildings surrounding us were rather contemporary, but white washed buildings with red clay roofs dotted a nearby hillside. An old stone castle rose above it all.

Rafael followed my gaze. "*Castelo de São Jorge.*"

I was so immersed in the city that I could only nod.

Rafael turned onto a wide avenue that reminded me of the Champs Elysees. "This is the *Avenida da Liberdade.* My flat is just a few blocks up, on one of the side streets."

I ignored the contemporary buildings and the high end stores, intrigued by the older, more historic buildings. The architecture was eclectic, boasting Moorish, Romanesque, Baroque, Renaissance, and Neoclassical designs. "What a fascinating city."

Rafael's smile widened. "I couldn't agree more." He came to an abrupt stop when he saw a parking space opening up.

I gaped at the sidewalk. Instead of concrete, black and white mosaic tiles formed an elegant design I felt hesitant to walk on. "Are all the sidewalks like this?"

Rafael helped me from the car. "Pretty much." He linked his arm with mine as we began walking.

I shook my head in disbelief. "I cannot imagine the work or the man power involved in laying all those tiny tiles." Some of the tiles had settled unevenly so they poked up out of the ground, digging into my shoes. "How do women navigate this sidewalk in heels?"

"I've seen a lot of people fall. Lisbon has some very steep hills, and these tiles can be very slick when it rains." Rafael ushered me inside the Confeitaria Nacional. He parked me at a table near the door. "You stay here. I'll order."

I glanced at the bakery counter where a mob of people were placing orders. Slowly, I nodded.

He kissed my cheek. "Do not leave this bakery."

I smiled while drawing a cross over my heart.

Rafael entered the fray. Ten minutes later, he deposited three pastry bags, two disposable coffee cups, and two small ceramic cups onto the table. He sat in the chair across from me. "I ordered the pastries and two large cappuccinos to go, but I thought you might like to try the *bica* before we leave."

I eyed the rich brown concoction. "I assume *bica* means coffee."

"More like espresso." Rafael took a sip and sighed appreciatively. "Remember the coffee we drank in the café along the Champs Elysees?"

I nodded.

His eyes sparkled. "This is even better than that."

"Impossible." I took a highly skeptical sip. *Bica* had a strong, smoky taste, but it lacked the bitter aftertaste that taints expresso. I took another sip. The warm, dark elixir felt creamy and smooth when it slid over my tongue. I felt robbed. In two sips, the *bica* was gone. "This is better than sex."

The couple next to us snickered.

Rafael and I exchanged glances. He burst out laughing.

We gathered the cappuccinos and pastry bags before scampering outside. "Clearly they speak English."

Rafael juggled the pastry bags and his coffee cup so he could help me into the car. "Most people do around here. And, just so you know, I'll be proving that statement wrong just as soon as we eat breakfast."

I rolled my eyes at him. "Tell me about your apartment. Why do you still maintain a place here?"

He handed me the pastry bags, climbed into the driver's seat, and eased into traffic. "I purchased it outright after selling my parents' house. I really like this area. It's close to cafés and restaurants but somewhat insulated from the nightlife and noise that is common in some of the more popular *bairros*. I kept long, odd hours when I was working for the police force, so I needed a place quiet enough to sleep day or night. I wasn't sure how long I'd be working for Michael when I left; and even after I opened the security firm in DC, I was certain I'd be returning here intermittently."

Rafael parked beneath a white historic building with tall windows and black wrought iron balconies. "I need to stop briefly on the first floor before we head up to the apartment." We grabbed the pastry bags and rode the elevator to the main lobby.

"*Senhor Garcia!*" The doorman boisterously exclaimed. He met us halfway across the lobby, abandoning the front door entirely.

Rafael shifted the cappuccino into his left hand so he could shake the man's hand. "*Bom dia, Matias. Este é o meu noiva, Senhorita Stone.* I'm afraid she doesn't speak Portuguese."

The doorman beamed. "Welcome to *Lisboa*, Senhorita Stone."

"Thank you. I look forward to exploring your city." I should have studied Portuguese when Rafael and I first began dating. I was going to have to download some books to my Kindle so I could at least learn the basics... after Rafael proved sex was better than *bica*, of course. Given how incredible the *bica* tasted, that could take a while.

He gently squeezed my hand before resuming his discussion with Rafael. "Senhor Brantuas stopped by last night to ensure everything is in order, but you will inform me if you need anything?"

Rafael smiled. "Certainly." He handed Matias one of the pastry bags.

Matias peeked inside the bag. "*Bolo Rei e pastel de nata?*" He patted his stomach. "It is good to have you back."

Rafael patted him on the back. "It's good to be back."

We walked back to the elevator. Rafael slid a card through a magnetic device rather than pushing a button when we entered the elevator this time.

I waited for the elevator doors to close. "You regularly plied the doorman with decadent pastries when you lived here, didn't you?"

Rafael chuckled. "Matias is very good at keeping unwanted guests away."

I eyed the plastic card he was holding. "You live in the penthouse, I presume?"

His eyes sparked with amusement. "You're quite the sleuth."

The elevator opened into a private lobby with a dark slate floor and charcoal walls. The room held three large tropical plants. Contemporary oil paintings in stark white, silver, gray, and black glowed beneath strategically placed lights. Two black leather chairs flanked a small table holding a white chunk of marble. The far wall featured a massive wall fountain. The black marble slab was housed inside a brushed steel frame. Hidden lights made the water shimmer as it trickled down the roughly hewn slab. "I want one of those."

Rafael swiped the card through the card reader before keying a code. He eyed the marble slab. "Where would you hang it?"

"In my bedroom, assuming I could find one in brown. I really like how soothing it sounds."

Rafael pushed the door open. Still balancing his cappuccino and the two remaining pastry bags, he pulled me into his arms. "Welcome to your new home, my love." He kissed me passionately before stepping inside the flat. He strode into the kitchen, grabbed some plates and silverware, and joined me at the counter. He folded his jacket over the back of his chair.

I settled onto a bar stool while Rafael pulled pastries from the bags. Black cupboards, black marble countertops, stainless steel appliances, a long stainless steel sink, and recessed lighting lent the kitchen a decidedly masculine feel.

I looked at the dining room. The far wall held a black, contemporary bar. The wall above the bar was lined with glass shelves where a variety of brandy snifters, wine, shot, rocks, beer, and martini glasses were glowing beneath recessed lights. The black dining room table and chairs were tall and anchored above a contemporary area rug in swirling strips of black, white, and gray. Black hard wood floors and charcoal walls framed the entire open concept flat.

I slid off the stool, unable to resist the pull of the living room. The black leather couch and chairs were anchored around a plush white rug. I tugged my boots and socks off so I could step on the rug. The soft fibers tickled my toes. A large flat screen television hung on the wall to my right. Two sets of French doors opened onto two separate balconies directly in front of me. I unlatched two of the doors and stepped out onto the balcony. This side of the building faced a large courtyard. I stepped back inside so I could continue exploring the flat.

"I'm brewing more coffee," Rafael announced from the kitchen.

I started toward him. Black and white photographs lined the wall behind the couch. I stopped to check them out. "What is this?" I pointed to a picture where black and white mosaic tiles formed a dizzying display of waves.

He joined me in front of the picture. "That's the pavement in front of Rossio Square."

"And this one?" The photograph contained mosaic

circles overlapping one another in alternating shades of black and white.

Rafael shrugged. "I can't recall which plaza that pavement surrounds."

"The sidewalks were stunning along the *Avenida da Liberdade*," I recalled. I followed him back to the breakfast bar. "Did you take those pictures?"

He poured two cups of coffee. "Yes."

I thought about the photograph he'd taken of me on the park bench. "You're very talented." My eyes swept over the apartment again. "I like this place. Your design choices are surprisingly contemporary for this historic building, bold but elegant in a minimalist sort of way."

"You don't think it's too dark?" He cut into a small yellow custard with his fork and held it up for me.

"I find the absence of color very soothing." I tried the custard. "What did you just feed me?"

"*Pastel de nata*, a traditional Portuguese pastry." He took a bite. "Do you like it?"

"The pastry shell melts in your mouth." I ate another piece. "The filling is creamy and very sweet."

"Try this." He offered me something that resembled a chocolate burrito.

My eyes widened. "Wow." I grabbed my own fork and took another bite. Chocolate and a salted caramel sauce had been rolled inside the chocolate cake-like pastry.

"I thought the *austriacos* would be more to your liking, given your affinity for chocolate." Rafael pulled a few more pastries out of the bag and set them on our plates. "Lamb and veal *croquettes*. They're a bit more savory."

I grinned. "Did you just serve dessert first?"

He heated the *croquettes* in the microwave. "Honestly,

would you have it any other way?"

I shook my head. Still smiling, we dug into the warm *croquettes*. "Do you mind if we just relax here today? I'm still pretty tired."

Rafael set our cups and plates inside the sink. "Sure. I'm not in a hurry to go anywhere, but I would like to take you out to dinner."

"That sounds perfect." I twined my fingers with his.

He led me down the hallway. I noted a bathroom and two guestrooms before we entered the last door on the left.

Rafael's bedroom was decorated in the same three hues as the rest of the house. The wall behind the bed was covered in large black and white suede tiles, similar to a chessboard. Three large chess pieces stood in the far corner of the room… a white king, his queen, and an elegantly carved knight. The other wall held a large stainless steel sculpture that appeared to be folding in on itself. All the furniture was black. The bedding was black except for the white throw pillows piled against the headboard. The most striking feature by far was a long gas fireplace that hung on the wall opposite the bed. There were three highly polished swords hanging above the fireplace. They weren't jeweled or embellished in any way. They looked old, which I found odd given Rafael's proclivity for contemporary things.

He tapped a button on a remote near the bed. The embers along the bottom of the fireplace glowed before the flames sprang to life. "What do you think?"

"That's even more impressive than the fireplace on the airplane." I felt the comforter, the pillows, and sheets.

"Clearly we share an affinity for fireplaces." He pulled his shirt off and tossed it on the chair.

My eyes snagged on a book sitting on top of the

nightstand. "A little light reading?" The book was entitled *Predators: Pedophiles, Rapists, and Other Sex Offenders.*

"I was working on a case involving an international pedophile ring before I went to work for Michael." He shoved the book inside the drawer. "That was not an easy case to walk away from."

I gently caressed his cheek. "Did you catch who you were looking for?"

He captured my hand. "It's a long, complicated, and repulsive story… not something I want you thinking about before you go to sleep." He pressed his lips against the palm of my hand.

My eyes remained on his lips.

"You know that statement you made about *bica?*" His fingers dipped beneath my waistband. He quietly unbuttoned my jeans.

"Vaguely." I stepped out of the jeans.

He removed my sweater. "I'm giving you a bye on that… for now. I vowed to prove that statement wrong, and I will prove it wrong once you've rested."

"We'll see," I mused matter-of-factly.

He collapsed onto the bed. "You're killing me."

"Those black satin sheets… that fireplace… this room… your entire apartment screams sex and you want to offer me a bye?" I rolled my eyes. Snatching my jeans and sweater off the floor, I turned toward the door. "I'm going to the bakery to get another *bica.*"

"The hell you are." Barreling into me, he swept me off my feet and threw me onto the bed. His eyes flared when he climbed on top of me. He opened the front clasp on my bra before pinning my wrists against the bed. "Challenge accepted."

* * * * *

My fingers raked through the curls in my hair while I pondered the closet. Rafael wore black, white, and gray. His color preferences had bled into the wardrobe he selected for me. Black cocktail dresses, black pants, black jeans… black heels, shoes, and boots… black, white, and gray sweaters and shirts. There were only two exceptions, a long-sleeved cocktail dress and a pair of heels, both in lipstick red.

I dropped my towel and pulled the red cocktail dress over my head. The dress had a wide scoop neck that pushed the sleeves just below the shoulder, so a bra wasn't possible unless Rafael had thought to buy a strapless one. Between the formfitting cut and the high quality fabric, I figured no one would be the wiser. "Naughty and convenient," I whispered.

"Did you say something?" Rafael called.

I stepped out of the closet. "I can't believe restaurants in Portugal don't open until eight o'clock."

His jaw dropped. "That dress…"

I kissed him on the cheek. "Yes. Thank you."

"Eva," he growled.

"What?" My shoulders tensed.

He tore his eyes from the dress. "I asked Eva, Benjamim's wife, to pick out some clothes for you. Benjamim pulled some money from my account so she could shop for us. I left detailed instructions about the clothes."

A smile tugged at my lips. "Let me guess. Your list didn't include a bright red dress."

"No, but I *really* like this dress." His hands slid over my hips, abdomen, and breasts. "You're not wearing a bra." He backed me toward the bed.

49

"Later," I laughed. "I'm starving."

"We're not lingering in Bairro Alto when dinner's over. We're coming straight home." He stalked down the hallway, across the dining room, and into the foyer.

I trailed behind him while admiring the sassy red heels. Eva was on the fast track to becoming my new best friend. "When do I get to meet Benjamim and Eva?"

He helped me into a black dress coat before tugging a black leather jacket over his shoulders. "We're eating dinner at Benjamim and Eva's house tomorrow night." He grabbed his keys from the counter and ushered me out the door.

Our fingers twined. "Tell me about them."

With a soft "ding," the elevator doors slid open. Rafael pressed the button for the garage. "They're good friends. Benjamim is an attorney and an accountant. He manages some of my finances and my property in Lisbon."

"Is this the Senhor Brantuas that Matias mentioned? The friend who manages your apartment so he can drive around in the Porsche?"

His hand slid to the small of my back. "Yes. Benjamim and I go way back. We've known each other since high school." The elevator doors slid open. Rafael strode toward the car.

I brushed a quick kiss against his cheek before sinking into the passenger seat. "And Eva?"

He folded himself into the driver's seat, backed out of the parking space, and eased toward the entrance to the garage. "Eva's from Madrid. They met when Benjamim was still in law school. They married within weeks of meeting one another. She moved to Lisbon, and they've been together ever since." He waited for a handful of cars to pass, then tore out of the garage. He stopped abruptly at a light before turning onto the *Avenida da Liberdade*.

I gripped the sides of my seat as he picked up speed. The Porsche moved with unfathomable precision while Rafael dodged pedestrians and darted in and out of traffic at warp speed. He didn't slow until we crested a small hill.

Rafael turned sharply in the center of the block so he could park in front of a white building. "Restaurante 100 Maneiras is one of my favorite restaurants."

I was still gripping my seat when he stepped out of the car. Rafael opened the passenger door. One by one he peeled my fingers from the seat. "Are you ready to eat?"

My legs wobbled when I stepped out of the car. I wasn't sure if it was the harrowing speed or those tiny little tiles throwing my heels off. "I think my stomach is still sitting in the garage."

"You don't like the Porsche?" He eyed the car uncertainly.

I started laughing. "Oh, I like the Porsche. It's the driver I'm not so sure about."

He cracked a smile as we stepped inside. "So I'm eager to get through dinner. Don't blame me. Blame the dress."

The restaurant glowed between the gleaming white floors, a white planked ceiling, white planked walls, and white tablecloths. Dark wood chairs and a dark granite bar stood in stark contrast against the white canvas. Wine bottles lined a shelf that circled the room above the windows and the artwork. Wine glasses hung suspended over the bar. The bar was lit and candles flickered from the center of each table.

The hostess escorted us to a table in the far corner of the restaurant. She set two menus on the table, said something in Portuguese, and returned to the front of the restaurant.

Rafael helped me out of my coat before pulling a chair

out for me. I eyed the other patrons and their entrees nervously. "Will you order for me?"

He kissed me on the cheek before dropping into his seat. "Why don't we let the chef decide? They have a nine course tasting menu with a wine pairing, like Komi."

I breathed a small sigh of relief. "That sounds perfect."

A waiter stopped by to fill our water glasses. Rafael visibly relaxed while he and the waiter engaged in friendly banter. The waiter retrieved two glasses of red wine from the bar and brought them to our table. Rafael raised his glass. "*Saude.*"

"*Saude.*" I hummed appreciatively. "What kind of wine is this?" I took another sip, savoring the rich cocoa, black cherry, and smoky notes in the full bodied wine.

"*Dao,*" Rafael replied. He reached for my hand after setting his glass aside.

The restaurant ceased to exist. "What do you want to do while we're in Portugal?"

He pulled my hand to his lips. "I'd like to spend a couple of days in Lisbon before taking you to Sintra. I thought we'd tour the Pena Palace, Monserrate Palace, Quinta da Regaleira, and the National Palace of Sintra while we're here."

"Monserrate Palace. Isn't that where your father proposed to your mother?" If I remembered correctly, this was also the place where Rafael dreamed of being married.

He brushed a feather soft kiss against my fingertips. "You remembered."

"Of course. How could I forget?" That wasn't the sort of revelation a woman would forget, although that evening had been a little crazy. Maxim had just negotiated Kadyn and Roger's release from the *sicarios*. Rafael was paying the ransom. I was terrified the exchange scheduled the next day would cost all our lives. I'd been desperate to forget the horrors we'd been through and those we were still facing, so I convinced Rafael to make love to me despite the fact that I hadn't been on birth control since crossing into Mexico. Rafael asked me to remain off birth control. More than anything, he wanted to see me pregnant.

The waiter delivered the first appetizer. I was too hungry to balk at the raw meat so I quickly snarfed it up.

Rafael ate the thinly sliced beef just as quickly as I did. "I can't wait to show you the gardens at Monserrate Palace. I also want to take you to Cascais and the Knights Templar City of Tomar but not until after Christmas."

"The Templar?" I sifted through what little I knew about the group. "The Christian knights who fought in the Crusades?"

"The Knights Templar fought to free Western Europe and the Holy Land from Islamic domination," Rafael explained. "They were an elite military organization that protected Christians and Jews. They also formed a charity, serving the sick and the poor."

The waiter removed our plates before delivering an artfully presented appetizer with two new glasses of wine. I drank the sweet pink rosé while studying the appetizer.

Rafael inhaled the lamb carpaccio. "The knights originated in France. They were richly rewarded for protecting pilgrims to the Holy Land. When they began inducting men from other countries, those men gifted all their cash and property to the Order. That's how they financed their charity work. The knights themselves were sworn to poverty. They gained a great deal of support throughout Europe. The organization grew to be quite large. The King of France, *Philippe le Bel*, became envious of the Templar's power and their wealth. He persuaded the pope to execute the knights by fabricating charges of heresy and sexual misconduct. He was trying to gain control over their assets, their land, and wealth. Thousands of knights were arrested. They were tortured into making false confessions. Many were imprisoned; hundreds were burned at the stake."

"That's how they were rewarded for helping people?" I thought about the violence and abuse perpetrated by the SVR. The SVR tortured Shae and me in an effort to secure false confessions so they could further their military objectives in Ukraine. They forced President Yanukovych and Prime Minister Azarov to extend the lease allowing the Russian naval fleet to remain in Sevastopol in exchange for our release.

Rafael's eyes softened. He knew what I was thinking. "Some things never change." He swirled his wine. "The King of Scotland and the King of Portugal refused to persecute them. King Dinis offered the Knights Templar refuge at their stronghold in Portugal. They formed a new order, the Order of Christ. Their headquarters in Portugal was relocated from Tomar to the Castle of Castro Marim during this time. Eventually, their original stronghold in Tomar was restored. They kept a magnificent castle and a convent in Tomar. We can visit both sites if you'd like."

I pushed my thoughts about the SVR and my plate aside. "I heard the Knights Templar protected religious artifacts like the Holy Grail. Is that true?"

"'Protected,' as in past tense?" A secretive smile tugged at his face. "The Knights Templar still exist. They protect people, free the oppressed, and safeguard sacred artifacts and holy sites to this very day."

I stared at him for a couple of heartbeats. I couldn't tell

if he was toying with me. "I thought the knights took a vow of celibacy."

Rafael's eyes sparked with amusement. "Knighthood isn't bestowed on descendants. Men are inducted."

The waiter removed our plates before delivering two new glasses of wine and the next course. Each of our plates contained a tic-tac-toe grid that appeared to be made from a thick paste or pâté. Sea scallops were perched across from one another, diagonally. Three separate squares in the grid had been filled with a green, orange, and red sauce. Another corner held a square shaped food that looked like it belonged in a box of chocolates. Green sprigs of some unidentifiable herb were scattered over the top.

The dish was so creatively presented, I couldn't bear to mess it up. I tried the wine instead. Rafael certainly seemed knowledgeable enough. Could it be? With the Knights Templar seeking refuge in Scotland and Portugal, odds were high the remaining members were Scottish or Portuguese. Rafael was a Christian and a member of an elite force, but he didn't adhere to a vow of poverty or celibacy.

"Aren't you going to try it?" Rafael had cut his scallop into four pieces and was dipping it into the sauce.

"Please tell me you're not a Templar." I cut into my scallop while diverting my eyes. The scallop was grilled to perfection, crisp on the outside and tender on the inside. The orange sauce exploded against my tongue. My grid was obliterated as I sought to experience every sauce and flavor combination the dish had to offer.

"Okay." He deliberately stretched the word out. "I'm not a Templar?"

My head shot up. "Why did your voice lift at the end?"

He shrugged.

My thoughts skipped back to the time we played twenty questions along the Potomac River, when Rafael revealed he'd been too busy avenging his parents' death and training for special ops to fall in love. My heart sank. "Please tell me I didn't sully a celibate knight."

I waited with baited breath while the waiter cleared our plates. He deposited two new glasses of wine and two wide rimmed bowls cradling poached quail eggs and black truffles on a bed of corn sand.

Rafael grinned. "You didn't sully a celibate knight."

"Quit responding like you're telling me what I want to hear," I half gritted, half whispered.

A single eyebrow rose along his forehead. "I'm pretty sure I've been sullying you."

I stared at him. Rafael was skirting the issue. There was something about the way he answered those questions..."

He leaned across the table. "They'll be serving chocolate mousse and *bica* tonight."

Wow. Talk about a diversion. My cheeks heated when my nipples pebbled through the dress.

Rafael laughed. "Perhaps we should head home."

I tried not to smile. "I suppose I deserve that." I endured the quail egg, the delicate slices of cod hung with clothespins on a miniature clothesline, fried lamb with a pistachio crust, some fruit dish called a pre-dessert, a red wine cake pop, the *bica*, and the chocolate mousse before Rafael agreed to take me home.

He drove like an old man.

I growled at him the entire way.

Rafael didn't show a bit of interest in me until we stepped inside the elevator. When the doors slid closed, he grasped my wrists and pressed me against the polished metal wall. He planted a well-muscled thigh between my legs. "How was the *bica?*" He layered open-mouthed kisses all along my neck.

"Good." My eyes slid closed. I was praying the elevator wouldn't stop on any other floor.

Rafael growled his rebuke before biting my neck.

"Awful," I amended. "The *bica* was awful."

"And this?" His tongue traveled the full length of my throat.

My legs clenched his thigh. "This… is good."

His teeth raked the sweet spot behind my ear. "How was the chocolate mousse?"

"Barely tolerable," I lied.

He released my wrists so he could slide his hands along my thighs. My dress inched up dangerously high. The elevator pinged. Rafael lifted me so that I was straddling his waist. He pulled the zipper down the back of the dress as he stumbled across the lobby.

I cried out as he yanked one sleeve down and latched onto my breast. My body trembled with need.

Rafael shifted me in his arms so he could swipe the card through the reader. "I could make love to you every minute of every day and still ache for you."

Our eyes met, and I knew. Knight or not, I belonged to this insatiable man. "I love you," I whispered.

His pupils dilated as he pushed the door open and kicked it closed. Rafael threw the card and the key fob on top of the counter. He pulled the dress up and over my head while he strode through the apartment.

I fumbled with the buttons on his shirt.

Rafael dumped me onto the bed. The cold satin sheets slid enticingly against my heated skin. Rafael made short work of his clothes before kneeling on the bed. He removed my thong and climbed back up my body until we were perfectly aligned. Then he allowed the full force of his muscular physique to settle on top of me.

I tried not to smile. He'd left the lipstick red heels on my feet. "I believe you were trying to prove something?"

Rafael forced my chin up with his forehead. He licked my neck again. "I intend to prove a lot of things to you." He pulled my legs around his waist.

I sighed contentedly. Rafael was right where I needed him to be. "Like what?" I demanded breathlessly.

"Like how we should never be parted again." He abandoned my neck and peered deep into my eyes. His coffee and chocolate infused breath mingled with mine, but his lips stopped just short of mine.

I moaned when he pushed just inside of me. "And?" I whispered across his lips. I tried to pull his head closer so I could kiss him, but he resisted. His mouth was still hovering just millimeters from mine.

His eyes grew dark and possessive. "I'm going to prove that this," he pushed a little further while still denying the kiss, "is where I belong."

My eyes fell closed as he began to fill me. I arched against him trying to encourage him along. "And?" I panted, still yearning for that elusive kiss.

"That you belong to me." His hands fisted in my hair, holding me in place so I couldn't kiss him. When my eyes opened, his eyes captured and held mine. He thrust deep enough to press against my womb.

My legs parted even more. "Kiss me. I want you to kiss me." I groaned as he began moving deep and slow. My nipples brushed against the fine hair on his chest. I tried to pull him closer.

He continued thrusting in long, satisfying strokes. "Say it."

"What?" I whimpered. With each stroke he pushed me higher, wound me tighter, left me yearning for more. I was already nearing release. Still he denied me.

He chuckled softly. I could feel the vibration against my chest. "That sex is better than *bica*." He pulled back, abandoning my body.

My thighs clenched as I tried to force him back inside of me. "Sex is a million times better than *bica*," I conceded, "but only with you."

He released my hair and grasped my hands. "It is," he agreed just before he slammed inside of me.

The world tilted. His tongue thrust deep inside my mouth, seeking... claiming... branding... everything. He kissed me long and hard... drove inside of me while devouring my mouth.

"Rafael," I gasped. I hated breaking the kiss, but I couldn't breathe.

His eyes darkened. He thrust even harder.

"Oh, God!" I screamed. The orgasm tore through me, sparked across every nerve ending, shot down every limb, before spiraling back and burrowing between my legs again.

Rafael's lips slanted over mine. His muscles tensed when he began kissing me again. He thrust one last time, then stilled as he flooded me with heat. He kissed me until our bodies quieted, but he didn't release me.

Rafael was still inside of me when we fell asleep, cocooned within those black satin sheets. The last thing I saw was the flickering of flames from the fireplace, dancing along those mysterious swords.

* * * * *

Rafael rose from the couch. "Dear God, what are you wearing now?"

I glanced down at what I assumed was a rather chic ensemble. "I'm not entirely sure." The gray fitted tunic, black leggings, and smoky looking infinity scarf had been draped around a single hanger. I briefly contemplated black heels but chose the knee high boots instead.

He walked a tight circle around me before running his hand up my leg. "I think I like these even better than your yoga pants. Why don't you wear pants like this at home?"

I shrugged. "I just never thought to shop for leggings."

"You should." His hand slid beneath the tunic while he kissed the sweet spot behind my ear. Within seconds he was fondling my breasts. "You should buy a lot of leggings."

"Remind me to thank Eva for this wardrobe," I murmured while his lips grazed my jaw. I wasn't taking a single kiss for granted, so I kissed him with everything I had when his lips sought mine.

Grudgingly, he ended the kiss. "Eva will never forgive me if we cancel dinner tonight. She's anxious to meet you." He twined his fingers with mine before retrieving his keys and a bottle of wine from the counter. He tugged me toward the door. "I promise we'll explore Lisbon tomorrow."

We'd spent the entire day in bed, intermittently drinking *bica*, eating pastries Rafael secured from the corner bakery, planning our wedding, sleeping, and making love. "I'm far more interested in meeting Benjamim and Eva," I confessed. I was hoping they'd offer some insight on the man I'd just agreed to marry.

My stomach did a little flip when he tucked me inside the Porsche.

"You ready?" Rafael asked after buckling up.

"As I'll ever be." Excitement won over fear when he turned the key.

The tires squealed when he peeled out of the garage. "They don't live far."

Curiosity got the best of me when Rafael drove outside the city center. We appeared to be driving along the Atlantic coastline. "They don't live in Lisbon?"

He shifted gears. "They live in a nearby parish called Cruz Quebrada."

We drove past a number of post-apocalyptic looking buildings. Low income housing I presumed based on the crumbling architecture, the decaying lawns, and the laundry draped outside the windows. "What's up with all the graffiti?"

He glanced at the building on our right. "Graffiti is considered street art here. It's encouraged in some areas, discouraged in others. The city council decided to make neglected and abandoned buildings available to street artists, so they'll leave the historic sites alone. Unfortunately, it doesn't always pan out that way."

I wished I could read Portuguese so I could decipher the words marring the buildings. Abruptly, the landscape changed. This area boasted large single family homes. Most of them were white with red tiled roofs. Rafael turned off the main road and climbed a small hill. He turned down another street before parking next to a house with a swimming pool overlooking the ocean.

"Rafael!" Eva cried warmly. She kissed him on both cheeks and offered him a fierce hug before lecturing him in both Spanish and Portuguese.

Rafael laughed. "This is my fiancé, Kristine."

Eva smiled and kissed both of my cheeks. "Welcome. Welcome." She tugged on my arm while pushing Rafael inside.

Benjamim strode across the room. "Rafael!" The two men hugged while exchanging hearty slaps on the back. "This must be Kristine, the woman who unwittingly stole your heart." He scoffed at my outstretched hand and pressed a kiss to my cheek instead. "Welcome to the family."

"Thank you, Benjamim, for everything. I understand you had the car serviced and the apartment stocked in advance of our arrival. We haven't had to worry about a single thing." I turned to Eva. "You must take me shopping while I'm here. I love your taste in clothes. Everything you picked out for me has fit beautifully. The red dress and heels…"

Eva laughed when a low growl rose from Rafael's chest.

"… had the desired effect," I finished with a lighthearted laugh.

Benjamim popped open a bottle of wine. "We're happy to help, although we do have an ulterior motive. We'd like you to spend more time in Lisbon."

Rafael pulled me close. "I'll admit, I miss being here. Paris was nice, and I do enjoy living in Alexandria, but there's no place quite like Lisbon."

"It has been too long," Eva scolded.

Benjamim handed us each a glass of wine.

I looked at Rafael. "How long have you been gone?"

"About a year. I spent the entire month of December here last year while you were with your cousin in Great Falls."

Eva snorted. "Four weeks was not enough, besides you've been gone far longer than that."

Rafael looked thoughtful, as if doing some additional

math. "I moved… well, it was two years ago in September. I spent the holidays in Lisbon that first year while Michael was in Virginia and returned again in March when Kristine was in the Bahamas. So, I've been gone a little over two years, but I've been back three times… four, counting this trip."

"They'll visit more once Kristine is done with school," Benjamim predicted. "You know how grueling school can be, and Kristine's working while attending school full time."

My eyes widened with surprise. This man, who I knew nothing about, appeared to know all about me.

"You're all he ever talks about," Eva explained. "He's also shared a few pictures. That's why it was so easy to shop for you."

They led us out onto a large patio where plush outdoor furniture framed a square coffee table. A variety of olives, bread, cheese, and thinly sliced meat were sitting on the table along with a stack of appetizer plates, cloth napkins, four sparkling waters, and two bottles of wine. The furniture was nestled between a palm tree and a large swimming pool with a built in hot tub. Two stainless steel patio heaters were glowing softly between the chairs and couch. "The temperature drops once the sun falls," Benjamim explained.

Rafael and I sat next to one another on the couch. Eva claimed the chair closest to the house, and Benjamim settled into the chair opposite her. The patio had an amazing view of the Atlantic Ocean, although it felt odd, seeing the sun set on the same ocean where it rose in Virginia.

I scooted closer to Rafael. "I'd love to hear some stories about Rafael."

Benjamim topped off our wine. "I assume she's heard about the GOE?"

"*Grupo de Operacoes Especiais*, the Portuguese Police

Special Operations Group," Rafael explained.

I nodded.

Benjamim smiled. "Rafael was the youngest officer to be admitted to the GOE. He applied shortly after securing his master's degree from the Higher Institute of Police Sciences and Internal Security. Only five percent of the applicants survive the first stage of training. Unlike Rafael, most of the candidates have spent years on the force. He'd been on the force for less than a year when he applied for the group."

Rafael snagged a couple of olives. "The first stage of selective training is brutal, but it only lasts seven days. The second stage of selective training takes two months. You still have to undergo basic training when you're admitted to the group, but that part was fun."

"Fun?" Eva repeated incredulously.

Rafael shrugged. "We were trained in VIP protection, precision shooting, hostage extraction, hostage negotiation, and martial arts. I learned how to drive fast, and I got to blow stuff up."

I laughed. "That explains why you're so adept at driving the Porsche." I knew Rafael was glossing over things, but I suspected he'd been trained to do that as well. He joined the special operations group because his parents were murdered. He wanted to protect others from that same dark fate. Those other candidates may have been more skilled and more experienced, but Rafael's demons had rendered him a fiercely determined candidate.

"He served in the special operations group for six years before agreeing to work for Michael," Benjamim continued. "Two years in counter-terrorism, four years in VIP protection."

I felt… guilty. I couldn't believe Rafael endured all that

training and relinquished that career so he could babysit me.

Rafael's eyes softened. "I wasn't planning to leave the force, at least not initially. I only agreed to use my personal leave to watch over you while Michael checked on the renovations in Paris. The day I decided to leave the force was the day I discovered you crying on that park bench." He scowled. "Michael wasn't entirely honest about where things stood between the two of you. Kadyn threw me for a loop. You went to Montana, and then Justin kidnapped you. Michael couldn't stay away after that. He sent me back to Paris to oversee the security installation for the mansion, and… well, you know the rest."

I grasped his hand. "I'm so sorry."

"I'm not." He brushed a tear from my cheek before he kissed me.

"I'm going to check on dinner," Eva interjected softly. She disappeared into the house.

"Rafael seems much happier," Benjamim mused, "despite all the horrific experiences the two of you have endured."

My eyes sought Rafael's. "So he knows?"

"He knows about your ex-husband, the Trout Lake incident, the attack in Paris, the Ukraine, and Mexico." He squeezed my hand reassuringly.

"In a way, I'm relieved. Although, I can't imagine what you must think of me." I forced myself to meet Benjamim's gaze.

"I see a strong and courageous woman who has given my friend a reason to choose life and love over death," Benjamim answered frankly.

Rafael glanced at him in surprise.

"Michael wasn't the only one questioning your decision

to join the force. I thought you joined so you could fulfill some sort of death wish," Benjamim explained. "Now the Order... that's an entirely different story."

Surprise turned to alarm.

Benjamim's eyes widened. "You haven't told her?"

Rafael didn't respond.

"The Order?" I repeated. "What Order?"

"You have to tell her," Benjamim whispered.

Eva returned with a large metal bowl. Tiny tendrils of steam curled in front of her. "*Arroz de Tamboril cons Gambas*," she announced cheerily.

Benjamim stood. He pinned Rafael with a stern look. "I'll get the bowls." He turned Eva around and steered her back inside the house.

Rafael looked at me. "I..." He swallowed nervously.

"Rafael?" My heart skipped a couple of beats. He was not the type of man to get nervous... about anything.

"Do you remember our conversation from last night?"

"Oh, God." I jumped to my feet. "You're not. Please tell me you're not."

He stood.

I backed toward the pool. "Rafael," I breathed. "You're not. Tell me you're not!"

Rafael took a single cautious step toward me. "I'm a Templar. I was inducted into the knighthood when I took a bullet for the Prime Minister five years ago."

"A bullet?" I took another step back. I'd seen the man naked multiple times. I couldn't recall any scars.

Rafael stepped closer. He lifted his arm and shirt. There, under his arm, was a thin white scar. "The bullet grazed me when I dove on top of the Prime Minister and shoved him to the ground."

Rafael's swords, the knight, the king, and queen all
flashed before my eyes. "You can't be," I argued. "You're not
poor or celibate."

He took another step, just as my heel struck the edge of
the pool. His words rushed out all at once. They sounded
rehearsed but jumbled up. "The Knights Templar were
dispensed from their vow of celibacy in 1496 and from their
vow of poverty in 1505. They were secularized under Queen
Maria's rule... Queen Maria I of Portugal." He took a deep
breath. "Globally, there are two orders; one civil, one
religious. The Templar faction in Portugal is strictly civil."

"Faction?" I edged away from the pool. I couldn't
believe the Knights Templar still existed, that they were *secular*
and *global*, and Rafael belonged to this archaic Order? What
did that even mean? I shook my head in disbelief. The man
standing in front of me was a complete stranger. I thought I
knew who he was... but I didn't. I'd agreed to marry him,
and I didn't even know who he was.

Rafael froze. He knew I was about to bolt. "I tried to tell
you last night, but you seemed upset by the idea. The
restaurant wasn't the best place to explain. I've been trying to
tell you all day, but..." He trailed off uncertainly. "I was
worried you wouldn't want to marry me."

A strangled sound caught in my throat. "I don't know
you," I whispered. "I don't even know who you are." He had
a home, a car, and friends I knew nothing about. That was
difficult enough, but this? This was...

Rafael lunged for me. His hands clamped over my arms
as he pulled me against his chest. "You do know me. You
know me better than anyone else. Look at me. Feel me!"

Every inch of his body strained against mine... his
muscular thighs... an abdomen and chest carved from

granite… broad shoulders… fiercely determined eyes. Every inch of this man screamed… *knight*.

He shook me gently, forcing me to meet his stormy gaze. "This doesn't change anything. I'm still the same person you fell in love with… the man who loves you more than life itself."

My heart beat against his chest. "What does this mean for you… for us?"

Rafael sighed. "My life is not entirely my own. I have certain obligations, and those obligations will obligate you."

"What does *that* mean?" I was thoroughly confused.

"The grand master granted my request to live and work in the United States so I can be closer to you, but he imposed some conditions." He willed me to understand.

"Conditions? What conditions?"

He loosened his hold on me, infinitesimally. "I've been asked to strengthen the faction in the United States, which is too small given your land mass and your population base. I still accept assignments from Portugal, and he retains the right to order me back to Portugal at any time."

"What about the security firm?" My eyes widened. Rafael's security firm protects foreign dignitaries. "Are they all…"

He nodded. "Ethan and I recruited those men to strengthen the eastern division of the Knights Templar in the United States. Ethan is my counterpart in the United States."

My breath whooshed out all at once. "This is unbelievable." I'd been surrounded by Knights Templar for months and had never even known. Ethan, Brady, Brogan, Aidan, Chance, and Jase… every single one of those men had been inside my home.

"I'm still the same man you fell in love with," Rafael

repeated.

"Who's the grand master?" For some reason it seemed important to know who it was that essentially owned Rafael.

"Each faction has its own grand master. My grand master is Anabal Cavaco Silva, the President of Portugal. I'm also required to answer to the grand master of the United States while working in the United States."

My knees nearly buckled. Rafael worked for the President of Portugal? And who, pray tell, was the grand master of the United States?

He pulled me back onto the couch. "This doesn't change anything."

I stared at him incredulously. "This changes everything."

"No, it doesn't," he argued forcefully. "We can still be married and have a family."

I shook my head. "Your life is not your own. You could be ordered to leave the United States... to return to Portugal."

His shoulders tensed. "I could... but as my wife, you would be welcome here. The Knights Templar of Portugal would welcome you with open arms."

"Is it safe?" Eva inquired from inside the doorway.

"It is," Rafael answered, although his voice remained strained.

She set the bowl on the table. "Benjamim!"

He stepped out onto the patio. "Is she okay?"

My eyes narrowed. "How does he fit into all of this?"

A single eyebrow rose along Rafael's forehead.

I huffed out a breath. "This revelation of yours wouldn't have been important to him unless he was somehow involved."

Rafael smiled. "Sometimes I forget how brilliant you

are."

"I'm not a knight," Benjamim clarified, "but I work for the Order. I am one of many inductees who manage assets." He set a stack of bowls and a handful of spoons on the table. "As such, I was required to swear an oath of fealty to the Order."

Eva perched on the edge of her seat while dishing an orange colored stew into the bowls. "It's not as bad as you might think."

"What isn't bad?" I wasn't sure whether she was referring to the savory smelling stew or being inducted into a secret organization.

"Being married to one of them." She distributed the bowls.

I dipped my bread into the warm stew. The rich, creamy sauce tasted like onion, garlic, white wine, and salty fish stock. Colossal size shrimp and white chunks of fish dominated the rice. "Is this why you brought me here?" I looked at Rafael.

He nodded, somewhat miserably. "I would have told you sooner, but I was forbidden. We are not allowed to reveal our identity to just anyone. The women we choose to marry must be approved by the grand master, and we cannot reveal our identity until she's agreed to marry us."

"The woman must be deemed worthy, demonstrate selflessness and a willingness to serve others, and she must show loyalty by making a commitment to her betrothed," Benjamim elaborated. "We cannot expose our identity in advance of that commitment because we cannot risk women pursuing a relationship with our brethren in an effort to infiltrate or destroy the Order."

Brethren? Betrothed? I couldn't shake the feeling I'd been dropped into the 12th century.

"We were persecuted once," Rafael reminded me. "The secrecy and the uncertainty surrounding our existence help keep us safe. We can work more effectively this way."

My stomach churned nervously. "So the grand master, the President of Portugal, has to approve of me?"

"He already has."

"Impossible," I breathed.

Rafael shrugged. "Maxim did not present the obstacle I thought he would. Inexplicably, the man passes scrutiny."

My eyes narrowed. "Maxim is selfless to a fault. He's devoted his entire life to helping the poor and the oppressed."

"As have you," Rafael noted softly.

Like a deer in headlights, I stilled.

He grasped my hand. "Think about it, Kristine. The advocacy work you did in Montana, the legislation you pursued in the Senate, and the peacebuilding you're doing through Seeds for Peace. You couldn't be a more perfect candidate."

"Candidate?"

"For marriage," Rafael clarified.

"She doesn't understand," Benjamim interjected. "You are not doing a very good job of explaining this."

"Neither did you," Eva chided. "This is not an easy thing to explain or comprehend."

It was Rafael's turn to blow out a breath. "This is why I hadn't considered the religious requirements you mentioned on the airplane. I was focused entirely on these requirements, the requirements imposed by the Knights Templar." He took a deep breath before continuing. "The grand master has approved my petition to marry you, but you will be required to swear an oath to the Order before I'm permitted to marry

71

you."

Rafael, Eva, and Benjamim eyed me expectantly.

I fidgeted nervously. "I think I can do that." I wasn't entirely sure what I was getting myself into, but if I was swearing an oath to a long standing security organization with a charitable component based on Christian principles, how bad could it be? I turned the idea in my head. "There's a catch, isn't there?"

This marked the moment when Rafael looked truly worried. "You must swear this oath to the same faction I serve, otherwise I will not be permitted to marry you."

I stared at him incredulously. "Are you asking me to swear loyalty to a foreign government… to relinquish my citizenship… my nationality?" The grand master was the President of Portugal. How could I declare my allegiance to the President of Portugal?

"You'll be granted dual citizenship," Eva interjected. "Like me."

"You'll be swearing loyalty to the Templar, not the government, and you won't be forced to choose between Portugal and the United States," Benjamim added.

"But if the President of the United States does something the President of Portugal disagrees with, then what? Will I be forced to choose?" I was assuming, of course, that the President of the United States was the grand master of the United States.

"No, Kristine. They would work out their differences. There are mechanisms in place. All of the grand masters would come together to ensure the situation is resolved in a way that is in the best interest of all humanity," Rafael answered confidently.

There was a long list of American foreign policies that

had received international condemnation as of late, so I persisted. "But what if he does. What then?"

"That has never happened," Benjamim argued. "The Templar do not allow politics to poison their mission, which is protecting and helping people in need. Very few disagreements ensue over those objectives."

A fire sparked in Rafael's eyes. Clearly, he'd had enough. "On the off chance that it does, you would be required to side with the Knights Templar of Portugal, to renounce your American citizenship, and reside permanently in Portugal with me."

And there it was. The big, terrible, awful thing he didn't want to tell me.

Chapter 3 – Stand by You

I stared at the landscape unraveling outside the Porsche. I couldn't imagine how opulent castles could exist less than twenty minutes away when all I could see were clotheslines weighted with tattered clothes and crumbling buildings marked with graffiti. We were driving to Sintra in search of a distraction from Rafael's obligations and mine.

Rafael, Benjamim, and Eva had spent the entire evening easing my fears about whether the Knights Templar of Portugal would require me to renounce my citizenship to the United States. I felt assured, in the end, that this would only happen if the United States engaged in genocide, committed mass atrocities against humanity, or persecuted the knights. I had enough faith in my government to conclude that those egregious crimes would never be pursued by my country.

So where did that leave me? Silently contemplating my oath. I was required to swear an oath to the grand master or his designee within the next thirty days. Apparently, I'd be doing so before leaving Portugal.

As surreal as it was to learn that Rafael was a modern day

knight, I'd learned something beyond this chivalrous designation. Rafael had an ego. He was a proud man who'd apparently had his fill of my insecurities, my waffling, and divided loyalties. Now that we were engaged, he expected me to put him first, to love and cherish him above all others, and to choose him above all things… even my country. It was a tall order from someone who couldn't deliver on the same requirements, given his fealty to the Knights Templar.

I peered out the window. The dilapidated buildings had been replaced by a handful of houses atop lush green hills. A cloud opened above us, misting more than raining on our parade.

I looked at Rafael, who appeared lost in his own thoughts. I admired his selflessness and his commitment to aid and protect others. Any other woman would have been swooning over the fact that he was a knight. The Knights Templar's mission was very much in line with my social and religious values. So, why did I view them as a threat?

One thing was certain. I now knew how Alice felt when she fell into that rabbit hole. Women who slept battered on bathroom floors didn't marry knights or visit castles. Maybe that was the problem. My life had grown unrecognizable once again.

"We're here," Rafael announced softly. We'd entered a quaint, hilly little town. The tourists who weren't climbing on and off buses were bartering with merchants who had jewelry and artwork on display along the cobblestone street.

I stared slack-jawed at an ominous castle while Rafael secured a parking spot. I couldn't imagine anyone wanting to live in such a sinister looking building.

Rafael peered up at the castle while helping me from the car. "Quinta da Regaleira," he revealed in a reverent tone. He opened an umbrella and tucked me beneath his arm.

I studied the gothic structure while he paid for our tickets. The castle was a fascinating conglomeration of spindly pinnacles, elaborately carved windows and terraces, an octagon shaped tower, and menacing gargoyles.

We crossed through a large wooden gate and were instantly transported into an exquisite garden. There were hundreds, if not thousands, of flowering trees, bushes, and plants surrounding us. Calla lilies sprouted straight from the ground.

The dirt trail we were on branched out in multiple directions, creating switchbacks along the terraced garden above and below us. The trail extended as far as the eye could see. "It's breathtaking."

The tension eased from Rafael's shoulders. The first genuine smile I'd seen in hours lit his face.

I turned a slow circle, trying to absorb the unspeakable beauty surrounding me. From this angle, the castle didn't appear ominous; it appeared inviting. The exterior looked whiter and brighter somehow. The back of the castle faced an ornately carved chapel. I couldn't resist touching the cool, wet stone before we stepped inside. I wondered how something so beautiful could withstand the test of time.

Angels, saints, and other religious figures were carved directly into the walls. Quietly, I pondered the scriptures reflected in the frescoes. "What's that?" I pointed to a large circular emblem on the floor. The contemporary design seemed sorely out of place in the ancient chapel. The emblem contained an armillary sphere surrounded by pentagons, which was unusual but not nearly as odd as the large squat cross that had been stamped over the top. A thick red line framed the thin white cross before flaring at each end.

Rafael leaned closer. "That, my love, is the Order of Christ Cross."

"Order of Christ," I murmured. Where had I heard that term before? My eyes widened. "The Knights Templar reorganized as the Order of Christ when they were being persecuted."

Rafael nodded. "Under King Dinis I."

"What does this mean?" I nodded toward the cross.

"The Knights Templar have sworn to protect this site." Rafael walked outside.

I stared at the cross for some time before joining Rafael outside. "How many buildings, artifacts, and people have your knights sworn to protect?"

Rafael shrugged. "More than I could possibly count."

We spent hours exploring the grottos, gazebos, fountains, and ornately carved benches scattered throughout the extensive grounds. We hiked down a winding staircase inside an initiation well that displayed another Order of Christ Cross. This squat white cross included a red circle in the center and red triangle shaped tips, sort of like a compass.

Rafael stood staring at the cross. "The Knights Templar met at Regaleira Palace. They held ceremonies in the chapel, along the lake, and inside this well. The initiation wells, grottos, tower, lake, chapel, and caves are connected by tunnels." He pointed to a dark cavern that was roped off.

We climbed the stairs so we could finish exploring the palace grounds. The lakes and gardens were well kept but still looked natural and wild. There was so much mystery and intrigue surrounding the place, I didn't want to leave.

The sun didn't come out until after we returned to the car. "I thought we'd eat lunch at Pena Palace." Rafael eased out of the parking lot. We wound through the town and looped around a mountain before another palace peeked through the clouds.

This palace was massive and bold. A weathered stone foundation loomed high above the ground just beyond the drawbridge. Above this foundation, one section of the castle was painted yellow, another section a deep coral color, and the center appeared blue from this distance. Scalloped windows and balconies wrapped around the castle beneath an elegant clock tower. There were multiple towers; some were square, others were round with mosque like domes.

"I feel like I've been dropped into another century." We hiked up the gravel path. The trail was very steep. At one point, I had to stop and catch my breath. Clouds formed wispy tendrils that wound around the massive rocks, lush ferns, and exotic trees.

"Are you hungry?" Rafael seemed invigorated and not at all winded.

"Starving." A competitive streak forced me to look a little less fatigued

"We're almost there." He grasped my hand and shortened his stride.

We crossed under a tall Moorish arch covered with four inch tiles. Each of the tiles depicted a knight. I peered up at the palace. I could picture women in opulent dresses strolling along the balconies, subtly flirting with knights. The arch emptied into a courtyard that held an ornate stone cross, multiple coats of arms, and gargoyles beneath prickly looking guard towers. "What is this place?"

Rafael chuckled. "Pena Palace has been a lot of things throughout the centuries; a monastery, a convent, and a palace. You'll find both Christian and Islamic culture reflected in this palace."

"That explains why the architecture is so eclectic." I reached for my cell phone, then shoved it back inside my purse. I knew if I started taking pictures now, we'd never eat.

Rafael led me inside the gift shop where we took an elevator to the second floor. The elevator opened into a modern cafeteria-style restaurant. I ordered the duck quiche with field greens. Rafael ordered *Linguas de Bacalhau*, fried cod cakes with Portuguese rice.

We carried our trays to a table next to a small window. "The architecture in my country must seem very boring to you." I was referring to our dull concrete sidewalks, asphalt streets, and unimaginative office buildings.

"Not at all." Rafael cut into his cod. He offered me a bite. "There are a lot of beautiful buildings in DC. Besides, your country has a lot of natural beauty, which I find far more impressive than these eccentric palaces."

Slowly, I nodded. I hadn't stopped to consider the Grand Canyon, the Grand Tetons, the Redwood Forest, the Na Pali Coastline, Yosemite, Yellowstone, or Glacier Park.

He eyed me curiously. "How are you feeling about our conversation last night?"

"Concerned," I answered honestly. I offered him a forkful of quiche.

He tried the quiche. "What are you concerned about?"

Although there wasn't anyone sitting close enough to overhear our conversation, I thought it best to remain vague. "I'm not sure I understand to what extent your involvement with this *organization* obligates you. I mean, is it like being in the military, or do you have more control over your life than service members do?"

Rafael looked thoughtful. "Being inducted is not all that different than receiving a meritorious service medal. I was awarded this honor for outstanding service to my country. My induction into the Order merely requires me to live up to that honor. It's not as demanding or as consuming as you might think. I vowed to protect and help those in need. In order to maintain my status, I need to deliver on those promises. Occasionally, the grand master requests my assistance in protecting our diplomats or in achieving national security objectives. I can marry, have children, and pursue my own career goals as long as they don't conflict with the goals and objectives of the Order."

"So how do you describe this organization to others, like when you're recruiting or inducting people in the United States?" Last night, I'd learned there were only three groups of people with whom Rafael could discuss Templar business; with people who were already working for the Order, his betrothed, and those he was recruiting. Since those working for the Templar and their betrothed were required to issue a vow of secrecy and support, the greatest risk occurred during recruiting because there was no guarantee that individual would actually join the Order. Understandably, they were extremely selective in their recruiting practices.

Rafael finished his rice. "I think the civil order is best described as an elite security force with humanitarian objectives." He walked back to the counter, placed another order, and returned with two cappuccinos and a small lemon merengue pie.

I ate every last bite of my salad and quiche. "You said there was a religious order as well?" I tried the lemon meringue pie. The tart filling bit at the taste buds just behind my jaw.

Rafael laughed when I moaned rather than spoke my appreciation for the pie. "I would describe the religious order as an elite security force charged with protecting religious figures, artifacts, and sites. Most republics and constitutional monarchies have a civil order. Some countries, like England, Italy, Spain, and Israel maintain a separate religious order."

I sipped my cappuccino. The froth was creamy and thick with nutmeg sprinkled on top. "Why do you have to strengthen the faction in the United States?"

Rafael frowned. "Your government didn't really see a need for us until recently. They already maintain several elite forces, far more than any other country. Additionally, your Department of State Bureau of Diplomatic Security offers protective services to foreign dignitaries, which fulfills your country's obligations under the Vienna Convention. With the recent economic crisis, your looming debt crisis, and the resulting budget constraints, it has become increasingly difficult for your government to fulfill its obligation to protect visiting dignitaries. They're allowing the Knights Templar to augment those services for some but not all visiting dignitaries, which is something my country has been doing for centuries. Additionally, your country doesn't offer protective services for those providing humanitarian aid except in war zones, so we've assumed that role."

"Who funds your work?"

"Centuries worth of investments, public and private donations allow us to absorb the cost of those services." He dug into the pie.

"So you formed a public private partnership that allows you to achieve your shared objectives."

Rafael nodded. "Increasingly, your government has shifted responsibility for social services and humanitarian aid to charity groups. This is no different."

Well, that was believable enough. "How do you decide

who to recruit or induct?"

Rafael smiled. "That's easy. We only approach former military members who have earned the Medal of Honor or law enforcement officers who have received a comparable award."

"Is the grand master of the Knights Templar in the United States the President of the United States?" I'd been dying to ask that question for hours now. Since the restaurant was nearly empty, I figured it was safe.

Rafael nodded. "I think that's enough information for one day. Are you ready to see the palace?" He chuckled when I stole the last bite of pie.

We spent the next few hours exploring the palace. As beautiful as the building was, it paled in comparison to the palace grounds. The walking trails extended for miles through what could only be described as an enchanted forest. Between the moss covered rocks and columns, the lush ferns carpeting the forest floor, and the fog drifting through twisted, exotic trees, I half expected unicorns and faeries to appear. I didn't want to leave, ever, but Rafael insisted we continue on to Monserrate Palace so we could watch the sunset over the palace gardens.

Monserrate Palace was hands down the most romantic building I'd ever laid eyes on. Never in a million years would I have imagined that stone carvings could be so intricate. The delicate arches were carved as finely as a filigree necklace. Those arches sat atop an endless array of elegant columns with floral capitals. The hallways, ceilings, balconies, and stairways were carved with such exquisite detail it made my heart ache.

I hadn't a clue who he was, but I mourned the loss of the romantic soul who had envisioned this masterpiece. What sort of man could turn that vision into a reality? I counted myself among the lucky ones, simply because I'd been fortunate enough to see this magnificent building. Someone had poured a lifetime of love into Monserrate Palace. His love had become a tangible thing.

Rafael and I were nestled close on one of his balconies, gazing out over the botanical gardens, a whimsical pond, and a lush forest that spanned as far as the eye could see. We were the only two people on the palace grounds. The lone man standing inside the gatehouse at the entrance to the park was in no hurry to chase us off.

The sun tugged every last bit of tension from my body before easing behind the trees. Rafael turned to look at me. "What do you think?"

It was some time before I could speak. "I can see why you'd want to be married here."

His smile was bittersweet. The pond where his father proposed to his mother was wreaking havoc on his heart.

"I think we should," I whispered. "I think we should marry in this very spot and at this very moment when the sun slips behind the trees."

He studied me uncertainly. "You still want to marry me, despite the secret Order and everything else you've learned about me?"

I smiled softly. "You're still the same man I fell in love with. Isn't that what you've been trying to tell me?"

His eyes traversed the many columns and arches, as if envisioning the ceremony, before gazing down at me. "You just made the only dream I've dared dream a reality." Then, like a knight charging into battle, he kissed me.

* * * * *

Rafael insisted on dining in a *casa de fados* in Alfama, the oldest district in Lisbon. Alfama was nestled beneath the São Jorge Castle. I'd gotten quite the workout climbing the steep cobblestone trails that were more appropriately labeled a medieval maze than passable streets. White-washed limestone buildings topped with red clay roof tiles were packed to bursting along the hillside. I had visions of medieval knights racing on horseback toward the castle only to get caught up in the clotheslines strung between the buildings. Of course, I had knights on the brain. Knights were all I could think about these days.

The small, dimly lit restaurant we'd wandered into felt warm and inviting, but the tables were set so close together I quickly surmised we'd be dining with strangers. Still, no one seemed to mind. "Tell me about *fado*," I beseeched as Rafael took his seat.

The waiter set a plate of cheese; some warm, crusty bread; and a small bowl of black olives between us. They had a brief conversation about wine before the waiter walked away.

"*Fado* is a traditional urban folk music that originated in Portugal. Some claim it's the oldest urban folk music in the world," Rafael answered.

The waiter returned with a bottle of wine. Rafael paused briefly to sample the wine. The waiter filled both wine glasses once Rafael nodded his approval.

"Three or four *fadistas* will sing at different intervals throughout the night. Out of respect, we don't eat while they're singing." Rafael raised his glass. "*Saude.*"

"*Saude.*" My eyes widened when I tasted the wine. "What kind of wine is this?" The wine was effervescent but far more

85

subtle than a sparkling or even a semi-sparkling wine.

"*Vinho Verde*," Rafael replied.

"*Verde?* Doesn't *verde* mean green?" I studied the wine, which was inarguably white.

"*Verde* does mean green, but green as in young, not the color green. *Vinho Verde* can be red, white, or rosé, but it's meant to be savored within a year of bottling. That's what sets it apart from other wines. Portugal is the only country in the world that produces *Vinho Verde*," he noted proudly.

"It tastes citrusy, like there's a twist of lime." I circled back to the previous topic. "So what does *fado* sound like?"

Rafael looked thoughtful. "*Fado* sounds sad, mournful even. The Portuguese are a melancholy people. This music reflects their sorrow and longing."

"Like singing the blues," I assumed.

Rafael shook his head. "*Fado* doesn't sound like the blues you're accustomed to. *Fado* is more traditional; and *fadistas* are only accompanied by a Portuguese guitar, an acoustic guitar, or both."

I adored B.B. King. I'd seen him perform in concert and couldn't fathom anything more sorrowful or traditional than the blues.

A rather imposing man stepped behind Rafael before I could inquire further. He barked some foreign command I didn't understand.

Rafael's eyes widened as he shot to his feet.

The man burst out laughing.

Rafael shook his hand excitedly. They slapped one another on the back and exchanged hugs.

Eventually, the man's eyes slid toward me. Rafael led him around the long row of tables so they could stand on the same side of the table as me.

I rose uncertainly.

Rafael wrapped his arm around me. *"Comandante,* I'd like you to meet my fiancé, Kristine Stone. Kristine, I'd like you to meet Leandro D'Souza, the Chief Superintendent of the Public Security Police."

I offered him my hand. *"É um prazer conhecê-lo, senhor,"* I recited hopefully. I'd been practicing my Portuguese.

Rafael beamed at me.

"The pleasure is mine," Chief D'Souza replied. "I do not wish to interrupt your dinner, Senhorita Stone, but I would appreciate a few moments with Senhor Garcia if you don't mind."

"Of course," I encouraged, meeting Rafael's eyes.

He kissed me on the cheek before easing me back onto my seat. "I'll be standing right outside the entrance." He stopped a waiter who was walking by. They spoke briefly before Rafael leaned over and whispered, "I just ordered, so you don't have to worry about deciphering the menu."

I forced a smile. "I'll be fine."

They walked toward the entrance and disappeared out onto the street.

A female vocalist approached the microphone. The gentleman accompanying her leaned against the stone wall on the opposite side of the fireplace. With his foot propped casually against the wall, he began strumming an instrument that looked more like a giant banjo than an acoustic guitar. I leaned forward in my seat. I counted twelve strings, although I wasn't certain I'd counted right given the dim lighting. I could only assume this was the Portuguese guitar Rafael mentioned earlier.

I studied the man's fingers. I was trying to discern how a single instrument could sound like two or three. My eyes widened when the woman began to sing. I almost wished she wouldn't sing so I could focus exclusively on the strings.

I looked around the restaurant. Rafael was right. Not a single person was talking, and no one was eating. Everyone was staring intently at the *fadista*. A few were sipping wine. I shifted uncomfortably. The woman's mournful song seemed more like an impassioned cry. I thought about the Chippewa pouring their grief into the ground and sky.

The woman visited with a few patrons after finishing her song. A waiter set two identical plates on our table.

"Grilled sardines," Rafael revealed, dropping into his seat.

I blinked in disbelief. "We're eating sardines?"

"Grilled sardines, potatoes, and red pepper salad to be more precise." His smile didn't quite reach his eyes.

Goosebumps pricked my spine. "What's wrong?"

"I can't. Not here." Storm clouds rolled through his eyes.

"Maybe we should leave," I suggested uncertainly.

"We're staying." He reached for his fork. "So, what do you think of *fado*?"

"The vocalist was a little too dramatic for me. I liked the guitar, but the singing was… I don't know… haunting?"

Rafael nodded. "That's a fair assessment. I'm not terribly fond of *fado*, but I thought you should experience it at least once."

We started eating. I peeked at Rafael when he wasn't looking. He was concerned about something. His entire body was tense. This wasn't the same man I'd entered the restaurant with.

The food was wonderful, but I could barely lift it from the plate. My arms felt leaden as if burdened by some invisible weight. I pushed the food aside. I couldn't swallow around the lump in my throat. I wanted to cry, but I didn't know why.

"You don't like the sardines?" Rafael looked angry, sad, and frustrated all at the same time.

"We need to leave." A million alarms were going off inside my head.

He eyed the half-eaten food. Slowly, he nodded. Rafael called our waiter over. He offered an apology and some assurances about the quality of the food before settling our bill.

A second vocalist approached the microphone as we began to leave. She didn't sing until we stepped outside. Still, her melodic lament clung to me.

Rafael strode from the restaurant. I tried to keep up. "What's going on?"

He didn't answer until we turned down an abandoned street. I glanced down at my feet. I was wearing comfortable shoes, but those tiny mosaic tiles kept poking through the soles. As beautiful as the sidewalks were, they were proving painful to walk on, and it appeared we'd be walking the entire way home.

Rafael slowed. "Do you remember the case I told you about when you discovered that book on my nightstand?"

I slipped my hand through the crook of his arm. "The one involving the international pedophile ring?"

He nodded. "That case involves several prominent and powerful individuals."

"You speak as if the case is still active," I interjected.

"It is." A tiny bit of tension eased from his face. "Hundreds of children from the Casa Pia Orphanage were victimized by this pedophile ring for more than forty years. Because the individuals involved were extremely wealthy and wielded a great deal of power, government officials and law enforcement officers turned a blind eye to the rumors that had been circulating for decades. Victims were intimidated, evidence was lost, and people were paid to sweep these claims under the rug."

"That's awful," I breathed.

"We identified over one hundred boys and girls who were violently abused; some were deaf and mute. That only includes the more recent victims… well, the ones who were willing to come forward. I'm sure there were more. Thousands of charges were filed against a handful of individuals. Most of these individuals have already gone to trial. Others have proven more elusive."

My brow knit with confusion. "How did you get involved with this case when you were working in VIP protection?"

Rafael sighed. "I was assigned to protect a former Portuguese ambassador. I was on duty when a child was brought to his flat. I assumed he was adopting the child. You have to spend some time living with the child you've applied to adopt in Portugal before the adoption is finalized, so I didn't think too much about it. The only thing that gave me pause was the man's age. He was older, in his sixties, and the boy was only nine." His voice broke on the boy's age.

I stepped in front of him so I could study his face. His eyes were steeped in pain. "Are you okay?"

Rafael shook his head. "I was protecting this man while he abused that little boy. I ignored the child's cries. I thought he was being rebellious, that he didn't want to be adopted. I just assumed he was missing his friends at the orphanage."

I grasped Rafael's hands.

Tears welled in his eyes. "I intervened the second night.

The boy's screams were just… more than I could bear. The ambassador didn't hear me when I entered the apartment. He was…" Rafael's eyes slammed closed. "He was raping that little boy while whipping him with a belt."

I pressed my dampened cheek to his chest. "I'm so sorry, Rafael. That's horrifying."

"I lost it. I couldn't believe I'd allowed such a monstrous thing to happen on my watch. I beat the ambassador until he was unconscious and left him lying there with his pants tangled around his legs. I didn't dare take the boy back to the orphanage. I knew there had to be some staff members at the orphanage who'd been bribed, who'd allowed this child to be violated. I didn't know who I could trust on the police force, given the ambassador's prominence and his wealth. So I took Manuel, the little boy, directly to Chief D'Souza. He was the highest ranking person I could trust."

"Is Chief D'Souza a Templar?" That would certainly explain the trust.

"Yes. Chief D'Souza is the one who petitioned for me to be inducted." Rafael wrapped his arm around me as we resumed walking. "He had his suspicions about who was involved in the pedophile ring. We took Manuel to the hospital before placing him in protective custody. Then we developed a plan for nailing the other members. I was assigned to protect the politicians and the celebrities we suspected were participating."

"Were you able to implicate anyone else?" I inquired softly.

"One other individual. Only seven individuals have been prosecuted so far, although I'm sure there were a lot more people involved."

I peered up at him. "Is this what Chief D'Souza wanted

to talk to you about?"

Rafael stopped walking again. "Yes. Benjamim told him I was in town. He wants me to come back and help him put an end to this pedophile ring once and for all."

My heart sank. "Is this a request from an old friend or an order from the Templar?"

"It's currently being framed as a request, which leaves some room for negotiation, but the President of Portugal has deemed this a national priority. Portugal has lost its standing among the international community for allowing these children to be violated for so long, and our citizens have lost faith in their government."

I hugged myself as I stepped in front of him. "I understand this is important."

Hope flickered briefly... then sadness... and fear. "Would you be willing to live here for a few months, possibly a year?"

My heart struggled in fits and bursts to start beating again. I knew. In my heart of hearts, I knew Rafael wanted this. He'd sacrificed so much for me, indulged and supported me in every way. I knew I should do the same. If I truly loved him, I'd stand by him. I'd support him in this so he could put this case to rest. But to walk away from my family and friends, my career, my degree program, and my country? Tears welled in my eyes. "I... I don't know, Rafael. How do you see this playing out?"

He pulled me close. "I don't see this taking more than a year, but it is possible. He wants me to return to work immediately."

My head fell to his chest. We stood holding each other for the longest time. Although we were standing in the middle of a long, narrow street, it felt as if we'd reached a fork in the road. We were going to have to choose between Rafael's dreams and mine.

My heart ached. The hands of time began to wind the wrong way. Months simply fell away. I was holding Michael. I could feel his pain. We'd just returned home from the hospital and were mourning the loss of our baby. I tried to comfort him, but he walked away.

Time surged forward with a violent jerk. I was kneeling in the snow in the middle of Lexie's driveway. Kadyn was hurt. He couldn't forgive me, not after everything that had happened with Michael. Tears streamed down my cheeks as he drove away.

Time twisted cruelly until I was kneeling at the edge of Michael's sailboat. Rafael was pouring Michael's ashes into the ocean. I reached out so I could feel Michael one last time. The only thing I could feel was Michael slipping away.

Somehow, this felt the same.

* * * * *

I was pacing across Rafael's living room, anxiously awaiting his return. I'd barely slept last night and was now running on fumes. Rafael left to speak with the police chief hours ago. With every minute that passed, I grew more fearful. I'd been doing some serious soul searching while he was away.

I decided I could walk away from Seeds for Peace. I was certain I could find a career in Portugal that would be equally rewarding. But I couldn't walk away from my degree program. I was only five months away from graduating. The faculty had been lenient with me, allowing me to complete assignments remotely while burying Michael and working out of country for Seeds for Peace, but George Mason wasn't an online university. Attendance was required. Short absences were tolerated as long as students remained on task. But five months? Five months was not an option.

My friends and family didn't present the obstacle I thought they would. Between the jet, Rafael's resources, and mine... *thanks to Michael*... I could fly back to see them anytime.

A plan had been unfolding inside my head, but I hadn't sorted through all the details yet. I spun on my heel when I heard Rafael slide his card through the door.

His eyes locked on mine. "Kristine?" He walked toward me as if he were approaching a frightened doe.

I took a deep breath and slowly released it. "What did he say?"

Rafael pulled me down onto the smooth leather couch. I found the cool material soothing. My skin felt heated, fueled by the tension and the panic building within me. "Chief D'Souza would like to reinstate me into the *Grupo de Operações Especiais* permanently. To the best of my knowledge, no operative has ever been reinstated before... at least not in Portugal."

I forced myself to breathe. I wasn't expecting this to be so permanent. Clearly, it was an honor to be reinstated into a special operations group... an unprecedented honor at that. I reached for his hands. "Do you want to be reinstated?"

Uncertainty flickered in his eyes. I maintained a firm hold on his hands when he tried to pull away. He glanced at me, surprised.

Tears welled in my eyes. "We're in this together, Rafael. I will support you either way, but I won't allow you to slip away."

He folded me in his arms. "I wish this didn't come at such a high cost."

Some time passed before either of us spoke again. Hesitantly, I began. "I'll resign at Seeds for Peace, and I'll move here, but I need to finish my degree first."

Rafael tucked a strand of hair behind my ear. "Few marriages survive special ops. I could be unavailable for weeks, maybe even months, on VIP protection missions. If they reassigned me to the counter-terrorism unit, you could be targeted, just like you were when you were with Michael. I can't put my wife or my children through that."

My heart stalled.

He grasped my hands. "I told Chief D'Souza that I would consider a temporary assignment, no longer than six months, to help them nail the scum who are abusing these children. He conceded, but he reserved the right to extend the assignment for another six months if we hit any roadblocks. I didn't commit. I wanted to talk to you first."

"So we would be separated for five months." I drifted toward the balcony. That was the length of time I needed to complete my degree. I could spend the remaining time in Lisbon while he wrapped up his investigation.

Rafael followed me. "I'm afraid so. We could visit one another over the weekends, but the timing could prove tricky. If I'm assigned to someone, I wouldn't be able to leave until that security detail was over. Assignments can run anywhere from a day to a few weeks, they often include weekends, and they can be extended unexpectedly."

I gazed unseeingly at the courtyard. "We can do this, right? I mean, it's only five months. We can reschedule the wedding so we're not getting married until after your assignment ends. That would be July or December if you wanted to play it safe."

I could feel the heat rolling off Rafael's chest when he stepped behind me. "We're not delaying the wedding. May 21st is already too far away."

I leaned against him when he wrapped his arms around me. "So we'll get married on May 21st and delay the honeymoon." I turned in his arms. "I think five months is doable. Oni's coming in a few weeks. I'll have midterms, Rwanda, finals, graduation, and the marriage preparation course. You'll be immersed in this case. We'll be busy planning the wedding, and we'll be flying back and forth to spend time together. Five months will be over in no time," I reasoned with forced optimism.

"Rwanda," he groaned. "How could I forget? I'm supposed to be joining you on that trip."

"You can send Jase instead or expand the security detail beyond Brogan and Aidan." I didn't know Brogan or Aidan very well, but they had served as the security detail for my colleagues when they were working in India and Pakistan a few months ago. "What are you going to do about the security firm?"

"You're speaking as if this is a done deal. I still haven't decided if I'm accepting this assignment," Rafael gritted. He blew out a breath. "Ethan can manage the firm. I'm more concerned about you. I can't leave you unprotected. I don't trust Maxim, and the SVR could still come after you."

"Jase is already serving as my bodyguard. Can't you just extend his hours or assign a second person to guard the townhouse at night?" I paused, surprised by how easily that suggestion had rolled off my tongue. I'd had a bodyguard for more than two years now, ever since Michael sent Rafael to watch over me in DC. I wasn't really aware that I had a bodyguard until I met Rafael in Paris. Still, that was eighteen months ago. Now, I didn't even think twice about having one.

Rafael shook his head. "If I do this, then I'm asking Brady and Jase to move in with you."

My voice rose three octaves. "Move in with me? Why?"

His eyes darkened. "While I may trust them to protect you, I don't want either of those men spending the night alone with you."

"But Brady and Jase aren't even remotely interested in me."

"You presumed the same about me when you were living with Michael," he noted drily. "If Brady and Jase are both sleeping there, they can keep each other in check *and* watch over you."

"Fine," I conceded. "I can live with that."

His eyes softened. "That helps, a lot. I'm just... I'm not so sure I can. Chief D'Souza gave me twenty-four hours to think this over. We should sleep on it and make our decision in the morning." He led me back into the living room.

"Do you want some time alone? I can read my Kindle or study Portuguese in the other room so you can think about this." I walked into the kitchen to pour some coffee.

He shook his head. "No. I would like to discuss something else."

"What do you want to talk about?" I handed him a cup of coffee before joining him on the couch.

"I want to host a party to celebrate our engagement."

"But you may not be returning with me," I noted softly.

His expression grew fierce. "Even if I accept this assignment, I will see you home."

I wasn't about to argue with that look. "Okay. We should

pick a date so we can send the invitations out. How soon do you want to do this?"

He rubbed at the stubble along his jaw.

"What about New Year's Eve?" I suggested.

A smile slid slowly across his face. "That's perfect."

I glanced at the calendar on my cell phone. "We're going to have to send electronic invitations. That's only ten days away."

Rafael opened the laptop he left sitting on the table last night. "If you can gather your friends' e-mail addresses, we can send the invitation now."

I scribbled their names and e-mail addresses on a piece of paper I snagged from his printer. "Your house or mine?"

"I need to make a phone call."

I looked up. Rafael was already walking down the hall. He disappeared into the bedroom with the laptop.

I fell back against the couch. "What was that all about?"

He returned a few minutes later. "I've secured a private yacht. We'll be ringing in the New Year and celebrating our engagement while cruising the Potomac River. That way, there's no prep work involved, and we don't have to clean up."

My eyes widened. "Are you serious? How did you secure a yacht this close to New Year's Eve?"

"Clearly, you don't know who you're marrying," he taunted with a cocky smile.

I snorted my coffee. "Clearly. I don't."

* * * * *

Rafael bolted upright. There it was again. A gentle rap on the door. He lunged out of bed and tugged a pair of sweats on. "Matias isn't getting any pastries this morning."

I glanced at my cell phone. It was eight o'clock in the morning, right on the nose.

Rafael's voice echoed briefly from the other room. Within minutes his broad frame filled the doorway to the bedroom. He was tapping an envelope against the palm of his hand.

I eyed the envelope. "What's that?"

He slid a formal looking invitation from the envelope. "Chief D'Souza has requested our presence at the PSP's charity ball tonight."

"PSP?"

"The Public Security Police. The event benefits those who are injured in the line of duty and the families of fallen officers."

I poked a single toe out from under the comforter and shivered. "Are we going?"

He tapped the remote for the fireplace. "I believe it's expected."

I planted both of my feet on the floor. "Is this a formal event?"

Rafael set the invitation on the nightstand. "Yes. You need a formal gown."

I joined him on the other side of the bed. "Can I have your cell phone? I'd like to see if Eva can help me shop."

Rafael grinned. "You don't want to shop with me?" He handed me his phone.

"I'd rather you be surprised by the dress." I kissed him on the cheek before scrolling through his contacts. "*Olá*, Eva?"

"*Bom dia*, Kristine. Is everything okay?"

I cringed. "Oh, God! I'm so sorry. It's crazy early."

"*Não, não.* It's fine. I've been awake for an hour."

"I was just wondering if you were free to go shopping with me. We just received an invitation for the PSP's charity ball..."

"Oh, you're going!" she squealed delightedly. "Benjamim and I are going too. Most of the Templar will be there as a show of support for those serving in law enforcement."

"Really?" I breathed. *No pressure there.*

"I'll pick you up in one hour. I know the perfect boutique. Oh, and I'll secure an appointment for you at the spa. My appointment is at noon. Don't worry, they serve lunch. Tell Rafael I'll have you back by five o'clock. *Adeus,*" she called cheerily.

I glanced at the phone. That woman had entirely too much energy for eight o'clock in the morning. I looked at Rafael. "I need lots and lots of coffee."

* * * * *

I stepped in front of the mirror. Truly, this was the most romantic dress I'd ever seen. The full, blush colored gown served as a canvas for deep forest green leaves, ivory, lavender, and burgundy flowers. The images were soft and faded like a Monet. The strapless gown forced a considerable amount of cleavage above the rib-crushing corseted top, which Eva assured me was okay. A blush crept over my cheeks. The corset pushed everything up so that my very average breasts looked much fuller than they really were.

With a slender shrug, I decided to let Rafael be the judge. He was waiting patiently in the living room, oblivious to the fact that I was wearing thigh high stockings, a light pink garter, and a matching thong beneath the filmy skirt. Soft

100

pink heels completed the ensemble.

Rafael scrambled to his feet. His jaw clenched while his hands circled my waist. "I don't know whether to kill or kiss Eva." His thumbs scaled the corset before grazing my breasts. "I'm going to have to beat the rest of the police force off with my baton."

"You have a baton?" I wondered if he knew his hands were clenching my breasts.

Rafael frowned. "Maybe I should bring one of my swords."

I laughed. "Good luck hiding that in your tux. You look gorgeous, by the way." The traditional black tux displayed his broad shoulders, trim waist, and muscular legs perfectly. He looked devastating in a tux.

His hands shifted, circling my neck. He forced my chin higher with his thumbs. "Kiss me," he demanded gruffly.

I stepped closer, so that every hard angle of his body was perfectly aligned with mine. I slid one flawlessly manicured hand behind his neck and forced his lips to mine. With painstaking precision, I traced his lips with the tip of my tongue. When I was certain he couldn't bear it any longer, I delved deep inside his mouth.

With a groan, Rafael wrested control of the kiss. My blood burst into flames as he thrust deep inside my mouth. He stroked my tongue again and again; circling... tempting... teasing until the kiss grew frenzied. He ventured lower, layering passionate kisses all along my jaw and thoroughly ravishing my neck.

My breasts swelled against the corset, demanding his attention. "We're going to be late." I prayed he didn't care. I wanted him in the worst possible way.

His thumbs dipped beneath the corset. "Everyone will

be late." He latched onto my breast.

"I'll never get enough of this… of you," I breathed.

Rafael's hands slid down my back. His eyes darkened when he cupped my bottom. "You're wearing a garter?"

I nodded, somewhat fearfully. The desire rolling off him was a little unsettling.

"If you value that thong, you'll step out of it. Now."

I dug beneath the beautiful skirt, unfastened the garter, and quickly removed the thong. My hands shook like a junkie needing drugs.

Rafael loosened his pants. In one fluid motion, he lifted me. Like a man possessed, he thrust. We slammed against the wall. I closed my eyes and savored the moment he lost all control.

He claimed everything at once; my breasts… my neck… and mouth… while destroying every nerve ending between my legs. He thrust harder than he ever dared before.

I welcomed every blow.

Rafael pinched my breasts, catapulting me toward release. I screamed deep inside his mouth. He groaned his response as he filled me. I fell slack, savoring the pulsing heat.

Rafael collapsed against me, his heartbeat as wild as mine.

I wiped lip gloss from his chin when my feet finally found the floor. "I… I need a minute to freshen up." I patted my hair, wondering how much damage had been done.

A warm chuckle rolled through his chest. "You look fine. A little mussed… like we just had sex, but that works for me. It'll keep the other officers away."

I just shook my head. Within ten minutes time, my makeup, thong, and dress were back where they belonged. I joined Rafael in the living room.

He pulled me in for a hug. "Thanks for indulging me."

A single eyebrow rose along my forehead. "Have you looked in the mirror recently? How could I possibly resist?"

Rafael twirled me around so my back was to his chest. He clasped a necklace around my neck.

"What's this?" My fingers skimmed the smooth, cool beads that sat too high to see. Slowly, I turned around.

He glanced at the necklace. "Those are my mother's pearls."

"Rafael," I objected.

He cupped my face in his hands. "Please. My mother would want you to have these."

I choked back tears. "I don't deserve you."

He smiled. "You do. You deserve me, and this, and so much more; and I'm going to spend the rest of my life proving it to you."

My heart clenched. "I love you."

"I love you too." He kissed me, gently. "Ready?"

"Yes," I answered breathlessly. We took the elevator to the garage. "Did you speak with Chief D'Souza today?" Rafael made his decision before I left with Eva. That decision had left me feeling vulnerable and sad, but I was trying to be supportive.

Rafael helped me into the car. "No, love. He'll be expecting an answer tonight."

"I can't believe we're going to live apart." We'd practically lived together for nine months, fourteen if you counted our time together in Paris. I forced my composure back into place. "I shouldn't complain. This is a small sacrifice to make. I'll finish my degree, and you'll nail every last man who abused those children. Then, we'll be together either here or in Virginia, and we'll never be parted again."

Rafael nodded although a scowl marked his face. He pulled out of the garage.

I pulled my skirt a little closer so it wouldn't interfere with the clutch. "What do you want to do about the wedding?"

He turned onto the *Avenida da Liberdade*. "We're going to proceed as planned. I reserved the Monserrate Palace. I told them we want to be married while the sun is setting. Should we plan to have the reception there? They offered to set up a large tent with tables and chairs."

I nodded. While we originally discussed having a small, intimate wedding, the guest list had taken on a life of its own. We were now up to fifty-three people; to include my family, Kimme and Dan, our friends from Virginia, Benjamim, Eva, and Rafael's friends from the police force, some of whom I suspected were knights. I hadn't given much thought to a reception, but I liked the idea of having everything in one place. "That sounds good. Will they allow us to bring in a caterer?"

He nodded. "Yes, but there's only one caterer who is allowed on the premises."

"Well, that's one less decision we have to make," I noted gratefully. I was still questioning how I was going to pull this off while immersed in school and working on the other side of the Atlantic Ocean.

Rafael glanced at me. "I'm happy to manage the logistics. Honestly, planning our wedding will help keep me sane while you're away. If you send the invitations, choose the dresses and the flowers for your bouquets, then I can manage the rest."

"I would like to choose your ring," I interjected. "Although, I do want your input. Maybe we can go ring

shopping after Christmas." I couldn't believe Christmas was
only three days away.

Rafael parked in front of the Four Seasons Hotel. He
helped me from the car before handing his keys to the valet.
"Shall we?"

I tucked my hand in the crook of his arm. "We shall."

Rafael nodded at the doorman. "*Boa noite.*"

He nodded politely while holding the door. "*Boa noite.*"

My heels clicked against gleaming marble floors. The
lobby offered several sitting areas anchored by sage and gold
embroidered rugs. Large windows lined the wall opposite a
contemporary painting depicting centaurs. "Interesting
décor."

Rafael surveyed the crowd while I admired the décor
inside the Pedro Leitão ballroom. Long ceiling to floor
curtains framed an entire wall's worth of glass doors. The
curtains were pulled back and the doors were open,
beckoning guests into a softly lit garden. Little specks of light
from the crystal chandeliers danced along the ceiling, the rose
colored walls, columns, and marble floor. "Wow," was the
only word I could muster.

Rafael handed me a glass of champagne just as
Benjamim called our names. Our friends stood beneath a
massive painting of a mythical tree with metallic gold leaves.
Rafael cut through the crowd with his hand planted
possessively on my lower back.

Eva kissed my cheek. "You look lovely, Kristine."

"Thanks, Eva. You look stunning." She was wearing a
red formfitting dress with a sweetheart neckline that revealed
even more cleavage than my corseted bodice. The
embroidered sleeves scrolled over her shoulders and arms as
if they'd been tattooed directly onto her skin.

Benjamim kissed my cheek. "Truly, you rival the artwork and the garden with that dress."

My cheeks flushed pink. "Thank you, Benjamim."

Rafael shook his friend's hand. "That reminds me. Are you available May 21st? That's the day we've chosen for our wedding, and I'd like you to be my best man."

"I would be honored." Benjamim's eyes glistened as the two men fell into a hug.

Rafael reached for my hand. "Now that I've secured my best man, would you like to dance?"

"I would love to." I set my glass on the table next to his.

He gave Eva a quick kiss. "Please forgive me, but I'm anxious to dance with my fiancé."

Eva offered a knowing smile. "Benjamim and I will be in the garden."

Rafael led me to the dance floor. With a playful twist, he pulled me into a waltz.

I smiled, thoroughly amused. "Any idea what we're dancing to?"

He moved closer to the violinists. "Tchaikovsky's 'Valse Sentimentale.'"

My eyebrows rose. I wasn't really expecting him to know. "What type of music would you like for our wedding?"

Rafael looked thoughtful. "A pianist or a violinist would be nice for the ceremony, but I'd prefer a band for the reception."

"That sounds perfect, although… I'm beginning to question the sunset wedding."

He stopped dancing. "Why? I thought you loved seeing the sun set over the palace gardens."

I stepped a little closer. "Do you remember when you took me to see the sunrise at Lewes Beach?"

Rafael nodded.

My hand slid from his shoulder to his chest. "You told me that sunsets make you feel sad, like you just lost something."

"That's true. They do." He gazed deep into my eyes.

"I don't want the sun setting on our relationship while we exchange our wedding vows," I admitted softly.

Slowly, we resumed dancing. "We can schedule the wedding a little earlier if you'd like."

I took a deep breath and slowly released it. "You told me you prefer to watch the sun rise. You like how the morning sun beckons new beginnings."

Understanding dawned in his eyes.

Mischief danced in mine. "I think we should drag all our loved ones out of bed in the dead of night so we can exchange our vows at sunrise."

Rafael laughed. Loudly.

I watched him turn the idea in his head.

Several emotions played across Rafael's face. Excitement won out in the end. "We can line the trail between the parking lot and the palace with luminarias. The palace is lit at night, so our guests would get to see Monserrate Palace glowing against the night sky… a glorious sight few people ever see… and imagine their surprise when the sun rises! Most of our guests would be unaware of the magnificent gardens surrounding them until the moment the sun crept over the palace."

I grinned. I knew it was crazy, dragging everyone out of bed so early in the morning, but with an evening wedding, our guests would arrive shortly before sunset. They would catch only the briefest glimpse of the palace gardens before the grounds grew dark. The entire reception would be held in the dark, which was truly a shame given all the natural beauty surrounding Monserrate Palace. If we were married in the morning, our guests could explore the gardens and the palace in the light of day. "Just think, with all the wonderful pastries Portugal is famous for, we could host a brunch instead of dinner... serve *bica*, mimosas, and *Vinho Verde* at the reception. We could still include a band and dance the morning away. We would have the entire day to celebrate."

"I think that's a brilliant idea." His lips slanted over mine.

"Ahem..."

Rafael looked up. "*Comandante*, I had a feeling you'd be cutting in, but I wasn't expecting it to be in the middle of a kiss."

Chief D'Souza laughed. "Please, by all means, finish your kiss."

Rafael looked at me.

I pressed my finger to his lips. "Later," I promised.

Chief D'Souza's smile widened. "May I have this dance?"

My chin rose ever so slightly. "You may."

Grudgingly, Rafael tucked my hand in his.

The police chief whisked me away. "Are you enjoying the ball, Senhorita Stone?"

"Yes, very much so." I surveyed the room. "I hope you secure enough donations to provide for your injured officers and their families."

He nodded thoughtfully. "What do you think of our city?"

My shoulders began to relax. Chief D'Souza was an adept dancer. "I love Lisbon. The people are friendly. The food is amazing. The weather is perfect. The architecture and art are fascinating. Even your sidewalks are pretty."

Chief D'Souza laughed. "That they are." He spun me under his arm. "Has Rafael made a decision?"

I glanced at him in surprise. "I think Rafael would prefer to answer that question for you."

"I'd prefer the answer came from you." A hint of amusement sparked in his eyes.

"Why?" I blurted incredulously.

"So I can gauge how you feel about the decision."

I stared at him for a couple of heartbeats. "Rafael will be returning on a temporary basis to assist with the investigation."

He nodded. Once. "And if he decides to remain on a more permanent basis?"

My eyes narrowed. "Then I will support him in that decision."

"Will you marry him regardless?"

"Of course," I bristled. "I love Rafael with all my heart."

His eyes darkened. "I was the first officer who responded… the one who found him kneeling in blood, praying for a miracle with both parents in his arms. I had to remove Rafael's father from his arms, force him to focus on his mother, and then re-direct his anguish when she passed away. I gave him a constructive outlet for all that anger and pain. I empowered him to save others and to make this world a better place."

I choked back tears. "You love Rafael… like a son."

"I do." He sighed. "I tried everything to piece that young man back together. He followed my advice. He welcomed every challenge, exceeded every expectation, and poured himself into his work."

"You did good," I whispered. "Rafael's a courageous man. He has a huge heart. He's selfless and kind. He's devoted his life to protecting others."

"But he still felt hurt and lost," Chief D'Souza noted, "until he met you."

I shook my head sadly. "I'm afraid I've hurt more than helped Rafael."

"You're referring to Michael," he surmised rather astutely. "You're not the one who shot Michael."

"I put everyone's life at risk when I went to work in Ukraine," I persisted.

"Including your own," he rebutted softly. "You were in Ukraine because you wanted to help others... because you wanted to make this world a safer place. Don't you see, Kristine? You were the missing piece."

I eyed him uncertainly.

"I gave the man a purpose, but that wasn't enough. You... you healed his heart." He tucked my hand against his chest. "There's one thing you should understand before you marry this man. Rafael needs you just as much as you need him."

Goosebumps trickled down my arms and back. Michael didn't want Rafael to join the police force. Benjamim claimed he had a death wish. And now, the man who recruited Rafael for special ops described him as hurt and lost. I knew he'd been deeply affected by his parents' death, but he'd always appeared so capable and strong. Not once had I considered the fact that Rafael might be every bit as broken as me.

Chief D'Souza stopped dancing, although my hand remained clasped to his chest. "You will love and support him in his efforts to protect those who are vulnerable whether through the police force, his private security firm, or the Templar."

I blinked back my surprise. "Yes. Of course." *Hadn't we*

already covered this?

"And you will continue to devote your life to helping others?"

I thought it odd that he was focusing on my goals, but I nodded all the same. "Yes. I'm afraid I'm hardwired that way."

He battled a smile. "You'll keep the Templar's secret?"

"Yes," I whispered. I glanced around nervously.

He lowered his voice even more. "Do you solemnly vow both secrecy and support for Rafael Tiago Garcia and his fellow knights?"

"Yes," I answered distractedly. Why was Chief D'Souza asking me this here? Was he questioning my willingness to follow through with the required vows?

He raised a single eyebrow.

"Yes," I answered more firmly.

This time he smiled. "In exchange for this vow of secrecy and support, the Knights Templar will aid and protect you, wherever you live for as long as you may live."

"V...vow?" I stammered.

Chief D'Souza lifted his hand and mine, revealing the service pin on his tux.

My eyes widened when I realized what it was. The ivory circle in the center of the pin displayed a white cross with red trim. The round pin was surrounded by a gold, fiery looking star. "The Order of Christ Cross," I whispered in awe.

"You were appointed the grand master's designee," Rafael stated from directly behind me.

I spun around. "What?"

Chief D'Souza clasped Rafael's shoulder. "Senhorita Stone has issued the required vows. She is everything you claimed and more. You have our blessing. I expect an invitation to the wedding, of course."

Rafael shook his hand before tucking me beneath his arm. "*Obrigado, Comandante.* We value your blessing, and you're already on the guest list."

Chief D'Souza smiled before adopting a business-like tone. "You will report to work January four?"

"Yes," Rafael assured him. "I will return to work on January fourth."

"Very well then." Chief D'Souza clasped, then kissed my hand. "I enjoyed spending time with you, Senhorita Stone. Thank you for the dance."

"Thank you," I answered softly. I looked at Rafael when he stepped off the dance floor. "What just happened?"

He turned me so that our bodies were flush. "Chief D'Souza has accepted your oath of fealty to the Order on behalf of the grand master. I wasn't expecting him to solicit those vows here. I thought there would be a private meeting."

I breathed a small sigh of relief. "Well, I'm glad that's over, but it would have been nice to have some sort of preamble or warning before he began asking those questions." He'd pretty much just blindsided me.

Rafael glanced curiously after the police chief. "He probably thought it would be less stressful for you."

I linked my hands behind his neck. "On the plus side, I've been authorized to marry a knight."

He dipped me back over his arm. "Not just any knight."

I chuckled softly. "No, Rafael. You're not just any knight. You're *my* knight."

With smoldering eyes, he claimed the kiss we'd been deprived.

* * * * *

I scooted forward. "I know what I want to do for Christmas."

"What?" Rafael slid his legs around me while easing into the steaming tub.

I leaned back against his chest. "I don't want to exchange gifts. I want to purchase gifts for the children at the Casa Pia Orphanage instead."

"There are over four thousand children at the Casa Pia Orphanage," Rafael warned. He reached for the cedar and sage soap we purchased at the outdoor market after securing pastries from the corner bakery.

"You don't think I can manage four thousand gifts? Clearly, you don't know who you're marrying." I thoroughly enjoyed throwing those words back at him.

He looked doubtful. "You're going to purchase four thousand gifts in two days?"

I turned and faced him while kneeling between his legs. "Give me your phone."

He set the bar of soap aside and handed me his phone.

I scrolled through his contacts with a ridiculously smug look on my face. My eyes met his when I hit send. *"Olá, Eva?"*

"Hálo, Kristine. Como vai?" Eva answered.

"Bem, orbrigada. E vocês?" I replied.

"Está tudo," Eva said, nearly exhausting my ability to speak Portuguese. "What are you doing?"

My eyes travelled Rafael's naked body and mine. "Um…" I decided an honest answer wasn't required. "I have a *huge* favor to ask."

"Really?" she replied. "Does this favor require

113

shopping?"

Rafael pulled the phone away from my ear and switched it to speaker so he could hear both sides of the conversation.

I grinned. "Yes. Actually, this favor is going to require a *ton* of shopping. Instead of exchanging gifts with Rafael, I'd like to purchase gifts for the children at the Casa Pia Orphanage. I want to deliver them in time for Christmas. Rafael is doubting my ability to pull this off."

"Oh!" she exclaimed excitedly. "I would love to help with that. What do you have in mind?"

"What was the name of that traditional cake? The one you gave to Matias?" I asked Rafael. He was gliding the bar of soap across my back. His Greek god-like body was glistening between the bathwater and the sun streaming through the open blinds. The cedar and sage scented soap smelled so utterly masculine it was muddying my mind.

"*Bolo Rei.*" He abandoned the bar of soap so he could work the lather into my shoulders and chest with both hands.

"*Bolo Rei,*" I repeated. I bit my bottom lip while suppressing a moan. I had to force myself to continue. "We should take the children *Bolo Rei*, books, and every board game we can find. We're going to have to hit a lot of stores in a short amount of time. I was wondering if you or Benjamim might have some *friends* who'd be interested in helping." "Friends" was code for "knights." Since Benjamim worked for the Templar, and the Templar ran a charity organization, I figured this would be right up their alley.

"Oh, I think our friends would be very interested in helping," Eva agreed.

"We need help shopping and wrapping," I murmured distractedly. I was trying to stay focused, but Rafael's ministrations had me longing for more elicit activities.

With a low growl, Rafael grabbed the phone. He said something to Eva in Portuguese and disconnected the call.

"What are you doing?" I objected.

"Eva and her recruits from the Knights Templar will purchase the *Bolo Rei*. I'm sure they'll wipe out every bakery in the city." He pulled my thighs around his waist before scrolling through his list of contacts. With one hand grasping my hip, he pressed the phone to his ear. He thrust inside of me the second the person answered the phone.

Desire pulsed through my entire body. I loved how this man felt inside of me... how thick he was... how consuming he was... and the way he so thoroughly possessed me. I moaned when he pulled our hips flush.

Our eyes locked. Rafael held a lengthy conversation in Portuguese while moving our hips. Water sloshed all around us.

I removed his hands from my hips so I could gain control. I wanted to see him unravel in the middle of the call.

Rafael's eyes darkened. He rasped out a few more instructions before ending the call. He latched onto my breast and the room faded to black.

My head fell back. "What did you just do?" I panted. Half of me didn't even care.

"I just recruited the Lisbon police force and their families to help. They'll purchase the games. We'll purchase the books, wrapping paper, and bows. Everyone who is available will meet at the station at six o'clock so we can wrap the presents." He thrust a little harder. "Does that work for you?"

"Yes," I groaned.

Rafael lifted my hips and pulled me down. Hard. We both cried out. I locked my arms around his neck as he spilled inside of me. The searing heat catapulted me toward release. His hips moved ever so slightly while he wrung every last bit of pleasure from me.

I waited for our hearts to quiet. "Thank you," I whispered.

"For what?" he laughed.

My arms tightened around his neck. "Everything. Thank you for everything." I knew then, I was hopelessly in love with this man.

* * * * *

We wiped out the children and young adult sections of every bookstore in town, as well as the bookstores in a few neighboring towns. The PSP Rossio Station was filled to bursting with officers, Templar, and their families. The gift wrapping event morphed into a full blown party. The children wrapped the presents while the officers organized the gifts into boxes marked for different age groups. The women supervised the color coded wrapping, ran errands for additional supplies, and served food. I made several new friends with whom I visited long into the night. The boxes were loaded into police cars and vans so they could be delivered the next day.

Rafael and I stumbled into bed during the early morning hours, which is why we were still lying in bed at ten o'clock in the morning. We were planning to join the rest of the officers who were delivering gifts to the Casa Pia Orphanage this afternoon.

Rafael was drawing lazy figure eights along my back. "Would you like to attend mass tonight? The *Igreja de Santa Maria at Belém* has a beautiful Christmas Eve service."

I thought about the mass Michael and I had attended at Notre Dame in Paris, France. I felt an overwhelming sense of sadness. I'd been avoiding church for far too long. "I would like that very much."

Rafael brushed my tears away after tucking me beneath him. "I love you, Kristine. I love you so much it hurts." His body trembled with the full force of his emotions. "I don't know how to survive this. You're the only family I have left."

Tears clogged my throat and flooded my eyes. In ten days' time we'd be living on different continents, an entire ocean apart. His sunset would be my sunrise.

Rafael buried his face in my neck. He let the full weight of his body relax onto mine. "Promise me we'll survive this."

My hands tangled in his hair as I lifted his head and peered into his eyes. "I'm not the only family you have left. The Templar, those other officers, Chief D'Souza, Eva, and Benjamim; they're you're family too."

"That may be so, but you hold the other half of my heart." His voice broke.

"I know." The ache in my chest told me that Rafael was hoarding the other half of mine. "It's only for a short while. I'll come to Lisbon just as soon as I graduate, and I'll visit every month until then."

"Promise me," he ordered.

"I promise. Now, make love to me before we go. I want your child growing inside my tummy by the time I return to Portugal."

Rafael's eyes flared with desire and hope. He tugged the camisole over my head and ravished my breasts before removing the rest of our clothes. We were naked, our arms and legs seeking purchase, when he slammed inside of me. His lips consumed mine as he thrust again and again.

I locked my arms and legs around him as he drove inside of me. My back arched on its own accord. We both screamed when he came. Rafael filled me with a searing heat, shattering me. Twice. Then, with painstaking precision, he knit us back together. He stole my breath, the other half of my heart, and my soul while offering me his own.

* * * * *

"You do realize I'm going to want to take them all home," I warned.

"All?" Rafael repeated with wide eyes. He helped me from the car.

I gazed up at the old historic building. The orphanage appeared to be housed within a convent or a monastery comprised of multiple buildings tucked behind a sharply pointed wrought iron fence. "Well, maybe not all," I teased. "Maybe four or five."

He spoke briefly through the intercom at the gate. After a low hum, the gate clicked open. Rafael left the gate open for the other officers.

A petite woman with steel gray hair met us at the door. Rafael introduced himself as we stepped inside the foyer. He spoke briefly in Portuguese before switching to English. "This is my *noiva*, Kristine Stone, the woman I told you about on the phone."

She reached for my hand. "I understand you organized this charitable donation, Senhorita Stone. Thank you, and welcome to Casa Pia. I'm the assistant director, Benedita Medeiros."

I shook her hand. "Thank you for permitting us to bring the children gifts. The rest of the officers are outside unloading boxes. Would it upset the children if they came inside? Some of them are wearing their uniforms."

She smiled. "I think it would be good for our children to see the officers doing such a kind thing. Please encourage them to bring the boxes inside."

"There are additional officers en route to the other campuses. They should arrive shortly," Rafael informed Senhora Medeiros. The Casa Pia Orphanage housed children on ten different campuses, which were scattered throughout the city.

I handed her my cheat sheet when Rafael stepped outside to help carry boxes. "We have color coded the gifts so it will be easier for you to distribute them. The gifts wrapped in green and gold are for the fourteen to eighteen year olds. The gifts wrapped in blue are for the nine to thirteen year olds. The gifts wrapped in red are for children between the ages of four and eight, and the gifts wrapped in white and gold are for the infant to three year olds."

"Senhorita Stone is extremely organized," Chief D'Souza opined from somewhere behind me. He set his box on a wooden pew before clasping Senhora Medeiros's hand. "It's nice to see you again, Senhora Medeiros. I would like to make this an annual event, with your consent." I suspected he was speaking in English for my benefit.

Her eyes widened when twelve other officers poured into the lobby. Each of the officers was balancing two or three boxes filled with gifts. "That would be wonderful. The children at Casa Pia receive so few gifts."

Benjamim and Eva stepped inside the lobby. They were joined by several people carrying large pastry bags. "*Feliz Natal*," Eva greeted cheerily.

Senhora Medeiros's eyes misted over. "Please you must

join us for *Consoada* and *Missa do Galo*."

Rafael tucked me against his chest. "*Consoada* is a traditional Christmas dinner, which is served on Christmas Eve. I think you'd like it."

"We'd love to join you," Eva answered.

"As would I," Chief D'Souza replied.

Rafael glanced at me.

I nodded. "We would too. Thank you for inviting us."

Some of the officers had to work. Others were expected to join their families at home, but three additional officers stayed behind to celebrate Christmas Eve with us. We stored the gifts inside the office adjoining the lobby until the children were called to the main dining hall for dinner. When Senhora Medeiros gave the signal, we carried the presents to the recreation room so we could stack them around the Christmas tree. A nativity scene was sitting next to the tree, but the baby Jesus was missing. I thought it odd, but I was so busy unpacking the gifts I forgot to ask about it.

We joined the children in the main dining hall as soon as we finished moving the gifts. We set a *Bolo Rei* in the center of each table before claiming our seats. Each of us was offered a plate filled with codfish, cabbage, hard boiled eggs, and boiled potatoes served with garlic sauce. Eva, Chief D'Souza, and the other officers shared some of their family traditions while we ate.

"What is *Missa do Galo*?" I finally asked.

"*Missa do Galo* is a special Christmas Eve service which is held just before midnight," Rafael explained.

My eyes widened. I hadn't realized it was going to be such a long night. Chief D'Souza pulled Rafael into another conversation. Eva was talking to Benjamim, so I sat back and observed the children.

The Casa Pia Orphanage was quite different from the orphanage I visited in Ukraine. The children seemed happier and healthier here, but there were a lot more children over all. The number of children in this facility was astonishing, and there were at least nine other campuses housing orphaned children in Lisbon. I wondered why so many children were being abandoned by their families in Portugal. The people living in Lisbon seemed far wealthier than those living in Simferopol. I reflected back on the decaying housing projects I'd seen on the outskirts of town when we drove to Sintra. Clearly, there was poverty here. Perhaps they were just better at hiding it.

I studied the staff. They were firm but kind toward the children. I wondered whether anyone who assisted the pedophiles in accessing these children was still working here. I couldn't fathom how someone who'd been entrusted to care for these children could allow such a horrible thing to happen. I prayed the PSP would be able to identify and arrest every last person involved in that heinous crime.

I turned around when I felt something brush against my back. A little boy, somewhere around the age of five, had his hand in my hair. I crooked my arm over my chair and smiled. "*Olá.*"

"*Olá,*" he repeated with a shy smile. He couldn't seem to take his eyes off my hair.

"*Falas inglês?*" I inquired hopefully.

He shook his head. "*Não.*"

Rafael turned and asked the boy a question in Portuguese.

The boy asked his own question while pointing at me.

"*Sim. Eu acho que ela é,*" Rafael replied.

"What?" I'd been trying to improve my understanding of

121

the language, but I hadn't a clue what either of them had said.

Rafael grinned. "He asked if you were an angel. I told him, 'Yes. I think she is.'"

The boy gaped at me before sprinting toward his friends. One of the staff members issued a sharp command. He slowed to a brisk walk while glancing worriedly at me.

Rafael laughed. He accepted a bowl of rice pudding from a young girl distributing dessert. "*Obrigado.*"

"*Obrigada,*" I repeated when she offered me a bowl.

"*Você é bem-vindo.*" She adjusted her tray and handed a bowl to the officer sitting next to me.

The cinnamon laced pudding tasted surprisingly good. "Are we staying for the midnight mass?"

"You might enjoy the service here more than the one at the *Igreja de Santa Maria,*" Rafael said, his head crooked thoughtfully.

I nodded my agreement.

"Will you be staying for the *Missa do Galo?*" Benjamim inquired from across the table.

"Yes," Rafael and I replied as one.

Benjamim laughed.

Rafael and the other officers sliced the *Bolo Rei*. Eva, Benjamim, and I helped distribute the cake. Excited squeals and audible groans sounded when the children cut into their cake. A few of the children held tiny objects in the air for all to see.

"The *Bolo Rei* holds two objects," Rafael explained, "a large bean and a small gift. The person whose slice includes the gift gets to keep the gift. The person whose slice includes the bean is supposed to purchase the *Bolo Rei* next Christmas."

"No way!" I exclaimed. "That sounds just like the King

Cakes we serve for Mardi Gras in the United States, only the King Cake contains a plastic baby that is meant to signify the baby Jesus. The person who finds the baby Jesus is considered lucky, but he also has to buy the cake the following year."

Rafael smiled. "Maybe our traditions aren't so different after all."

We returned to our table once the children and staff were served. I was anxious to try the *Bolo Rei*. "*Obrigada*," I purred when a staff member delivered coffee.

Senhora Medeiros educated us about their program while the children prepared for church. We toured the campus while we waited for the service to begin.

We joined the children in the sanctuary shortly before midnight. There were no frescoes or stained glass windows adorning this building. Stone walls, arched windows, wooden pews, and kneelers defined this church. A large crucifix hung at the front of the church. Hundreds of votive candles were lit along the altar, at the base of the statues of the Virgin Mary and the saints, and upon the window sills. The candles bathed the dark, cavernous sanctuary in a soft, warm light. Heated wax and frankincense scented the musky air.

Rafael translated the sermon as best he could without appearing rude. For the most part, the service was structured the same as the Christmas Eve masses I'd attended in the United States, but that changed after communion.

After communion, the priest lifted a swaddled doll from a manger that had been sitting in front of the altar. Everyone lined up to kiss the doll. I didn't want to kiss the doll, but I relented because I didn't want to offend anyone. While they sang worship songs, I calculated how many of us would end up with the flu. With hundreds of people sharing the same wine goblet and kissing the same doll smack dab in the middle of cold and flu season, it was bound to happen.

The service was fascinating. I truly enjoyed praying while kneeling; it helped me stay focused. The music was nice, even if I couldn't sing along, and I loved the benediction at the end; but that wasn't the best part. The best part was celebrating Christmas with all those children. That was truly awesome.

Senhora Medeiros invited us to watch the children open their gifts. Miraculously, the swaddled doll beat us to the recreation room. He was, in fact, the baby Jesus who had been missing from the nativity set. Rafael explained that the children in Portugal do not receive their gifts until baby Jesus appears in the manger. No one knows how he gets from the churches where the masses are held into the homes where the children live. I liked how their Christmas gifts were tied to Jesus.

I curled up next to Rafael. We were sitting on the floor since there weren't a lot of chairs to be had. There wasn't a dry eye to be counted among the grownups when the children opened their gifts. The children couldn't comprehend owning their own books. They tried giving the books to the staff, assuming they were meant for the library. While they were encouraged to share, they were also encouraged to record their names inside the books. Only then would they trust the books truly belong to them. I'd never seen a child prize a book so much.

We laughed when they opened the board games. They were beyond ecstatic. The younger children shoved their games toward the older kids, demanding to be taught how to play. The older kids turned to the adults for help. Before long, we were all sprawled out on the floor playing board games.

We didn't leave until three o'clock in the morning. I hugged Rafael long and hard when we got to his car. "That was, hands down, the best Christmas I've ever had."

"Me too," he whispered.

"Our first Christmas together," I murmured with some surprise.

"Our first Christmas," he marveled. "*Feliz Natal.*"

* * * * *

"What's this?" Rafael asked.

"A present." I'd woken up early so I could make him breakfast in bed. Only he wasn't in bed. He was standing in front of the breakfast bar eying the gift sitting on the breakfast tray next to his eggs.

"But you said you didn't want to exchange gifts." He stole the coffee cup from the tray.

My hands fisted on my hips. "Would you get back in bed? I didn't wake up early so you could eat in the kitchen."

He hid his smile behind the coffee cup before sauntering into the bedroom.

I followed with the tray. "You gave me your mother's pearls, and you purchased books for more than four thousand children at my request. I think I'm entitled to buy you a gift."

He set the coffee cup on the nightstand before climbing back into bed. "Can I open it now?"

I set the tray on his lap, retrieved my tray, and climbed in next to him. "Sure, why not?"

Rafael ripped the green and silver foil from the box. His eyes widened when he lifted the lid.

I pulled the gray leather bracelet from the box. "I know you don't typically wear jewelry, but I thought this was masculine and casual enough that you might like it." I showed him the inscription on the back of the silver medallion.

He smiled. "Mine."

I wrapped the leather strap around his wrist three times before cinching the clasp. "You're always telling me I'm yours. I thought it was about time you heard you were mine."

"It's perfect. Thank you." He dropped a quick kiss on my lips before opening the nightstand. "I have a gift for you."

"So much for not exchanging gifts," I laughed.

"Merry Christmas, love." He handed me a small wooden box.

I opened the lid. "A Viana's heart necklace." I'd been admiring the filigree heart necklaces at the open market.

He sought a kiss so tender it brought tears to my eyes. "So you'll remember you hold my heart."

I fought to keep my emotions in check. "When are we heading back?"

He cut into the French toast. "The day after tomorrow. I need to go over a few things with Ethan since he'll be managing the security firm while I'm away."

I took a deep, steadying breath. We'd been in Portugal for nine days. Still, it wasn't enough. "What do you want to do on our last day?"

He licked maple syrup from his fingers. "I was debating between the City of Tomar and Cascais."

I peeked at him from over the top of my coffee. "A relaxing day at the beach sounds nice."

Rafael nodded. "Cascais it is then. Is there anything special you'd like to do today?"

I shrugged. "Not really."

He set our trays aside. "I want to make a baby."

"Oh, I'd like a baby," I admitted playfully.

"Then let's make one," Rafael suggested huskily.

I buried my hands in his hair and pulled his lips toward mine.

* * * * *

Rafael and I spent our final day in Portugal on a sandy beach in Cascais, savoring a thermos of Portuguese coffee and a bag full of decadent pastries under a brilliant blue sky. The weather was cool, so there were very few people on the beach. We were wearing sweaters and blue jeans. Still, we kicked our boots off so we could dig our toes into the sand. The sunshine, the salty sea air, and the sound of gently lapping waves helped loosen the vise on my heart.

The clock was ticking. Loudly. We were flying back home tomorrow. We'd have six days together in Virginia before being parted for five months. *Five months.* Half a year suddenly felt like an eternity. I hated the thought of being separated from Rafael. I wanted to stay in Lisbon with him, but I'd soaked so much time and money into my degree, I couldn't bear to throw it all away.

My graduate program wasn't the only commitment forcing my hand. Oni was moving to Virginia in fifteen days. I helped her secure admission to the Institute for Conflict Analysis and Resolution. Oni would be safer in the United States, but she didn't have a support system in Virginia. I wanted to help her through that transition, see her settled into her new life.

I rested my head on Rafael's shoulder with a dejected sigh. His responsibilities were even more daunting than mine.

Destroying an international pedophile ring, especially one that involved influential individuals, was no small undertaking. Rafael was personally vested in the case. I doubted he'd ever forgive himself for allowing that child to be violated while he stood guard over the perpetrator, even though he'd done so unknowingly. Still, if he could ensure that every last monster in that pedophile ring was taken off the streets, he might find peace.

"How are you holding up?" Rafael asked. He'd been quiet while grappling with his own thoughts.

"I miss you already," I admitted tearfully.

He pulled me close. "Me too."

The waves lulled us back into a tumultuous silence. We gathered our strength while seeking refuge from the impending storm.

Chapter 4 – Little Talks

I turned a slow circle in the mirror while admiring the sumptuous gown. Large chunks of jeweled confetti trickled down the nearly transparent bodice and a single sleeve. The heavily jeweled bodice was slanted, so my left arm was bare. Liquid gold poured from my hips all the way down to my toes. A deep slit along the side revealed strappy gold sandals and artfully painted toes in black and metallic gold. My hands shook as I smoothed the gown over my hips.

I sank onto the edge of the bed. That image of a daring, confident woman couldn't have felt more wrong. Beneath the perfect hair, the glittering nails, and dress; I was a mess. I didn't feel like celebrating, not with Rafael leaving in three days. I was also worried about Kadyn. He was invited to the celebration because he remained one of my most cherished friends. I was shocked he was actually attending the party. I still loved him, and I couldn't bear to see him hurt. Still, Rafael deserved a fiancé who celebrated the fact she was marrying him. I hadn't a clue how to soothe both their egos, how to honor one without hurting the other. With a deep, shuddering breath, I grabbed the faux fur wrap and walked downstairs.

I'd banished Rafael from the bedroom so he wouldn't see the dress before I was completely pulled together. I found him standing inside the kitchen with a San Pellegrino in his hand. I froze just inside the entrance. I couldn't grasp how he managed to look so refined with all that raw power rolling off his lethal frame.

Rafael's eyes widened. He muttered something in Portuguese… a benediction, a few choice curse words, or something in between. In three long strides, he stood before me. He caressed my arm while studying the bodice. "Those jewels best cover all the important parts."

"They do." A chill ran down my spine.

He stepped a little closer. His hand slid beneath the slit in the dress. His fingers skimmed my hip before curling around the gold lace thong.

"We'll be late," I objected. This was the PSP charity ball all over again.

His lips grazed my shoulder. "Perhaps we should stay home."

My eyes slid closed. "We should be there to greet everyone."

"I'll take a rain check," he grudgingly conceded, "but consider yourself warned. I'll be collecting within the hour." He herded me out the door. We were walking since the pier was less than two blocks away from the house.

Rafael spoke with a crew member before we boarded the yacht.

The captain greeted us when we stepped onto the deck. "Welcome aboard."

Ethan and his wife, Dakota, joined us a few minutes later.

Rafael shook Ethan's hand. "You clean up nice, my friend."

"Yeah, right." Ethan tugged at his collar. I suspected his wasn't the only bow tie that would be tossed aside before the end of the night.

"You look gorgeous." I hugged Dakota carefully so the jewels on my dress wouldn't snag her silky taupe gown. Dakota's pale blond hair was pulled back into an elegant twist that mimicked the ruched design of her dress.

"Congratulations on your engagement," Dakota gushed.

Rafael kissed her cheek when Ethan pulled me in for a hug.

We gave them a quick tour of the saloon before returning to the deck. Brady and Chance were boarding the yacht with their dates. Brady shook Rafael's hand. He gave me a hug while introducing his date. "Heidi, these are my friends, Rafael and Kristine. Heidi has graciously agreed to be my date this evening."

Rafael and I shook Heidi's hand. She was wearing a crushed velvet gown in midnight blue that looked gorgeous against her porcelain skin. Her dark blond hair was piled on top of her head in a messy but sexy upsweep. She looked flushed, and her blue eyes sparkled, which left me questioning what she and Brady had been up to before boarding the yacht.

Chance planted a quick kiss on my cheek. He shook Rafael's hand before introducing his date. "Jessica, I'd like you to meet my friends, Rafael and Kristine."

She smiled. "Congratulations. I understand you two were recently engaged."

Rafael drew me closer. "Yes. Thank you for celebrating with us."

"Jessica looks an awful lot like Shae," I noted when they walked away. Both women had warm skin tones that made it difficult to pinpoint their ethnicity. They were both petite but curvy enough to cause men whiplash. Their hair tumbled down their backs in soft brown, auburn, and gold waves. The most noticeable difference appeared to be in their eyes. Shae had warm brown eyes and an even warmer personality. Jessica's eyes were an impossible shade of green. The color was so improbable I suspected she was wearing tinted contacts. Still, her eyes were captivating, especially when paired with that emerald green dress.

"I don't think Chance has gotten over Shae." Rafael stepped in front of me. He bent to kiss me but paused millimeters away when his eyes snagged on something. "Your colleagues have arrived."

I grasped his face with both hands. "Don't you dare renege on that kiss."

A smile tugged at his lips. Slowly, Rafael fit his lips to mine. He took his time savoring the kiss.

My toes curled against the deck. I stared at him, speechless.

"Your friends..." He nodded toward Sammi and Cory.

Sammi's silver sequined gown glittered in the moonlight. The silver vest and necktie Cory was wearing complemented her gown and his dark skin tone perfectly.

Sammi stepped forward to give me a hug. "Congratulations, Kri." She grasped my hand. "Wow. What a beautiful ring!"

"Thanks." My pulse fluttered. I loved the sense of belonging that fell over me every time I caught sight of that ring.

Cory pulled me in for a hug. "You're literally glowing, Kri." He shook Rafael's hand. "Congratulations. Truly, we couldn't be happier for you."

Cenia, Roger, Phil, and Marie arrived together. Cenia was wearing a red satin gown that looked striking with her long dark hair. Marie was wearing a black lace evening gown that offered tiny glimpses of skin along her shoulders, waist, and hips. Her light brown hair was pulled into an elegant upsweep that showcased her long, delicate neck. Phil and Roger looked surprisingly comfortable in their tuxes. We spent a few minutes exchanging hugs.

Shae arrived on Konstantin's arm. She was wearing a silk champagne gown that draped around her shoulders before plunging dangerously low across her back. Konstantin looked handsome in his tux.

Jase stepped onto the yacht with his date, Emma. Silver sequins formed the straps, cinched the waist, and framed the back of her stark white dress. She looked angelic in the white evening gown, especially when standing next to Jase. His daunting frame was in no way tempered by the tux. With his short cropped hair and piercing blue eyes, the man still screamed special ops.

Kadyn was the last to arrive. His RSVP had indicated a "plus one," so I knew he was bringing a date. Still, my breath caught when I saw the woman on his arm. Rafael watched me while I observed them.

Kadyn's date was wearing a deep merlot gown. In all reality, she was the polar opposite of me. My skin was pale. Hers was dark. My eyes were blue. Hers were chocolate brown. Light blond hair tumbled down my back in waves. Her straight brown hair was cut in a stylish A-line that fell just below her chin. I forced myself to ignore the ache in my chest, my roiling stomach, and all the objections bubbling up inside of me so I could welcome them to the party.

Rafael squeezed my hand encouragingly. "You got this." He kissed me just above my temple.

I nodded, took a deep breath, and slowly blew it out. Kadyn's eyes grudgingly met mine. I was fumbling with a greeting when Rafael shook his hand. "Thanks for coming, Kadyn."

I didn't want to make Kadyn uncomfortable by hugging him in front of his date. He pulled me in for a hug anyway. "Welcome back, Kri. How was Portugal?"

I smiled gratefully. "Portugal was beautiful, especially Sintra. I could have spent months exploring those palaces."

Kadyn reached for his date. "Brianna, this is Rafael and Kristine, the friends I was telling you about."

I shook her hand. "It's a pleasure to meet you, Brianna."

"How do you know Kadyn?" Rafael asked, grasping her hand.

"We're collaborating on a project for CBP. Kadyn's overseeing the project and managing the purse strings." She nudged his shoulder with hers. "This man has made my life difficult the past few months. I think he's trying to make amends by inviting me to your party."

Kadyn chuckled. "You're a contractor. I'm supposed to make your life difficult."

The captain cleared his throat. "I'm sorry to interrupt, Mr. Garcia, Ms. Stone. Are you expecting anymore guests?"

"No. Everyone is here," Rafael confirmed.

The captain nodded toward a couple of crew members who were eying us expectantly. They began casting off the lines. "Please, make yourselves comfortable. We'll be departing shortly." He spoke to one of the crew members before returning to the bridge.

"Shall we?" Rafael ushered us inside. We joined Konstantin and Shae at the bar. "Brianna, what would you like to drink?"

"Pinot Grigio, please." She studied the saloon with her hand tucked inside the crook of Kadyn's arm. The room was richly appointed with glossy mahogany paneling, tables, and chairs. Ivory and gold upholstery softened the chairs. The lights had been turned down low. Candles cast a romantic glow from the center of each table.

The band was singing a lively rendition of Jimmy Buffett's "Margaritaville" near the dance floor. The bar, where we were standing, was tucked in a corner against the back wall. A chocolate fountain was churning above an impressive display of strawberries, shortbread cookies, homemade marshmallows, and pretzel rods dipped in caramel in the opposite corner.

The saloon had a long bank of windows on all four sides, so we could see the monuments and the fireworks igniting against the night sky when the clock struck midnight. Still, I suspected we'd wander outside to watch the display.

Rafael looked at Kadyn. "The usual?"

Kadyn nodded.

"Chianti?" Rafael raised a single eyebrow while smiling at me.

"Yes, please." I kissed his cheek. "Brianna, I'd like you to meet our friends, Konstantin and Shae."

She shook their hands. "Pleased to meet you."

Kadyn hugged Shae. "How was your Christmas? Are you enjoying the time off?"

She smiled. "Christmas was nice. Konstantin purchased a

135

condo in Arlington, so we've been shopping for furniture and getting him settled into his new place."

Kadyn grasped Konstantin's hand. "How are things at the embassy?"

"A bit too civilized for my blood," he admitted with a wry smile.

Shae laughed. "You've only been working there for a couple of weeks. Give it time."

His eyes narrowed on my ring. "Does Maxim know that you've agreed to marry Rafael?"

Kadyn stilled.

I averted my eyes. "Maxim will be arriving with Oni on the tenth. I plan to inform him then."

An ominous growl rolled through Konstantin's chest when he caught Chance admiring Shae from a few feet away.

Chance's gaze turned scathingly.

Konstantin tensed.

Kadyn edged between the two men.

Rafael handed Brianna their drinks. "Excuse me." He spoke with Chance.

Chance tensed, but he steered Jessica toward the table where Jase was sitting with his date.

Konstantin and Shae joined Sammi and Cory at a table on the opposite side of the room. Kadyn took Brianna to meet Cenia and Roger.

"Crisis averted." Rafael retrieved our drinks from the bar before escorting me to our table.

I draped my wrap over a chair and followed him onto the dance floor.

Rafael waited for the song to end before retrieving the microphone from the band.

The room quieted.

Kadyn and Brianna settled in at our table.

Rafael pulled me close. "I'd like to thank everyone for coming. We're pleased to be celebrating our engagement and ringing in the New Year with friends both old and new. The staff will be serving dinner shortly. Please enjoy the music, the dance floor, and the bar. There will be a champagne toast at midnight. Until then, I'd like to offer a toast to my future bride."

My cheeks heated.

His eyes softened when he gazed at me. "Every single one of you has come into my life because of her..."

Shockingly, Rafael was right. He wouldn't have opened his security firm, met my colleagues, my friends, or Konstantin if he hadn't moved to Virginia to be closer to me. I studied our friends. Aside from Sammi, Cory, and some of the guys' dates, nearly every person in the room had fought to keep me safe. I'd endured so much violence, faced countless threats, and somehow acquired the kindest and most fiercely protective friends. I slowly released my breath.

When my eyes met Rafael's, I knew. We'd been led to believe we were celebrating New Year's Eve, but that wasn't Rafael's intent. Rafael was gathering the troops, pulling everyone together so I'd remain safe while he was working in Portugal; and the vast majority of our guests didn't even know we were about to be separated. Yet.

Rafael smiled when my eyes lit with understanding. He raised his glass. "I just want to thank you for agreeing to marry me and for gifting me with so many remarkable friends."

We tapped glasses and drank to Rafael's toast. He handed the microphone to the lead vocalist. The band slid into the prelude for "Stand by Me." Rafael set our glasses aside. He led me to the center of the dance floor, twirled me under his arm, and pulled me close as we began to dance. Cenia, Roger, Shae, and Konstantin joined us midway through the song.

Warm dinner rolls and crisp green salads were waiting for us when we returned to our table. Rafael waited until Brianna went to the lady's room to draw Kadyn into the loop. He lowered his voice. "I've accepted a temporary assignment in Portugal. The police chief has pulled me back onto a case I was working before I met Kristine. They're trying to nail some elitists involved in an international pedophile ring that's been sexually abusing children from Lisbon's largest orphanage."

Kadyn's jaw clenched. "Preying on orphans? Why would anyone..." He stopped abruptly and looked at me. "Are you going?"

I shook my head.

"She's going to stay here and finish her degree. The assignment is temporary. I should be back within six months," Rafael explained.

Kadyn set his Sprite aside. "Look, I admire your determination to nail these guys, but you can't just leave Kri unprotected. The threat posed by the SVR is reason enough, but when Maxim gets wind of this..." His eyes slid toward Konstantin.

"So you understand my predicament," Rafael surmised.

Kadyn folded his arms against his chest. He knew Rafael was about to request something of him.

Rafael reached for his glass. "I've asked Brady and Jase to move into Kristine's townhouse until I return. They'll be sleeping in the guestrooms and accompanying her to work."

Kadyn rose from his chair when Brianna returned. He

dropped back into his seat once she was settled. "What do you want me to do?"

Rafael glanced at Brianna. He seemed uncertain as to how much he should divulge in front of her. "I know this is awkward, Kadyn, but there isn't a man on this planet I trust more than you. I know you have your own career, your own life, and responsibilities but would you mind serving as their back up?"

Kadyn leaned against the table. "Define 'back up.'"

Brianna studied the three of us over the top of her wine glass. The waiters removed our salad plates.

Rafael set his wine glass aside. "I'd like you to strategize with them, serve as a sounding board, check on Kristine regularly, and establish a presence at her place when Maxim is in town. You can stay at my place if you'd like."

Kadyn locked eyes with Rafael.

I fidgeted nervously. Kadyn had once confessed that he wished Rafael didn't trust him so much because it made him feel obligated to maintain that trust when he preferred to act less honorably. Less than two months had passed since Kadyn kissed me. I wondered whether either man was considering that misstep.

"Who knows about this?" Kadyn finally asked.

A waiter arrived with our dinner plates. He topped off our drinks and walked away.

"Ethan, Brady, Chance, and Jase," Rafael answered.

"I'd like to tell Cenia, Roger, Phil, and Marie. Not here. Elsewhere. So we aren't overheard." Kadyn looked at me. "How long do you think you can keep this from Shae?"

I rubbed my forehead irritably. "I don't know. A month... maybe two?" I looked at Rafael. "I'll tell her you're tied up with an assignment if she comes over. She doesn't have to know you're working out of town. I hate lying to her, though."

He reached for my hand. "I know, but if she says anything in front of Konstantin, it'll get back to Maxim. If Maxim thinks you're vulnerable, he'll exploit the situation."

"What am I supposed to do about Oni?" I asked. "Maxim is bringing her on the tenth. You'll be in Portugal by then. How do I explain your absence over the ten days that she's staying with me? And how do we know she won't report your absence to Maxim?"

Kadyn dug into his food. "Have you heard anything more about this favor Maxim's planning to ask?"

Rafael blew out a long, frustrated breath. "God. I just don't see how I can do this."

"You have to nail the creeps who've been sexually abusing those children," I insisted. "This case means so much to you. Rafael, you have got to see this through."

"I'll do it," Kadyn interjected. "I'll help protect Kri, but I have some conditions."

My jaw fell slack.

Rafael leaned forward. "Name the conditions."

"I'll stay at your place while you're gone, check in on Kri, consult with Brady and Jase, and serve as their back up should either of them become unavailable... under three conditions."

Rafael raised a single eyebrow.

Kadyn's face proved completely unreadable. "I stay at Kri's place during the ten days that Oni is there and every night that Maxim is in town." He looked at me. "Is Jase still accompanying you to work?"

I choked down a mouthful of loaded baked potato. "Yes."

"Then you'll do nothing without one or more of us joining you." Kadyn's tone brokered no room for argument.

Dread pooled in my stomach, making me feel nauseous.

"And?" Rafael prompted.

Kadyn's shoulders relaxed. "I get to drive the Enzo and the Vyrus while you're gone."

Rafael didn't even blink. "Agreed, but I'm going to add my own condition." His eyes slid toward Brianna. "I'd prefer to discuss that condition in private."

Kadyn studied him. "I know what the condition is. You don't want a repeat of McAllen."

Rafael nodded.

Kadyn looked at me. "Done."

Rafael breathed a sigh of relief before settling in to eat.

All of their strategizing over my security was making it difficult for me to breathe. I excused myself from the table so I could walk downstairs to the restroom. The door swung closed behind me. Finally, I was alone.

I grasped the vanity. Haunted eyes regarded my ashen face as panic bubbled up inside of me. Rafael was leaving in three days. *Three.* I trembled violently. Horrific things happened every time we parted. Several violent images set out to prove this very thing. The madman who tried to drown me... the Russian operative who interrogated me while his comrade shoved a stun gun between my legs... men dressed in camo, khaki, and black hanging out of SUVs with machine guns while bullets ricocheted all around me.

I splashed cold water on my face in an attempt to drive the images away. I thought about the little boy who was raped while Rafael kept his abuser safe. Those children at the Casa Pia Orphanage wouldn't be safe until every last monster in that pedophile ring had been locked away. I grabbed a face cloth from the silver tray next to the faucet and dabbed my face. As much as I wanted Rafael to stay, I couldn't ask him to abandon this investigation. Rafael needed to see this through or he'd never forgive himself for allowing that child to be abused. I had three extremely capable men standing guard over me while those children were a million miles from safe. My shoulders and spine straightened as I turned from the mirror.

Rafael was pacing in the hallway. "Your hour is up."

My eyes widened. I'd totally forgotten about the rain check. "You want to…" I swallowed nervously. "Here? *Now?* With all our guests upstairs?"

He planted his hands on either side of my head as he cornered me against the wall. "Yes. Here. Yes. *Now.* And I don't care who's upstairs."

I grasped his wrists. My heart beat wildly as he lowered his lips to mine. The kiss he stole was inexplicably soft given the aggression and the possessiveness rolling off his unyielding frame.

My hands fell to his chest, then linked behind his neck. I pulled him toward me so I could deepen the kiss.

Rafael's restraint crumbled. He devoured my lips… my chin… my neck. His hand carved a trail from my breast to my hip. His fingers slid beneath the slit in the dress.

He nudged my foot aside, forcing me to widen my stance as he stepped between my legs. In one fluid motion he had my legs around his waist. The kiss grew frenzied as he stumbled down the hallway. He slipped inside a bedroom, threw the lock, and pinned me against the door.

His tongue thrust deep inside my mouth as he tore my thong. Rafael shifted me in his arms while freeing himself from the tux. Still, he kissed me. With a groan, he sank inside of me.

I stilled, mortified that someone might hear us.

His hands raked over my breasts. He shifted the bodice so he could play with my nipples through the thin, sheer fabric. Slowly, he began to thrust.

My breath caught when Rafael's eyes pierced mine. Something primal was lurking just behind his eyes. He thrust even harder. "Mine," he growled. "You're mine, Kristine. Not Maxim's. Not Kadyn's. Mine."

"Yes." My breath rushed through my lips in short panting breaths. The amount of force he was using was frightening, but it felt so amazing I no longer cared who was listening. *God*, I thought, *how will I live without this... without him... for the next five months?* I locked my arms around his neck and kissed him frantically.

I lost myself in that exquisite place between pleasure and pain. Rafael was no longer capable of gentle. He was every bit as lost as I was. "Kristine," he cried. He tilted my hips and slammed inside of me. I shattered deep inside. The room sheeted white. Pleasure pulsed between his body and mine. Like a rag doll, I collapsed.

Rafael took his time releasing my legs. "I will never get enough of this... of you," he rasped. He kissed every square inch of my face before gently pulling away. "God help me. I don't know how to live without you."

I burrowed into his chest as tears threatened. "I promise, we'll get through this."

"Every chance," he whispered. "Every chance I get, I'll come back to see you."

We straightened our clothes. I grasped his hand when he unlocked the door. "I love you, Rafael." I wasn't sure I said that often enough.

He planted a tender kiss on my swollen lips. "I love you too."

We stepped inside the bathroom to freshen up before walking arm in arm to the main floor. Kadyn and Brianna were dancing by the time we returned. We visited with some of our other guests before joining them on the dance floor.

Before I knew it, we were filing outside so we could watch the fireworks pierce the night sky. My heart filled with joy while we counted the last remaining seconds before the clock struck midnight. I'd never felt safer or more loved than I did in that moment. There was no questioning how blessed I truly was.

* * * * *

"I'm sorry," Rafael whispered for the hundredth time.

I memorized every angle and shadow that formed his face while my eyes filled with tears. "Please don't apologize. As difficult as this is, we both know you're doing the right thing." The words were hollow, even to my ears.

Rafael shook his head. "Promise me you'll be safe, that you'll listen to Brady and Jase."

A soft sigh escaped my lips. "I'll be safe. Promise me you'll do the same. You're not allowed to jump in front of any bullets or take any unnecessary risks."

"I'll do my best." He brushed my tears aside with his thumbs. "Please don't cry."

I forced back my remaining tears. "Call me as soon as you land. I want to know you arrived safely."

"I won't land in Lisbon until after six o'clock your time. Are you cooking dinner for Brady and Jase tonight?"

I shook my head. "Jase is taking care of dinner tonight."

I doubted I'd even eat. I was planning to crawl straight into bed.

Rafael chuckled. "So you'll be eating burgers from Five Guys."

I laughed. "That sounds about right."

He held me tight. "I'll try to be here when Maxim arrives. Hopefully, he won't stay for more than a day or two. Please, don't agree to anything without speaking to me first."

I nodded my consent.

"Hey," Rafael whispered. He lifted my chin toward his. "You're in good hands with Brady and Jase. We'll Skype every night, and I'll come back just as soon as I can."

Another tear stole down my cheek. I was trying to be strong so it would be easier for him to leave. "I love you," I whispered hoarsely.

Rafael brushed a kiss on each cheek before slanting his lips over mine. He demanded nothing. Instead, he poured every emotion imaginable from his heart into mine. We clung to each other for the longest time. Grudgingly, he released me. "You're going to be late for work. Brady and Jase are waiting downstairs."

We walked downstairs to the garage. Rafael opened the passenger side door to my Jeep. He popped his head inside. "Don't worry about retrieving the SUV from the airport. Ethan and Chance are going to swing by and pick it up this afternoon."

Jase nodded. Once. "Travel safe."

"Take good care of my girl." Rafael pulled me in for one last hug. "You, behave." He fastened my seatbelt.

I made a big show of rolling my eyes. "Like I don't behave."

Brady barked out a laugh. He was sitting directly behind

me. "You weren't behaving in Ukraine."

"You weren't behaving when you tried sneaking into Mexico behind Kadyn's back either." Jase frowned. "If you so much as look mischievous, I'll chip you in your sleep."

Rafael chuckled. "Now why didn't I think of that?" He kissed me one last time. With a gentle shove, the door closed between us.

Rafael's eyes held mine while Jase backed out of the garage. He followed us out of the garage, then waved as Jase pulled away.

I burst into tears when Rafael disappeared from sight.

Brady handed me a box of tissues.

Jase continued driving. "Where'd you get the tissue?"

"From the townhouse," Brady answered. "Come on. You had to know she'd cry."

"Do you need me to pull over or anything?" Jase offered uncertainly.

"No. I'll be okay. Just… drive."

Brady shoved a paper cup at me. "Grande skim toffee nut latte, extra shot, extra hot."

Jase spun toward the back seat. "You went to Starbucks?"

He laughed. "You've been her bodyguard for how many months? Seriously, Jase. How could you not know that she'd need coffee on a day like this?"

Jase scowled at the road. "I was planning to stop at the coffee shop next to her office."

A grateful smile tugged at my lips. "Thanks, guys. For everything."

Jase merged onto I-395. "How are you going to explain Brady's presence at the office? Shae's going to know something is up when you walk in with two bodyguards."

I took a sip of coffee. "I'm going to tell her that Rafael insisted on having two bodyguards at the office since Chance isn't protecting her anymore."

He nodded admiringly. "That sounds believable enough."

"Because it's the truth," Brady chimed in. "Rafael would have insisted on having two men assigned to her office regardless. She's more vulnerable at the office than anyplace else since the SVR knows where she works."

I turned around in my seat. "It's been six months since we fled Ukraine. If the SVR was going to pursue me, wouldn't they have shown up by now?"

He shook his head. "That's not how SVR operatives work. They watch and wait until the moment is ripe so they can maximize their gains."

"That's why we call them 'sleeper agents,'" Jase explained. "They'll spend months building a cover, establishing their position, blending in, and building trust. If anyone new applies for a job at your office or tries to strike up a friendship with you, he'll be our first suspect."

My heart sank. I'd mistakenly presumed I'd be safe once a decent amount of time had passed.

"If the SVR believes that Maxim still cares for you, then they'll keep monitoring you. They won't hesitate to use you in order to manipulate him, and he's influential enough for them to want to do so," Brady stated.

Jase turned onto Constitution Avenue. "Maxim killed the operative who shot Michael and the ones who tortured you and Shae. Those acts won't go unpunished."

I shivered when those memories reared their ugly heads. "Why hasn't Rafael mentioned this?"

"He doesn't want you any more frightened than you

already are," Jase admitted softly. "This is why he doesn't want Maxim near you. It's not the threat posed by Maxim that concerns him. It's the SVR."

"What about Oni?" I inquired hesitantly.

"Rafael doesn't trust Oni, and neither should you," Brady stated matter-of-factly. "Even though you facilitated her admission into your degree program, and she is moving to the United States, she still has family in Ukraine. The SVR can and will manipulate her to get to you."

My gaze shifted to the window. Maxim was delivering Oni next Tuesday, precisely one week from today. She'd be living with me until the dorms opened. I really liked Oni, and I wanted to trust her, but I couldn't argue Brady's point. If someone threatened to kill my family, I'd do just about anything to ensure their safety.

Jase parked the Jeep. "I know you consider Maxim and Oni friends, but the sooner you distance yourself from those two, the better."

I unfastened my seatbelt with a harsh sigh. I felt even more miserable now than when I climbed inside the Jeep. I hadn't a clue how I was going to survive the next two weeks.

Brady and Jase escorted me into the building.

"Welcome back, Kri," Alyssa greeted cheerily. She was standing next to the reception desk. She raised a single eyebrow in Brady's direction.

"This is Brady. He's assisting Jase since Chance was dismissed by Shae," I explained. "Alyssa is our administrative specialist. She's the glue that holds our office together. She also manages the office calendar."

"Are you expecting any visitors today?" Brady asked.

"No. It should be quiet around here today." Her eyes slid toward me. "You have a team meeting on Rwanda in thirty minutes. Paul has blocked off the entire morning for that meeting, so you might want to grab some coffee before you go in there."

"Thanks, Alyssa."

Jase followed me to my office while Brady hung back in the lobby.

I stashed my purse inside the file drawer. "Feel free to use my desk and the computer. I'll be in the conference room the rest of the morning."

"I'm sitting in on that meeting. I want to know what your plans are for Rwanda so I can plan the security detail." He walked me to the break room.

I pulled three mugs from the cupboard. "Hey, Sammi. How's the coffee?"

She eased away from the coffee pot. "Not bad. I was just debating whether I should brew another pot."

"We'll probably finish this off, so I'll start another pot." I poured a cup for Brady and Jase, replaced the coffee grounds, and brewed another pot while Jase delivered Brady's coffee. I sent a text message to Rafael, poured my own cup of coffee, and joined the rest of the staff in the conference room.

Shae stood and gave me a hug. "That was one awesome party, Kri." She tugged me into the seat next to her.

"Thanks." Frankly, I was relieved that Chance and Konstantin hadn't caused a scene.

Paul shuffled his paperwork. "I'm sorry I missed it."

"I hope your wife is feeling better," I offered with a hopeful smile.

"Turns out she wasn't sick." He blushed.

Cory, Sammi, and I exchanged glances.

"She's pregnant," Paul announced with a sheepish smile.

Everyone jumped up at once. "Congratulations!" I

149

rushed forward to give him a hug.

Shae followed with her own hug. "I'm so happy for you!"

Cory shook Paul's hand.

Sammi kissed his cheek. "Do you know if you're having a boy or a girl?"

"No. It's still a little early for that. Vanessa's only ten weeks pregnant."

Jase pushed off from the wall so he could shake Paul's hand. "Congratulations."

Paul's expression warmed even more. "Thanks, Jase. Why don't you join us at the table?"

Jase claimed the chair next to me.

"So, Rwanda…" Sammi began eagerly.

"Yes. Rwanda." Paul sounded as if he'd swallowed something bitter.

I looked up from my padfolio. "What's wrong?"

He handed each of us a copy of a United Nations OHCHR report. "There have been some disturbing developments since President Kagame's reelection last August. I thought the human rights violations and the increase in government violence would die down after the elections, but the situation has deteriorated even more."

Cory eyed Paul intently. "President Kagame's former army chief was shot in the stomach for disagreeing with him, the acting editor of the Umuvugizi newspaper was murdered for reporting the incident, and the Vice President of the Democratic Green Party was stabbed and nearly beheaded days before the election. How much worse could it be?"

Frustration shone in Paul's eyes. "A number of senior government and military officials who have spoken out against President Kagame have disappeared. Others have fled the country and are now living in exile. They're being tried in absentia by a military court."

Sammi shoved the report aside. "For what crimes?"

Paul studied her over the top of his coffee. "For publically criticizing President Kagame and the Rwandan government."

"That's insane." I tossed my pen on the notepad.

"President Kagame is using their laws against genocide to punish anyone who speaks out against the government," Paul elaborated.

"That's not what those laws were intended for," Shae objected. Her frustration was evident.

"Regardless, the law is being used to silence and incarcerate critics. Reporters and government officials aren't the only ones being punished for criticizing state policies. They just arrested a priest for speaking out against the government's new family planning restrictions during his Christmas Eve sermon. He's been charged with endangering state security and inciting civil disobedience." Paul leaned back and crossed his arms over his chest.

"The UN has noted a spike in extrajudicial killings, torture, disappearances, violence against children, human trafficking, gender based violence, and unlawful detention," Jase read from the report.

I winced at the mention of torture.

"So it's safe to assume that anyone criticizing President Kagame or the Rwandan government will be incarcerated or killed regardless of their prominence," Cory concluded.

"But we can't teach university students how to resolve conflict if they can't even discuss the problems plaguing their country." I huffed out a breath.

"You're not going," Jase gritted.

I spun around to look at him.

His muscles were coiled tight. Clearly, he wanted to fight.

Paul sighed. "Jase is right. Not only would we be endangering your lives, but we'd be risking the life of every student participating in the training. It's too dangerous. We have to shelve this trip."

"So what are we going to do? Are we going to schedule a different training?" Shae prodded impatiently.

He opened his laptop. "That's why I blocked off the entire morning. We're going to spend the next few hours choosing a new location."

My eyes widened. "I need a refill on my coffee."

Shae stood. "I'm going to get my laptop."

Paul smiled as the mood lifted. "Sky's the limit here, folks. I'd like each of you to choose a different country. You have one hour to assess the need and the risks surrounding your location so we can debate the merits of each selection. We should be ready to hit the ground running with the new training assignment before we break for lunch. We have to work hard and fast to get this training organized before April."

I rose from my chair. My brain was already spinning with the possibilities.

* * * * *

"What did you guys finally decide?" Rafael asked. I'd already summarized the day's events while trudging up the stairs.

"Sierra Leone." I stepped out of my work clothes and tugged a camisole over my head as soon as I stepped foot inside my bedroom. "English is their official language, so we don't have to learn a new language. That should free up time to research the issues and develop the training materials."

"Sierra Leone," Rafael repeated contemplatively.

"There have been no reports of government killings, no politically motivated disappearances, and the government doesn't punish people for criticizing their policies," I offered reassuringly. I climbed into bed thoroughly exhausted.

"Well, that's certainly an improvement over Ukraine."

"And Rwanda." I rolled over and hugged his pillow.

Frustration road his next breath. "Jase was in the meeting?"

"Yes. Jase thought Sierra Leone was a good choice," I assured him.

"What type of conflicts will you be discussing in the training?" A cupboard door closed while he spoke.

I glanced at the phone. I could have sworn I heard the crinkling of a pastry bag. "We're going to discuss vigilante violence, human rights violations in mining communities, forced initiations into tribal secret societies, and the excessive use of force by law enforcement."

"Interesting," Rafael mumbled around a mouthful of food.

A pained expression claimed my face. "Please tell me you're not eating *croquettes*."

He laughed. "That is precisely what I'm eating."

"No fair." I really missed those savory little pastries.

"I found your note," he murmured. "Very sweet."

"Which one?" I'd hidden a bunch of notes in Rafael's flat while he was showering so he'd know I was thinking of him when he returned to Lisbon.

"There's more than one?" He sounded surprised. "I

found the one inside the cupboard." Several cupboards and drawers thudded all at once.

I tried not to laugh. "I hid forty-five notes, but I don't want you looking for them all at once. I was hoping you'd find a few each day."

"Okay," he agreed. "I'm game."

"I miss you," I confessed in all seriousness. "How am I supposed to sleep without you lying next to me?"

"I don't know." Rafael sighed. "I was wondering the very same thing."

I burrowed under the sheets. "Are you going to bed after you eat?"

"Yes. I have to go into work early tomorrow morning," he answered sullenly. "Where are you? Have you climbed into bed yet?"

"Yes. I wasn't up to doing anything else. I miss you too much." A single tear crept through my lashes.

"I miss you too, baby," Rafael whispered softly.

I swallowed around the lump in my throat. "I hope everything goes well at work tomorrow. Say 'hi' to Chief D'Souza for me."

"I will," he agreed. "Dream of me."

I took a deep breath and sighed contentedly. I'd found the soothing scents of his cologne on his pillow. "I already am," I whispered. "I love you."

"I love you too." Rafael ended the call.

I rolled over and plugged my phone into the charger. The room blurred as my eyes filled with tears. I curled around Rafael's pillow.

Jase popped his head inside the doorway a few minutes later. "Rafael asked me to check on you. Are you okay?"

"Yes," I answered, but my raspy voice betrayed me.

"Need tissue?" Brady pushed past Jase. He set the tissue box on my nightstand before checking the windows.

I grabbed a couple of tissues from the box before propping myself up. "I miss Rafael."

"You just need to stay busy; bury yourself in work." Brady strode toward the closet.

Jase glanced inside the bathroom. "Can you purchase your books and get an early start on your coursework?" Spring semester was still seventeen days away.

I rubbed my red rimmed eyes. "That's a really good idea."

"The more coursework you complete now, the less you'll have to do when Rafael visits," Brady encouraged.

I checked the bookstore's schedule on my phone. "The campus bookstore is closed."

Jase shrugged. "So. Order the books from Amazon."

I requested the syllabi from my professors and had the books overnighted the very next day.

* * * * *

I sliced the French bread, wrapped it in tinfoil, and tossed it inside the oven. The two pans of lasagna I'd layered last night were already bubbling inside the oven, scenting the house with oregano and garlic. I glanced at the clock. Maxim and Oni were due to arrive any minute.

"Does this look like enough?" Brady gave the salad a final toss.

I joined him at the center island. "That looks great. Thanks for chopping everything up."

"Table's set." Kadyn reached inside the refrigerator and popped open a Sprite.

I pulled the cork out of a bottle of Chianti. "Thanks, Kadyn. Where's Jase?"

He leaned against the black and copper speckled countertop. "Outside. He wants to see how many men Maxim plants around your house when he arrives."

I took a deep breath and blew it out. "You guys act like Maxim's planning a hostile takeover. He's not here to kidnap me. He's delivering Oni."

As if on cue, the doorbell rang. I set the corkscrew on the counter. "I'll get it."

Kadyn pinned me with a look as he pushed off the counter. "Stay. Put."

I followed him into the foyer. "That would be extremely rude."

Kadyn peered out the window before opening the door. "Maxim."

"Kadyn." A single eyebrow rose along Maxim's forehead. "I wasn't aware you lived here."

"I don't." Kadyn didn't elaborate.

I fisted my hands on my hips. "Behave. Both of you."

Maxim cracked a smile as they shook hands.

I gave Maxim a hug after tugging him inside. "Where's Oni?"

"Here," she answered in a small voice. She followed Lev inside.

I pulled her close. "I can't believe you're here. I'm so excited to see you. Did you have a good flight?"

Oni laughed. "Yes. The flight was fine."

Lev reached for my hand. "Kristine. It's nice to see you again."

I followed his handshake with a hug. "What? No coffee?"

He laughed, recalling an inside joke from Simferopol. "No, although we still make the occasional coffee run." He shook Kadyn's hand. "I was happy to hear you survived Mexico."

Kadyn nodded. Once.

Lev patted Brady on the back. "It's good to see you on your feet again."

I pulled Kadyn closer. "Oni, I'd like you to meet Kadyn. He's one of my dearest friends."

Oni's cheeks pinkened when she reached for his hand. "Hi, Kadyn."

Kadyn studied the two of us with an inscrutable look on his face. "Nice to meet you, Oni."

"Where's Rafael?" Maxim inquired from directly behind me.

I turned around and collided with his chest. I took a step back. "Rafael's working tonight." Thankfully, that wasn't a lie. He was still working... in Portugal.

Jase tugged the storm door open before Maxim could ask any more questions.

Maxim's eyes narrowed. "And you are?"

"Your worst nightmare," Jase announced flatly.

Maxim laughed. "My nightmares make you look like a fluffy bunny."

I choked down a laugh. "Maxim. Be nice. This is my bodyguard, Jase. Jase, these are my *friends*; Maxim, Oni, and Lev. Please note the emphasis on 'friends.'"

Jase offered a brief nod. "Are you going to invite the rest of your men in?"

Maxim shook his head. "No. They're guarding the perimeter."

Jase locked the door just as the timer went off on the

stove. He didn't mention that Ethan, Aidan, Brogan, and Chance were also guarding the perimeter.

"Oh! That's dinner." I bolted toward the kitchen. "Feel free to wash up or grab a seat at the table. Bathroom is on your right."

Jase was on my heels in a single stride. "Maxim has nine additional men positioned outside this house. Why the large security detail?"

"He had a large security detail in Ukraine," I answered dismissively. I pulled the lasagna out of the oven.

"I don't like it." Jase grabbed the salad bowl. "And that," he nodded toward the wine, "is a very bad idea." He strode toward the dining room.

I uncorked a second bottle of wine halfway out of spite. I knew Kadyn, Jase, and Brady wouldn't be drinking, but the rest of us could easily drink two bottles of wine. Brady and Kadyn carried the lasagna. I followed behind with the aforementioned wine.

Jase pulled out the chair at the head of the table. He used every last one of his nonverbal communication skills to demand I sit in it. Of course, Maxim was sitting at the opposite end of the table.

I sidestepped Jase so I could set a bottle next to Maxim. "Would you mind doing the honors?"

Maxim's hand clamped around my wrist. "Where's my ring?" His eyes darkened as he rose to his feet.

I raised my left hand before Jase could intervene. "Here, on my left hand." I'd retrieved the ring from my jewelry box this morning because I knew he'd react like this.

"So, Rafael finally proposed." He released my wrist.

"Yes. Shortly before Christmas."

"Then we should celebrate," Maxim conceded in a dark

158

tone. He sampled the wine, then motioned for my glass. He poured wine for Lev and Oni before filling his own glass. Kadyn, Brady, and Jase weren't drinking wine. They were drinking Sprite.

Maxim tucked a glass of wine in my hand before raising his glass. The room fell away when his penetrating eyes met mine. "To those who dare to love despite the tragedies surrounding them."

My heart stalled. I couldn't tell if Maxim was referring to himself, Rafael, or me as the one who dared to love. He worded the toast so that it could be perceived either way. "To those who dare to love," I repeated cautiously.

Lev and Oni joined in the toast. Kadyn, Brady, and Jase did not.

Maxim kissed both of my cheeks before whispering in my ear. "You still owe me a kiss, *kotyonok*."

I backed away. "Kadyn, do you mind cutting the lasagna?" I sank into the chair between Brady and Jase. Oni was sitting between Kadyn and Maxim. Lev was sitting on the other side of Jase.

Brady heaped salad onto his plate before passing the bowl to me. "How are things in Ukraine?"

Maxim's eyes darkened. "Aside from the fact that President Yanukovych embezzled more than one hundred and thirty billion dollars' worth of public funds and fled the country?"

I handed the salad bowl to Jase. "When did he flee the country?" I'd been following the protests in Ukraine, but I hadn't seen the news over the past few days.

"Yesterday," Maxim growled. "He fled to Russia after ordering our security forces to kill the protestors."

"Yanukovych belongs in Russia," Oni opined, "since

every domestic and foreign policy he's ever implemented has helped Russia destroy Ukraine."

"His decision to seek refuge in Russia will bring a fitting end. Putin will have him killed for his cowardice and for compromising his ability to manipulate Ukraine," Lev weighed in.

Kadyn dug into his lasagna. "Who's serving as president in Yanukovych's absence?"

"The Chairman of the Ukrainian Parliament will serve as the acting president until the special election in April," Lev answered over the top of his wine.

An awkward silence fell over my Ukrainian friends.

My eyes narrowed. "What?"

"The People's Front has asked me to run as their presidential candidate," Maxim revealed rather stoically.

My jaw dropped. Everyone stopped talking at once.

"But you're in the mafia," Jase sputtered.

"Not anymore," Lev rebutted. "He resigned from the mafia so he could run for president."

"You resigned from the mafia?" Kadyn repeated.

Maxim nodded.

I felt extremely nauseous. Running for office seemed far more dangerous than working for the mafia, especially in Ukraine. "Do you *want* to be president?"

A shadow passed briefly through his eyes. "I will do whatever it takes to free my people from the corruptive elements that hold my country hostage."

"What is your political platform based on?" Kadyn inquired curiously.

"I intend to strengthen our economy, improve democracy, end government corruption, end Russia's meddling in our domestic and foreign affairs, join NATO, and join the EU," Maxim replied.

Brady whistled. "How are you going to accomplish that?"

Maxim's eyes locked on mine. "By collecting on a promise."

My heart bounced against my toes. "*What?*"

"We'll discuss this later," Maxim answered dismissively. "I would prefer to enjoy the meal you so thoughtfully prepared."

I glanced at his uneaten lasagna and mine. "Okay. What would you like to discuss then?"

He relaxed into his seat with a disarming smile. "How was Portugal?"

Like that would evoke a pleasant conversation. I stabbed my lasagna with my fork. "Portugal was nice."

"Surely you can do better than that," Maxim countered with a chuckle.

I forced a shrug. "I enjoyed visiting their palaces."

"You should see Mariyinsky Palace, the presidential palace in Kyiv," Oni interjected.

Maxim's gaze remained squarely on me. "Would you like to live in a palace?" he inquired softly.

"Please don't," I whispered fearfully.

"Every president needs a first lady." He studied me over the top of his wine.

"She's already engaged," Jase gritted. He stood, menacingly.

"Engaged is not the same as married," Maxim rebutted coolly. "I'm simply ensuring she's aware of her options."

"Stop trying to get everyone riled up," I chided. "Jase, please sit. We are not discussing this."

Reluctantly, he sat.

"Is there anything special you'd like to do before school begins?" I asked Oni. I figured that was a pretty safe topic.

"I'd like to familiarize myself with the university campus, see some of the monuments, and visit the Capitol," she answered hesitantly.

I breathed a small sigh of relief when the tension eased. "I'll call my friend Patrick to see if he can give you a VIP tour of the Capitol next week. We can visit the campus this weekend. Have you received your dorm assignment yet?"

Oni nodded. "They offered me a studio apartment in Beacon Hall."

"You might want to show her how to access the metro and the bus from George Mason," Kadyn suggested.

"That's a really good idea." I reached for my wine. I was trying to ignore the fact that Maxim was watching me so intently.

We pushed through dinner, as nerve-wracking as that was. Brady and Oni offered to clear the table and wash the dishes afterwards. I asked everyone else to sit in the family room while I brewed coffee and served dessert.

Lev's eyes widened when I handed him a plate. "What is this?"

"Chocolate and pistachio cake." The miniature cakes glistened with a dark chocolate glaze, edible gold shavings, and gold leaves. This was, hands down, the most exquisite dessert I'd ever made.

"A dessert fit for a king," Maxim announced decidedly. He patted the couch. "Please, Kristine, sit next to me."

Jase scowled when I complied.

I'd promised Maxim anything... well, anything but sex... when he agreed to help me find Kadyn in Mexico. I was anxious to know how that promise could possibly factor into

162

his bid for the presidency. "Maxim," I began hesitantly.

He reached for my hand after setting his dessert aside. "Kristine, I want you to know this is not what I intended to ask of you." He eyed Rafael's engagement ring and sighed.

My heart clenched when his eyes met mine.

He peered deep into my eyes. "You're aware of the difficultly we've experienced in extending the Odessa-Brody pipeline."

"Yes." I'd studied the issue before traveling to Ukraine. I glanced at Kadyn and Jase while I made an effort to explain. "The Ukrainian government has been trying to extend this pipeline to Plock, Poland so they can transport oil from the Caspian Sea into the EU. This would strengthen their economy and reduce EU dependence on Russian fuel."

"This project has proven difficult to fund," Maxim noted bitterly. "Now I know why."

"With the amount of money Yanukovych was embezzling, there weren't enough funds to complete the project," I surmised.

Lev braced his elbows against his knees. "Putin paid Yanukovych to connect the Odessa-Brody pipeline to the Druzhba pipeline. They reversed the flow of oil so the Odessa-Brody pipeline now transports Russian oil to Mediterranean countries."

"But that would only strengthen Russia's economy and hurt Ukraine," I objected. I hadn't heard the flow of oil had been reversed.

"Precisely," Maxim agreed. "I want to disconnect the Odessa-Brody pipeline from the Druzhba pipeline, reverse the flow of oil, and complete the extension into Plock so we can transport oil from the Caspian Sea into the EU as was originally intended."

"Putin will fight you every step of the way," I stated speculatively.

Kadyn cracked open another Sprite. "How does Kri factor into this?"

"Kristine knows Senator Rockefeller, the great-grandson of an oil tycoon. She has connections in the U.S. Senate, she believes in this cause, and she knows how to lobby Congress," Maxim said, swiftly connecting the dots.

My jaw dropped. "You want the U.S. to help fund this project."

Maxim nodded.

"How much?" I held my breath.

Maxim fingered the gold leaf on his cake. "Seven hundred eighty million dollars."

I turned the idea in my head. "That's a lot less expensive than I thought it would be."

He eyed me thoughtfully. "The terrain is relatively flat."

"Why would the United States fund another country's pipeline?" Brady inquired before polishing off his cake.

"Not only would this cripple Russia's economy, thereby reducing the threat they pose to the United States, but this would reduce EU dependence on Russian oil so Putin can't force them to side with him in international politics. He wields fuel like a weapon, cutting oil and gas supplies off when political leaders don't do what he wants," I answered easily.

Maxim smiled. "You are the perfect person for this job."

"Konstantin and I want to help," Oni insisted. She was sitting in the chair across from Lev.

"Konstantin and Oni can serve as your support staff. They can conduct research and help craft the bill, but I want you to take the lead with Congress," Maxim amended.

My eyes remained fixed on his face. "How long do I have to accomplish this?"

"Sixty days," he answered apologetically. "I need to incorporate this into my campaign, and the election is in ninety days."

I took a deep breath and blew it out. "We can't introduce this as a bill, Maxim. Even the most pressing bills don't pass Congress within sixty days. We've got to identify another bill that is really close to passing and attach this as a rider."

"You're already working and attending school full time," Jase reminded me. He'd been following the conversation closely.

"I'll invite the congressmen out to lunch or take them out to dinner. Those types of meetings are far more productive than lobbying on the Hill." I was already generating a mental list of all the congressmen I wanted to meet with.

"So you'll do it?" Maxim pressed. "You'll help me secure the funds?"

"I want to speak with Rafael before I commit to this," I hedged. "Oni, do you mind brewing another pot of coffee while I call him?" I rose from the couch.

Maxim's eyes darkened. "I'd like to hear your thoughts on how we might strengthen security along our eastern border," he said, shifting his attention to Kadyn.

Jase followed me upstairs. "Kristine, what he's asking... it's too much."

"Too much? Maxim saved Kadyn's life... and mine. That counts for something, Jase. Besides, this doesn't just benefit Ukraine. This benefits the EU and the United States. I want to help Maxim free Ukraine and put Putin in his place."

"You want to punish Putin for what the SVR did to

you," he countered softly.

I released a long overdue breath. "Maybe," I confessed. "I'd like to reduce his power and influence... limit his ability to hurt others the way he hurt me."

He stopped just inside the doorway to my bedroom. "This is going to make you an even bigger target."

I grabbed my cell phone off the nightstand. "I'll be flying under the radar for the most part." I thumbed through my recent calls and tapped on Rafael's name.

Jase shook his head. He pulled the door closed as he stepped into the hallway.

Rafael's voice drew me back to the phone. "How's it going?"

"Oh, just ducky," I answered in a saccharine sweet voice. "Maxim's called in his favor, and I promised to run it by you before committing."

"Well?" he pried impatiently.

I bit my lip while trying to suppress a nervous laugh. "Maxim is running for president, and he's asked me to serve as the First Lady of Ukraine."

"What?" Rafael exploded across the phone line.

My eyes squeezed shut. "Actually, it's not quite that bad... although he was hinting around about that."

"Kristine," Rafael growled. "What exactly did Maxim ask?"

"He wants me to lobby Congress so he can secure funds to extend the Odessa-Brody pipeline into Plock. He feels he can win the election if he secures that funding."

"Wait," Rafael interjected. "He's really running for president?"

I blew out a breath. "Yes. The Ukrainian President fled the country after embezzling billions of dollars' worth of

public funds. They're holding a special election, and The
People's Front has asked Maxim to run."

The line grew quiet.

"Rafael?"

"I can't believe he's running for president."

"Do you mind if I help him with this? There's so much
good that could come from this... for his country and mine. I
really want to help him secure that funding, Rafael. Please? I
want to help."

He sighed. Loudly. "He's not asking you to serve as first
lady?"

I laughed. "No. He was just trying to get everyone riled
up when he said that. Maxim isn't in love with me. He's in
love with his country. He's asking me to secure the funding
so he can win the presidency, strengthen their economy, and
lift his people out of poverty."

"How are you going to find time to do this?" he queried
reluctantly.

I paced across the room. "I'm not in this alone.
Konstantin and Oni are going to help. I can juggle this with
school and work. I'll meet with the congressmen over dinner
and lunch."

"Could you be any more ambitious?" Rafael bemoaned.
"Let me talk to Jase."

I tugged on the door. Jase nearly fell on the floor.
"Rafael wants to talk to you." I handed him the phone.

I stepped inside the bathroom so I could freshen up. Jase
handed me the phone when I returned. "Well?" I inquired of
Rafael.

"You can help Maxim secure funding on one
condition..."

"Oh, God, not another condition," I blurted. "Why?

Why does everyone have conditions?"

He ignored my rant. "If Jase determines you're being monitored or followed by the SVR, you end this."

I met Jase's piercing gaze. "Fine. If Jase discovers we're being followed, I'll stop lobbying Congress."

Jase's eyes narrowed. He didn't believe me.

"Text me when Maxim leaves," Rafael reminded me.

I glanced at the clock on my phone. It was two o'clock in the morning in Portugal. "Okay," I agreed. "I love you."

"I love you too," Rafael answered softly.

Maxim and Kadyn were hunched over a hand drawn map of Ukraine when Jase and I returned to the family room. Maxim motioned for me to join them.

Kadyn scrutinized the map. "Where's the pipeline going?"

Maxim sketched Poland to the left of Ukraine before drawing two lines across his country. "The pipeline begins here, at Odessa. Currently, it ends here, at the Druzhba Pipeline. I want to disconnect the Odessa-Brody pipeline from Druzhba and extend it up to here." He lengthened the first line until it crossed into Poland. "Poland plans to extend it from their border up to Plock."

Kadyn studied the diagram. "You're going to need an early warning system, surface to air missiles, and an anti-ballistic missile system to protect this pipeline."

Maxim and Lev exchanged glances. "We have surface to air missiles and an ABM system, but the ABM system is only capable of tracking fifty targets at once."

Kadyn hid his surprise. "What's the deployment time?"

"Eight minutes," Maxim replied.

Kadyn scanned the diagram again. "How long are you going to be in town?"

"Two maybe three days," Maxim estimated. "Why?"

He met Maxim's penetrating gaze. "Would you be willing to discuss your economic strategy with the United States Secretary of Defense, Robert Gates?"

"Are you offering to arrange a meeting with him?" Maxim countered. His voice dripped with sarcasm.

Kadyn nodded, slowly. "Do you recall the missile defense system we were planning for Poland?"

Maxim laughed. "How could I forget? Russia threatened to bomb Poland if you installed that system."

Lev leaned forward, thoroughly captivated. "I still cannot believe you abandoned those plans."

Kadyn braced his elbows against his knees. "We'd like to install that defense system in your region so we can protect Europe against an attack from Russia and Iran. You need a defense system capable of protecting your eastern border and the pipeline you're building to transport fuel into Europe. Seems like a pretty good fit to me."

The smile slid from Maxim's face. "Putin would attack us."

Kadyn shrugged. "Putin is going to attack either way. He'll bomb the Odessa-Brody pipeline the same way he bombed the Baku-Tbilisi-Ceyhan pipeline in Georgia in 2008. Wouldn't you like to have that defense system in place before he does?"

Maxim stood abruptly. "Why would you help me?"

Kadyn glanced at me before pushing onto his feet. "I'm not making any promises, Maxim. I'm just offering to arrange the meeting. I was working for Secretary Gates when we developed the defense shield for Poland. He was livid when that deal fell through. Ukraine seems like a viable alternative, given your proximity to Poland. This would allow both of our countries to achieve our objectives, as long as this system is installed discretely. If Putin were to get wind of this…" he trailed off ominously.

Maxim stared at Kadyn for a couple of heartbeats. "The enemy of my enemy…"

"…is my friend," Kadyn agreed. "We want Putin contained as much as you do."

His eyes locked on me. "And you, *kotyonok?*"

My heart beat a thunderous score. "I'll secure the funding."

Kadyn pulled me close before Maxim could touch me. "And I'll arrange a meeting with the Secretary of Defense."

Lev slapped Maxim on the back. "See? You will make a great president."

His eyes remained steadfast on me. "Not without a first lady."

* * * * *

Shae tackled me in the hallway. "Kri! I can't believe Maxim is running for president. Like, seriously running for president. And he left the mafia!"

Jase groaned. "I'll meet you in your office."

I followed Shae into her office. "I know. How crazy is that?"

"I want in on whatever it is you're doing for him. Konstantin said you're trying to secure funding for the pipeline," she prattled on excitedly.

I dropped into the chair across from her desk. "Yes. Oni is researching legislation on congress.gov now. She'll have a list of energy and oil bills along with the names of the congressmen supporting those bills by the end of the day. I

plan to request meetings with those congressmen, but I want
to speak with Senator Rockefeller first."

She eased into the black leather chair behind her desk.
"What can I do to help?"

"You can help me generate talking points over our lunch
break. I'd like to have talking points and a one page briefing
crafted by the end of the day."

She blocked that time slot on her calendar. "Where's Oni
working?"

"At the house, on my laptop. Brady's there too. Jase
didn't like the idea of her staying there by herself while
Maxim was in town. He was worried she'd let Maxim plant
bugs or cameras inside my house."

Shae rolled her eyes. "Maxim asked Konstantin to
establish an internship position for Oni when he stopped by
last night. She's supposed to begin next week."

"I should show her how to access the metro sooner
rather than later then." I typed a reminder in my phone.

Shae tapped her pen against the desk. "What did Rafael
think of her?"

I met her inquisitive gaze. "Rafael's been working
twenty-four seven the last few days, so he hasn't met her yet."

Her pen stopped mid-tap. "Maxim was inside your
house, and Rafael wasn't there?" Her eyes narrowed. "There's
no way Rafael would allow that to happen. What's going on?"

I forced a shrug. "He'd already committed to this
assignment."

Her eyes narrowed even more. "We've known the date
Maxim was delivering Oni for weeks now. When did he
commit to this assignment?"

"In December." I hated dancing around the issue, but at
least I was still being honest. "Did Maxim mention what

Kadyn's doing for him?"

"No," Shae admitted grudgingly. Clearly, she didn't want to change the topic.

I leaned forward and lowered my voice. "He's helping Maxim secure the pipeline and their eastern border."

Her jaw dropped. "Are you serious?"

I nodded. "Kadyn's going to arrange a meeting between Maxim and Secretary Gates. He thinks the Secretary of Defense might be interested in positioning the defense shield we developed for Poland in Ukraine."

"Kri," she breathed. "That's brilliant."

I pushed up from the chair. "I'm worried Secretary Gates will refuse to work with Maxim when he discovers his ties to the mafia."

"Our government has collaborated with far sketchier people," Shae bristled. "Maxim is pro-democracy, pro-NATO, and he wants to join the EU. Besides, that defense shield and the pipeline further a lot of U.S. objectives."

"I hope you're right," I stated sincerely. "I need to finish developing that simulation for Sierra Leone. Stop by when you're ready for lunch."

"Will do," Shae called. Her voice followed me down the hall.

* * * * *

"What took you so long? You were supposed to be here a half hour ago," Kadyn growled.

I tossed my keys on the counter. "We stopped by ZPizza so I wouldn't have to cook dinner." Jase lugged all six boxes in behind me.

"ZPizza!" Brady cheered. "Please tell me there's a ZBQ

Chicken."

"ZBQ Chicken, Thai Chicken, Tuscan Mushroom, Italian, Mexican, and Santa Fe," I bragged. I'd pretty much covered all the bases.

Oni nearly slammed into Kadyn when she rushed into the kitchen. He caught her when her socks slid across the hard wood floor. She quickly steadied herself. "Oh, good! You're here. Maxim called. He's on his way. Can you review this list of bills and congressmen before he arrives?" She handed me a stack of paper.

I set my purse on the counter. "I need wine."

"I'm on it," Brady replied.

My phone buzzed with an incoming text. I glanced at the message. "Konstantin and Shae are coming over. Maxim asked them to meet him here. Do I have enough pizza?"

"Eight people and six pizzas should be fine," Jase gritted. "Can I speak with you? Privately?" He set the pizza on the counter and pulled me toward the stairs. "How are you going to explain Rafael's absence for the second night in a row?"

"He's still working?" I offered hopefully.

"Maxim has converted your house into campaign headquarters. Mark my words, you guys are going to be pulling an all-nighter, if not tonight, then tomorrow night. There's no way you can hide Rafael's absence under these circumstances. Call Rafael. Tell him to fuel that souped-up jet of his and get over here. Now."

"It's nearly midnight in Portugal," I objected. "I don't want to add to his stress."

"You call him or I will," Jase growled.

I shot him the stink-eye before tapping on my phone. Rafael's phone transferred me to voicemail. I took a deep breath and forced a chipper tone. "Hi, handsome. Please give me a call when you get a chance. Things are getting a little crazy on this end of the planet. Love you. Bye."

Jase nodded his approval before stalking back to the kitchen. I made an attempt to follow him, but the doorbell rang.

"I got it." Kadyn muscled past me.

I crossed my arms, ticked that I couldn't even answer the door to my own home. "This protective custody routine is getting way out of hand."

"Hey, Kadyn! Good to see you." Shae rolled onto her tiptoes and gave him a hug. "Kri, I hope you don't mind that we're crashing your party. I brought wine."

"Who needs wine?" Konstantin blustered. He brushed a quick kiss against my cheek before handing me two bottles of Ukrainian vodka.

"So you do live here," Maxim ribbed while shaking Kadyn's hand. "Were you able to schedule a meeting with the Secretary of Defense?"

"Secretary Gates will meet with you at three o'clock on Friday at the Mayflower Hotel," Kadyn answered. "He asked me to join you."

"That's perfect. Thank you for arranging the meeting." Maxim's eyebrows rose as he surveyed the house. "Where's Rafael?"

"Working," I answered curtly.

"Your fiancé's neglect is unforgivable," Maxim murmured. I offered him my cheek, but he grasped my face with both hands and kissed me squarely on the lips.

"Rafael's working. There's nothing neglectful or unforgivable about that." I tugged his hands from my neck. "I'm meeting with Senator Rockefeller on Friday. I'd like you to read through my talking points and the issue brief to ensure I haven't misrepresented anything. I'm going to review the bills and the list of congressmen Oni pulled together so we can strategize about the legislation and the congressmen we should lobby for this rider."

"We'll discuss work when the meal is over," Maxim rebutted firmly.

We filed into the kitchen. I stopped short when I saw Brady folding a slice of ZBQ Chicken pizza into his mouth. "I'm afraid it's each man for himself."

* * * * *

"Kri!" Patrick's voice echoed across the cavernous lobby.

"Hey stranger!" I gathered my briefcase and the restaurant bag from the conveyor belt before giving him a hug.

Jase strode through the metal detector clearly agitated. He was used to carrying a gun, but they weren't allowed inside the Senate Hart Building.

"Patrick is a friend from Senator Rockefeller's office," I explained. "Patrick, this is my bodyguard, Jase."

Patrick's eyes widened when he catalogued Jase's six foot three frame. "Bodyguard?"

"Long story." We walked toward the stairs.

Patrick eyed the sack nestled in my arms. "Jamie said you were meeting with Senator Rockefeller. Are you buying him lunch?"

"I've got two *nigirizushi* sets, rainbow rolls, and *miso* soup," I recited. "One of the *nigirizushi* sets is for you."

He nodded his approval. "Sushi. Smart girl. What prompted this meeting with the Senator?"

I shifted the bag to my other arm. "I'm looking for

money just like everyone else."

He glanced at me, surprised. "Money? For what?"

"A friend of mine is running for President of Ukraine. I'm trying to help him win the election by securing funds to extend an oil pipeline into Poland."

Patrick froze mid-step. "You're doing what?"

I nudged him up the stairs. "I'm trying to help the government of Ukraine extend their oil pipeline into Poland so they can improve their economy and lift their people out of poverty."

"That's a far cry from health policy," he noted admiringly.

A secretive smile tugged at my lips. "That it is."

He opened the door to the Senator's suite. "Clearly, we have some catching up to do."

I pulled one of the *nigirizushi* sets from the bag and handed it to him. "I'll stop by your cubicle after I meet with the Senator."

He gave me a hug. "Thanks for thinking of me, Kri."

Jamie leapt from behind her desk when I neared the Senator's private office. "Kri! I'm so happy to see you."

Jase took the bag so she wouldn't squish the food.

I gave her a hug. "Thanks for getting me in to see the Senator so quickly."

Jamie gasped as she grabbed my hand. "Kadyn proposed?"

Jase and I shared an awkward glance. "No. I'm engaged to Rafael."

Her cheeks flushed pink. "I'm so sorry. You must be Rafael."

Jase offered a sympathetic smile. "No. I'm Kristine's bodyguard, Jase."

Her jaw fell slack.

I patted her back. "I'll be offering the CliffsNotes to Patrick after my meeting with the Senator. Maybe you should join us."

She nodded before lifting the handset on her desk. "Ms. Stone is here to see you, sir."

"Do you mind if I join you?" Jase asked. "I'd like to hear what he thinks of this plan."

"The Senator doesn't know you, you're kind of intimidating, and I'm worried that could impact his willingness to get involved." This was the very same argument I'd presented to Maxim and Konstantin. I felt my odds of winning the Senator over were better if I approached him alone.

He handed me the sushi.

Jamie opened the Senator's door. "Good luck," she whispered for my ears only.

I took a deep breath before approaching his desk. Senator Rockefeller was one of the kindest but also one of the most intimidating men I knew. His position on the Senate Finance Committee; the Subcommittee on International Trade, Customs, and Global Competitiveness; and the Select Committee on Intelligence rendered him the single most influential congressman I could possibly recruit. This rider would die without his support.

Senator Rockefeller towered over his desk. "Kristine. What a pleasant surprise." He clasped my hand in his. "Let's sit over here." He motioned toward a group of chairs nestled beneath a large ink wash painting. The painting depicted a whimsical Japanese landscape.

"Thank you so much for squeezing me in. I've missed eating at Yamato, so I stopped for sushi on my way over.

Would you like to eat while we visit or should I put this in the refrigerator?" He kept a small refrigerator in his office.

"We should eat the sushi while it's fresh." He strode toward the refrigerator. "What would you like to drink?"

I pulled the soup and sushi containers from the bag. "Sprite, please."

Senator Rockefeller set two Sprites on top of the coffee table before settling into the chair next to me. "I reviewed the issue brief you e-mailed to Jamie yesterday. Would you mind explaining your interest in Ukraine?"

I eased back into my seat. "I spent some time in Ukraine last June, teaching conflict resolution at the Tavrida National Vernadsky University for Seeds for Peace. I witnessed Russia's meddling in Ukraine's governance while I was there. I met with Prime Minister Azarov. I know how much he and the Ukrainian people want to end Putin's stranglehold on them. The Odessa-Brody pipeline will enable them to do so, but they need help funding the extension up to Plock, especially now that Yanukovych has absconded with billions in public funds."

He sipped a spoonful of *miso* soup. "When you say you witnessed this meddling…"

Tears threatened to fall. I blinked them back forcefully. "The SVR kidnapped me and a colleague the day after Prime Minister Azarov offered me a job with their ministry of foreign affairs. The SVR accused us of being spies. They injected us with truth serum and tried to force a false confession by subjecting us to electric-shock torture. They refused to release us until Prime Minister Azarov and President Yanukovych agreed to extend the lease allowing the Russian naval fleet to remain in Sevastopol. They were renegotiating the terms of that treaty the day we were seized.

We had to pay ten million dollars to secure our release even though they signed the treaty."

Senator Rockefeller set his soup aside. "I'm sorry, Kristine. I didn't know."

I nodded stiffly. "With the ousting of President Yanukovych and the upcoming elections, we have a unique opportunity to improve human rights and human security in Ukraine. Maxim Markov, the man nominated by The People's Front, is the same man who negotiated my release from the SVR. His entire family was killed by the KGB. He wants to end these human rights violations, end Russia's meddling in their governance, improve democracy, strengthen civil liberties, lift his people out of poverty, join NATO, and strengthen ties with the EU. This pipeline will help him achieve those goals, but Ukraine is not the only country that would benefit from this economic aid package."

"This pipeline would help reduce the EU's reliance on Russian oil," the Senator observed.

"Precisely," I agreed. "If we can secure this alternative fuel source for the EU, we can reduce their dependence on Russian fuel. This would limit Putin's ability to manipulate them in international politics."

He stirred wasabi into his soy sauce. "While this economic aid package clearly benefits the EU and the United States, you're going to have a difficult time securing funds from Congress in this economic environment. I think you'd fare better with the IMF, the European Investment Bank, or the European Bank for Reconstruction and Development."

"There's another potential benefit to the United States, which I didn't mention in the briefing," I confessed.

He arched a single eyebrow while savoring the sushi.

"Mr. Markov has expressed an interest in allowing the

United States to position the missile defense shield we had planned for Poland in Ukraine. He's meeting with Secretary Gates this afternoon."

The Senator nearly choked on his food. "Mr. Markov is meeting with Secretary Gates?"

I slathered wasabi across the top of my sushi. "Kadyn arranged the meeting after Maxim requested his assistance in securing their eastern border."

"He's worried Putin will bomb the pipeline," he noted astutely. "Do you think Mr. Markov can win the election?"

"He's been working with Prime Minister Azarov for years. He's highly respected. The media treats him like a celebrity. He's got the support of The People's Front, a pro-Western, anti-Russian, pro-democracy movement. These are the same people who forced Yanukovych out of office. So, yes. I think he can win this election, especially if he secures funding for the pipeline."

"Seven hundred eighty million dollars' worth of economic aid wouldn't be all that unreasonable for a country willing to house our missile defense system," Senator Rockefeller mused. He pushed his lanky frame from the chair and strode toward his desk. "What time did you say that meeting was?"

I tried not to smile. "They're meeting at the Mayflower Hotel at three o'clock."

He lifted the handset on his phone. "Jamie, clear my schedule for this afternoon, secure a driver for two-thirty, and get Secretary Gates on the phone." He returned the handset before folding himself in the chair next to me. "I want to know everything you know about Maxim Markov."

My heart plummeted. This was the part of our conversation I'd been dreading most. "Maxim Markov saved my life. He also saved Kadyn's life. He loathes Putin and everything he stands for. He values democracy. He is fiercely protective and loyal to the citizens of Ukraine, but..." I swallowed nervously, "he used to work for the Russian mafia."

Senator Rockefeller's disappointment was nearly palpable. "I was afraid you were going to say that."

"He severed ties with the Russian mafia when he was asked to run for president," I added hopefully.

"And that was?" he inquired with a sigh.

I cringed. "Five days ago."

He shook his head. "Five days? How do we know he's truly severed ties? Kristine, what you're asking is political suicide. I cannot support a former mafioso in his bid for the Ukrainian presidency. I'd be forced out of office."

"I'm not asking you to fund Maxim's campaign, and the money isn't going to the Russian mafia. This economic aid package would go directly to the Ukrainian government," I argued softly.

"Surely, Mr. Markov will take credit for securing this aid. He is weaving this into his campaign?"

"Yes," I admitted grudgingly.

"I'm sorry, Kristine. As much as I'd like to decrease the EU's reliance on Russian fuel, I cannot sponsor an economic aid package that arguably benefits the Russian mafia."

I forced an even tone. "What about the defense shield?"

He ate another piece of sushi. "Secretary Gates won't pass up this opportunity, but he will insist on working with the interim government, or he'll wait until the new president is elected to install the missile defense system."

My eyes widened when the solution whacked me upside the head. "What if Maxim was working for the interim government?"

Senator Rockefeller looked surprised. "Is he... working for the government?"

I shot to my feet. "Senator, will you excuse me? I need to make a quick phone call."

He stood politely. "Of course."

My heart raced. I hurried from the room.

Jase rose from his chair. "Are we leaving?"

I looked at Jamie. "Is the conference room free?"

She glanced at her computer screen. "Yes. It's available until one o'clock."

"I just need five minutes to make a phone call," I promised.

Jase followed me down the hall. "What happened? Is everything okay?"

"Yes. No. I don't know." I ducked inside the conference room. "Just... give me a minute. Okay?"

He followed me into the room. "Okay."

I scrolled through my list of contacts until I found Maxim's name. My foot tapped anxiously while I waited for his phone to ring. .

Jase pulled the door closed. He folded his arms across his chest and studied me intently.

"How was your meeting?" Maxim answered.

I began pacing. "Is Mykola Azarov still serving as the Prime Minister of Ukraine?"

"Yes," Maxim replied. The word was drawn out as if he were hesitant to say more.

My feet slowed, briefly. "Does the Prime Minister support you in this bid for the presidency?"

"Yes. I am the only candidate Prime Minister Azarov is publically supporting," Maxim boasted. "Why?"

"Is Leonid Kozhara still serving as the Minister of Foreign Affairs?" I couldn't believe I was plotting to get the man who'd previously offered me a job canned.

"Yes," he admitted hesitantly. "Why do you ask?"

I tried to ignore the frustration in his voice. "Is Mr. Kozhara supporting you in this bid for the presidency?"

"Yes," Maxim gritted. "Why do you ask all of these questions?"

"Are you and Mr. Kozhara on good terms?" I continued.

"*Kotyonok*," Maxim warned. "I would not have encouraged you to work for him if we were not on good terms."

I took a deep breath and blew it out. "Okay. Can Prime Minister Azarov appoint you the Minister of Foreign Affairs while you are running for president?"

"No. The Minister of Foreign Affairs is nominated by the president, not the Prime Minister," Maxim corrected, "and that nomination must be approved by the Ukrainian Parliament."

"Would the Chairman of the Ukrainian Parliament be willing to nominate you, since he's acting as president, and would the Ukrainian Parliament approve this nomination?" I quickly amended.

"Kristine, why do you ask these questions?" Maxim demanded.

"Because Senator Rockefeller will not support an aid package that can be perceived as benefitting the Russian mafia. He's far more likely to support an aid package solicited by the Ukrainian Minister of Foreign Affairs. And, Maxim? I think you're going to run into the same problem with Secretary Gates this afternoon. He's clearly interested in positioning that defense shield in Ukraine, or he wouldn't have agreed to the meeting. But he isn't going to negotiate a deal with the Russian mafia. He'll insist on dealing with the interim government, or he'll wait until the new president is elected."

Silence ensued.

"Maxim?"

"I'm here," he answered gruffly.

"You have to be working for the Ukrainian government in some formal capacity in order to negotiate these deals. Can you make that happen?"

"Is your meeting with Senator Rockefeller over?" he countered.

"No. I stepped out of the meeting so I could call you. It's beyond rude for me to walk out of a meeting like this, but I... I just wanted to warn you. Senator Rockefeller plans to attend the meeting with Secretary Gates. I think they'd both like to work with you, but you need to proceed in some formal capacity."

"I'll call you back."

I gaped at the phone. Maxim had ended the call.

"What happened?" Jase asked.

"He's calling me back." My voice turned shrill. "Why is he calling me back?"

Jase shrugged. "Maybe he had another call."

I stood frozen with indecision. "What time is it in Ukraine?"

He glanced at his phone. "It's twelve-thirty. They're seven hours ahead of us, so it's seven-thirty in the evening in Kyiv."

I frowned. "Their government offices are closed. There's no way he can get this problem resolved now."

Jase stepped aside when I started toward the door.

"Where are you going?"

"I can't keep the Senator waiting." Sadly, I hadn't a clue how to handle the rest of the meeting.

My phone vibrated with an incoming call by the time I reached Jamie's desk. I stopped just outside the Senator's office. "Yes?"

Maxim's voice slid through me like a salve. "Leonid Kozhara has appointed me the Deputy Minister of Foreign Affairs. This position does not require a presidential nomination or approval by the Ukrainian Parliament."

The tension eased from my shoulders. "Thank God." I grabbed Jamie's business card from the card holder on her desk. "Can you ask Mr. Kozhara to fax confirmation of this appointment to 202-224-6384 on official government letterhead as soon as possible?"

A low growl emanated from the phone.

"Please, Maxim?" I persisted sweetly.

"You will have documentation shortly." Maxim disconnected the call.

I stepped inside the Senator's office. "I'm sorry for the interruption."

He stood and beckoned me toward our chairs. "Is Mr. Markov working for the Ukrainian government?"

I dropped into my seat. "Yes. Mr. Markov is currently working as Ukraine's Deputy Minister of Foreign Affairs."

He reclined against the back of his chair. "How long has he been working in this capacity?"

I stuffed a rainbow roll inside my mouth so I could buy a few more seconds. "He's been serving as Ukraine's Deputy Minister of Foreign Affairs for approximately five minutes."

My revelation was met with a hearty laugh. "Well played, Ms. Stone."

I smiled. "Ukraine's Minister of Foreign Affairs will be faxing written confirmation of this appointment to your office within the hour."

Senator Rockefeller rose from his chair. "I'll attend the meeting with Secretary Gates this afternoon. I can't make any promises about the economic aid, but I'll see what I can do."

I shoved the empty sushi containers back inside the bag. "Thank you so much for meeting with him… and me."

He walked me to the door. "Thank you, Ms. Stone. Next time, lunch is on me."

* * * * *

My eyes flashed open in the darkened room.

"It's me," Rafael whispered soothingly. He pulled a long-sleeved heather gray Henley over his head. The moonlight slipped between the blinds to dance along his chiseled abs.

I pushed up from the pillow and smoothed my wildly tangled hair. "What time is it?"

"One-thirty. I'm sorry. I didn't mean to wake you." He kicked his jeans aside.

I burrowed into his arms, savoring his warmth, when he climbed into bed. "Why didn't you tell me you were flying in tonight? I would have waited up for you."

Rafael's chest rose and fell with a tired breath. "I didn't think I'd get my report finished in time to fly out tonight; and when airports started closing along the east coast, I didn't know if we'd be able to land here or if we'd be diverted someplace else. I didn't want to get your hopes up."

I snuggled a little closer. "Is it still snowing outside?"

He tucked the covers beneath my chin while nuzzling the top of my head. "There's a foot of snow on the ground, and it doesn't look like this storm is going to end anytime soon."

"Good. I hope we get buried under mountains of snow so you can't fly back to Portugal." I tried not to yawn. "God, I've missed this... and you. I'm so happy you're home."

"Me too," Rafael murmured sleepily. Within seconds, he was snoring softly.

I pressed my nose to his neck, sighing contentedly when I smelled the cloves from his spicy cologne. I whispered a small prayer of thanksgiving before surrendering to sleep. The snow continued to fall while we slumbered safely in each other's arms.

* * * * *

I kissed the stubble shadowing Rafael's jaw. "I can't believe you're really here." I'd assumed I'd been dreaming last night. When I discovered him lying next to me, I woke with a burst of energy and in an insanely good mood.

He smiled without opening his eyes.

I climbed on top of him. "Are you still sleeping?" I lifted one of his eyelids.

His chest vibrated when he chuckled. "Not anymore."

"Why are you still sleeping? Isn't it like two o'clock in the afternoon in Portugal?" I leaned back, still straddling his lap.

"I'm jet lagged," he complained. "Why are you so awake? Did you sneak out for coffee?"

"No. I'm just excited you're home." My smile faded. "When do you have to fly back to Portugal?"

His warm brown eyes sought mine. "I fly back Tuesday night."

Four days wasn't nearly enough. I forced another smile.

"You said something about a report last night. Did you catch one of the bad guys?"

"Yes, a wealthy businessman." He shook his head. "I still can't believe he asked me to secure the child for him."

"Not bad for your first ten days on the job," I stated admiringly.

His hands caressed my thighs before settling on my hips. "Any idea how the meeting went between Maxim and Secretary Gates?"

I shrugged uncertainly. "Kadyn said the meeting went well. Everyone's mulling over the possibilities, but they haven't agreed to anything. Maxim left after the meeting. He had to get back to Ukraine to campaign. Kadyn confirmed Maxim's flight before he left last night."

Rafael nodded. "Jase told me, well, he texted me last night. I suppose we should head downstairs so I can meet the infamous Oni."

I bit my lip. "I don't want to go downstairs."

"Why?" Curiosity and hope sparked in his eyes.

I pressed my lips to his ear. "I need to feel you inside of me."

His fingers gripped my hips. "I don't know. Once we start we may never stop."

My tongue traced a circle just behind his ear. "Please?" I whispered.

"Kristine," he groaned. His body hardened right where I needed him most.

I let the full weight of my body settle against his. He rolled over, pinning me beneath him before thoroughly ravishing me with a kiss. I managed to wiggle out of my sleep shorts without breaking the kiss. He slid his boxer briefs off.

We both moaned when his deliciously naked body

settled against mine. Need pinged across every nerve ending and pooled between my legs.

I was forced to break the kiss when Rafael lifted the camisole over my head. His warm, wet tongue circled my breasts. He drew them deep inside his mouth. My body arched, demanding more, while pleasure pulsed deep and low. I was already dangerously close to climaxing. "Now," I whispered pleadingly.

His lips forged a trail along my collarbone, shoulder, and neck. He pinned me with his gaze before filling me inch by glorious inch. "Is this what you need?"

"Yes," I whispered. I loved the way he forced my body to accommodate him despite his intimidating size. I breathed a sigh of relief when our hips finally met. The tension eased and the pain subsided with that one, single breath.

With a groan, he pulled us even closer. "You're so tight. I love how your body tries to resist mine." Our lips met in a heated kiss. His fingers coaxed my breasts into sensitive peaks; tugging, twisting, and pinching until I writhed beneath him.

My knees lifted instinctively, allowing him greater access as he thrust. He demanded more with every stroke. The room wavered in and out of focus. Rafael pushed me to the edge in long, slow strokes, tore me away, then sent me back again. Three times he denied my release. "*Please*," I whimpered shamelessly.

He slowed even more. "Open your eyes." His arms shook while he fought for control.

My heart stalled when I saw the determination in his eyes.

His eyes darkened as he began to swell. With impossible precision, he thrust once... twice... three times. The room exploded when he struck my womb. A million jagged stars danced between us.

Rafael swallowed my scream as we found our release. He pulsed inside of me, anchoring his seed with a searing heat. My body trembled as he wrung every last bit of pleasure from me.

I sprawled face down in the pillows too sated to move when he rolled me over. He blanketed my body, chest to my back, grasped my hands, and pushed inside of me again. His thick limbs held me in place. There was no questioning this man's strength or his power over me. I found that thought soothing. Rafael moved deep and slow. He took his time, savoring every move, while he stitched our bodies together. With hands still clasped, he sent us careening toward an exquisite end.

When our bodies finally quieted, Rafael scooped me up and carried me to the shower. He turned all twelve jets on while cradling me in his arms. Steam enveloped us as we stepped inside. We took turns washing each other's hair, lathering each other up, kissing, and holding one another while the jets sent the soap spiraling down the drain.

Rafael wrapped me in a thick, cotton towel before drying himself off. We both donned sweats, long-sleeved shirts, and thick socks before heading downstairs.

"Feeling better?" Jase inquired when we stepped inside the kitchen. He was perched on a stool at the center island.

"Lots," I boasted. I'd gone to bed without dinner the night before, although I couldn't say whether it was fatigue or depression that had sent me there. The meeting with the Senator had left me feeling drained, and I was missing Rafael terribly.

Rafael crossed the kitchen, poured two cups of coffee,

and handed one to me. "You two are welcome to stay, but don't feel like you have to stick around here today. You've been working twenty-four seven. I'm sure you would enjoy some time off."

Brady glanced up from his spot in front of the television. He'd been hunched over, watching the screen intently, when we walked into the kitchen. "Have you looked outside the window recently?"

Rafael and I exchanged glances. "No."

Jase laughed. "There's two and a half feet of snow out there. Most of the roads have yet to be plowed, so emergency travel only."

I pulled the blinds up on the window and was nearly blinded by the sun. "Maybe you'll get snowed in after all."

Brady nodded toward the television. "The snow has slowed, but they're expecting it to pick up again this afternoon. Hey! Check this out."

Rafael, Jase, and I joined him on the sectional.

"They're having a snowball fight on King Street in front of City Hall," Rafael noted with a hint of envy.

Jase burst out laughing. Someone off screen had just beamed the reporter upside the head with a snowball.

The four of us exchanged glances. Brady was the first to move. "Let's go."

Oni yelped when he bolted past her. "What's wrong?"

"Oni, Rafael, Rafael, Oni," I said excitedly. I pulled her toward the television so she could see the snowball fight. "Get your coat. We're going to play in the snow."

We giggled and plotted like nine year olds as we trekked up King Street. We had to walk in the middle of the street because the plows had forced all the snow up onto the sidewalks. We stopped and made snowballs along the way, piling them inside plastic bags. Our gloves were sticky with snow by the time we arrived at City Hall.

Brady and Jase wasted no time jumping into the melee. They pelted every man standing. Rafael hung back, seemingly conflicted. I could tell he wanted to join Brady and Jase, but he also wanted to protect us.

I nudged Oni, who was staring slack-jawed at the crowd. "Ready?"

Her eyes were bright, her cheeks flushed from the cold. "No."

I piled a bunch of snowballs into her arms. "I'll never pull it off alone."

She shoved a few snowballs into her coat pockets before grinning. "Okay."

We ran opposite one another while attacking Rafael. "Take that," I yelled.

"Hey! You're not supposed to attack your own team," he protested laughingly. He ducked and danced between the ammunition but refused to throw a snowball.

One of Oni's snowballs hit Rafael in the arm when he was protecting his head. I caught him in the hip.

"Girls against the boys!" Brady yelled. He beamed me in the chest with a snowball, then danced on his toes like he'd just scored the winning touchdown.

"Hey! That's my girl!" Rafael threw his first snowball, nailing Brady in the head.

Jase came to Brady's rescue, throwing snowballs rapid fire toward Rafael, Oni, and me. We returned fire, instinctively forming our own team.

It wasn't long before we collapsed in a heap, caked in snow.

"They're handing out free hot chocolate at Bread and

Chocolate," a well-bundled woman shared excitedly on her way up the street.

The five of us exchanged glances. Rafael laughed. "Let's go."

Oni and I strolled arm in arm, flanked by the three rambunctious men. "Are you okay?" I asked when she suddenly grew quiet.

She nodded. "I really miss my family and friends in Ukraine, but this is nice. I think I might be okay."

"I'm sorry, Oni. I've been so focused on helping Maxim, I'm afraid I've been neglecting you. We'll get you square with the metro and school, just as soon as the snow clears. You're going to make all kinds of friends once school begins." I gave her a hug.

She brushed away a tear with her snow encrusted glove. "I still can't believe I'm here. How will I ever repay you?"

"You don't repay friends," I said, repeating Rafael's words from long ago.

Rafael slowed. "I love you," he whispered when Oni's attention was diverted.

I sighed contentedly as the world righted itself. "I'm so happy you're home."

* * * * *

Oni offered to cook dinner after we toured the campus and rode the metro. Rafael mapped her bus and metro routes so she'd know how to travel between the Ukrainian embassy and the campus for work. I sampled the *borshch*. "Are those dumplings?"

"This is *varenyky*." She handed me the platter. "They're filled with mashed potatoes, sautéed onions, and mushrooms."

I added the *varenyky* to my plate before passing the platter to Rafael.

"*Pierogis*," Rafael murmured appreciatively. He popped another *pampushky* into his mouth. "I love Ukrainian food."

"Oni, you are an amazing cook." I dipped the little garlic ball into the savory soup. "Oh, Rafael, that reminds me, are you going to be around for the Super Bowl?"

His spoon paused just above his soup. "When's the Super Bowl?"

"Three weeks from today. Cenia is hosting her second annual chili cook-off. The men compete for best chili. The women bring appetizers and dessert." I glanced at Oni. "You're invited too."

Her eyes grew round. "Who's Cenia?"

I smiled. I absolutely adored Cenia and her spunky attitude. "Cenia's a very good friend of mine. She used to serve in the Air Force with Kadyn. She works for the Department of Defense now."

She glanced shyly from her soup. "Will Kadyn be there?"

My heart stalled, recognizing the look. "Yes. Kadyn will be there."

Rafael's gaze slid smoothly between Oni and me. "Does Kadyn make you nervous?"

"No." She blushed. "Well, maybe. A little. I was just curious if he was going."

I fought to remain impartial while countless emotions rioted inside of me. "Kadyn is one of my dearest friends." I admired Oni, but I questioned whether any woman was good enough for Kadyn, including me.

Oni simply nodded.

Rafael cleared his throat. "I'm not sure I'll be free for the

Super Bowl. It depends on how long my next assignment is in town." By "town," he meant Lisbon. He didn't want Oni to know he was working in Portugal.

"I'll RSVP for all three of us just in case." I tried the *varenyky*. "Is the embassy open tomorrow?"

Oni nodded. "Yes. Konstantin assured me the embassy will be open tomorrow. He offered to drive me to work since it's my first day. I think he is staying down the street with Shae tonight.

"What kind of work will you be doing for the embassy?" Rafael inquired curiously.

She chuckled softly. "Officially? I will be working in the press room. Unofficially? I will be campaigning for Maxim."

"Maxim certainly knew what he was doing when he positioned Konstantin at the embassy," Rafael mused. "Between Konstantin, Kadyn, and Kri, he has established some surprisingly useful connections in the United States. It's almost as if he knew he'd be running for president."

My spoon stalled right in front of my mouth. I wasn't one to buy into conspiracy theories, but Rafael's point sent goosebumps rocketing down my spine. Maxim researched me. He knew I worked as a policy advisor for Senator Rockefeller before he pursued a relationship with me. Had his interest been politically motivated? What about his decision to help Kadyn?

"Maxim has established similar connections in Ukraine, Belarus, Poland, Germany, and Great Britain. He has helped a lot of people who now owe him favors. If he wasn't collecting on those favors to strengthen his campaign, he'd be using those favors to help Ukraine in some other way," Oni explained.

I tried to ignore the cloud of suspicion hovering over

me. "How is his campaign going in Ukraine?"

She reached for another *pampushky*. "Maxim and Yulia are tied for first place in the latest polls."

"Yulia Tymoshenko was the first woman to serve as Prime Minister of Ukraine. She helped lead the Orange Revolution," I informed Rafael. I wasn't sure how familiar he was with Ukrainian politics.

Oni nodded. "She's pro-Western, like Maxim, but a lot of Ukrainians don't trust her. Until recently she was serving time in prison for embezzlement and for abusing her power. I believe those charges were politically motivated, but not everyone agrees. Besides, there are a lot of men who won't support a female president. Prime Minister is one thing, but the presidency is something else entirely."

"I still can't believe an individual with ties to the Russian mafia could receive so much support," Rafael remarked.

"The Russians elected a former KGB operative for their president. This is not so different. Maxim is one of the few people who maintains enough power and influence to end Putin's meddling in our governance," Oni noted dismissively.

Rafael's eyes met mine. "It will be interesting to see if the U.S. government views this election the same way."

My thoughts turned inward with a slight chill. I suspected they would.

* * * * *

I burrowed against Rafael's chest. My body felt like it was filled with lead. "I wish you didn't have to leave tonight." We'd made the most of the last two hours, making love in his bed. Brady and Jase thought we were packing. Or not. They were settled in over at my house since Rafael's flight was scheduled to depart in a couple of hours.

"Me too." He gently caressed my back. "At least Oni is settled in at the dorms. Maxim is gone. You're going to be busy with school, lobbying for Maxim, and preparing for your trip to Sierra Leone."

My thumb skimmed his cheekbone. "Can you join me in Sierra Leone?"

"I'll try. Do you have any vacation time remaining?"

"Three or four days," I estimated. "Why?"

"I'd like you to fly to Portugal for Valentine's Day." His fingers teased my arm.

"I'd love to spend Valentine's Day with you." I reached for my cell phone so I could check the calendar. "Valentine's Day falls on a Friday this year. If I take Thursday, Friday, and Monday off from work, we'd have five days together."

"I'll send the jet back for you." He frowned. "How will that affect your coursework?"

"I'm already halfway through the assigned readings, and I plan to work on my midterms this weekend." My final semester didn't even begin for three more days, but I'd requested the syllabi and ordered my books early so I could stay busy while Rafael was working in Lisbon. Of course, those studies had ground to a complete stop when Maxim dropped his presidential bomb. "I only have nine credit hours this semester, and I purposely chose classes that were scheduled on Tuesdays, Wednesdays, and Thursdays." I'd been hoping to snag some long weekends with Rafael.

He tucked me beneath him. "Good. I'll plan something special."

A moan escaped my chest when he sank inside of me again. There was no denying how perfect the world felt when our bodies were joined like this. "You are the only something special I need."

We made love slower than I ever dreamed possible, with eyes and hands locked. Rafael pushed me to that place where nothing else mattered... nothing but the feel of his body driving deep and determinedly into mine.

My nipples pebbled against his chest. Our bodies wound tighter and tighter. "Rafael," I cried. My knees rose. My back arched as if begging for the next thrust.

He released my hands so he could grasp my breasts. "Let go, baby. Let me see you lose control." He rolled both nipples between his fingers and thumbs.

Pleasure tore through me, shredding my emotions, my body, and mind.

Rafael captured me in a fierce embrace. "Mine," he whispered hoarsely. With one final thrust, he filled me.

Softly, I began to cry.

Chapter 5 – Never Gonna Let You Down

I blinked back tears. I couldn't believe the jalapeno and habanero peppers in Jase's chili had literally driven me to tears.

"Can I taste?" Oni inquired hesitantly.

Jase shrugged. "Sure." He pulled a soup spoon from the drawer and handed it to her.

"Iz spy-ee," I warned with a slightly swollen tongue. Jase had aptly named his chili "A Slow and Painful Death." I was still trying to numb the pain with a piece of bread.

Oni's eyes teared. "Oh!" The spoon clattered against the granite countertop as her hand flew to her mouth.

I handed her a piece of bread. "Water won't relieve the pain. Try Brady's chili. It doesn't hurt as much."

Brady stood there expectantly while Oni worked up the courage to try his chili. His "Shark Bait" chili stood a good chance of stealing first place with clams, shrimp, bite size chunks of orange roughy, and Old Bay Seasoning.

"That is good," Oni agreed. These recipes are very

different. How do you choose?"

I laughed. "You can't choose yet. You have at least five other recipes to taste when we get to Cenia's house."

Jase tugged a pair of oven mitts over his hands. "Are you ladies ready to leave?"

Oni retrieved the bright pink *Dulce de Leche* Ukrainian Waffle Cake she'd crafted from the center island. "I'm ready."

"I'll get the door." I grabbed the bacon cheddar scones from the counter before following them into the garage. I climbed into the back seat next to Oni.

Jase set his Crock-pot on the floor between my feet. He handed me the oven mitts before sliding into the driver's seat. "Be careful. That chili is hot."

"Too hot if you ask me." Brady secured his chili on the floor between his feet.

"Chili is supposed to be hot. That ocean brew you concocted shouldn't even be called chili." Jase backed out of the garage.

Brady looked offended. "There's chili powder and beans in there. You're just bitter because you didn't think to cook something more original."

I typed Cenia and Roger's new address into the navigation system on my phone before settling in to visit with Oni. "Did you finish your homework?"

"Yes. I've completed the reading and the assignments for the next two weeks." She looked relieved. Oni was so much like me, it was scary.

"I finished writing my paper. Rafael's taking me someplace special for Valentine's Day, so I'm afraid we won't be around next weekend." Since Oni had spent the last two weekends with me, I figured some advanced warning was in order.

Oni was under the impression that Rafael worked most weekends. She never questioned the fact that Brady and Jase were living with me. Rafael assigned bodyguards in Ukraine, and she knew what the SVR had done to me. "Where are you going?"

Jase sent a subtle warning through the rearview mirror.

"I'm not entirely sure. Last I heard, he was considering someplace in Portugal." I'd become quite adept at telling the truth while still being vague.

Brady shared some unspoken communication with Jase before changing the topic. "How do you like your courses?"

"My professors and classmates are nice, but the courses are difficult," Oni replied.

He shifted so he could face the back seat. "Because everything is in English?"

"Because students are expected to voice their opinions and participate in class," Oni clarified. "University students aren't permitted to speak in Ukraine."

"They aren't even allowed to ask questions," I added. "It's considered disrespectful." That had proven one of our biggest challenges while teaching in Simferopol.

"Really?" Brady looked at me.

"I don't like speaking in front of the other students," Oni admitted. "I'm afraid they'll laugh or think I'm stupid."

"I feel the same way," I assured her. "So does Shae."

"I felt the same way when I was in school," Brady revealed.

"Me too," Jase agreed. "I think we all do."

Oni smiled appreciatively. "I thought it was just me."

"Nope. That feeling is pretty universal," Brady assured her.

Jase's eyes sought mine in the rearview mirror. "Is your

meeting with the Senator still scheduled for tomorrow?"

"Yes. We're meeting at Ten Penh at one o'clock. I asked Jamie to add you to the reservation, so Senator Rockefeller knows you'll be joining us for lunch."

"Do you think he'll support the rider?" Brady asked.

"I don't know." Jamie called to schedule the meeting, but she didn't reveal what the Senator's decision might be. I glanced out at the barren trees. "If he's willing to support this rider, then I'm going to have my work cut out for me lobbying Congress over the next few weeks. There will be no guarantees, no way of knowing if we've chosen the right bill to attach this rider to, whether it will pass, or how long it might take."

"Sounds impossible," Brady noted skeptically.

"It would be possible if we had all the time in the world, but Congress doesn't move quickly. I just don't see how we're going to secure this funding before the election," I admitted worriedly.

"But we chose bills with a lot of support, bills that are very close to passing," Oni reminded me.

"We're still fighting an uphill battle with very little time on the clock." Three and a half weeks had passed since I ran the idea by Senator Rockefeller. Each day that passed left me feeling even more anxious and depressed. Between the impending election and Rafael's absence, I was a mess.

"What if he doesn't support the rider?" Jase asked.

"He thought I'd fare better with the IMF, so I'd approach them rather than pursue anything further in Congress. I don't know anyone who works there, but I'm guessing Senator Rockefeller does. I've encouraged Maxim to reach out to the European Investment Bank and the European Bank for Reconstruction and Development. Maybe something will pan out there."

"What is IMF? Is that a government office?" Oni asked.

"The IMF is an international organization that helps fund projects that stimulate growth, improve economic stability, and reduce poverty for member countries. And, yes, I've already checked. Ukraine is a member of the IMF. So, if Maxim approached them for a loan, as Deputy Foreign Minister of Ukraine, and the U. S. supported him in this endeavor, odds are high he'd get the loan. The U.S. has more voting power than any other country in the IMF. There's just one problem."

"What?" Oni inquired breathlessly.

"Russia is a member of the IMF. So if we approach the IMF for a loan, and they put it to a vote, Russia would vote against us. Russia holds a small percentage of votes, so I doubt they could stop us, but the damage would be done. Putin would know what Maxim was planning. He would destroy Maxim and the pipeline the second he got wind of this."

Oni's eyes widened. "Putin has positioned troops along our eastern border. He's planted people inside Ukraine. They're pretending to be Ukrainian protestors, but their accents give them away. They're from Moscow and St. Petersburg, not Ukraine. My father said they're threatening people, trying to force Ukrainians to vote for the pro-Russian candidate in the upcoming election. If we don't vote the way Putin wants us to, he's going to invade Ukraine."

"Which is why you need the missile defense system," I reasoned. "Sadly, there are no easy answers. We'll just have to wait to see what Senator Rockefeller says tomorrow."

Jase turned onto an unfamiliar street. "Which house is theirs?" Cenia and Roger purchased a new home shortly before their wedding. This was our first time visiting their new place.

I studied the house numbers on the mailboxes. "Over there." I pointed toward a brick house with black shutters on the other side of the street.

Jase parked alongside the curb. He stepped from the Jeep and opened my door. Brady helped Oni from the vehicle before grabbing his Crock-pot from the front seat.

Cenia met us at the door. "Kri! I thought you'd fallen off the planet." She planted a quick kiss on my cheek. "Hey, Jase, Brady. I can't wait to try your chili." She hugged them around their Crock-pots before beckoning them inside. "Hi, Oni. I'm so glad you could join us."

"Thanks for inviting me." Oni handed her the cake.

"This looks too pretty to eat." Cenia nudged the door closed with her toe. She nodded toward the adjoining office. "You can leave your coats in here. I'll show you around the house after everyone gets settled."

The foyer opened into a great room. I set the bacon cheddar scones on the dining room table so I could give Kadyn a hug. "Hey, handsome. Where's that award winning chili of yours?"

Roger laughed. "You're speaking to the wrong guy. My chili is the *only* award winning chili in this house." He pulled me from Kadyn's arms so he could give me a hug. He kept me tucked under his arm as he reached for Oni's hand. "You must be Oni. I'm Roger, Cenia's husband."

"It's nice to meet you." She peeked at Kadyn. "It's good to see you again."

He nodded politely. "How's school going?"

Her eyes widened. She seemed surprised he would ask. "Good. How are your classes?"

Kadyn shrugged. "They're okay."

"Hi, Kri." Marie smiled and gave me a hug.

"Where's Phil?" I scanned the room.

"Right here." He'd snuck up behind me. "This must be Oni. Wow. Kadyn wasn't kidding. You really do look like sisters." His eyes narrowed while he studied her. "Only your eyes are green."

"Thank you," Oni answered uncertainly.

"Nothing gets by this guy." I laughed. "Phil's one of the most brilliant men walking the planet."

"Not even close, but I'm glad you think so." He gave me a hug.

Marie's hand brushed gently against Oni's arm. "Would you like a glass of Chianti?"

"Yes, please." The tension in Oni's shoulders eased.

"I'll go with you. Kadyn…" I prodded expectantly.

He grinned. "Five Alarm Fire, third Crock-pot on the right."

"You're not supposed to know which chili is his," Phil objected. "This is supposed to be a blind taste test."

"Since when?" Roger scoffed. "Forget the Five Alarm Fire. Try the Smoking Gun. It's in the stainless steel Crock-pot next to the stove."

"I guess we know who's winning the award for the manliest Crock-pot," Jase teased. He and Brady sauntered by with their beer.

"There's an award for that?" Matt yelled from the living room.

"Read your e-mail!" Cenia quipped from inside the kitchen.

Oni followed us into the kitchen. I dipped a spoon into Kadyn's chili while Marie poured the Chianti. "Wow! That is good." Kadyn had confided that he was using a recipe that won best chili at the Chicago firefighters' chili cook-off last year. The sauce was thick and meaty with the perfect amount of heat.

Marie handed me a glass of wine before grabbing a spoon and giving it a try. "Poor Phil." She sighed dejectedly.

I handed Oni a spoon. "What do you think?"

"It's quite good," she agreed.

Marie handed Oni a glass of Chianti. "Have you tasted chili before?"

Oni shook her head before sipping the wine. "No. We cook with beans, but nothing spicy like this."

"You should sample all of the chilies." Cenia handed us a stack of paper cups. "Once you find your favorite, grab a bowl and dish up. Cornbread, scones, and chips are on the dining room table. Sour cream, onions, and cheese are over there." She pointed next to the stove. "Oh, and don't forget to vote. We'll announce the winner at half time." Cenia strode into the living room, where she made the same announcement.

We sampled each of the chilies in turn. Cenia, Roger, and Kadyn followed suit. The remaining guests waited until the commercials. Kadyn joined Oni and me on the floor when we settled in front of the television to eat.

I nudged his shoulder with mine. "Any news on the missile defense system?"

Kadyn kept one eye on the television. "Last I heard, Secretary Gates was running it by the White House. I doubt I'll hear anything further."

I figured as much. A plan of this magnitude was only discussed on a need to know basis. "If we decide to position the defense shield in Ukraine, do you think we'll be able to get it installed before Putin discovers what we're doing?"

Kadyn eyed Oni, then me. "Maxim will have to position the shield in an area that minimizes the chances of pro-Russian forces passing human intelligence back to Putin. They'll have to work quickly. Mobile launch pads and munitions convoys can be detected by satellite. Putin could discover what he's doing before the defense shield is operational."

My stomach turned when I considered the ramifications. "This could lead to war, not just between Ukraine and Russia but between Russia and the United States."

Oni paled.

I set my food on the coffee table. I felt too nauseous to eat.

Kadyn's arm braced my back as he whispered discretely. "You'll see the U.S. position a carrier group in the Black Sea. We'll run training exercises simultaneous to the installation as a precaution, a show of force, and a distraction." He squeezed my shoulders reassuringly.

A chill stole through my bones. I feared what we'd begun so much so that I barely registered the football game and the tour of Cenia's house. I perked up when the results for the chili cook-off were announced. Kadyn won best chili, Brady came in second place, and Jase came in third. Of course, Roger scored the award for the manliest Crock-pot.

* * * * *

I twisted the strand of pearls Rafael had given me. The black dress suit with the white silk camisole and pencil skirt fit my mood perfectly. I was dreading the meeting with Senator Rockefeller, in part because I finally grasped the consequences in terms of human lives. If we chose not to fund the pipeline, it would prove difficult for Ukraine to strengthen its economy and sever ties with Russia. With Russian forces already amassed along the eastern border and poised to invade, Putin could easily take Ukraine in its weakened state. While funding the pipeline would enable Ukraine to improve its economy and sever ties with Russia, this strategy was even more likely to lead to war. Either way, war seemed inevitable for Ukraine and possibly the United States.

"Are you okay?" Jase slid effortlessly into a parking space.

"I'm fine. I'm just tired. I was too worried about this meeting to sleep last night." I researched alternative funding streams nearly the entire night. Congress was still Plan A since it was the only place where I maintained useful connections. USAID was Plan B, although I didn't know anyone working for that agency. IMF was Plan C, an option of last resort. I was planning to run the alternative funding streams by Senator Rockefeller if he shot down the rider. Even if we couldn't secure congressional funding, I was certain he could help me establish the necessary connections at IMF and USAID.

Jase helped me from the Jeep. "Perhaps an early bed time is in order since you don't have school tonight." He fed the meter before escorting me inside the restaurant.

Senator Rockefeller was sitting next to a man I didn't recognize. Both stood as we approached. Senator Rockefeller reached for my hand first. "Ms. Stone, thank you for joining us."

"Of course, Senator. Thank you for inviting me to lunch. I'd like you to meet my friend and my bodyguard, Jase

Adkins. Jase, this is Senator Jay D. Rockefeller."

Senator Rockefeller shook Jase's hand before introducing the man with the salt and pepper hair. "This is Mark Sondell. He represents the United States on the IMF Executive Board."

I squared my shoulders as I grasped his hand. "Pleased to meet you."

Jase held my chair before claiming his seat. Our waiter handed us tightly rolled steaming washcloths with bamboo tongs before taking our drink order. My stomach felt too queasy to order anything more than sparkling water. We agreed on the set menu while placing our drink order.

Senator Rockefeller began as soon as the waiter walked away. "As Mr. Sondell's presence might suggest, I think it would be beneficial to pursue funding for the Odessa-Brody pipeline through the IMF."

"In lieu of the rider or in addition to congressional funding?" I inquired warily.

"I've run this proposal by the senate democratic leadership. I believe we can garner enough support to pursue the rider, but I don't believe we can accomplish this in time for the upcoming election," Senator Rockefeller replied. "I'd like to ensure a pro-Western candidate wins the election in Ukraine. Funding the pipeline may help us achieve that objective, but you know how this works. There's no way we can get this rider and whatever bill it's attached to through committee, the full House, and the Senate before the election. The IMF can act more swiftly, and this is precisely the type of project their organization funds."

Mr. Sondell braced his elbows against the table. "I can add this to our agenda and secure a vote from the executive board as soon as Ukraine files their letter of intent. We should be able to obtain the funding within a week to ten days."

We paused briefly when the waiter returned with our drinks and a platter of steamed dumplings.

I studied the two men while they transferred steamed dumplings onto their plates. "How detailed would Ukraine have to be in this letter of intent? Would Mr. Markov have to reveal that the loan will be used to extend the pipeline?"

"Yes. The letter of intent must provide sufficient detail to ensure a favorable vote." Mr. Sondell dunked his dumpling in the dipping sauce before popping it into his mouth.

I shook my head when Jase offered me the dumplings. "With all due respect, I feel that would be a grave mistake."

Senator Rockefeller's chopsticks stalled just above his plate.

"I'm certain we can garner enough votes to approve funding for this pipeline," Mr. Sondell assured me.

I forced an even tone. "Russia's Aleksei Mozhin sits on the IMF Executive Board."

His brow lifted. "Russia does not wield enough votes to block this."

"I'm aware of that fact, but Mr. Mozhin would undoubtedly alert President Putin of these plans. Putin has been trying to block the extension of the Odessa-Brody pipeline for years. He paid Yanukovych to connect the Odessa-Brody pipeline to the Druzhba pipeline. He blocked trade with Ukraine until they reversed the flow of oil, so the Odessa-Brody pipeline transports Russian oil to Mediterranean countries instead of transporting Ukrainian fuel as was originally intended. This has crippled the Ukrainian economy and left them even more vulnerable to Russia's influence. Putin has troops stationed along Ukraine's eastern border. He's just itching to invade. Mr. Markov and I are concerned that he will bomb the pipeline or invade Ukraine when he gets wind of this project. We need to secure funding, get the missile defense system in place, and complete the project as discretely as possible."

"Ukraine has expressed an interest in housing the missile defense shield we developed for Poland. This would enable them to protect the pipeline among other things," Senator Rockefeller explained.

Mr. Sondell eyed my empty plate. "Russia has grown increasingly hostile toward them. I fear they will invade either way."

"I appreciate your willingness to fund this pipeline, but I have another option I'd like to discuss with Senator Rockefeller before settling on a course of action." I pushed my plate aside. "USAID was granted seventeen billion dollars in discretionary funding last week. I'd like to see if they'd be willing to fund this project. This would enable us to proceed a bit more discretely. They already have staff assigned to the embassy in Ukraine who could provide oversight and monitoring."

Senator Rockefeller stroked his jaw. "Your objectives are consistent with their mission."

Mr. Sondell grew pensive. "Would they be willing to fund the entire project?"

I winced. "Seven hundred and eighty million dollars is a lot of money for USAID to invest in a single country. I'm still holding out hope the European Investment Bank or the European Bank for Reconstruction and Development will finance a portion of this project."

"Have you approached them?" The Senator claimed the last dumpling when the waiter arrived with the main course.

My stomach growled when I smelled the flounder and bok choy smothered in crab. "Mr. Markov is meeting with them tomorrow."

He fished his phone from his coat pocket. "Do you know anyone over at USAID?"

"No." I bit my bottom lip. "I was hoping you could recommend someone."

He typed out a brief text. "You'll have a name by the end of the day. I'll do what I can to pave the way."

Gradually, I released the breath I'd been holding. "Thank you, Senator."

Mr. Sondell handed me his business card. "You're welcome to call if that doesn't pan out."

I tucked his card inside my wallet. "Thank you, Mr. Sondell. I truly appreciate your help."

The lunch ended amicably with coffee and a chocolate torte.

* * * * *

"Hi, love. How'd it go?"

"Well, Maxim's a month into his campaign and we still haven't secured any funding." I turned the light off in the bathroom and padded off to bed. "Senator Rockefeller has been incredibly supportive, but he doesn't think we can secure the funding before the election if we go through Congress."

"What are you going to do?" There was some rustling over the phone while Rafael settled in for our call.

I glanced at the clock on my cell phone. It was eight o'clock in Virginia, one o'clock in the morning in Lisbon. "I'm going to pursue grant funding through USAID. I'm meeting with the executive director of their Global Development Lab on Thursday. Maxim's meeting with the European Investment Bank and the European Bank for Reconstruction and Development tomorrow morning, so we'll have a better grasp of our options by the end of the week."

"Are you still flying to Lisbon Thursday night?"

I shivered when my legs slid between the cool sheets. "Yes. Are you still free this weekend?"

"I'm free," he assured me. "I'll have the jet fueled and waiting for you at Reagan National Airport by five o'clock Thursday. I'll make sure you're pre-cleared so you don't have to go through customs, and I'll meet you at the jet so you don't have to walk through the airport by yourself."

"I don't want to see anybody. I don't want to go out to eat. I just want to stay home and cuddle with you." Work, school, and Maxim's campaign had proven exhausting. If the truth be told, I just wanted to crawl under a rock and never again see the light of day. I was *that* tired.

"I have something very low key planned for Friday and Saturday, just the two of us, but we're meeting with the priest on Sunday so we can begin the marriage preparation course."

I'd totally forgotten we were going to squeeze that in when I returned to Lisbon. "Sounds good." Hopefully, I could sleep during the flight. I sighed, recalling the first time we flew on Rafael's jet. It seemed wrong, flying on that jet without him.

"What's the matter, baby?" Rafael could read me, sight unseen, from thousands of miles away.

"Nothing. I just miss you. A lot." Thursday could not come soon enough.

"I miss you too," he whispered soothingly.

"Tell me about your case," I pleaded around a throat full of tears.

"Well, the celebrity I'm currently investigating has declined police protection while in Lisbon, so we've had to monitor him through a series of stakeouts. I'm practically living in this unmarked car."

My eyes widened. "You're in the car now?"

"Yes," he grumbled. "We've been sitting here for six hours."

I fluffed my pillow and burrowed beneath the duvet. "So you're working with a partner?"

"Vasco is with me." Vasco helped us wrap presents for the orphanage. He was jovial then, probably fun to hang out with.

"*Boa noite*, Kristine," Vasco called out cheerfully.

"So, what are you doing now?" I pictured them hunkered down in the car with high powered night vision binoculars.

"Playing cards and eating *natas*," Rafael revealed with a chuckle. "The guy rented a house with glass walls, which makes it easier for us to monitor him. He's sleeping now."

I groaned, recalling how creamy those decadent little pastries were. "Be sure to stock up on *natas* Friday morning *before* you come to the airport."

Rafael laughed. "I'll send some back with Captain Anderson. They'll be waiting for you when you board the jet."

"God, I love you." My arm looped around his pillow.

"I love you too. Call me tomorrow."

"I will," I promised. "*Boa noite.*"

"*Boa noite, meu amor.*"

Sleep found me curled around his pillow with the cell phone lodged beneath my head.

* * * * *

A well-muscled arm coiled around my waist, tugging me back against a granite chest. *"Dobryy den'."*

The little glass shaker filled with nutmeg tumbled into the frothy cappuccino. "Maxim?" Goose bumps pricked my skin when he nuzzled my neck.

"Release her," Jase growled.

His arm tightened when I turned around. The entire length of his body pressed me back against the condiments bar. "No."

I glanced at Jase. His back had been turned for all of two seconds while the barista brewed his latte. Now, two men restrained Jase so he couldn't intervene. His face was red, his eyes beyond livid. I forced an exasperated breath. "He's just doing this to make you mad."

"Not true," Maxim purred. "I'm doing this because I love the feel of your body pressed against mine." He shifted ever so slightly.

The room spun when I felt how aroused he was. "Maxim," I pleaded. "Let me go."

His breath tickled my neck. "Never." He sought the sweet spot behind my ear. His arms loosened, but he didn't step back. He chuckled when I slid out from beneath him.

I glared at the men restraining Jase. "Release him."

Their lips curved into half smiles. Still, they awaited Maxim's order.

Maxim shrugged. "You should aspire to stay on her good side. She will soon be the First Lady of Ukraine."

I stood in front of Jase when they released him. "I'm fine. He's just trying to provoke you."

"Why are you here?" Jase demanded angrily.

"I'm here to speak with Kristine." Maxim swiped Jase's coffee from the bar and motioned toward a table in the far corner. "Shall we?" Amusement danced in his eyes while he awaited my response.

"I have to leave for USAID in fifteen minutes." I fished the bottle of nutmeg from my coffee, wiped it down with a napkin, and handed it to the barista. "I'm sorry. You might want to refill that." I tossed the cappuccino in the trash before staring at Maxim.

He steered me toward the corner table and pulled a chair out for me. He set Jase's coffee directly in front of me, as if it were some sort of peace offering. "You look beautiful."

I glanced down at my clothes. I was wearing a heather gray sheath dress and the pearls Rafael had given me. This conservative ensemble was framed by a black ankle length coat that puddled against the floor on either side of me. I turned briefly. Jase was glowering a few feet away. My eyes widened when I noticed the contingent of men standing guard outside the coffee shop. Thankfully, there were no guns drawn. Still, their postures were just menacing enough to dissuade others from entering the shop. I handed Jase his coffee while ignoring the compliment. "Do you want me to cancel the meeting?"

Maxim relaxed into his seat. "No, but I would like to join you."

My eyebrows shot up. "You want to attend the meeting with USAID?"

His smile widened. "If you don't mind."

I searched his eyes. "What happened yesterday?"

He leaned forward conspiratorially. "The European Bank for Reconstruction and Development offered to loan us five hundred million dollars to extend the pipeline into Poland."

"Maxim, that's awesome." I was so happy for him.

He beamed, obviously pleased. "Maybe this will help persuade USAID to loan us the remaining two hundred and eighty million dollars."

"They don't issue loans. They issue grants, so you wouldn't have to pay that portion back."

He smiled. "Even better."

One of the men from his security detail handed me a cup of coffee. "Cappuccino with nutmeg."

"So the mafia still makes the occasional coffee run," I teased.

"They do," Maxim conceded.

I studied the contingent of men while pondering whether those ties were truly severed. "We need to leave, or we'll be late for the meeting."

Maxim stood. "Will you ride with me?"

"We'll meet you there," Jase gritted.

I grasped Maxim's hand as I rose from my chair. "I'll meet you in the main lobby." I rolled onto my tiptoes and kissed him on the cheek. "You might want to lose the gun before you walk through security."

His jaw clenched.

I tucked my hand beneath Jase's arm as we walked away. "Thanks."

"For what?" he demanded irritably.

I waited until we left the coffee shop. "For resisting the urge to punch him out."

A frigid gust of wind tugged at my coat when Jase swung the door to the main building open. "Why are you friends with that man?"

I sighed, knowing full well he'd never understand. "Aside from the fact that he saved my life?"

Brady had retrieved my Jeep while Jase and I were ordering coffee. He was now idling curbside in front of my office building. Jase opened the rear passenger door. "I don't trust him."

I climbed into the back seat. "Maxim behaves outrageously to assert his dominance, to throw people off, and to gain the upper hand. Just ignore him. He's not interested in a relationship with me. Well, he might be on some level, but he knows I'd be miserable in Ukraine, and he's not the type of man to force me there. He's way too proud for that."

Jase snorted his disbelief. He joined Brady in the front seat. "Thirteen-hundred Pennsylvania Avenue."

Brady eased into traffic. "What's going on?"

I leaned back in my seat. "Maxim's joining us at USAID."

His eyes shot toward Jase. "Maxim's in DC?"

"He mauled Kristine when we stopped for coffee." Jase looked pointedly at me.

My eyes narrowed. "He wasn't mauling me. He was trying to make you mad by acting a little too friendly. *Acting* would be the operative word in that sentence, in case you were wondering."

"Why is he here?" Brady resumed driving after idling at a red light.

"He obtained a partial loan for the pipeline and wants to secure the rest of the funding." I swiped a thin layer of gloss over my lips while peering into the jeweled mirror Kimme sent me for Christmas.

"We should let Kadyn and Rafael know he's here." Jase reached for his cell phone.

"Why? I'm leaving in a few hours." They were driving me to the airport after the meeting. My suitcase was sitting in the back of the Jeep.

"I'm letting them know, regardless." His thumbs flew over the phone.

I couldn't resist the groan or the eye roll. I turned my cell phone off so the onslaught of texts that were likely to ensue wouldn't disrupt the meeting.

Brady pulled alongside the curb outside USAID. "I'll meet you in the lobby."

Jase shoved the phone inside his pocket, stepped outside, and opened my door.

"Thanks for driving, Brady." I eyed the sidewalk cautiously. I hadn't bothered with snow boots. I was wearing three inch heels, and there was a thin dusting of snow on the ground.

Jase was still scowling when he offered me his arm. "I can't believe Maxim snuck into that coffee shop. What was I thinking, turning my back on that door?"

"Jase, it's fine. Maxim's not a threat. He'd never hurt me, and he's not going to force me into something against my will. The SVR? Now that's a different story." I paused in front of the door.

Jase tugged forcefully on the clear glass door. "You don't get it."

"Get what?" I hated the way he was beating himself up.

"Maxim wanted to be caught. He could have dragged you out that door without making a sound. If Maxim could pull that off, imagine what the SVR could have accomplished in that same amount of time. That was a rookie move, turning my back to that door. I'm pissed. My stupidity could have cost you your life. I need to find a refresher course and get my head square while you're away." He scanned the security guards, the metal detector, and the lobby before allowing me to proceed.

"I'm sorry, Jase. I'll ask Maxim to give me a heads up next time he's planning to be in town." I set my briefcase on the conveyor belt.

He followed me through the metal detector. "Maxim won't comply. He thrives on the element of surprise."

We signed in at the reception desk and retrieved our visitors' badges while waiting for Brady.

Maxim arrived a few minutes later. "Miss me?"

Jase folded his arms over his chest. "Where's the rest of your security detail?" He was only accompanied by two other men.

"They're around." Maxim signed for his visitor's badge. "Shall we?"

All six of us squeezed onto the elevator with a handful of other people. "Do you mind leaving your security detail in the reception area with Brady and Jase?" I whispered. "I don't want to intimidate this woman by dragging all these men into her office."

Maxim nodded.

We stepped off the elevator, crossed the hallway, and entered the suite of offices that managed USAID's Global Development Lab.

The receptionist's eyes widened. She half-sat, then stood while gaping at us. "H-how may I help you?"

"Hi. I'm Kristine Stone, and this is Maxim Markov, Ukraine's Deputy Minister of Foreign Affairs. We're meeting with Ms. Dickson." I smiled encouragingly.

She eyed the glowering towers of testosterone standing behind me. "Are they joining you?"

I leaned forward and whispered, "I was kinda hoping they could hang out here with you."

"Oh." The air rushed from her chair as she sank back onto the faux leather seat. "I'll let Ms. Dickson know you're here."

Maxim reached for my arm. We strategized in hushed tones.

"Kristine Stone?" Ms. Dickson looked up from her notes.

"Please, call me Kristine." I shook her hand. "This is Maxim Markov, the Deputy Minister of Foreign Affairs for Ukraine. He's in town unexpectedly, but I thought you might like to meet him. He can answer far more questions about the pipeline than I can."

Maxim clasped her hand in his. He bowed slightly, as if tempted to kiss her hand. "It's a pleasure to meet you, Ms. Dickson."

Her mouth fell open just a little. A faint blush crept over her skin.

I bit back a smile. It was nice to know I wasn't the only woman affected by Maxim's presence. Or was it his accent?

"Mr. Markov." She glanced at the remaining men.

"Our security detail," I admitted apologetically.

She nodded politely. "Kate, please offer these gentleman a drink."

The receptionist rose from her chair. "Yes, Ms. Dickson."

"This way, please." Ms. Dickson turned and walked down the hallway. She paused in front of their breakroom. "What would you like to drink?"

"Water, please." I unbuttoned my coat.

"Water," Maxim agreed. He coaxed me from my coat, removed his coat, and folded both over his arm.

Ms. Dickson returned with the bottled water. We entered an office on the other side of the hallway. She waved toward the chairs opposite her desk. "Ms. Stone, I've reviewed your letter of inquiry and the issue brief you submitted in support." She dropped into the chair behind her desk. "This development project has some interesting implications."

"Yes." I eased into the chair Maxim was holding out for me. "The influx of fuel from Ukraine will decrease the price of oil for European consumers, which should increase their standard of living and reduce poverty in several European countries. More importantly, this pipeline will reduce the economic and political damage that results when Putin cuts off their oil supply. As I'm sure you're aware, he cuts their fuel supply so he can force them into siding with him in international politics, which adversely impacts the United States. But that isn't the only benefit for the United States."

Her eyebrows rose. "What other benefits do you see for the United States?"

I glanced at Maxim.

He nodded encouragingly.

I took a deep breath and continued. "This oil pipeline will strengthen Ukraine's economy… substantially. This will allow them to reduce their dependence on Russia for trade, and it will limit Putin's ability to meddle in their domestic and economic policies. This will enable them to improve governance, strengthen democracy, and grow their military. Ukraine must improve in all three of these areas in order to meet NATO membership requirements, which has long been a goal of the United States and Ukraine."

She jotted a few sentences in her padfolio before shifting her attention to Maxim. "Will Russia retaliate?"

"I am certain Russia will retaliate," Maxim answered honestly. "Putin is preparing to invade my country, even as we speak. He is determined to squash the pro-democracy movement in Ukraine. He does not want his own people aspiring to such things. He stands to lose valuable assets in Ukraine, such as the naval base in Sevastopol which houses their Black Sea Fleet. The economic impact would be devastating. Russia would no longer be the sole source of fuel for European countries, this pipeline would no longer transport Russian fuel to Mediterranean countries, and Russia would see a reduction in trade with Ukraine."

She set her pen aside. "That is my primary concern, aside from the expense, of course. How can we justify funding a pipeline that will be seized or destroyed by the Russian government? How can we fund a project that will lead to war?"

I glanced at Maxim. He nodded, so I responded. "We are pursuing a precautionary measure that will prevent Russia from destroying the pipeline... from attacking Ukraine and other European countries."

She leaned forward, her interest clearly piqued. "I'm listening."

"Mr. Markov has spoken with Secretary Gates. He's offered to house the missile defense shield the United States developed for Poland. This defense system would prevent Russia from attacking Ukraine and our European allies. There's just one problem." I paused dramatically. "The Ukrainian government requires a revenue stream that will ensure adequate staffing, training, and maintenance for this equipment. This pipeline is that revenue stream."

Maxim resisted the urge to smile. "The European Bank for Reconstruction and Development has offered to loan us five hundred million dollars to extend the Odessa-Brody pipeline into Poland. We require only two hundred eighty million dollars to fully fund this project. Once we secure this funding, we can extend the pipeline and install the defense shield in a relatively short amount of time."

Ms. Dickson's breath rushed through her lips. She looked as if she'd been sucker punched. As subtle as the message was, I had clearly conveyed how Maxim's plans to install the defense shield were riding on her decision to fund this pipeline.

Inside, I was doing the happy dance. While Maxim and Kadyn had identified how critical the defense shield was to protect the pipeline, no one had really considered how vital the pipeline was to the defense shield... until now.

Ms. Dickson appeared to be at a loss for words.

I handed her my business card. "We don't expect an answer today, Ms. Dickson. We thought you might like to speak with Secretary Gates before making your decision."

She smiled shakily.

We stood. Maxim extended his hand. "Thank you for your time. I do hope you will consider funding this pipeline."

"Thank you, Mr. Markov, Ms. Stone." She escorted us to the front office.

Jase pushed off from the wall next to the door. He was the only man who wasn't sprawled out in a chair with a soda in his hand. "Ready?"

I shook Ms. Dickson's hand. "Thank you for meeting with us on such short notice. I look forward to hearing your decision."

Maxim helped me into my coat.

Jase opened the door.

Quietly, we filed into the hallway.

Maxim grabbed me by the waist and spun me up into the air the second the door closed. He caught me and held me close. "You were... amazing."

I giggled, equally elated.

He gazed up at me. "I knew we would make a good team."

Jase yanked me out of his arms. "I don't care how well the meeting went, you're not kissing Kristine."

"You would intervene?" Maxim seethed. "Why? Do you fear she is in love with me?"

My heart beat anxiously. "I'm engaged to Rafael."

The elevator dinged. The lone passenger scurried down the hall.

Brady and Jase wedged between us as we stepped onto the elevator. I tapped Jase on the shoulder. "I need to speak with him."

He moved. An inch.

I huffed out a breath. "I'm serious, Jase. Please?"

"He touches you and the conversation is over." Jase switched places with me.

The elevator dinged, signaling our arrival on the ground floor. Brady held the door.

I stepped through the heavy metal doors. "Does Secretary Gates want the defense shield in Ukraine?"

"Yes." Maxim fell in beside me.

"I think you should ask him to call Ms. Dickson, to answer any questions she may have about the defense shield. Make sure he understands how much Ukraine needs this pipeline. Take the same approach I did with Ms. Dickson. Explain how the revenue generated from the pipeline will help ensure adequate staffing and maintenance of the defense system." I handed him the business card I snagged from her desk.

"I'll request his assistance with Ms. Dickson." He stopped abruptly. "Are you free for dinner?"

My heart skipped a few beats. "Rafael and I are spending the weekend in Portugal. I'm heading to the airport now."

He looked... lost.

I briefly touched his arm. "I'm sorry, Maxim. I wish you would have told me you were going to be in town."

He forced a shrug. "Another time, perhaps."

I glanced at his security detail and mine. "Can you guys give us a minute?" All four of them had been standing there awkwardly, trying not to listen to our conversation.

Maxim nodded when his security team looked to him for confirmation.

"One minute," Jase relented. He glared at Maxim. "I'll be watching you the entire time." He typed something into his cell phone as he and Brady walked away.

I swallowed nervously. "I... um... I want to ask you something, but I don't want to offend you."

He offered a single, solemn nod. "Proceed."

"Did you pursue a relationship with me because of my political connections?" This question had been eating at me for weeks, ever since the dinner with Rafael and Oni. I wasn't sure why, but the thought bothered me. It tainted my perception of Maxim, and left me questioning how much I could trust him.

Maxim barked out a rich and boisterous laugh. His eyes darkened when he saw my expression remained serious. With a single step, he closed the distance between us. "You believe this?"

"I don't know what to believe," I confessed in a barely audible whisper.

He remained silent for a very long time. "At first... it was this." He caressed my cheek with the back of his hand. His fingers sifted through my hair before he pressed my palm to his chest. "Your compassion for others breathed hope and life into my hardened heart." His fingers pressed into my temples as he framed my face with his hands. "But this... this is what causes me to pursue this relationship."

"My brain?" I was more than a little surprised.

His eyes closed when his forehead dropped against mine. "It is the way you think... the way you view the world... your intelligence, your selflessness, all the good that is inherently you."

"What do you want from me?" I breathed between thunderous heart beats.

"Everything," he whispered.

My heart ground to a complete stop.

Warm, soft lips brushed against mine. I fought briefly to pull away, but his kiss was filled with so much longing it shredded every last one of my defenses. I very nearly drowned as I sank against his chest. Maxim's lips remained achingly tender, but they carried a promise... and a very clear threat.

For within that kiss, Maxim revealed who he really was. He was a man who would fight for a presidency... who would annihilate an insidious threat... and amass an entire army... so he could steal my heart.

* * * * *

"I tried to tell you," Jase persisted.

My face remained hidden behind my knees, which were tucked against my chest. "How could I be so stupid?" My fingers clenched around fistfuls of hair.

"You're not stupid," Brady argued, "just naïve." Like that wasn't the understatement of the century.

Our flight leveled off.

All hell had broken loose when Maxim kissed me. Jase shoved Maxim off me and punched him in the face. Maxim was furious but hesitant to cause any more of a scene. Still, the way he looked at me when Brady and Jase dragged me away…

They were so convinced he would intercept my flight or have it diverted from England, they drove straight to my house, packed their bags, and stormed the jet.

I didn't argue their decision. For the first time in my life I was terrified of Maxim, not because I thought he would hurt me, but because I finally grasped the true depth of his feelings for me. "But I'm in love with Rafael," I repeated for the hundredth time.

Jase shrugged when I peered at him through tear swollen eyes. "I suspect that makes you even more appealing."

Kari set a mug of herbal tea next to me. "This should help settle your stomach. Let me know when you're ready to eat."

I warmed my hands against the mug and sniffed the steam. *Green tea with mint.* I took a tentative sip. All those provocative statements I'd dismissed meant something to Maxim. It wasn't like he'd hidden his feelings. He laid them out there again and again. How could I misinterpret that?

"Why didn't you take Maxim more seriously?" Brady easily read my thoughts.

The extravagant plane with the smooth leather seats, the built in chess board, and fireplace faded away as my thoughts turned inward. Suddenly, I was standing on the tarmac in Sevastopol, my hands clenched in Maxim's shirt while the pillowcase was tugged from my tear streaked face. His eyes sought mine as he steadied me. *"I'm releasing you from that promise, Kristine. I don't want you returning to Ukraine."*

"I didn't think he wanted me in Ukraine, not after everything that happened with the SVR." The voice that answered was too far away to be mine.

"I think you should lie down." Jase walked me to the back of the plane.

I blinked, thoroughly disoriented. The reel was still moving in my head. Michael's plane. The guns. Mirrored lenses. Bullets and blood. My legs buckled as a strangled sound tore through my chest.

Jase scooped me up and placed me on the bed. He tugged my heels off, grabbed the plush brown blanket from the foot of the bed, and draped it over me.

I curled onto my side while tears poured from my eyes. I shivered beneath the blanket.

Jase tapped the remote for the fireplace. "Rest," he said. He sank onto the floor next to the bed. "I'll be here if you need me."

The reel skipped. My mind spiraled toward another time, an equally horrific time, when Rafael stood guard over my bed. "Rafael," I whimpered.

Hushed voices.

Firelight… but which fireplace?

The room faded in and out of focus.

I shrank even smaller.

Someone was sobbing.

I think she lost a baby.

She lost so much more than a baby.

The reel flipped back to the airplane.

There was a kiss filled with blood.

"What's wrong?" a man whispered.

"I don't know," another man answered.

It sounded like they were standing inside a wind tunnel.

My eyelids wouldn't budge.

"Maybe it's the PTSD."

Hushed voices again.

Darkness claimed me before I figured out who it was.

* * * * *

I sat in a zombie-like state while the wheels skipped against the tarmac. Kari insisted I buckle up before the plane landed in England. We had to refuel the jet.

Brady and Jase stared at me while I stared at nothing. Somewhere in the back of my brain a clock started ticking. The clock was counting down to something. There was a finite amount of time. *Before what?*

My eyes grew feral when the door opened unexpectedly.

Jase ripped me from the seatbelt and shoved me to the back of the plane. Brady raced to the front with his gun drawn.

Kari yelped when she caught sight of him. "What? What's wrong?"

"What are you doing?" Brady yelled. "Why are you opening the door?"

Kari's jaw fell slack. She slowly backed away.

"Brady! What are you doing?" Rafael stepped inside the plane.

Brady tucked the gun into the back of his pants. "What are you doing here?"

Rafael laughed. "This *is* my aircraft." He stopped laughing when he saw Jase trying to coax me from the floor. "What's wrong?" He strode toward the back of the plane.

"We didn't know it was you," Brady answered.

Rafael looked confused. "Didn't you get my text message? I texted all three of you."

"Our cell phones died hours ago," Jase gritted. "You scared the crap out of us."

Rafael sized Brady up.

He folded his arms against his chest. "Don't give me that look. It's not like we knew we were taking an overseas trip."

Rafael sighed as he knelt beside me. "Kristine, baby, it's me."

I flinched when he caressed my face.

"Maxim," Jase growled.

Tears streamed down my face.

Rafael's eyes widened. "He hit her?"

"No, but he caressed her face..." Brady's voice trailed off when he saw the look on Rafael's face.

I longed to crawl into Rafael's arms, but my body refused. *Anger.* There was so much anger, and I wasn't entirely sure these men weren't angry at me. I tugged my knees to my chest as I began to rock. Rafael should be angry with me. I cheated on him when I let Maxim kiss me... *how many times?* I was a cheater. I was a cheater, and I was stupid. *Stupid, stupid, stupid* echoed in my mind. I pressed my hands to my ears, but the words grew louder. They were so loud, they drowned everything else out.

Rafael tried to scoop me up.

I fell against the wall after scrambling away. I felt...

cornered. "Don't... don't touch me."

Rafael glared at Brady and Jase. "What the hell happened? What haven't you told me?"

"She's been like this ever since..." Jase eyed Rafael nervously. "Maxim said something to her... before kissing her. I think she's afraid he'll force her back to Ukraine."

Brady's voice dropped to a mere whisper. "She hasn't been entirely... *here.* She's been vacant, like she's trapped inside her head. I think it triggered some memories. I... I've seen this before with combat vets."

Rafael sat next to me with his back against the wall. "Can you guys give us a minute?"

I burst into tears.

Brady and Jase quietly walked away.

"We don't have to talk," Rafael assured me. "I just want to sit next to you for a while."

We sat like that for the longest time, with me crying and Rafael sitting silently beside me. Rafael linked his pinky finger with mine when my hand finally fell to my side.

I stared at our entwined fingers. "I don't deserve you," I finally whispered.

His entire hand blanketed mine. "Jase told me what happened. You weren't the one who initiated that kiss."

"I shouldn't have asked to speak with him in private. I shouldn't have accused him of using me for my political connections. I should have kept my distance. I wanted to help him... to return that favor... but that encouraged him to pursue something more. I didn't mean to encourage him. God, how could I be so stupid? How could I dismiss all his previous advances as harmless? How could I not know?"

"Do you still love me?" Rafael demanded.

My heart shuddered beneath the weight of his question.

"Yes. Of course."

His knee grazed mine as he turned to face me. "Do you still want to marry me?"

"Yes," I whispered brokenly. The thought that Rafael might not want me... that he'd refuse to marry me... was what I feared most. That thought wielded more pain than I could possibly bear.

"Then don't let Maxim ruin this for us." He pressed his lips to my hand. "We'll get through this, just like everything else, and we'll be stronger for it."

My head fell to his shoulder. I felt so tired and defeated, I could no longer argue how unworthy I was.

Rafael's arm slid beneath my knees. He pulled me to his chest and stood with very little effort. "I'm sorry, love. We need to take our seats so the plane can depart." He sat me in the seat furthest from Brady and Jase, then snapped my seatbelt into place. He dropped into the seat next to me and fastened his seatbelt.

Kari placed a basket of pastries, two steaming mugs of coffee, and two bottled waters in front of us while the plane taxied down the runway.

I glanced at Brady and Jase. "I feel bad, dragging them to Portugal."

Rafael quirked an eyebrow. "You would deny them a trip to Portugal?"

"No, not if they wanted to go." I held my coffee so it wouldn't slide against the table.

The nose of the plane lifted. "Their departure may have been a bit unexpected, but I think they're looking forward to this trip. I've arranged for them to train with some of my friends while they're in Lisbon."

"Are they staying with us?" I fought a yawn and lost.

"They'll be staying in our flat, but *we* won't be joining them until Sunday." He cracked open a bottle of water and handed it to me.

I drank half the bottle. "Where are we staying?"

"Someplace safe," he assured me.

I nodded wearily.

"Come lie with me." He released his seatbelt and mine.

I quietly considered him. "Why did you fly to London?"

"I was worried Maxim would do something stupid." His arm slid beneath my knees. Gently, he lifted me.

My arms wrapped loosely around his neck. "More stupid than the kiss?"

"More stupid than the kiss." He carried me to bed.

I shrank against the bed. "I'm scared."

He pulled the blanket over us and drew me to his chest. "I won't allow any harm to come to you."

Like a pendulum my life swung between fairytales and nightmares.

* * * * *

"We're here," Rafael announced softly.

Grudgingly, my eyes opened. I'd fallen asleep within minutes of climbing into Rafael's Porsche. "How long was I asleep?"

"About forty minutes." Rafael stepped out of the car.

My eyes widened when he walked in front of the car. Rafael opened my door and offered his hand, but I didn't budge. "We're staying here?"

His broad shoulders filled the doorway as he knelt beside me. "Is that okay?"

I gaped at the medieval castle towering before me.

Rafael's Porsche seemed sorely out of place parked in front of this ancient fortress. I counted five stone towers, two square and three round, although there could have been more on the other side of the building. The castle was enormous. I slowly stepped from the car. "It's... a castle."

"It is." Rafael chuckled.

The wind whipped my hair while I surveyed the rugged landscape and the massive stone wall winding away from the castle. I half expected an archer to shoot an arrow between one of the merlons forged atop the castle. Dark clouds formed an ominous backdrop behind the rocky hilltop. "This place is huge. Where are all the tourists?" Not a single soul walked the treacherous looking grounds.

Rafael anchored a duffel bag over his shoulder before reaching for my carry-on luggage. "Obidos Castle is not open to visitors unless they're staying the night." He offered me his arm.

We picked our way through the loose pebbles and the uneven ground. "But there are no cars. Where did the staff and the other guests park?"

"A valet parks the cars in the village located on the other side of that wall. The front of the castle overlooks a very quaint town."

I was stunned. The castle and the castle wall had hidden the town so well, I'd assumed we were the only two people around for miles. The only other building I could see from this angle was a white limestone chapel peeking over the hillside. "This place reminds me of the Moorish Castle in Sintra, only bigger."

Rafael smiled. "The Moors built Obidos Castle during the 8th century. This castle was in ruins, much like the Moorish Castle, but it was renovated after the earthquake and eventually converted into a luxury hotel."

I thought he might be using the word "luxury" a bit loosely, given the rustic structure looming before us. Still, I was ecstatic. I couldn't believe we were staying inside an 8th century castle.

The heavy wood door creaked open as we approached. Rafael spoke with the distinguished looking gentleman who held the door for us. He took Rafael's keys while another man claimed our luggage.

I clung to Rafael's arm while my eyes adjusted to the dim lighting. The inside of the castle was dark and ominous, which I found oddly soothing. Rafael checked in while I admired the tall, scenic tapestries hanging against the stone walls. The place smelled musky, like soil after a storm.

Rafael linked his hand in mine. "They're sending food up so we can eat in our room and rest awhile."

"This place is amazing." We walked down a long, windowless hallway, dimly lit by thick candles in rustic metal sconces. Shadows danced along the stone walls and floor. "It certainly feels authentic," I whispered. The atmosphere demanded a whisper.

"There's electricity and Wi-Fi, but they prefer to keep things as authentic as possible," Rafael replied.

I smiled. It was my first genuine smile since the fiasco with Maxim. I rather liked the idea of turning back time with my modern day knight. We had yet to see another guest, so I doubted anyone would think to search for us here.

I clung to the stone wall while Rafael and I climbed a steep flight of stairs. There was no banister or railing to speak of. Each candle we hiked by flickered, casting shadows that made it difficult to see the stairs. My thighs were burning by the seventy-eighth step. I lost count after that. "I'm glad they're sending food up. These stairs are a bit much."

Rafael buried his shoulder in my stomach so he could carry me the rest of the way. I was too tired to object.

The stairs emptied into a large stone room. The room righted itself when my feet touched the floor. The hard wood floor was stained the same dark color as the open beam ceiling, the window frame, and bed. A masculine four-poster bed was anchored over a rich burgundy rug. The white duvet and pillows stood in stark contrast against the heavy furs draped across the foot of the bed. The room felt toasty warm. A very real fire was already crackling inside the fireplace. A stack of wood lay between the fireplace and an ancient metal chest. Our luggage was sitting on top of the chest.

I peered out the only window I'd seen inside the castle. The thick, wavy glass revealed a raging storm. The thunderclouds had finally broken, but the wind and the driving rain were barely audible through the eighty inch thick walls.

Rafael swept my hair aside so he could nuzzle my neck. "What do you think?"

I tore my eyes from the storm. "This place is everything I needed and more."

"You should check out the bathroom." He walked backwards while leading the way.

"Oh!" I gasped. "This... this..."

"It's unbelievable," Rafael agreed.

The large copper tub was simply breathtaking. I crossed the room so I could examine the decorative handles. My fingers trailed along the smooth copper rim. The oval tub was large enough to fit both of us. The tapestry that hung against the stone wall behind the bathtub depicted two maidens bathing a young woman with porcelain skin. A narrow, arched entryway sat on either side of the tub. Both entryways led to a cavernous marble shower with more jets than I cared to count. I walked slack-jawed through the shower, from one entryway to the other. Thankfully, a very modern toilet was hidden behind a stone wall on the far side of the bathroom.

Rafael was studying a simply constructed wood vanity with the same dark stain as the open beam ceiling and the hard wood floor inside the bedroom. The bathroom floor was stone. The sink appeared to be half of a large round stone, hollowed out and polished so the inside was smooth. Wall sconces bracketed the ornate copper mirror. The fire crackling inside the bedroom extended into the bathroom. The windowless room literally glowed.

I reached for his hand. "Thank you."

"I'm glad you like it." He pulled me close.

My eyes filled with tears. "I missed you so much. My heart hurts when we're apart. I don't want to live apart anymore. I want to move to Portugal."

"I want you to finish school." Rafael looked sad when he cupped my cheek in his hand. His thumb lifted my chin as he fit his lips to mine.

My body surged to life.

Rafael's hands tangled in my hair. There was no give and take, only take. Warm, firm lips demanded my chin... my jaw... my ears... and neck. He unzipped my dress.

"Rafael," I groaned. My dress pooled on the floor.

"Now," he ordered. With an unyielding grasp, Rafael forced me toward the bed. He unclasped my bra, dragged the straps down my arms, and let it drop to the floor. He eased my panties over my hips. They slid to the floor.

I pulled Rafael's shirt over his head when he lowered me onto the bed. Our lips met in a feverish kiss. My hands branded his shoulders, abdomen, and back while I drank him in.

Our eyes locked while Rafael removed his remaining clothes. The determination in his eyes made me tremble. The muscles in his shoulders bunched when he lifted my foot. He licked the arch of my foot, my calves, and thigh before settling between my legs. His tongue stroked, tasted, and teased while I pleaded for release.

His fingers clenched my hips when I squeezed my breasts. "Please, Rafael. I need you. *Now.*"

Still, he denied me. His tongue dipped inside my belly button, circled my breasts, and carved a trail to my neck. He feasted on my neck.

My eyes slid closed when our bodies aligned. My arms and legs clenched his back as I urged him closer.

"Kristine," he breathed. Determinedly, he filled me. He pinned my wrists over my head when our hips finally met. His eyes darkened. With a groan, everything spiraled out of control. Our bodies slammed together, ravishing one another, until we fractured.

The air rushed from my lungs when Rafael collapsed on top of me. I relished his weight. He wrapped his arms around me, held me close, and rolled so that I was lying on his chest. I tucked my head beneath his chin and listened to his thundering heart while we tried to catch our breath.

Rafael shifted unexpectedly. "When did the food arrive?"

I followed his gaze. "That food was there when we stumbled into bed."

"Thank God," he whispered. "I was afraid someone walked in on us."

I laughed, although that would have been embarrassing. "Are you hungry?"

"Yes." His response contradicted the sated look on his face.

I sat up. Rafael was still inside of me, so that one simple move forced him even deeper.

His eyes hooded.

I braced my hands on his chest and curled my hips against his. "You're mine now."

He chuckled. "I have always been yours." He sat up and pulled our hips even closer.

My hands tangled in his hair while he suckled my breasts. My head fell back. My hair had grown so long, it brushed against his legs. "God, I love making love to you."

He murmured his agreement while coaxing my lips into another passionate kiss. His tongue chased mine in a dance as old as time.

I could feel him swelling inside of me. Our hips barely moved, but he was buried so deep I could feel him brush against my womb. That had to be the most erotic feeling in the world. When he came, I knew. He was part of me now... the only part anchoring me to this world.

We were both spent, but Rafael climbed out of bed so he could throw another log on the fire. The room was cold so we wrapped ourselves in the fur throws before inspecting the food they'd delivered for us.

The bench under the window held a wooden bowl filled with grapes, oranges, apples, and pears. A wood cutting board held two blocks of cheese and a crusty loaf of bread. A dagger had been stabbed directly into the board. A small metal bowl offered a variety of olives. A jug of wine and a ceramic pitcher filled with water sat next to two pewter wine glasses and two medieval tankards.

The dagger made me smile. "Is that for the cheese?"

Rafael grinned. "I believe it is."

I poured the water and wine while he moved the food to the stone hearth in front of the fireplace. He spread his fur blanket over the floor and wrapped the two of us in mine. We picked at the food, talked, and made love long into the night.

* * * * *

The staff snuck into our room during the early morning hours. We were shocked we didn't hear them deliver breakfast. "They take room service to a whole new level," I mused. "What kind of food did they deliver?"

"Mulled wine, meat, fish, and bread." Rafael poured the wine. He filled two metal plates and carried everything to bed.

"What an odd breakfast." My stomach growled regardless. "I can't believe we're drinking wine for breakfast."

"What do you want to do today?" Rafael threw another log on the fire and joined me beneath the blankets.

"I want to take a bath in the copper tub." The roast beef nearly melted in my mouth. "How is this still warm?"

"They lined the bottom of the ceramic pot with hot rocks." Rafael sipped his wine.

I tried the hearty wheat and nut filled bread. "This is really good."

"Anything else, besides the bath?" He cut into the flaky fish.

"I'd like to explore the castle. Maybe we can find the key and open the chest." Obidos Castle was filled with ancient chests. Rafael had informed me there was one chest in particular, an iron chest, that had yet to be opened. All guests were encouraged to search for the key that would unravel its secrets.

"How do you feel about eating in the dining room tonight?" Rafael tossed a piece of rye bread into his mouth.

"What sort of attire is required? Aside from the dress I wore to work yesterday, I don't really have anything to wear. My carry-on contains textbooks. I thought I'd be reading and knocking out some coursework while I was on the plane. I assumed I'd have access to my wardrobe at your place, so I didn't pack any clothes."

"No wonder your suitcase was so heavy," Rafael murmured. "I'll see if Eva can stop by the flat and deliver some clothes today. We're only forty-five minutes away."

"I'm sure she has better things to do on Valentine's Day." I frowned. "I really should have thought of this yesterday."

Rafael shook his head. "*I* should have thought of this. I just assumed when I saw your suitcase that you packed what you needed from home. Would you prefer I ask Brady or Jase?"

I nearly choked on the warm wine. "God, no. I don't want those two sifting through my panties."

Rafael laughed. "Eva it is then."

"I can make do with what I have. I'll wear one of your shirts while we're in the room and ask housekeeping to clean my dress."

He continued typing on his phone. "I'll sweeten the deal by reserving them a room in the other tower, assuming one's available."

"But they'll want to eat with us, and I don't want to share you," I grumbled. I climbed out of bed so I could refill our wine. The orange and clove infused wine tasted surprisingly good for breakfast.

Rafael rolled his eyes. "I'm sure Benjamim has other plans."

I handed him his wine when he finished the text.

He eyed me over the top of his glass. "You better drink fast."

My brow furrowed. "Why?"

He guzzled his entire glass of wine. "So we can have make-up sex."

I laughed. "Are you saying *that* was a fight?"

Rafael nodded. A boyish smile lit his face.

I downed the wine. "I like the way you fight."

He pulled the pewter wine glass from my hand. "Shower first, then bath."

* * * * *

"I'm pretty sure I would have remembered seeing this in the closet." I spun while admiring the filmy black gown. The wrapped halter neckline was anchored over a sparkling jewel encrusted collar. I was praying the jewels weren't genuine diamonds.

"I asked Eva to make a purchase along the way." He'd also requested his tux. I loved the way his muscular physique looked inside that tux.

I poked my toe out from under the gown. "I'll put these back on at the bottom of the stairs." Six glittering strands swirled around the bottom half of my foot. The top half of my foot was bare, but a soft velvet cuff encircled my ankle above a five inch silver stiletto heel. As breathtaking as they were, the heels seemed more appropriate for an S&M club.

Rafael swallowed. Hard. "I'll take them off for you." He knelt in front of me so he could remove the shoes.

I laughed. "Maybe we should just save them for bed."

His eyes flew to mine. "Oh, you're definitely wearing them in bed."

My body hummed its agreement. I wondered if I'd ever tire of sex with this man.

Rafael slid his fingers through the cuffs so he could carry the shoes. He offered me his arm. "Ready?"

"Ready," I agreed. We picked our way down the long flight of stairs. "I want to continue our search for the key tomorrow." We'd found several keys, but none of them opened the chest.

"You don't want to explore the village?" Rafael asked. The candles flickered in the narrow passageway.

"No. I rather like kicking around this old castle." I'd discovered that while some parts of the castle were primitive, other areas were downright opulent. I was guessing the dining room was opulent given the way we were dressed.

Rafael nodded. "That's probably best. They're expecting more storms tomorrow."

"Maybe we should just stay in bed then." We'd crossed very few people while exploring the castle, and the staff were practically invisible. I had a feeling we'd find more people in the dining room.

"Whatever your heart desires." Rafael smiled.

I stopped mid-step. "My heart desires you and only you."

He kissed me like a man possessed. Grudgingly, we continued down the stairs.

"I was serious when I said I wanted to move to Portugal," I whispered.

Rafael frowned. "I don't want you quitting school when you're so close to graduating. Kristine, you've fought tooth and nail for that degree."

My eyes glistened. "School doesn't feel important anymore. Neither does work. I just... I feel so lost without you. I didn't realize this would be so difficult."

He took a deep breath and slowly released it. "You'll regret it. Maybe not today, tomorrow, or next week... but someday you'll regret walking away from school when you were so close to earning your degree."

I diverted my eyes. "Three months feels like an eternity."

"I won't argue that point. Three *weeks* feels like an eternity these days." He stopped me on the third step from the bottom so he could slip my heels on. "Maybe I should try to find a way out of this assignment."

I braced myself against the stone wall while Rafael fastened my shoes. I thought about my conversation with Chief D'Souza.

"There's one thing you should understand before you marry this man. Rafael needs you just as much as you need him."

I gazed at the man kneeling before me.

"You will love and support him in his efforts to protect those who are vulnerable whether through the police force, his private security firm, or the Templar."

My heart clenched as Rafael rose and reached for my hand.

"Do you solemnly vow both secrecy and support for Rafael Tiago Garcia and his fellow knights?"

A single tear slid down my cheek.

"Kristine?" Rafael inquired worriedly.

"No." I grasped his shoulders as he lifted me from the stairs. "You have to put every last one of those predators away so those children will be safe."

He offered a solemn nod. "And you have to stay in school. That degree helps you reduce violent conflict. That's important too."

I burrowed against his chest. "I love you."

His fingers slid soothingly over my hair. "I love you too." We walked arm in arm down the dimly lit hallway. "Did you bring the invitations?"

"They're in the suitcase." I'd brought samples so Rafael could weigh in. I wanted to ensure our wedding invitations reflected both of our personalities.

He veered into the red carpeted hallway we'd explored earlier. "Did you decide on the flowers?"

"Yes." That was easy. "Wisteria with deep purple roses and calla lilies."

He smiled. "That sounds pretty. I'll let the florist, the palace staff, and the pastry chef know."

I eyed the tapestry depicting the Knights Templar on the wall to my right. "Did Chief D'Souza agree to be one of your groomsmen?"

"Yes." Rafael frowned. "I can't seem to decide on the other two."

"Who are you considering?" I inquired curiously.

His frown deepened. "Ethan, Brady, and Jase."

I nodded thoughtfully. "I can ask Marie to serve as a fifth bridesmaid so you don't have to choose." Lexie, Kimme, Cenia, and Shae agreed to be my bridesmaids back in January.

Rafael looked relieved. "Really? That would make things so much easier."

"I adore Marie. I'll ask her as soon as I return to Virginia," I assured him.

He wrapped his arm around me. "What happened to our small wedding?"

I laughed lightheartedly. "I haven't a clue." We stopped in front of the dining room.

"It's very contemporary," Rafael observed. The upholstered arm chairs, contemporary light shades, and finished walls seemed sorely out of place in the medieval castle.

He spoke with the hostess. She led us through a set of wooden doors and out onto a small, intimate balcony.

I was so drawn to the view I walked right past the chair Rafael pulled out for me. A large white church glowed beneath us, framed by rolling hilltops and a moonlit sea. The clouds had cleared, the moon was full, and a billion stars pierced the sky. Very few lights flickered beneath the hilltops, which made the view all the more spectacular. "It's breathtaking."

The hostess slipped away unnoticed.

Rafael propped his shoulder against a braided stone pillar when he joined me. "That's Our Lord Jesus of the Stone Sanctuary."

"Why is it shaped like a hexagon?" Actually, the church contained three hexagons, a large hexagon for the main sanctuary and two smaller hexagons, one on either side.

Rafael shrugged. "King Joao V commissioned the sanctuary after surviving an accident where he evoked our Lord Jesus of the Stone. No one knows why he chose this particular design." He turned to face me. "There's an ancient stone cross inside the sanctuary that is rumored to have miraculous power. If you'd like, we can see it tomorrow."

My palm brushed against his lightly stubbled cheek while I pressed the faintest of kisses onto his lips. "A cross that yields miracles. I think I might like to see that." We settled in at the table. I still couldn't believe we had this breathtaking view all to ourselves.

The candles on the table flickered when Rafael reached

for my hand.

A waiter slipped quietly through the heavy wooden door. He was carrying two champagne flutes filled with what appeared to be pink champagne and a small metal bowl filled with strawberries.

"Cherry Kir," Rafael explained.

He set the champagne flutes and strawberries on the table.

"*Obrigada,*" I murmured softly.

"*Você é bem-vindo.*" He exchanged polite nods with Rafael before disappearing through the heavy door.

Rafael handed me a strawberry and raised his glass. "Happy Valentine's Day."

I met his gaze. "Happy Valentine's Day." We tapped our champagne flutes, bit into the juicy strawberries, and sipped the Cherry Kir.

Rafael quietly considered the sparkling cocktail.

"I can't believe this is our first Valentine's Day together." He'd lavished me with so many romantic escapes, it felt as if we'd shared a lifetime of Valentine's Days together.

He set his drink aside. "This isn't the first Valentine's Day we've spent together."

My brow furrowed. "I'm pretty sure it is."

He smiled but offered no further response.

The waiter returned with bread and two bowls of spicy vegetable cream soup.

I tore a piece of bread and dipped it into the soup. "Okay. Explain."

Rafael feigned offense. "I'm crushed you don't recall."

My spoon hovered above my bowl.

A secretive smile played on his face. "It was the first time we slept together."

I abandoned the spoon altogether. "Your birthday was the first time we slept together, and *that* was March 14th."

He chuckled softly. "I distinctly recall sleeping in your bed on February 14th." He shook his head. "I really should have hand delivered those roses."

I raked through my memories from that night. Rafael had sent the most beautiful long stemmed roses I'd ever seen to Dr. Sandstrom's classroom. He'd written a romantic note, but he didn't sign the card. I didn't discover he was the one who sent them until we started dating in March. I gasped when the light finally clicked on. "That was the first night you snuck into my bedroom... the first night I smelled your cologne."

Rafael laughed. "Behavior hardly becoming a knight."

I shook my head. "Well, I'm glad you stopped sneaking around. I prefer knowing you're in my bed."

The waiter returned with breaded green beans and a bottle of wine. He held a brief conversation with Rafael in Portuguese while he poured the wine.

I tried the green beans. They were crunchy and nutty tasting, like parmesan cheese. "How many times do we need to meet with the priest?"

"Twice," Rafael answered. "I think we should schedule the second session in March. We just need to pick a weekend when you can return to Lisbon."

I reached for my wine. "I'll be in Sierra Leone over spring break. Are you still planning to join me?"

"Yes. Chief D'Souza approved my leave." He sounded relieved.

I breathed my own sigh of relief. "Why don't I fly to Lisbon first? We can meet with the priest before we leave."

He smiled, obviously pleased. "I'll see if Father Ramires

is available on the thirteenth."

I leaned forward excitedly. "We can celebrate your birthday in Lisbon since we don't have to be in Sierra Leone until the fifteenth."

"Sounds good." Rafael piled a few more green beans onto his plate.

I studied him over the top of my wine. "What would you like to do for your birthday?"

He laughed. "The same thing we did on my birthday last year."

"Rafael!" I gasped. "What would Father Ramires say?"

The smile slid from his face. We'd had sex eight times that day.

I narrowed my eyes at him. "You do remember Cenia and Roger abstaining from sex before they were married?"

"Yes." He choked down a green bean.

I folded my arms across my chest. "And who do you think encouraged them to abstain from sex?"

"Their priest?" he answered weakly.

I offered a solemn nod.

His face blanched. "The priest is going to talk about sex?"

He sounded so incredulous I nearly snorted my wine.

The waiter returned with crab pot pies. He topped off our wine.

I waited until he was out of earshot. "I'm afraid our days are numbered. You should enjoy it while you can."

Rafael's reaction was priceless. At first he looked physically ill. He didn't say much until the lamb arrived. Then, he just seemed frustrated. By the time the waiter delivered dessert, he was eyeing me like I'd thrown down the gauntlet.

I rather enjoyed the sexual tension, so I dragged coffee

and dessert out as long as I could. I informed Rafael, "*Crepe Flamejado* should not be rushed." The crepes were stuffed with apples, kiwi, and strawberries, all of which were swimming in a rich, buttery sauce.

Imagine my surprise when the waiter delivered a second dessert, *Sobremesa Namorados*, a brownie type pie topped with toasted meringue and drizzled in a tart cherry sauce.

I was beginning to question whether we'd make it back to our room before we had sex.

Sadly, we did not.

* * * * *

"What did you pray for?" Rafael asked. We were lying side by side in the soft grass watching eagles and falcons soar through the crisp blue sky. We'd stumbled across the castle garden after exploring the romantic village tucked inside the castle wall. The weather held after all.

I curled onto my side so I could study his handsome face. "I prayed we would survive this separation, marry in May, and live happily ever after." I felt guilty about my greedy little prayer. I should have prayed for world peace, a cure for cancer, or an end to pedophiles everywhere. "What did you pray for?"

Rafael's hand found mine as he rolled onto his side. "I prayed for a baby."

A smile tugged at my lips. "Well, you've certainly been working diligently toward that goal." My eyes shifted toward the castle wall. A falcon had just landed on one of the merlons. His head cocked while he studied us. "Can we come back here some day?" Obidos castle had proven the perfect escape.

Rafael smiled. "We'll spend every Christmas in Lisbon, every Valentine's Day in Obidos, and our summers in Saint-Tropez."

My eyes held his. "Even when we have a baby?"

He pulled me closer. "We'll ask Benjamim or Chief D'Souza to babysit on Valentine's Day."

My shoulders relaxed. "I'm irrevocably in love with you."

His smile widened. "I'm hopelessly in love with you too."

The falcon cried when Rafael's lips slanted over mine.

* * * * *

I sneaked a peek at Rafael. Father Ramires was quietly comparing our answers on the compatibility test. The first few questions were designed to rule out abuse. The remaining questions explored our religious beliefs, our perceptions toward one another, our communication and conflict resolution styles, our physical attraction, our plans for having children, our thoughts on discipline, and how we plan to manage our finances. We'd spent the first two hours praying; discussing the sacrament of marriage; discussing my previous marriage, the abuse, the annulment, and how we first met. Then we took the test.

Father Ramires chuckled while turning the page.

Rafael and I exchanged glances.

The clock ticked on the mantle.

Father Ramires cleared his throat when he returned to the first page. "I don't believe I have met a more compatible couple."

Rafael slowly released his breath.

He looked thoughtful. "Your conflict resolution styles

are surprising given the violence you've both endured."

"I've received extensive training in crisis negotiations, and Kristine is working on a master's degree in conflict resolution," Rafael explained.

Father Ramires nodded. "How do you typically work through your disagreements?"

"We discuss the problem and generate solutions we're both comfortable with," I answered. Really, there were very few disagreements between us.

He jotted a few sentences in his notebook. "Do you work through these problems face to face, from across the room, by e-mail, or over the phone?"

Rafael's brow furrowed. "We sit next to one another, hold hands or touch in some other way."

Father Ramires looked pleased. "A reassuring touch can help immensely. It is difficult to be angry with someone who is holding your hand." He made another notation. "What do you see as the most challenging part of your relationship?"

"The fact that we're currently living on two different continents," Rafael answered.

"My past," I added softly.

Father Ramires nodded. "Let's discuss Rafael's concern first. "How do you plan to resolve this problem?"

"I'll be joining Rafael in Portugal as soon as I graduate in May. We're getting married the weekend after I graduate," I explained.

He leaned back in his seat. "Will you remain in Portugal once you are married?"

I glanced questioningly at Rafael. "I don't know. I guess it depends on how long this assignment lasts."

He twined his fingers with mine. "We should be able to wrap up our investigation by the end of June, although a new lead could always extend things. I'll know more by the time we're married."

Father Ramires eyed me curiously. "Are you willing to remain here indefinitely?"

I reflected on my family, my friends, and my position with Seeds for Peace. "Yes, as long as I can do something constructive with my time and visit my family and friends in the United States."

Rafael turned so he was facing me. "Something constructive? Like work?"

"I could volunteer at the orphanage or work for that charity organization you're affiliated with." I was hesitant to mention them by name in front of Father Ramires.

Rafael smiled. He knew I was alluding to the Templar's charity organization. "I think that's a wonderful idea."

Father Ramires penned another sentence. "How will you maintain your relationship over the next three months while you're apart?"

"We'll talk on the phone every night and travel to see one another every two or three weeks like we do now," Rafael answered.

"Is that sufficient for you?" he asked me.

I smiled confidently. "We'll make it work."

His tone softened. "What is it about your past that concerns you?"

I sifted through my thoughts. "Sometimes my past taints my perceptions. I get scared easily, and those memories can make it difficult for me to see the things that are truly in front of me. And my instincts are off. I trust people I shouldn't trust. I seem to swing between the two extremes… trusting and not trusting…scared and refusing to be scared. It's like I'm overcompensating because I don't want my past to limit me or dictate who I am."

Father Ramires looked thoughtful. "You've endured a number of traumatic events. Have you sought counseling in the past?"

I nodded.

He set his pen aside. "Do you think you could benefit from additional counseling?"

"Maybe," I admitted, although I wasn't sure when I'd find the time to add that to my schedule.

"Rafael?" he asked. "How do you feel about this?"

Rafael took a deep breath and slowly released it. "I've taken enough psychology classes to recognize that she's struggling with PTSD. I think the worst of it is behind us, but I know there are certain triggers that increase her anxieties. Her coping skills have improved immensely, so I believe this will get better in time."

He retrieved his pen. "Does this put a strain on your relationship?"

Rafael shook his head. "Not at all. I love Kristine regardless. I'll stand by her regardless. I am confident that God will work this for a greater good, and he will see us through."

A single tear slid down my cheek. Rafael's response loosened a vise on my heart, one I hadn't even known existed.

"Your testimony reminds me of the message found in Corinthians 13:13," Father Ramires noted softly. "'And now these three remain: faith, hope, and love. But the greatest of these is love.' Clearly, you love one another very much."

A few more tears moistened my cheeks.

Rafael tugged a couple of tissues from the box and handed them to me. "Are you okay?"

I swiped at my tear stained cheeks. "Yes. I'm just... relieved and very happy."

"You're crying because you're happy?" He smiled and kissed the top of my head.

"There is one more issue I'd like to discuss." Father Ramires reached for our compatibility tests. "Have you two discussed how many children you would like to have?"

"No," we answered cautiously.

Father Ramires chuckled. "Kristine, would you mind telling Rafael how many children you would like to have?"

"Two." Two seemed like a fairly solid number.

He nodded. "Rafael, would you mind telling Kristine how many children you would like to have?"

"Five," he admitted softly.

"Five?" The color drained from my face.

"I thought maybe we could adopt some." His expression remained hopeful.

I stilled. "Are you serious?"

He reached for my hand. "Yes, but only if you're willing. I'd be ecstatic just to have one, but I'd be lying if I didn't admit to wanting at least five. Whether they are ours or adopted doesn't matter. I just want a house full of children."

I tried not to panic. "At *least* five?"

He cringed. "I only wrote five because I was afraid to write eight."

"Eight?" I nearly leapt from my seat. "How will I work? Rafael, I *need* to work. I cannot just sit at home all day wiping bottoms, and noses, and... and *stuff!* I need some sort of intellectual stimulation. I *need* to have a job." I didn't dare look at the priest. I knew Catholics were supposed to want a lot of children, but eight seemed a little extreme.

"I could stay home," Rafael offered.

My jaw dropped. I spent a few precious minutes gathering my thoughts. "You can't stay home." I glanced at Father Ramires, wondering just how much I could reveal. My voice lowered to a mere whisper. "Rafael, you swore an oath. You vowed to protect those in need. I vowed to support you in this, and I promised to continue helping others. How can we do that when we're raising eight kids?"

His eyes brightened. "We could create our own NGO so we could both work from home."

I shook the confusion from my head. "What?"

He leaned forward excitedly. "You wanted to help political refugees. We can create an NGO that helps refugees. I could manage the security aspects and you could serve as their advocate. We could both secure the necessary funding, accommodations, and any support services they may need."

The air rushed from my lungs, right along with any arguments that may have been lingering on the tip of my tongue. I glanced at Father Ramires. "I need to think about this. I'm not saying this would dissuade me from getting married." I looked at Rafael. "I want to marry you no matter what. I just need to think through how we might accomplish this... how we could manage all those children, work, and... everything else."

"If I may..." Father Ramires interjected.

We both nodded.

"The Grand Master of the Knights Templar ensures that every Templar within my diocese is on my prayer list. The same holds true for their wives, their children, and their betrothed. Rafael has been on that prayer list for some time. Kristine was added back in December. So I am aware of the vows you've made. There was a time in our history when the Templar were required to take a vow of celibacy. Thankfully, we have learned from our mistakes. Now, Templar are encouraged to have children because we know they will pass their values onto them. By having children and teaching them your values, you honor your vows to serve and protect those in need… perhaps a bit more indirectly than you are accustomed to, but you are still honoring them."

Rafael and I exchanged glances.

Father Ramires continued. "Children are a blessing, and they are only home for a short while. They are in school before you know it, so any sacrifice you might make is temporary. I encourage families to savor that time before their children are enrolled in school. Most find the experience incredibly rewarding."

I grasped Rafael's hand. "I'm sorry I reacted so strongly. You know how much I adore children. I want to raise a family with you, and I don't mind adopting. It's just… the number was a little surprising."

He gently kissed my hand. "I'm sure we can settle on a number that works for both of us. We don't have to decide today or even next year. We'll take it one child at a time. I just… I don't want you thinking you're on your own in this. I plan to take a very active role in raising our kids."

I grinned. "I can't wait to see you change your first diaper."

Father Ramires chuckled. "I think I might like to see that as well." He retrieved two workbooks from the corner of his desk. "I'd like you to answer these questions together. You can discuss the questions over the phone or the next time you're together. Flag any problem areas, and we'll discuss them in March. Please bring the workbooks in March."

We eyed the workbooks curiously.

"One more thing." He handed us the workbooks. "I

want you to start praying together, and I want to see you in church. You need to reserve a place for God in this relationship."

We nodded dutifully. This was, perhaps, our greatest shortcoming.

"Shall we pray?" Rafael and I were already holding hands, so he walked around the desk and clasped our hands in his. "Heavenly Father, I lift this couple unto you. I pray that you will strengthen them... guide them... and bring them peace. Allow them to feel your presence in their relationship so that your light may shine in them. We pray this in the name of the Father, and of the Son, and of the Holy Spirit. Amen."

* * * * *

I climbed onto the stool. My hair was still dripping from the shower so I squeezed the ends with my towel.

Rafael slid an omelet onto my plate before joining me at the breakfast bar. "Your phone is blowing up."

I'd shut my phone off on Thursday and had been vigorously ignoring the outside world ever since. When I turned my phone on this morning, the battery was drained down so I plugged it in before jumping in the shower. I plucked it off the cord, checked the screen, and frowned. "Maxim."

Rafael froze.

"I have six missed phone calls and eight text messages from him." I thumbed through the messages. "He's been trying to reach me since Thursday." I paused briefly so I could finish reading. "He's threatening to send the Russian mafia after me if I don't respond by twelve o'clock today.

He's worried I've been kidnapped or am lying in a pool of blood." I met Rafael's gaze. "I'd better call."

He rose from his seat. "I'll give you some privacy."

I grabbed his arm. "No. I want you to hear what I have to say."

He settled back onto the stool.

I hadn't a clue what the time difference was between Portugal and Ukraine, but I figured Maxim would answer either way. I dialed his number without listening to my voice mail, set the phone on speaker, and placed it on the counter.

He answered on the first ring. "Kristine! Are you okay? Where have you been? Why haven't you called me?" His voice thundered through the room.

"I'm fine, Maxim. I told you I was going away for the weekend with Rafael. Why? Is there a problem?" I tried the ham and Gouda omelet and offered Rafael a thumbs up. He made a mean omelet.

"I thought you were dead. How could you not answer your phone?" Maxim demanded. He sounded genuinely upset.

I tried to keep my voice as even as possible. "I turned my phone off before the meeting with Ms. Dickson and forgot to turn it back on. I was a little shook up after everything that happened Thursday. I didn't mean to worry you, I just needed some time away from work, and school, and my phone."

The phone grew silent.

I frowned. "Maxim, is everything okay? Did something happen? Are you okay?"

He blew out a breath. "Nobody has made any assassination attempts, if that is what you are asking. But no, I am not okay."

I glanced at Rafael.

He shrugged while sipping his coffee.

"I was calling to apologize. I did not mean to upset you on Thursday. I was so pleased with how our meeting went, and when I saw how good we were together, I'm afraid I got carried away."

I set my fork down. "Maxim, I want to help you secure this funding so you can build the pipeline. I want to help you win the presidency because I believe you would make a very good president. I care about you, Maxim, as a friend, but I cannot offer you anything more than that. I don't want you flirting with me, and I don't want you bad mouthing my relationship with Rafael. And, while I am honored that you would think I am worthy, I do not want to be the First Lady of Ukraine. I'm in love with Rafael. I'm engaged to Rafael. And I plan to marry Rafael. If you have a problem with that, then I will be forced to remove myself from this project. Do you understand?"

Rafael's jaw dropped.

I waited breathlessly for Maxim's response.

"I do not believe Rafael is worthy of you. He is neglectful and absent from that relationship. You deserve more. I want more than a simple friendship with you, but my country remains unsafe. Even if I were elected president, I question whether I could keep you safe. Our last president was driven from the country after multiple assassination attempts. The previous president was poisoned and nearly died. His Prime Minister, Yulia Tymoshenko, was incarcerated under politically motivated charges and beaten relentlessly for two and a half years. So, yes, while I believe you would make a worthy first lady, I do not believe my country is worthy of you." He sighed. "I will keep my feelings mute, not out of respect for your relationship with Rafael but out of respect for you. You see the good in me. Your faith in me has been unwavering. I do not wish to lose that too."

I eyed the phone warily. Maxim had just bad mouthed my relationship with Rafael again, but it appeared he was relenting. "So… we're okay?"

"I will abide by your conditions so that we may work together, but Kristine…"

Alarms sounded in my head. "Yes?"

"If I lose the presidential election on April 10th, I will move to the United States and pursue you relentlessly. Do you understand?"

"Yes," I gritted. As if I weren't working hard enough to get the man elected.

Chapter 6 – All of the Stars

"Yes!" I leapt from my chair, grabbed a handful of air, and pulled it to my chest.

Shae rose hesitantly from her chair. "Yes, what?"

"Yes, this!" I turned my computer screen so she could see.

Her eyes widened. "She sent you a grant application?"

I smiled so wide it made my cheeks ache. "She sent me a grant application."

Shae threw her arms around me. "You did it!" She stepped back and shoved my shoulder. Hard. "Holy crap! You did it."

I laughed. "Don't get too excited. USAID still has to *approve* the application."

She reclaimed her chair on the other side of my desk. "I guess I know what we're doing over lunch."

"I have to call Maxim." I dug the cell phone from my purse, scrolled through my contacts, and tapped on his name.

"Dobroye utro, kotyonok."

I rolled my eyes at his seductive tone. "I have good news."

"You're leaving Rafael?"

"What? No. I am not *leaving* Rafael. Maxim, could you please try to behave?" I huffed out a breath, my excitement dulled. "Ms. Dickson e-mailed a grant application."

Shae looked up from her phone.

"What does that mean?" Apparently, Maxim had very little experience with grants.

I opened the PDF file attached to Ms. Dickson's e-mail. "It means Ms. Dickson is seriously considering our request. We're one step closer to funding the pipeline and winning the election."

"I'm not so sure I want to win the election," Maxim grumbled. "I think I may prefer the alternative."

"Maxim," I gritted. "Do you want me to work on the grant application or not?"

Shae eyed me worriedly.

A heavy sigh sounded over the line. "How long will this take?"

I glanced back at my computer screen. "The grant application is twenty eight pages. I have most of the information they need on hand. Shae's helping so we should be able to submit it tomorrow."

"And once it's submitted?"

I scrolled through the guidelines in the PDF file. "They have thirty days to respond."

Maxim did the math. "That would be twenty days before the election."

"They could ask for revisions, and there's no telling how long it would take for them to release the funds," I warned.

"We'll make it work," Maxim answered.

"Okay," I agreed. "I'll e-mail you a draft before I submit it to USAID."

"*Spasibo.*"

"*Pozhaluysta,*" I answered softly. "I'll touch base with you tomorrow. Be safe, Maxim."

"What's going on between you and Maxim?" Shae demanded the second I ended the call.

"Nothing." I saved the PDF file to my hard drive and e-mailed her a copy.

She raised a single eyebrow.

"I don't want to talk about it." I folded my arms across my chest so she'd know I was serious. "How are you coming along on Sierra Leone?"

"I hate this issue," she finally relented. "How do you *resolve* female genital mutilation?"

I cringed. As boring as it was, I was thankful I was working on human rights violations in mining communities instead of secret societies and tribal initiation.

Shae leaned forward in her seat. "Did you know ninety-four percent of women over age fifteen have been cut?"

I shuddered. That was far more than I anticipated.

"Nearly everyone living in Sierra Leone's provinces belongs to these secret societies. Anyone who refuses to join is threatened or beaten until they agree to become an initiate. The initiates are forbidden to discuss society affairs with non-initiates, so I don't have a clue how we're going to discuss these human rights abuses with them," Shae fretted.

"What if we map the problem and ask them to identify solutions?" I suggested. "It would be interesting to see if they can develop a strategy for resolving this. If they're unable to propose solutions, we could suggest strategies and see if they can predict the outcomes."

"So no simulation," Shae concluded.

I shook my head. "I think that would be a bad idea unless we perform the simulation as a model and they simply observe the process."

Shae frowned. "This issue could have a chilling effect on our dialogue."

"Then we should raise this issue last. How's Cory coming along on vigilante violence?"

"He's done mapping. He and Sammi are already working on their simulations." Sammi was working on the excessive use of force by law enforcement.

"I should be finished with my simulation by the end of the week." I glanced at my computer briefly. "How are things going between you and Konstantin?"

"I don't want to talk about it," she replied in kind.

My eyebrows shot up. "What? Why?"

A stubborn look settled over her face. "You first."

"Fine." I huffed out a breath. "Maxim kissed me. Jase punched him. I had a coming to Jesus talk with Maxim. He promised not to flirt with me or bad mouth Rafael between now and the election. He's also threatened to move to the United States and pursue me relentlessly if he loses the election."

"Wow." Shae studied me for a couple of heartbeats. "Has he?"

My brow furrowed. "Has he what?"

"Stopped flirting."

I barked out a laugh. "Absolutely not."

Shae sighed. "I'm questioning whether Konstantin has severed ties with the mafia. He's acting suspicious. He's gone most evenings, and he refuses to discuss what he's doing."

"Maybe he's out drinking. He is rather fond of his

vodka," I offered skeptically.

She shook her head. "I don't think he's out drinking. He doesn't come home drunk. We hardly go out, although he sleeps over more often than not. The only thing he seems interested in is…" Her cheeks flushed.

"Sex?" I guessed.

"His sex drive is…" Her voice trailed off again. "He's really attentive in bed, but he's always seducing me. Every time I try to talk, he seduces me. Physically, we're fine, but emotionally? I thought we'd be closer by now."

I frowned. "Have you shared your concerns with him?"

She nodded. "Every time I bring it up he apologizes, he starts kissing me, and we end up in bed."

I reflected on the workbook that Father Ramires had given me. "Why don't you write him a letter, explain the problem, and tell him what you need. Sometimes it helps for people to see it in writing, and he won't be able to interrupt or distract you if he's reading. You should offer concrete examples of what you need so it's clear what he has to do to improve the relationship. Instead of discussing it, ask him to write you a letter back, telling you what he needs out of this relationship."

She gaped at me. "That's perfect."

I laughed. "That's in the marriage preparation workbook."

Shae rose from her chair. "I'd like to borrow that when you're done."

"I'll make a copy for you." I glanced at my computer screen. "I e-mailed the grant application. Let me know which sections you want to work on."

She stopped at the door. "Will do. Are we still going dress shopping this weekend?"

"Yep. We're meeting at my house, Saturday at ten." I sat staring at the doorway long after she'd left, wondering just how much danger my friend was in.

* * * * *

Brady sidled up to the center island. "What are you making?"

"Pear and pomegranate mimosas." I scattered pomegranate seeds into the bottom of the champagne glasses.

The doorbell rang.

"I got it." Jase jumped from the couch.

I followed him into the foyer.

"Hey, Jase. Ready for a little dress shopping?" Cenia teased. She gave each of us a hug.

"Hardly," he grumbled. "I'd rather rip my toenails off."

Marie followed her inside the house. "Hi, Jase. It's good to see you again. Kri, you look beautiful as always." She pulled me in for a hug.

I stashed their coats inside the office and followed them into the family room. "I hope you're hungry."

"I am now," Marie confessed. "Look at all this food!"

I waved toward the scones, mini quiches, Andouille sausage, and chocolate dipped strawberries. "Grab a plate. Would you like some coffee or a pear and pomegranate mimosa?"

"Both," Cenia answered. "Kri, you didn't have to do all this."

"I know. I just thought it might be fun." I handed Cenia and Marie their mimosas before pouring the coffee.

"I'll get it," Jase yelled when the doorbell rang again.

Shae followed him into the kitchen a few minutes later.

"Sorry I'm late."

I hugged her tight. "You're fine. Grab a plate." I shoved a mimosa at Brady and Jase.

Brady glanced awkwardly at Jase.

Jase shrugged. "I won't tell if you don't."

I poured two more mimosas, handed one to Shae, and kept one for myself. "I have a confession to make."

The room grew quiet.

I took a deep breath. "I've arranged for the bridal shop to bring the dresses here. They'll be arriving at ten-thirty."

Marie's jaw bounced off the granite countertop.

"That's awesome!" Cenia shouted.

Shae glanced at me, confused. "So we don't have to schlep through the bridal shop?"

I shook my head. "I thought this might be easier and a bit more fun." I looked at Cenia. "Jase still has nightmares about scary face Barbie."

Jase shuddered. "That woman was truly frightening."

Cenia laughed. "Will you still serve as our judge?"

He eyed Brady.

Brady chuckled. "I won't tell if you don't."

I patted Brady on the back. "You're both serving as judges." I handed him a plate.

Marie carried her plate into the family room. "How many dresses are they bringing?"

"I asked them to bring ten different wedding and bridesmaid dresses in sizes six and eight." I bit into a chocolate covered strawberry. "Thanks for agreeing to wear purple." I was pretty certain I knew which bridesmaid dress they were going to choose.

We were just finishing up breakfast when the doorbell rang. I smiled when I saw it was the dress consultant who'd assisted me at the store. "Hi, Gloria. Thanks for coming."

She was carrying a portable tri-fold mirror. "Hi, Kristine. These are my assistants, Emily and Nicole"

I would have shaken their hands, but they were loaded down with dresses. "Do you mind taking the dresses upstairs?"

"Not at all," Gloria assured me.

Brady and Jase tried to lighten their load before they tackled the stairs.

"We want to see the wedding dresses first!" Cenia called from the living room. "Do you need help?"

"No. I'm good. I'll be back down in a minute." I followed everyone upstairs. I'd selected eight dresses at the bridal shop without trying any of them on and then asked Gloria to surprise me with two additional dresses.

Brady and Jase strode from my room. "We'll be downstairs."

I removed my clothes while Emily and Nicole organized the dresses. Gloria slid a delicate lace dress over my head. The lace edging above the bodice and down the arms was so fine it looked air-brushed.

"That looks gorgeous on you," Emily cooed. "Are you wearing your hair up or down?"

"I'm not sure," I answered. Gloria was still buttoning me up.

"Let's pull it up and see how it looks," Nicole suggested. She grabbed a large clip from her bag, twisted my hair around her hand, and secured the roll against my head.

I smiled, utterly impressed. "Wow. That was fast." And the up-sweep looked surprisingly good.

Gloria turned me toward the mirror. "How do you like the dress?"

I admired the dress while turning to the right and left. "I love the bodice, but the skirt is a little too filmy for me."

Gloria's head tilted while she studied the dress. "Would you like to show your friends?"

I nodded.

She gathered the train and followed me downstairs. Stand with your back to your friends while I position the train, then turn around."

I smiled sheepishly at Brady and Jase when I stepped into the family room. They joined the girls on the couch. My friends studied me intently while Gloria positioned me. All five of their heads ducked unexpectedly. I started cracking up when they held numbers in the air. They'd recorded their scores on printer paper with thick black Sharpies. "You're scoring the dresses?"

"We're tallying our scores so we can choose the best dress," Marie answered in far too innocent a tone.

I glanced pointedly at Cenia. "Gee, I wonder who came up with that idea."

"I'm negotiating the final agreement and mediating disputes," Shae stated happily.

I shook my head before scrutinizing their scores. "Fives, sixes, and seven... that seems about right. Okay, next dress."

Gloria followed me out of the room. "Your friends are hysterical."

"That they are." I schlepped up the stairs and shimmied into the next dress. This was one of the few satin dresses that I'd selected. I was trying to steer clear of dresses that resembled the one I'd chosen in Paris. The formfitting bodice was strapless. The hips and waist were embellished with a soft floral embroidery that tiptoed toward the bodice. A wide satin sash framed my hips before falling in elegant folds. The dress was nearly straight, with the subtlest flair as it fell toward the floor.

"Hair down for this one," Emily announced. She removed the clip from my hair and fluffed it with her fingers. "Perfect."

We traipsed downstairs.

"Oh! That's gorgeous," Marie breathed.

"Very pretty," Shae agreed.

I turned briefly while awaiting their scores. The dress was elegant, but I couldn't picture Rafael's jaw dropping when I walked down the aisle.

Brady and Jase rated the dress a five while all three girls awarded a nine. I smiled. "Just as I suspected. Let's see how you like the next dress."

The next dress looked innocent and sweet. I was a million miles from innocent so I removed it immediately.

Gloria pulled one of the dresses she had selected from the garment bag and eased it over my head. "I've got my fingers crossed on this one."

Nicole pulled my hair in a twist and clipped it up again. Emily tucked a pearl tiara in my hair. The three women stood breathlessly awaiting my response when Gloria nudged me toward the mirror.

My heart stalled. The embroidered dress was beyond exquisite. The entire dress was heavily beaded with ivory sequins and pearls. The formfitting bodice dipped well below my breasts, but a built in bra and delicately embroidered straps held everything in place. The dress hugged my hips before flaring into an incredibly romantic train. I turned to admire the back, and my vision blurred. The train was much longer than I expected and delicately scalloped along the edges. A thin strand of embroidered ivory leaves trailed down my shoulders before delicately framing my waist. The back was cut in a low V that dipped below my hips. Four strands of pearls draped from one shoulder to the next, trailing all the way down my back. I reached for the chair as my knees began to weaken.

Nicole eased me onto the chair while Emily fanned my face.

Gloria pressed a handful of tissues into my hand. "Never in a million years did I think I'd find a woman who could carry this off, but you do in a surprisingly elegant way. This gown is so exquisite, I couldn't resist ordering it. I know it's a little risqué. Are you brave enough to wear it?"

My heart was pounding. This elaborate dress pushed the boundaries between romance and seduction just like Rafael. "It's perfect," I finally breathed.

Emily and Nicole cheered.

Gloria smiled as she knelt in front of me. "Would you like to show your friends?"

I studied her kind face. "You know, Gloria, I don't think I will. I'd like to keep this dress secret. I don't want anyone to see it before Rafael."

"I think that's a wonderful idea." She helped me remove the tiara and dress after one last look in the mirror.

I threw my blue jeans and sweater back on so I could break the news to my friends. I rifled through the bridesmaid dresses before I went downstairs. "We might as well present this one first. I doubt they'll look at another dress after seeing this gown."

Gloria smiled. "I'll make sure they try that one first. Go ahead and send them up."

My heart was singing by the time I reached the bottom of the stairs. I was so in love with my dress.

My friends' eyes widened when I stepped into the room.

Shae jumped from the couch. "What happened? Why aren't you wearing a dress?"

I grinned. "I've found the perfect dress, but I don't want you to see it."

"What?" Cenia exclaimed. "You can't do that. We... we have to tally our scores."

I laughed. "No, you don't. You have to go upstairs and try on your bridesmaid dress."

Marie glanced at me uncertainly. "Are you serious? You're keeping your dress secret?"

I walked into the kitchen so I could pour a cup of coffee. "I want Rafael to see the dress first." I frowned. "Well, maybe not first but at the same time as everyone else."

Jase joined me in the kitchen. "I think that's a great idea."

"I kinda liked being a judge," Brady objected.

"You can be a judge for the bridesmaids' dresses." I glanced at my friends. "Gloria's waiting for you upstairs."

They moved reluctantly toward the stairs.

I lowered my voice. "Either of you willing to wager a bet?"

Jase leaned against the counter while pressing a coffee cup to his lips. "What kind of bet?"

I bit my bottom lip. "I bet they choose the very first dress."

Brady joined us in the kitchen. He appeared to be weighing the odds.

Jase's eyes narrowed. "I'm not betting on this. You have an unfair advantage. You've seen all the dresses."

"They're women," Brady scoffed. "No way are they choosing the first dress they try on."

I joined him at the center island. "So Jase is out and you're in. What do you want to bet?"

"Dinner," Brady stated. "Winner chooses dinner, and the loser buys."

"You got it." We shook hands before joining Jase on the couch. "I'd like to go ring shopping for Rafael tomorrow. Are either of you willing to tag along?"

"I'll go," Brady offered.

"Sure, why not?" Jase bit into a chocolate dipped strawberry.

I patted their knees. "You guys seriously rock."

Their jaws suddenly dropped.

Cenia, Marie, and Shae filed into the room. They looked stunning in the deep purple gowns I'd selected. The bodice, a sheer lavender material, was embellished with a beaded purple and ivory floral applique that strategically covered the chest and framed the back of the dress, which was cut in a V just above the waist. A ruched eight inch strip of fabric defined the waist. Large black roses swirled throughout the dark purple skirt which pooled on the floor in a subtle train. The dress was elegant, sexy, and unabashedly romantic.

"This dress is unbelievable," Shae murmured dreamily.

"Absolutely gorgeous," Marie agreed. She turned a slow circle, admiring the train.

"I may never take it off," Cenia announced defiantly.

"Maybe you should try the other dresses," Brady suggested.

Shae looked horrified. "No. This... this is the dress I want to wear."

"Me too." Marie looked pleadingly at me.

"I told you I wasn't taking it off," Cenia very nearly growled.

I laughed. "I'm so relieved. I was secretly hoping for that dress." I snapped a picture for Lexie and Kimme, who had agreed to wear whatever we chose.

"Who knew dress shopping could be so easy?" Marie exclaimed as they walked upstairs.

I looked pointedly at Brady. "You're buying ZPizza for dinner."

"Works for me," he conceded with a grin.

Jase just shook his head.

* * * * *

"What do you think of this one?" I tapped on the glass above the brushed titanium band.

The jeweler pulled it out of the case. "Black titanium wedding bands are quite popular these days."

Jase slid the ring on his finger. He was modeling rings since his coloring was similar to Rafael's. "I don't know. There's nothing really distinctive about this ring."

I frowned at the ring. "I agree."

"Why don't you try this one?" Brady pointed to a rustic looking ring.

The jeweler pulled the ring out and set it on top of the counter. "That ring is handmade, hammered silver with antiquing."

Jase returned the titanium ring to the jeweler before slipping the hammered band on his hand. "This looks like Rafael."

The ring had an old world feel about it and certainly looked masculine enough. "I don't know about silver, though. Isn't silver soft?"

The jeweler nodded. "Titanium and platinum are more

scratch resistant. Have you ever seen a tungsten carbide ring? They're completely scratch proof, our most durable rings by far." He pulled a highly polished silver ring with a black inlay from his case. "The only problem with these rings is they can't be resized."

Brady slid the ring on his finger.

I studied both of their hands. "I don't know whether to go with contemporary or rustic." I looked at the price tags and released an exasperated breath. "Neither of these will work."

Brady frowned. "Why not?"

I pointed to the price tag. "That ring is a hundred dollars. I can't buy Rafael a hundred dollar ring, not when he bought me this." I held my ring out for everyone to see.

"I've been admiring your engagement ring," the jeweler confessed. "Is that a Verragio?"

I nodded. "My wedding band is a Verragio as well." Rafael had shown me the braided band to ensure I liked it. I nearly fainted when I saw all the diamonds.

The jeweler collected the rings and returned them to the case. "I have some Verragio wedding bands in my other case."

We followed the jeweler to the other side of the store and quietly studied the rings. "That's the one," I finally whispered.

My heart leapt when the jeweler pulled it from the case and placed it in my hand. "This ring is available in platinum or eighteen karat gold."

The ring was solid, heavy even. The trim along the edges was highly polished and set against a black enamel line with a brushed platinum finish in the center. The ring was deeply notched. Each notch formed a square that framed a diamond.

Five diamonds were set flush inside the ring. The design was masculine and refined, which seemed fitting for a man who preferred cargo pants and jeans over his tux but still enjoyed the finer things in life. "This is perfect."

"Would you like to see it on my hand?" Jase inquired hesitantly.

"Sure." I handed him the ring. "How does it feel?"

Jase slid the ring into place. "Solid and comfortable." He clenched his hand and twisted the ring around his finger. "I really like the way it feels."

I placed my hand over Jase's hand. "It looks good with my engagement ring. Can you see Rafael wearing this?"

"Absolutely," Brady agreed.

Jase slid the ring off his finger and placed it in my hand. "I think this ring is perfect."

I handed the ring to the jeweler before digging out my credit card. "I'd like this ring in a size eleven. Platinum, please."

He nodded his approval. "You've chosen a very handsome ring. Would you like to have it engraved?"

"Yes, please." I followed him to the register where he handed me a slip of paper. I carefully printed the two words I'd been considering ever since Rafael proposed and whisked me off to Portugal.

The jeweler read the inscription he would later engrave. His eyes glistened when they returned to mine. "I'm so happy you found one another."

"Me too," I answered sincerely.

* * * * *

"Rafael!" I sprinted around the corner and ran smack dab into Jase's chest.

He tried not to laugh. "Let me make sure it's him." He strode past the center island just as Rafael opened the door into the kitchen.

I darted past Jase and jumped into Rafael's arms. "You're four hours early!"

"I was trying to surprise you." His hands speared my hair and clenched my waist as he pressed his lips to mine. He forced my lips open. The kiss grew possessive. There was an underlying current that made me tremble with anticipation. "I've missed you," Rafael admitted while his lips still blanketed mine.

"I missed you too." I buried my face in his neck and hugged him again. God, how I loved this man.

"We're going to head out," Jase announced, as if we might not notice.

Rafael tucked me under his arm.

"Are you going to see Emma?" I pried curiously.

"Maybe." He very nearly blushed.

I peered at Brady. "Are you seeing Heidi?" Both men were fairly tightlipped about their girlfriends, but they'd been loosening up over the past month.

"Heck yeah." Brady patted Rafael on the back. "I'll see you Sunday."

"Have fun." Rafael locked the door behind them.

I linked my fingers with Rafael's and led him into the family room. "I cannot imagine how they're maintaining those relationships when they're watching over me day and night. The only break they get is when Kadyn comes to visit, and even then, they take turns leaving. They take their responsibilities here very seriously."

Rafael sank onto the couch. "As well they should."

I plopped down next to him. "Can someone else cover for them every once in a while? This job shouldn't cost them their personal lives."

He pulled me close. "I hate to ask Ethan, since he's married, but I can ask Brogan, Aidan, or Chance to spend the night a couple times a week so they can have more time off. Do you have a preference in whom I ask?"

"I've spent more time with Chance, but Brogan and Aidan would be fine too. I should get to know them better since they'll be joining us in Sierra Leone." I burrowed beneath his arm.

"I'll see what I can do." A contented smile settled on his face. "We caught another one."

My eyes widened. "You did? How?"

"One of the staff members at the Casa Pia Orphanage reached out to me. A movie producer from Spain became enamored with one of the boys after seeing him on the playground. He wanted to use the child as an extra in a scene he was filming in Lisbon. He requested medical records to ensure the child was healthy and asked that he be tested for sexually transmitted diseases. When she refused, he tried to bribe her. He said he might be willing to adopt the boy if they spent time together on the set. He came to the orphanage multiple times, so we fit her with a wire. When she reiterated their children could not be filmed or used for commercial purposes and could only be released for personal relations, he revealed his true interest."

My jaw dropped. "He admitted his intentions?"

Rafael's eyes darkened. "He had heard the orphanage released children for sexual purposes. He went on and on about how important sexual intimacy is and how he could help this child reach his full potential."

I shook my head, thoroughly disgusted. "Is that recording admissible in court? I thought both parties had to consent to a recorded conversation in order for it to be admissible."

He shook his head. "Only one party has to consent to the recording in Portugal, and what she said was carefully worded so it cannot be viewed as entrapment."

"Good." Frankly, I was relieved. "I'm happy to hear you're making progress on the case."

Rafael smiled. "We should go out and celebrate."

I studied his face. "Aren't you tired from the flight?"

He shrugged. "Not really. I'd like to take my fiancé out for dinner."

"Okay," I agreed. "Anywhere in particular?"

"Old Ebbitt Grill?" he suggested.

I peered at the time on the microwave. "Sure. What time?"

Rafael dug his cell phone out of his pocket. "Eight o'clock?"

I didn't doubt he could pull it off. "I'm going to change, then."

He snagged my arm when I rose from the couch. "Hold on. I'd like to help you with that." He made the reservation and tossed his phone on the couch.

"We've got two hours," I giggled. He was already removing my shirt.

* * * * *

"So how many people do you think will mistake this time, five-thirty in the morning, for five-thirty in the evening?" I wondered aloud. Rafael and I were sprawled on top of the ivory rug in front of the fireplace in my formal living room addressing invitations for our wedding.

"About half." Rafael chuckled. "Don't worry, I'll schedule a wake-up call for the whole lot of them once they check in at the hotel." He assembled another invitation.

"Did you find a hotel large enough to accommodate all of our guests?" I checked another name off the list.

"I've reserved forty rooms at the Penha Longa Resort for May 19th through the 22nd," Rafael confirmed.

I looked up from my envelope. "Is forty rooms enough? We have fifty-eight guests."

"Most of those guests are couples, so forty should be enough." He finished addressing his envelope.

I checked another invitation off the list. "I need to call Eva to see if she knows anyone who'd be willing to do makeup and hair at two o'clock in the morning." Since sunrise was at five forty-five, the wedding party had to be at the palace no later than four-thirty in the morning.

Firelight danced in his eyes. "I've already taken care of that. The Penha Longa Resort has a world renowned spa. I scheduled massages, manicures, and pedicures for ten o'clock in the morning on the twentieth and hair and makeup for two o'clock in the morning on the twenty-first for you, your mother, and our bridesmaids. I also hired a limousine service to drive everyone to the palace."

I shook my head while a smile tugged at my lips. "You're always one step ahead of me."

He laughed. "Eva has been helping me."

I assembled another invitation. "What are we going to do about the rehearsal?" A practice run at the palace would give the view away before the wedding.

"I don't think we need one. The wedding party will be at the palace an hour early. The chairs, the runner, and the luminaries will already be set up, so it will be obvious where everyone walks. We can show them where to stand when we arrive. We can still do a rehearsal dinner if you'd like, either in the courtyard or by the pool at the Penha Longa Resort. I have several pictures on my cell phone, if you want to see what the resort looks like." He opened his photo gallery and handed me the phone.

I stared at the picture, confused. "What building is this?"

He glanced at the phone. "That's the Penha Longa Resort."

I gaped at him. "This isn't a hotel. It's... It's..."

"It's a nineteenth century palace built on monastery ruins." Rafael chuckled. "Don't worry. This isn't like Obidos Castle."

I sifted through the pictures. The rooms, the lobby, the restaurants, and spa were truly luxurious. They offered a surprisingly contemporary décor and modern day amenities while drawing on the natural beauty of the palace and the surrounding forest. "This place is unbelievable. The courtyard is beautiful, but I think the patio surrounding the pool might be better for the rehearsal dinner."

Rafael leaned closer so he could take a look. "I like the pool. That picture doesn't do it justice, but the view is spectacular. The resort is located inside a national park. That side of the hotel overlooks the mountains and the ocean. There are several restaurants and a catering service on site. Their menus are on the website."

I handed him the phone. "Why don't we schedule the rehearsal dinner for sunset on the twentieth since the pool overlooks the ocean?"

He reached for another envelope. "I'll find out when the sun sets in May and schedule the dinner a half hour before that time. You do realize we won't be getting any sleep that night?"

"We'll nap before the rehearsal dinner." Hopefully, the jetlag would work in our favor.

Rafael propped his head on his hand as he rolled onto his side. "What do you want to do about Maxim?"

I rolled onto my side so I could read the expression on his face. "I feel conflicted about inviting him. He's hardly predictable, often inappropriate, and he enjoys pushing buttons. I don't want him to ruin this day for us."

A single eyebrow crept up his forehead. "But..."

"But," I conceded with a sigh, "Maxim saved my life. He saved Kadyn's life, and he avenged Michael's death. If anyone deserves to be there, it would be him."

Rafael nodded. "I agree that it would be rude not to include him. I think it's better to send the invitation and let him decide whether to attend."

I added Maxim's name to the list and made a quick mental note to ask Konstantin for his address.

Rafael snatched my pen and tossed it aside. My shoulders sank into the thick, plush rug when he rolled on top of me. A well-muscled thigh slid between my legs as he lowered his body onto mine. "If Maxim tries to kiss you..."

My hands tangled in his hair as I pulled his lips to mine. "The only man who's kissing me is you."

* * * * *

I shoved another waffle fry into my mouth. I wasn't sure I liked waffle fries, but I was ravenously hungry, and Oni was in love with Chick-fil-A.

Oni popped a chicken nugget inside her mouth sans sauce. "Have you heard from USAID?"

"No. I submitted the grant application two weeks ago, and they have thirty days to decide." I dipped my chicken strip in barbeque sauce before sinking my teeth into the juicy meat.

"How's Maxim doing in the polls?" Shae asked around her straw. I was surprised she stopped guzzling her sweet tea long enough to join the conversation. The three of us decided to meet for dinner after class. Brady and Jase were eating at a nearby table, offering what little privacy they could.

"He's still tied with Yulia." Oni frowned. "The election is only a month away. We need something to happen, something that will help him gain the lead in those polls." She eyed me thoughtfully. "Can you fly to Ukraine and pretend to be his girlfriend again?"

My jaw bounced off the table.

"Oni!" Shae bristled. "Have you lost your mind?"

"I'm sorry." Oni's cheeks flushed pink. "I just... I remember all the press he got when the two of you were together."

My heart stalled. Several disturbing images came to mind. Bare light bulbs, metal chairs, and cold cement floors. I swallowed. Hard. "I can't go back there. Even if it were pretend, I can't put Rafael through that again."

"I'm sorry," Oni repeated. "It was a stupid idea."

Shae and I exchanged glances. I hadn't shared any of the gruesome details about the torture we endured while held captive by the SVR. Oni knew that we had been abducted, but I wasn't sure how much she knew beyond that. "It's fine, Oni. You just want what's best for your country."

She picked through her waffle fries. "Would you go back if he were elected?"

"I don't know." I shifted uncomfortably.

"Speaking of dating," Shae segued, "have you met anyone you're interested in dating?"

"No. Not really." Oni snuck a peek at me.

"Really?" Shae teased. "You haven't met any intriguing men at work or at school?"

"No." She folded three waffle fries inside her mouth.

"We should take Oni out for a night on the town," Shae announced.

"Not we. You. Oni's not going to meet any men with me tagging along." I jerked my head toward Brady and Jase. "No one would dare approach us with those two hovering over us."

Shae looked thoughtful. "Maybe…"

I shook my head. "Nope. I'm not ditching them. I've grown rather fond of my security blanket."

"Security blanket, huh? Now that paints a yummy visual." Shae fanned herself with a napkin.

"Gagh! Don't go there!" I slunk down in my seat when Brady and Jase narrowed their eyes at me.

"Maybe Kadyn could join us," Oni suggested.

Shae stilled. Her eyes slid questioningly toward me.

I took a deep breath and blew it out. "Are you interested in him?"

Oni leaned forward excitedly. "Is he dating anyone?"

Shae gaped at her. She took one look at me and snapped her mouth shut.

I reached for my sweet tea. "He was seeing Brianna back in January. I don't know if they're still dating."

Oni sighed. "Is there any way to find out?"

"I can ask him," I offered reluctantly. I wasn't sure I liked where this was heading. I tossed my empty containers on the tray. "I need to head home so I can call Rafael." I bit my lip when I realized my mistake.

"I would have thought he'd be home by now," Shae mused. "Is he working nights again?"

"That man works day and night," I answered irritably. I hoped it was enough to cover my mistake. I returned my tray and gave Oni a hug.

Shae eyed me suspiciously.

I gave her a hug before I could hang myself any further.

Brady and Jase herded me out the door.

* * * * *

"I can't believe you cooked clam linguine," Kadyn moaned appreciatively. "You need to teach me how to cook this stuff."

I piled a second helping onto both of our plates and joined him at the center island. "Anytime, although I do enjoy cooking this for you."

Kadyn reached for another piece of sourdough bread. "Any news on the grant application?"

"No." I frowned. "I was really hoping to hear from them before we leave for Sierra Leone."

Kadyn twirled the noodles around his fork. "When do you leave?"

"Next Wednesday after work, but I'm flying to Portugal to celebrate Rafael's birthday first. We fly out from Lisbon late Saturday night so we can join Shae and the rest of my team in Sierra Leone Sunday morning." I shoved another forkful of linguini into my mouth.

Kadyn sopped up the sauce from the linguine with his bread. "I've always wanted to visit West Africa."

I chased my linguini with Sprite. "You're welcome to tag along."

Kadyn's eyes widened while he chewed the bread. "Really?"

I shrugged. "As long as you have the vacation time."

Kadyn shook his head. "I have plenty of vacation time but not enough funds. What does a trip like that run? Five... six thousand dollars?" He gathered another forkful of linguini.

I set my napkin on the counter. "I don't know. Seeds for Peace covers my expenses." I studied Kadyn. He seemed genuinely interested in going. "If you flew to Portugal with Jase and me, you wouldn't have to pay for a plane ticket. We're using Rafael's jet. Rafael's flat has two guestrooms, so you and Jase would have your own rooms. You could tour Lisbon with Jase while Rafael and I meet with the priest on Thursday and join us for dinner Friday night. I've invited some of Rafael's friends from Lisbon to join us for dinner since it's his birthday, but he doesn't know that. I'd like to keep that a surprise."

Kadyn set his fork down. "Are you taking Rafael's jet to Sierra Leone and back home?"

I nodded. "I'm sure Jase wouldn't mind if you crashed with him in Sierra Leone. Brogan and Aidan are sharing a room. Jase was the odd man out because Rafael's staying with me." I frowned when I realized Shae was without a roommate. I made a quick mental note to request adjoining rooms.

Kadyn leaned against the high back stool.

I propped my feet on the bottom of his stool as I turned

to face him. "Think about it. If you shared a room with Jase in Sierra Leone, the only expense you'd have is food."

His eyes met mine. "You just made this trip impossible to resist. I'll see if I can take leave during that time, but I want you to make sure Rafael and Jase are okay with this. Is there something I can help with while in Sierra Leone?"

I patted his knee before grabbing our plates. "You can help keep us safe."

"That's easier said than done," he groaned in an exaggerated tone. He smirked when I shot him a dirty look.

I set our dishes in the sink. "Speaking of flights, I spoke with Kimme last night. Dan's not coming to the wedding. He hasn't been able to board a commercial flight since meeting us in the Bahamas. His PTSD is too bad."

Kadyn joined me at the sink. "I didn't realize his PTSD was that disabling."

"Dan tries to hide it as best he can. He doesn't want other people thinking he's broken. He begged Kimme to come up with some other excuse. He didn't want me to know it was the PTSD." I rinsed the plates and passed them to Kadyn.

He shoved them inside the dishwasher. "I could get him there."

I stilled. "How?"

"I know a couple of Vietnam vets who serve as volunteer pilots for the Veterans Airlift Command. The VAC provides free air transportation to wounded veterans and their families to hospitals and special events." His eyes glinted with mischief. "I could chloroform Dan, load him onto the plane, and fly him to Virginia so he can join us on Rafael's jet. Do you think he'd be okay on Rafael's jet? He'd be surrounded by friends."

Kadyn caught the glass I nearly dropped in the sink. "That's your solution… to chloroform him?"

He laughed. "Sure. Why not?"

I just shook my head. Dan would probably admire Kadyn's strategy and his stealth. "Why don't we see if he's willing to board the VAC plane and Rafael's jet on his own steam before we start talking chloroform?" I washed the pan and handed it to Kadyn.

"Where's the fun in that?" Kadyn tossed the towel on the counter. He followed me into the family room.

I took a deep breath before sitting next to him on the couch. "Are you still dating Brianna?"

He shook his head. "Technically, we weren't dating."

I chuckled. Kadyn and I used to deny the fact that we were dating even though we were. "That was quite the kiss on New Year's Eve for two strictly platonic friends."

He grinned. "She's a contractor. We decided to dial it back a notch since she's arguably working for me."

I swallowed. Hard. "Are you dating anyone else?"

Kadyn looked amused. "No. Why?"

I bit my lip while trying to suppress an audible groan. "Oni is interested in you."

His eyes widened. "Oni?"

I nodded.

Kadyn frowned. "I can't date Oni."

I glanced at him, surprised. "Why?"

"She's a foreign national. That could mess up my security clearance. I'm already required to report my interactions with Konstantin and Maxim. Trust me, that's bad enough."

"I don't think I should reveal that." I sighed. "I'll just tell Oni you're dating someone."

He eyed me curiously. "Wouldn't that violate the girlfriend code?"

"The girlfriend code?" *What girlfriend code?*

Kadyn rolled his eyes. "You know. Girlfriends aren't supposed to date a man their friend has dated. I thought that rule was etched in stone."

My brow furrowed. "Isn't there some sort of expiration date on that? We haven't dated for two years."

Kadyn laughed. "Do I look like a carton of milk?"

"Maybe. Chocolate milk," I teased.

He shoved me off the couch.

I ignored his hand as I pushed off the floor. "Jeesh! I was just trying to hook you up."

He patted the cushion next to him. "So you really wouldn't mind if I dated one of your friends?"

I sank onto the far end of the couch instead. "Honestly? I doubt there's a woman on this planet who's good enough for you, but I'd never stand in the way of your happiness, Kadyn. You, more than anyone I know, deserve to be happy. Friend or not, as long as that woman treated you like gold, I'd support your decision to date her."

Kadyn studied the coffee table.

My breath caught. "Who? Who are you interested in dating?"

"Shae," he admitted softly.

My heart battled a confusing array of emotions. "How long?"

He met my gaze. "Since we fled Ukraine."

I scooted closer to him. "That was nine months ago. Does Shae know?"

He shook his head. "I haven't breathed a word. I... I didn't want to hurt you."

"If there was a woman who I thought *might* be good enough, it would be Shae," I confessed. "She's beautiful, intelligent, witty, and she has a very kind heart. Better still, she respects and admires you."

Kadyn shrugged. "She's dating Konstantin, so it's a moot point."

I took a deep breath and blew it out. "That relationship isn't going as well as you might think."

He lifted an inquisitive brow.

"Shae's questioning whether Konstantin has severed ties with the mafia. He's gone most evenings and refuses to discuss what he's doing. Unless he's working a second job so he can save for an engagement ring, I'm afraid she may be right."

"I knew that relationship would put her in danger," Kadyn gritted.

"I've never been too keen on that relationship," I agreed. Early on, I'd been nudging her toward Chance. He had a major crush on her.

"Do you think Konstantin will return to Ukraine if Maxim's elected president?" Kadyn asked.

"I don't know." I looked him square in the eyes. "What I do know is that I'd fully support you in pursuing Shae. Can I tell her you're interested?"

Kadyn shook his head. "Absolutely not."

I opened my mouth to object.

He leveled me with a fiercely determined look. "Trust me, I got this."

* * * * *

I filled my coffee cup before claiming the chair next to Shae. I was still having a hard time looking her in the eyes. Like one secret wasn't bad enough. Now I was keeping two secrets from her. "I purchased forty bags of snack sized candy last night; Skittles, Starburst, Tootsie Pops, and Sour Patch Kids."

Sammi's eyes widened. "Why so many?"

"I figured ten bags for our students and twenty bags for the orphanage. I thought we could hand the remaining candy out to street kids when we're out in public. Did you know that most children in Sierra Leone have never even tasted candy?" I would have preferred to bring chocolate but I was worried it might melt. Electricity and air conditioning were unreliable, even in Freetown.

Cory strode into the breakroom. He joined us at the table. "The printer called. The training manuals should be completed by the end of the day." He looked at Shae. "Did you get the pens?" She was planning to purchase pens depicting the monuments in DC as a parting gift for our students.

She took a swig of diet coke. "I have thirty pens, thirty key chains, and thirty gift bags."

Sammi eyed me over the top of her coffee. "What time are you flying in?"

"Sometime around six o'clock in the morning," I estimated.

"I'll make sure one of our drivers is waiting for you at the airport," Cory promised. Public transportation was extremely limited. Taxis were so poorly maintained, they were discouraged by the Department of State. It wasn't all that uncommon for tourists to be attacked and robbed in taxis, so as pretentious as it seemed, we needed reputable drivers to help ensure our security.

I warmed my hands on my coffee mug. "Kadyn is coming so there'll be four of us."

Shae smiled. "Good. I'm happy to hear he got the time off."

"I reserved SUVs, so there should be plenty of room," Cory assured me.

"Rafael and Kadyn have offered to help Brogan and Aidan with their portion of the training. They're still flying in with you on Saturday?"

"Yep. Should be fun," Shae chirped.

"Yeah. Like Brogan clearing out public bathrooms so you can pee qualifies as fun," Sammi grumbled irritably.

Shae's brow furrowed. "Speaking of bathrooms, does anyone know what the toilet situation is there? Are we squatting over holes again?"

"I don't think so," Cory answered. "While Freetown still lacks plumbing and proper sanitation in impoverished areas, the hotel and the university have modern toilets. Oh! Everyone should bring bottled water. I don't want to take any chances with that Cholera outbreak." He looked at me. "Make sure Kadyn, Rafael, and Jase bring water and know to avoid ice, fresh fruit, and vegetables. You guys should brush your teeth with bottled water and keep your mouths closed in the shower."

"Did you complete all your travel vaccines?" Sammi interjected.

Shae and I nodded.

"Have you started the antimalarial medicine?" Cory prodded.

"Yes." I smiled, anticipating his next question. "Kadyn, Rafael, and Jase have also started."

Cory stood. "I think we're set, then."

I rose from the table as well. "I'm worried about Shae staying in a room by herself. I'm going to call the hotel to see if they offer adjoining rooms, so she can be close to us."

Sammi frowned. "What if they don't offer adjoining rooms?"

I glanced at Shae. "You can sleep in our room. It's not like we'll be using the other bed." Each of the rooms we'd reserved was supposed to include two beds.

Shae looked appalled. "I do not want to be all up in your business when the two of you start feeling amorous."

I laughed. "I'm sure we can manage to keep our hands off one another. We're only there for a week. If you prefer, I could ask Kadyn to sleep with you." I patted myself on the back for planting that tasty little morsel in her brain.

Her eyes widened even more. "I... I'll sleep with you... if they don't have adjoining rooms."

I smiled. "I'll let you know what I find out." I walked back to my office so I could call the hotel.

After securing adjoining rooms, I opened my e-mail. My breath caught.

"What is it?" Shae inquired softly. I hadn't even heard her enter the room.

"USAID," I breathed. "I have an e-mail from Keshia Dickson from USAID."

She joined me in front of the computer screen. "Maybe you should open it."

I winced. "I'm afraid."

"I'm sorry, but the suspense is killing me." She clicked on the e-mail notification.

My heart stalled. We both stared slack jawed at Ms. Dickson's message.

"What's wrong?" Sammi asked. I hadn't a clue where she came from. When neither of us answered, she joined us in front of the computer screen. "Holy. Crap. You did it."

Shae's wide eyes met mine. "Maxim's going to be president."

Tears abruptly filled my eyes.

Shae yanked me to my feet. She gave me a fierce hug. "Do you have any idea what you've done? You've changed the destiny of an entire country."

Sammi rubbed my arm. "You're trembling."

"What if this leads to war?" I choked on a throat full of tears.

"Then that's Putin's doing, not yours," Shae insisted vehemently.

Sammi looked confused. "Why would this lead to war? It's an economic aid package."

I took a deep breath and blew it out. "I have to call Maxim."

Shae pulled Sammi from the office. "I'll explain. Let's give her some privacy."

"We should be celebrating," Sammi argued. "We're going out to lunch after you call Maxim. You don't secure funding for a pipeline every day!" she yelled down the hallway.

I sank into my chair. I couldn't believe this was happening. I was terrified for Maxim and the citizens of Ukraine. With trembling hands I dragged the cell phone from my desk, retrieved his number, and hit "send."

"*Kotyonok*," Maxim purred. "I was just thinking about you."

The dam inside of me broke as I began to cry.

"Kristine! What's wrong? Why are you crying? Have you

been hurt?"

His concern made me cry even harder.

"Where are you?" Maxim demanded. "I'm sending someone to get you."

"No!" I gasped. "No. God, I'm sorry. I... I don't know why I'm crying. I should be happy, but I'm not happy. I'm completely terrified."

"If you don't explain what is going on..." Maxim growled.

"The grant. USAID awarded us the grant," I blurted.

Maxim didn't breathe a word.

I swiped at my eyes. "Maxim?"

"Can you read it to me?" he pleaded softly.

"I can e-mail it to you." I turned toward my computer.

"No. My phone is secure, but I am not certain about my computer. If you could read the correspondence to me, print a copy, and give it to Konstantin, then he will ensure a hard copy is securely delivered to me."

"Okay," I agreed. "Should I ask Ms. Dickson to refrain from making an announcement?"

"Please," Maxim answered. "For at least two weeks."

He listened attentively while I read the award letter. "What are you going to do?" I finally breathed.

"I'm going to expedite training and installation for the missile defense system. The equipment is being housed in a secure location in Poland and is nearly operational. If I can get that equipment in place and begin construction on the pipeline within the next two weeks, I should be able to announce both accomplishments a week before the election."

I fought to steady my breathing. "I don't want you to get hurt. Please, Maxim, it's not too late to withdraw from the election. You can proceed with both projects discretely and still achieve your objectives."

"I will not hide like a coward," he argued. "I made my father a promise, and I intend to see it through."

My eyes closed against the images that provoked. "Please be safe, Maxim. I'm so scared this pipeline will lead to war."

"*Milaya kotyonok*, your concern humbles me, and your tears are like an arrow in my heart. I wish…"

"I know." I couldn't bear to hear the words.

"I will make my country safe," Maxim vowed. "Perhaps someday you will tire of Rafael."

I shook my head, unable to conceive such a thing. "I'll ask Ms. Dickson to hold off on making the announcement, and I'll make sure Konstantin gets a hard copy of the award letter today. Let me know if you have any difficulty accessing the funds through the USAID office at the U.S. Embassy in Kyiv. Those funds should be available by the end of the week."

"I do not know how to repay you for this." Maxim's voice broke with unwanted emotions. All that bluster about collecting on a promise? Nothing more than smoke and mirrors.

Tears filled my eyes once again. "You don't repay friends, Maxim."

Chapter 7 –Fix My Eyes

I sat with my knees tucked to my chest, staring silently out the window while the clouds bathed in the early morning sun.

"Is she always like this?" Kadyn whispered.

"Our last flight was a bit more turbulent," Jase murmured.

I tore my eyes from the window so I could gauge the expression on his face.

Jase winked, assuring my colossal melt down from our previous flight would remain our secret.

I smiled. As hard headed as he was, the man was growing on me. "Who's winning?"

Jase grunted. He'd started defending my side of the chess board after Kadyn slaughtered me... twice.

Kadyn grinned.

I laughed. "So Kadyn remains undefeated?" I untangled my legs so I could change into the pretty black, white, and blue floral skirt I discovered on the bed when we boarded the plane. Rafael had paired the skirt with a fitted black sweater, a thin Tiffany blue belt, and black kitten heels.

A melodic "ding" sounded over the intercom. "*Bom dia*. This is your pilot, Captain Anderson. Crisp blue skies and a cool sixty-two degree temperature await us in Lisbon. The local time is eight-ten a.m. We'll be landing in thirty minutes."

I changed into the skirt and sweater and did a cursory check in the mirror before returning to the main cabin.

The intercom dinged again. "We've been cleared to land at the Lisbon Portela Airport. Please make sure your seatbelts are fastened, seat backs are in the upright position, and all inanimate objects are stowed. I'll be collecting cups, glasses, and plates shortly." Kari stepped from the galley. "Sorry, Jase. I know how much you wanted to win that match."

Jase shrugged. "We've got an eight hour flight to Sierra Leone where I can even the score." The flight was only five and a half hours, but we had a two and a half hour layover in Morocco.

Kadyn chuckled. "We'll see about that."

I handed Kari my cup and plate. "Will you be joining us?"

She barked out a laugh. "Like I'd miss an opportunity to fly on this jet."

I smiled. I liked having the same personable flight crew on every flight.

The wheels touched down smooth as glass. We shook hands with the flight crew before tackling the stairs. Rafael had reserved a vehicle for Kadyn and Jase, so he was meeting us near the rental counters.

I stopped when the crowd parted just short of the car rental area. "Rafael?"

He picked me up and spun me around. "You look

stunning." He pressed a quick kiss to my lips before allowing my feet to touch the earth again.

My fingers sifted through the silken strands that tapered just above his ears. "You cut your hair."

He smiled that panty dropping smile of his. "I thought this might look a little more presentable for the wedding." The wedding was still two months away.

"You look..." Seriously, there were no words to describe how delectable this man looked. While trimmed short on the sides, his hair was longer on top, and it looked mussed. I tugged on the unruly waves. "You look..."

His eyes sparked with amusement. His strong features were perfectly balanced between the shorter hairstyle and the five o'clock shadow he regularly sported. Handsome was an understatement. Sinful was more like it. "Sexy," I concluded.

A chuckle rolled through Rafael's chest. He tugged the computer bag off my shoulder, tucked me under his arm, and shook Kadyn's hand. "I'm glad you could join us." He patted Jase on the back before leading us to the rental counter. "I hope you don't mind. I rented a Porsche."

"I'm driving!" Kadyn and Jase shouted as one. They slapped their driver's licenses on the counter at the exact same time.

Rafael laughed. "We have to head out. We're supposed to meet Father Ramires in Sintra at ten o'clock. We'll be back in time for dinner."

I gave each of them a hug. "Have fun." I linked arms with Rafael as we stepped through the automatic doors. "We're meeting Father Ramires in Sintra?"

He strode toward the parking garage. "He wants to see our wedding venue. We'll plan the ceremony while we're there. Do you have your workbook with you?"

I nodded toward the computer bag he'd slung over his shoulder. "Right there."

He slowed, allowing my eyes to adjust to the dim lighting in the garage. "Good. Nervous?"

I squeezed his bicep. "No. I'm excited to see Monserrate Palace again. Can we stop by the hotel while we're in Sintra?"

The lights flashed on his car. "That's precisely what I was thinking. We need to firm up the menu for the rehearsal dinner." He reached for the passenger door, then boxed me in against the Porsche. "Maybe we should reserve a room."

My hands slid over his well sculpted chest before linking behind his neck. "Sounds good. We could order room service and sample their food."

His eyes fell to my lips. "Only if I'm allowed to feed you in bed." His lips brushed against mine.

My eyes slid closed while I savored Rafael's warmth and his spicy cologne. "I've missed this… and you."

He kissed the Cupid's bow at the top of my mouth before pulling my bottom lip between his teeth. Gently, he bit down.

My eyes flew open.

The full length of his body pinned me against the Porsche. With hooded eyes, he fit his lips to mine. His tongue swept through my mouth, plundering every crevice. He stroked, tempted, and teased; drugging me with deep, intoxicating kisses until my knees weakened.

Rafael stepped back. An inch. "I'm sorry. I… I didn't mean to get carried away. I don't think I could look Father Ramires in the eye if we… *you know*… right before our meeting." He planted a chaste kiss on my cheek. "I'll make it up to you when we get to the hotel." He helped me into the Porsche before climbing behind the wheel.

I took a deep breath and slowly released it.

Rafael's hand raked through his hair. He glanced at me worriedly, and we both burst out laughing.

I relaxed into the buttery soft seats. "What time did you get off work last night?"

He slid the key into the ignition. "I didn't get home until three o'clock this morning. Did you sleep on the plane?"

"A little. Not much." I felt fatigued more often than not. I would have thought I'd be sleeping better after securing the grant, but I tossed and turned when I slept alone. I missed sleeping with Rafael.

He eased out of the parking garage. "Did you submit your midterm papers?"

I breathed a small sigh of relief. "Yes. I'm done with midterms. I just need to get through this training in Sierra Leone so I can start writing my final papers. I'd like to submit my remaining coursework early, so I can focus on our wedding."

"Once we firm up the menu for the rehearsal dinner, we're done. Everything else has already been taken care of." He turned onto the highway.

"I know it's your birthday, but I'd like to go shopping tomorrow. I want to find amethyst earrings and necklaces for my bridesmaids. Have you thought about what you're giving the groomsmen for their gifts?"

He looked thoughtful. "Monogrammed cufflinks?"

I nodded my approval. "I'd like to take you out to dinner tomorrow night, just the two of us, so we can celebrate your birthday."

The Porsche sped by the post-apocalyptic looking buildings that dotted the outskirts of town. "What about Kadyn and Jase?"

"I've already warned them. I want you all to myself tomorrow night." I tried not to smile over the little white lie.

"Would you like me to make a reservation?"

"Nope. I've already made a reservation," I answered smugly.

Comforted by his presence, I drifted off to sleep.

* * * * *

"Wake up, sleepy head."

"Ten more minutes," I pleaded without opening my eyes.

"The sooner we meet with Father Ramires, the sooner we can head to the hotel," he stated enticingly.

My eyes opened on a sigh. "I need coffee." I rifled through the computer bag so I could retrieve my workbook.

"I'll see if I can scrounge some up." Sadly, Monserrate Palace didn't have a café or a restaurant like Pena Palace. Rafael unfolded himself from the car. He strode to the passenger side, tugged the door open, and extended his hand. "Milady."

Now how could I be grumpy with that? "Why thank you, kind sir." I smiled and reached for his hand.

Rafael popped the hood so he could retrieve his workbook, a blanket, picnic basket, and thermos from the trunk.

"Brunch," I gushed. "I just fell in love with you all over again!"

He tucked the thermos and our workbooks inside the picnic basket before slinging the blanket over his arm. "I thought we could picnic by the pond."

Father Ramires was leaning against one of the columns

overlooking the pond. He was wearing the same white collar, black shirt, black jacket, and pants he wore the first time we met him. He looked remarkably at peace when he clasped our hands. "Rafael, Kristine, it's wonderful to see you again." His eyes swept over the expansive grounds. "You have chosen a beautiful wedding venue."

"Are you sure you don't mind performing the ceremony so early in the morning?" I inquired worriedly.

"Not at all," Father Ramires assured me. "Now tell me, where do you envision the ceremony?"

We walked toward the front of the palace while Rafael explained. "We'd like to be married in front of the fountain. There's a trail hidden behind those trees where Kristine and her bridesmaids can move unseen from the back of the palace, so they can enter behind our guests once everyone is seated. The palace staff have arranged for the women to dress in a room near the back of the palace. We don't want to see each other before the wedding, so the groomsmen and I have been assigned a room near the front. We'll enter from the staircase on the left."

He stopped in front of the fountain. "Will your father be escorting you down the aisle?"

Rafael and I hadn't really discussed this. "My parents are attending the wedding, and we're marrying with their consent, but I'd like to walk down the aisle by myself since I'm the one giving Rafael my heart."

Father Ramires smiled. "The question of who gives away the bride is not permitted in a Catholic ceremony even when the bride's father walks her down the aisle. We believe the bride and groom should give themselves to one another of their own free will, not at the will of others. So I admire your decision to walk down the aisle by yourself."

Rafael beamed. "So do I."

He quietly considered the two of us. "Would you like to receive communion during the ceremony?"

My eyebrows shot up in surprise. "I didn't think I could receive communion in the Catholic Church." I joined Father Ramires's church as a non-Catholic member when we met last month. Although our beliefs were closely aligned, I was still Lutheran, not Catholic.

He patted my arm reassuringly. "You are a member of my flock, and we share the same shepherd. As long as you fast and make your confessions before the wedding, you can both receive communion during the ceremony."

Tears welled in my eyes. "That would mean the world to me." I had never shared communion with my first husband or with Michael, both of whom were Catholic. This would be a first for me. I loved that it was happening with Rafael.

Rafael wrapped his arm around me. "We would cherish the opportunity."

Father Ramires noted the picnic basket and the blanket still dangling from Rafael's arm. He started toward the pond. "You should stop by the church a couple of days before the ceremony so that I may receive your confessions and offer the sacrament of reconciliation. Have you been praying together?"

I smiled. "Every night… unless one of us is on an overnight flight. I really treasure that time with Rafael. Since we're apart more often than not, it sheds light on the issues troubling his heart."

Rafael held my arm as we made our way down the stairs. "I enjoy praying when we're together. I believe it has strengthened our relationship with one another and with God."

"Praying always does." Father Ramires led us across the large swath of lawn.

Rafael spread the blanket near the edge of the pond. We settled onto the blanket while he dug through the picnic basket. He pulled three coffee mugs, pastries, and a container of berries from the basket.

Father Ramires reached for our hands. We bowed our heads as he led us in prayer. "Bless us, Heavenly Father, and these thy gifts we are about to receive for the nourishment of our bodies. Through Christ our Lord we pray. Amen."

"Amen," Rafael and I repeated.

I pulled the thermos from the picnic basket.

"May I?" Father Ramires nodded toward the workbooks. "Were there any sections that proved troublesome?"

"Not really." Rafael handed him the workbooks. "That section on managing finances proved very useful. We've opened two joint accounts, one in Portugal and one in the United States. We've already added one another as beneficiaries for our investments, retirement plans, and life insurance policies. I still need to add Kristine as a joint owner for my properties."

I poured each of them a cup of coffee. "We still need wills."

"Benjamim can help us with that." Rafael handed me a white pastry bag filled with *natas*.

Father Ramires pulled a ham and cheese croissant from the other bag. "Have you made any decisions regarding children?"

"We're tentatively planning on three, but we're willing to consider more if the opportunity presents itself." I set two *natas* on my napkin before passing the bag to Rafael.

"You have agreed to raise your children Catholic."

Father Ramires picked at his croissant while reviewing our handwritten responses.

"Our children will be baptized and complete the required sacraments in the Catholic Church," Rafael confirmed.

Father Ramires quietly considered our work. "Very well, then. There are a few matters I would like you to take under advisement before we discuss your wedding vows and practice the ceremony."

Rafael and I exchanged glances.

"I would like you to attend church whether together or apart. I would like you to keep praying together, and I would like you to read the Bible together. This will strengthen your relationship with one another and with God." Father Ramires took a deep breath and blew it out. "This may not be an issue for you, since you live so far apart, but I would be remiss if I did not advise you to abstain from sex. Please honor one another by waiting until you are fully united in the sacrament of marriage."

My cheeks heated while Rafael's face sheeted white. Our plans to reserve a room were promptly tossed aside.

* * * * *

Rafael eyed the black satin sheets uncomfortably. "Maybe I should sleep on the couch."

I joined him on the other side of the bed. "We can still hold one another. We're fully capable of sleeping together while abstaining from sex."

He gently caressed my face. "I'm so sorry, Kristine. I should have respected you instead of seducing you like some desperate fool. Will you forgive me for treating you so poorly?"

"You haven't treated me poorly. You've treated me like gold. Everything we've done, I've done willingly. I regret that we didn't wait, but I shoulder that blame." I planted a kiss in the center of his hand when he cupped my face. "Of course, I forgive you, but I must ask that you forgive me too. I never meant to hurt you or to demean our relationship with my indiscretions."

Rafael pulled me into his arms. "I hardly think that requires my forgiveness when Kadyn and Michael came before me. You haven't hurt me, and you haven't sullied our relationship. Our relationship is everything I dreamed of and more."

I swallowed. Hard. "I crossed the line with Maxim. Can you forgive that?"

His eyes captured and held mine. "I'll admit, your willingness to put up with his advances has hurt at times. I understand there were some extenuating circumstances. Still, it means a lot that you would ask my forgiveness for this. Yes. I forgive you, Kristine."

I sank against his chest. "Thank you."

He kissed the top of my head. "Sleep well, my love."

My jaw dropped when he strode from the room.

* * * * *

My nose twitched. I smelled bacon, coffee, and something I couldn't quite put my finger on... something... *floral?* My eyes popped open. A stunning display of white roses and fresh lavender filled a crystal vase on the nightstand. A white envelope sat propped against the vase. I broke the seal and read the inscription.

*Kristine, there is no me without you… for every last
one of my dreams, my hopes, and heart reside in you.
Happy anniversary, my love. Always and forever,
Rafael.*

The handwriting blurred. I'd been so immersed in work,
in school, and Maxim's pipeline that I'd completely forgotten
Rafael's birthday marked our one year anniversary.

I fell back against the bed. Pinpointing our anniversary
wasn't easy. Rafael served as my bodyguard before we even
met. We became friends, and then? Our relationship evolved
into something far more difficult to comprehend. He
breathed life into me after the attempted drowning. He
served as my guardian angel while I mourned the loss of my
child. He fell in love with me long before I fell in love with
him. Still, he denied his feelings. He encouraged Michael to
mend our relationship because he thought it would make me
happy. After waiting five months, he decided he'd had
enough.

One year ago today, Rafael confessed his love for me. He
staked his claim on my heart. Dating proved tumultuous.
Michael's death nearly ripped us apart. Rafael pieced together
my broken heart, and yet here we were living an ocean apart.
Like angry waves during a violent storm, life kept throwing us
together and tearing us apart.

Still, my guardian angel, who was really a knight, was
commandeering a palace where he planned to make me his
wife, all while slaying the monsters who preyed on vulnerable
children at the Casa Pia Orphanage. Violence and tragedy
marred our pasts, but Rafael was still fighting for the happy
ending that all fairytale romances promised. What gift could I
possibly give to a man like that?

If the smell of bacon was any indication, Rafael was in the kitchen cooking breakfast. Kadyn and Jase were staying with us, and Rafael's surprise birthday party was less than twelve hours away. I sifted through some extremely limited options before settling on an anniversary gift that Rafael might consider romantic and thoughtful. I texted Eva, followed up with a phone call, and breathed a small sigh of relief when it actually proved feasible. I buried my nose in the fragrant bouquet and forced myself from bed.

Kadyn and Jase were sitting at the breakfast bar. They were deeply engrossed in a conversation about Sierra Leone when I padded into the kitchen. Rafael was facing the stove, so I planted a kiss in the center of his back. "Thank you for the flowers."

He turned and folded me in his arms. "Happy anniversary."

I rolled onto my tiptoes so I could kiss him on the lips. "Happy birthday. Do you have to work today?"

He shook his head. "No. I need to pack for Sierra Leone. Other than that, I'm free. Would you like to go shopping?"

"Maybe," I conceded. We still had to purchase gifts for our groomsmen and our bridesmaids. "I would like to treat you to a heated stone massage at eleven o'clock if you're free."

His eyes sparked with interest. "Will you be joining me?"

I nodded.

He grinned. "I'm all in then."

I stole a piece of bacon when Rafael began scrambling the eggs.

"You're not arguing?" Jase inquired over the top of his coffee.

311

I nearly choked on the bacon. "Why would we be arguing?"

He jerked his head toward the living room. "Why else would Rafael sleep on the couch?"

Kadyn's eyebrows rose.

I laughed while Rafael and I exchanged glances. "Rafael doesn't want to sleep with me before we're married."

Jase looked stunned. "But…"

"Father Ramires has advised otherwise," Rafael answered drily.

Jase rubbed his prickly jaw. "Where are you going to sleep in Sierra Leone?"

Rafael groaned. Judging from the pained expression on his face, he hadn't thought that through.

I topped off his coffee. "Surely, we can share a room."

He bit his bottom lip.

My eyes widened. "There are two beds in the room."

"I can share a room and *not* sleep with her," Jase offered, "so you don't… *you know*... burn in hell."

Kadyn snorted orange juice out of his nose.

* * * * *

Rafael gaped at me. "Guilty? There's a restaurant named Guilty within a stone's throw of my flat? How could I not know that?"

I scanned the storefronts, searching for the sign. "Because it's new. Eva claims the chef is famous… someone named Olivier."

Rafael slowed. "Chef Olivier as in Olivier da Costa?"

I smiled. "Yes. That's it. Have you heard of him?"

Rafael laughed. "Yes. Chef Olivier is one of the most

successful restaurateurs in Lisbon. His food is phenomenal."

My smile widened. "Good, then we're in for a real treat." I admired his attire from the corner of my eye. Rafael was wearing black slacks, a crisp white dress shirt sans tie, and a brand new pair of Italian dress shoes. He looked like he'd stepped off the cover of GQ Magazine with his five o'clock shadow and his lightly tousled hair. I was wearing a black cocktail dress with lace bolero sleeves and heels that were way too high for me. The stiletto heels had proven downright treacherous against the tiny mosaic tiles that formed the sidewalk, which is why Rafael maintained a death grip on me.

Rafael stopped in front of the restaurant. A pulsing, contemporary beat greeted us when he opened the door. A long line of people separated us from the bouncer who was sitting on a stool at the far end of the hallway. Cocktail dresses, high heeled shoes, slacks, and dress shirts were standard attire. The bouncer waved us through after checking our names off the list.

I took one step inside the restaurant and froze. A large, semi-circular cocktail bar sat in front of us. The bartenders were shaking martinis, drizzling champagne over long-stemmed fruity looking drinks, smiling, and dancing around one another while filling drink orders. A DJ sat to their right, spinning the type of music you'd expect from a dance club… only there wasn't a dance floor.

Flames leapt through large stainless steel ovens in the open concept kitchen to our right. A ritzy looking lounge sat between the kitchen and the cocktail bar. Panels from wooden wine crates covered the far wall. Cowhides lay scattered across the bare cement floor between plush brown leather couches, contemporary chairs, and tables. Another seating area sat to our left between the cocktail bar and the outdoor patio.

I spotted Kadyn and Chief D'Souza before the hostess returned from seating the other guests. Rafael was still admiring the décor, so I tugged on his arm. "This way."

He hesitated until he saw Chief D'Souza. "You planned a surprise party?"

I grinned. "Turnabout is fair play."

He stopped just short of our table. "I've never had a surprise party."

I kissed his cheek. "This is long overdue, then."

He pulled me in for a hug. "I love it."

"*Feliz aniversário!*" Chief D'Souza greeted cheerily.

"*Obrigado, Comandante.*" Rafael reached for his hand, but the police chief gave him a hug instead.

Chief D'Souza was still chuckling when he pressed a kiss against my cheek. "Kristine, this is my wife, Mariana. Mariana, this is Rafael's fiancé, Kristine."

"Hi, Mariana. Thank you for coming." I paused uncertainly. I wasn't sure whether to extend my hand or kiss her cheek.

She kissed my cheek. "I'm sorry I missed you at Christmas. I would have joined Leandro at the orphanage, but I was in Porto, caring for my mother."

I stepped back so Rafael could greet her. "I hope your mother is feeling better. Perhaps you can join us this year?"

Mariana smiled as he kissed her cheek. "I would love to. We're so pleased this has become an annual event."

"The officers and their wives still talk about the gift wrapping party," Chief D'Souza remarked. "Such a brilliant idea and a heartwarming experience for everyone involved."

Benjamim slapped Rafael on the back. "*Feliz aniversário, meu amigo!*" They bantered in Portuguese.

Eva joined me. She was wearing a red cocktail dress that hugged her curves in all the right places. Her bottom lip jutted out in an adorable pout. "Kristine, when will you move to Lisbon for good? I miss shopping with you."

Kadyn frowned.

"We'll be dividing our time between both countries," I assured him while kissing Eva's cheek. "Have you met my friend, Kadyn?"

She linked arms with me. "Yes. Jase introduced us."

Jase shook Rafael's hand. "Happy birthday, old man."

I wondered how much younger Jase could possibly be when Rafael was only thirty-three.

Eva tugged me toward the bar. "I've been dying to try their sangria. I heard they make it with champagne." She ordered seven glasses for our table when she learned they didn't offer it in a pitcher or carafe.

I ordered a Sprite for Kadyn.

The bartender scooped a handful of berries, a crushed mint leaf, a cinnamon stick, and ice into each glass. He poured Sprite, vodka, brandy, rosé wine, cranberry juice, and grenadine on top of the ice before topping everything off with champagne.

I shook my head, thoroughly impressed. "That's got to be the most elaborate sangria I've ever seen." We were sampling the fruit laden concoction when Rafael joined us. I handed him a glass. "You have to try this."

He brushed a kiss against my temple before trying the drink. "Sangria." He hummed appreciatively.

I barked out a laugh. "Sangria... on crack."

We carried the drinks back to our table, where our friends were just getting settled into their seats. I sat between Rafael and Kadyn. Eva joined Benjamim and Mariana on the opposite side of the table. Chief D'Souza sat at the head of the table, and Jase sat opposite him.

A waitress stopped by with menus. She explained how to use the small push button console to request additional service before fading into the crowd.

"Check this out." Kadyn slid his menu in front of me.

"It's printed in English." I smiled. "Most restaurants in Lisbon print their menus in a variety of languages."

He tapped on the section listing their pizza.

I read the first few items and gasped.

Kadyn laughed.

"Check this out." I elbowed Rafael.

He read the menu and laughed. "Well, that certainly seems fitting."

Eva eyed us curiously.

"Look at the pizza," I told her. "They're named hell, desire, seduction…" I read the rest of the list to myself.

Benjamim peered at his menu. "Anyone want to join me in hell?" Hell was a thin crust pizza with three types of sausage, a variety of peppers, and a spicy sauce.

"Hell sounds good," Chief D'Souza agreed, "but I want to try one of their gourmet burgers first."

"How funny," I mused. "Everything on this menu can be considered a guilty pleasure."

I don't know whether to order pizza or pasta," Eva complained. "Everything sounds so tempting."

We chose a variety of appetizers, pushed the button on the console, and placed our orders.

Chief D'Souza raised his glass. "I'd like to propose a toast. Mariana and I have long considered Rafael our son. We are so proud of the man he has become. So, here's to a remarkable young man, whose good deeds now span two continents."

There were murmurs of agreement all around. We tapped our glasses and drank to Rafael.

He leaned over and kissed my cheek. "Thank you."

I pressed an envelope into his hand. "You haven't opened your present yet."

He eyed the envelope uncertainly.

"Open it," I encouraged. Everyone else was busy talking.

He read the card before opening the certificate I'd tucked inside. "You arranged for me to race an Indy car?"

The table suddenly quieted.

My cheeks heated. "Yes. I've arranged for you and two of your friends to race Indy cars at the Richmond International Raceway. They offer some instruction before setting you loose on the track."

A boyish grin played on his face. "I love it."

"I figured, what with the Porsche, the Enzo, and the Vyrus," I teased.

He eyed Kadyn and Jase. "I don't suppose either of you would want to join me?"

Jase choked on his drink. "No way am I passing that up."

"I don't know," Kadyn waffled. "That could prove embarrassing for you."

Rafael laughed. "I'm going to make you eat those words, right after you eat my dust on that racetrack."

* * * * *

I squinted against the early morning sun. I couldn't believe I'd forgotten my sunglasses. The temperature in Sierra Leone was in the low eighties. There was a decent breeze and a teensy amount of humidity. Still, goosebumps pricked my skin because our driver had his air-conditioning cranked all the way up.

The truck in front of us veered right. "Absolutely not," Rafael growled. I couldn't gauge his expression because he was wearing mirrored lenses, but he appeared to be referring to the rusted ferry docked at the end of the street. The dilapidated vessel was listing to one side.

Rafael had acquired his disagreeable mood at the airport when we were bum rushed by prospective attendants hoping to earn a tip. He'd caught three complete strangers sifting their fingers through my hair while he was momentarily distracted by all the men attempting to assist us. When our driver, Momka, stumbled across us, he shooed the other men away. After the hair petting fiasco, all four men walked in a tight formation around me with Momka leading the way. Sadly, this drew even more attention.

I eyed the crowded vessel and the long line of vehicles idling in front of us. "The ferry takes one hour. The road is much longer."

"Dee road between dee airport and Freetown is treacherous and requires six hours," Momka confirmed. His voice held a melodic lilt. He carefully articulated each word, but his "th" sounded more like a "d," and his "r's" were barely audible.

"That ferry doesn't look safe," Jase countered. "Maybe we should rent a speed boat."

"A water taxi will be more to your liking," Momka replied. "Dee speedboats will make you wet."

"What will we do about Momka's vehicle?" I persisted.

"Please, do not worry about me. I can drive you to dee water taxi and take dee ferry to Aberdeen. Dee hotel can send a shuttle to retrieve you from dee boat station if you do not wish to wait for me. Dee water taxi is dee safest way to travel," Momka assured me.

"Thank you, Momka. Please allow me to compensate you for the inconvenience." Rafael handed Momka fifty thousand Leones.

Momka eased the vehicle out of line. "My cousin operates a water taxi at dee udder end of dee terminal. I promise he will take good care of you. Dee water taxi requires only a dirty minute journey." He eyed the branches swaying on a nearby tree. "It may be a bumpy ride, but he will offer you a fair price."

Rafael and I exchanged glances. I presumed "dirty" meant "thirty" with Momka's accent.

"I will call dee Radisson to ensure a shuttle is waiting for you in Aberdeen." Momka handed each of us his business card. "I should arrive at dee hotel in two hours. You may call me at any time. Your colleagues have ensured my availability for dee entire week." He put a lot of effort into pronouncing his "h's" but not his "r's." For some reason, that made me smile.

Momka's cousin was very accommodating. He loaded our luggage onto the bright yellow water taxi before helping us step onto the boat. Rafael paid extra so we wouldn't have to share the taxi with anyone else. I'd been looking forward to observing local customs and listening to the dialect, but I wasn't about to argue after what had transpired at the airport.

"Kadyn and I are going to purchase SIM cards and the other items you requested after we're checked in at the hotel. Do you mind if we ask Momka to drive?" Jase had to yell in order to be heard over the boat.

"That's fine," Rafael replied. "We're going to sleep for a

couple of hours. We'll eat at the hotel restaurant around noon. You're welcome to join us. We're touring the university at two o'clock with Cory, Sammi, and Shae. Brogan and Aidan are going with us, so you two can stay at the hotel and get some sleep."

Jase nodded.

Kadyn didn't look tired. He looked excited.

I burrowed beneath Rafael's arm. I was having a difficult time keeping my eyes open. None of us slept last night. Instead, I briefed Kadyn and Rafael on Sierra Leone. We reviewed the training manual so they could identify areas where they could help. The first chess match began shortly after Kari served breakfast. The guys were talking so much smack, sleep proved futile after that.

The water taxi drew closer to Aberdeen. The city center was far more developed than I'd anticipated. I eyed the trees struggling to survive among the odd conglomeration of buildings. They seemed to fare better along the hillsides. If I squinted, I could make out the shanty towns on the outskirts of town.

We docked at the boat station a few minutes later. Momka's cousin assisted us with the luggage before attempting to carry me off the boat. I thought he was offering me his hand, but he wrapped his arm around me instead.

"What are you doing?" Rafael demanded. He grasped the man's arm while tugging me closer.

Momka's cousin looked confused. "I am carrying dee lady off dee boat."

Rafael seemed agitated so I forced a soothing tone. "I'm fine. I don't need any help."

He tried reasoning with Rafael. "I assure you, dis is customary. I do not want any passengers falling in dee river, least of all dis lady. She will get hurt." He eyed my heels accusingly.

I glanced at the dramatically tailored wrap dress and the three inch heels I'd so carefully selected. Did I look incompetent?

"I'll help her off the boat," Rafael responded.

Momka's cousin scowled. "Dee wind is blowing, and dee waves are rough."

While they argued, I climbed onto the pier using my own two feet. Well... Kadyn assisted me.

The hotel shuttle was idling at the boat station, as promised. We loaded our luggage onto the shuttle and climbed aboard. A motorcycle carrying five passengers crept by, just before we turned onto the main road. A tiny white car veered in front of us. The occupants had stacked so many baskets on top of the car, they'd nearly doubled its height. As if that weren't impressive enough, three gangly kids sat perched on top of the baskets, holding on for dear life.

Our driver dodged several potholes. There were so many, he eventually gave up. The streets were crowded and narrow. Most were in need of repair. We were caught in stop and go traffic, which I found odd because there weren't any traffic lights. Driving appeared to be a lawless endeavor for the most part. There were no sidewalks, so pedestrians were walking in the street. If an individual drifted anywhere near our vehicle, our driver would lay on the horn. He really liked honking his horn.

Jase tapped Rafael on the shoulder. He was sitting in the third row. "Vehicles must have the right of way here. Have you noticed? Our driver speeds up every time a passenger crosses in front of him." Jase wasn't kidding. People were quite literally running for their lives.

I studied the pedestrians. The men seemed to prefer button down shirts, khaki shorts, loose cotton pants, or jeans. The women were wearing long dresses or skirts with geometric designs. Most of the women tied scarves around their hair. No wonder the men were petting my hair. They probably thought I was flashing them. I added hair scarves to my shopping list, although I questioned how that might look with silk blouses and pencil skirts.

I tucked the shopping list back inside my purse before peering out the window again. Nearly every woman was carrying something on her head. Many were balancing three or four packages without using their hands. It was as if the packages had been cemented onto their heads. Not a single woman lost her bundle when our driver tried to mow her down. He laughed as if it were all in good fun.

The driver and I were about to have a serious falling out, but he came to an abrupt stop in front of our hotel. I gaped at the stunning hotel… the palm trees… the tropical flowers… and the pristine beach. This was a marked improvement over our accommodations in Simferopol.

"Welcome to dee Radisson Blu Mammy Yoko Hotel," our driver announced cheerfully.

The doorman intervened when we tried to collect our luggage. "Please. Dee bellmen will retrieve your dings."

My heels clicked across the marble lobby. I stopped to speak with the concierge while Rafael and Jase checked in at the reception desk. Kadyn joined me. "You have a beautiful hotel. Is there a story behind the name?"

A bright white smile flashed against his ebony skin. "Yes. Names are very important in Sierra Leone. Dee Radisson Hotel was named after dee Queen of Senehun, Mammy Yoko, who helped bring peace to dee Lpaa Mende region. To dis day, dee Radisson Blu Mammy Yoko Hotel draws peacekeepers from all over dee world."

I extended my hand. "My name is Kristine. I work for Seeds for Peace."

He clasped my hand. "See? I speak dee trude. My name is Emmanuel, which means 'God is wid us.' Do you know dee meaning behind your name?"

I shook my head. "No, sadly, I don't."

His smile widened. "Kristine means 'follower of Christ.'"

My shoulders relaxed. "I like that." I tucked my hand in the crook of Kadyn's arm. "This is my friend, Kadyn."

He shook Kadyn's hand. "I do not know dee meaning behind your name, but I will find out. Where are your people from?"

Kadyn chuckled. "Chicago, Illinois."

Emmanuel frowned. "Where are your ancestors from?"

"A few places, but mostly Cameroon." Kadyn looked thoroughly amused.

Emmanuel nodded. "I will find dee meaning behind your name."

"I see you've made a new friend," Jase mused from directly behind me.

I grinned. "Emmanuel, this is my fiancé, Rafael, and my friend, Jase."

He shook their hands. "I am not familiar wid dis name, Jase, but dee Archangel Rafael is considered dee supreme healer in dee angelic realm. Rafael is God's healer."

Rafael's eyes widened with surprise. "My mother explained the meaning behind my name when I was a little boy. She often encouraged me to live up to my name."

"You are Portuguese?" Emmanuel surmised.

Rafael nodded. I could see the wheels turning in his

head. Emmanuel was so unexpected.

"A Portuguese explorer, Pedro de Cintra, named dis country Serra Lyoa," Emmanuel revealed.

"Lion range," Rafael translated. "I know very little about Pedro de Cintra. You have inspired me to learn more."

"We should all aspire to learn more." Emmanuel smiled. "If dere is any ding I can do to make your stay more enjoyable, please let me know."

Rafael shook his hand again. "Thank you, Emmanuel."

I linked arms with Rafael as we walked away. "What an intriguing man."

"What inspired you to speak with him?" Rafael held the door as we boarded the elevator.

"This hotel has such a unique name. I wanted to know the story behind it." I pulled the shopping list from my purse and handed it to Jase.

"Well?" Rafael pressed the button for the fourth floor.

I glanced at his reflection in the mirror. "They named the hotel after the Queen of Senehun because she brought peace to this region."

Rafael smiled. "Well, that certainly seems fitting."

"The sunglasses I can do. I'm not buying hair scarves," Jase growled.

"Suit yourself." I shrugged. "You're the one who has to fight off all the men trying to pet my hair."

Kadyn chuckled.

"Fine," Jase muttered, "but I don't want to hear any complaints if you don't like the color or the patterns I pick out."

"You won't hear any complaints from me." I rested my head on Rafael's shoulder. All the adrenaline I'd acquired through the chaotic airport, the bumpy boat ride, and the harrowing drive dissipated all at once. I was stifling a yawn when the elevator dinged.

"I've got you," Rafael whispered. He scooped me into his arms. Within minutes, he was tucking me beneath the most luxurious sheets. "Sleep well, my love."

"God is with us," I whispered sleepily.

"That he is," Rafael agreed. My archangel lay on top of the sheets while cradling me in his wings.

* * * * *

"So what do you think?" I pushed against one of the desks, but it wouldn't budge.

Cory shook his head. "I don't know. This isn't at all what I expected."

"Do we have to use this room?" Shae frowned. "Maybe there's another room where the desks aren't bolted down."

A broken tile slid beneath my foot.

Sammi caught me. "Kri!"

"Sorry," I murmured.

Rafael obliterated the distance between us. "This building isn't even remotely safe."

He wasn't wrong. The floor, the ceiling, walls, and stairs were crumbling around us. The electricity had flickered off twice since we arrived. Fourah Bay College, once touted as Sierra Leone's ivory tower, was bordering on uninhabitable. Dr. Jalloh, head of the Peace and Conflict Studies Department, revealed the dorms, which he called hostels, were so badly vandalized after the last student election that students could no longer live on campus. The university banned student elections after that, so there was no student government to advocate for improvements.

Shae jumped when loud voices echoed down the hall. "I hope Dr. Jalloh is okay." Three students had rushed into the room, shortly after we arrived, begging him to help break up a fight.

Jase peered down the hall. "I think we should wait outside." Kadyn and Jase had decided to forego sleep so they could inspect the campus and evaluate the security risks.

Rafael noted our new location on the chalkboard so Dr. Jalloh would know where to find us.

I followed Jase down the cement stairs. "Why don't we hold the training outside? The campus grounds seem nice enough."

"I think that's a great idea," Shae echoed behind me. "We can purchase rugs for everyone to sit on and donate them to the university when we're done."

Cory didn't weigh in until we stepped outside. "We're two weeks away from their rainy season. Any idea what the weather is supposed to be like?"

Kadyn walked backwards while studying the building. "They're not expecting any rain. Mostly sunny, upper seventies, and low humidity."

Brogan and Aidan joined us. They'd been walking the perimeter while we were inside. They remained close after speaking with Rafael.

Shae eyed the busy street. "The other side might be quieter."

We walked to the side furthest from the street. There was a wide swath of grass, but it was strewn with litter. We stopped short when we caught sight of the hostels hiding behind the building. The broken and boarded up windows proved deeply unsettling. This was unlike any vandalism I'd ever seen. Someone had set out to destroy this university.

"What's that smell?" Shae covered her nose.

Jase frowned. "Sewage, maybe?"

Sammi smacked Cory's arm. "Sorry, honey. I didn't want that mosquito to get you."

Rafael and I exchanged glances. "Did you remember your anti-malarial medicine?" I asked.

He nodded. "You?"

"Yes," I assured him. "Kadyn?"

He nodded while turning in a slow circle. "I think it's safer inside."

We returned to the front of the building, where a disheveled Dr. Jalloh was searching for us. "I dought maybe you had returned to dee hotel."

"No. We were thinking about holding the training outside. The weather is nice, and we really like the view," Cory answered politely.

Dr. Jalloh considered the view. "Dere will be far more students on campus tomorrow. Dis will make it difficult for your students to focus if you are outside."

I forgot today was Sunday. No wonder there were so few students milling about.

Shae fidgeted nervously. "Is there another classroom we could use? We would like to seat our students in a circle. We've found this helps promote dialogue and improve student participation."

Dr. Jalloh sighed. "When fights break out between dee Blacks and Whites…" He paused when he heard our collective intake of breath. "In Sierra Leone, dese terms do not represent skin color. Dey represent political ideologies. Dee Whites hold a European worldview and align wid dee APC, which is mostly comprised of dee Temne and Limba ethnic groups from dee north. Dee Blacks practice hard line

327

Africanism and align wid dee SLPP, which is mostly comprised of dee Mende from dee south. Dare is a great deal of animosity between dese political groups. Desks or chairs may be drone if dee wrong person enters dee classroom first."

My eyes widened. I'd been mapping conflicts in mining communities when our students could barely tolerate one another? I could see the wheels turning in Cory's head. There were going to be some last minute changes to our agenda. "Are students from both groups attending our training?" I inquired hesitantly.

Rafael squeezed my hand. "I'm going to make a phone call." I watched him walk away, curious as to who he might be calling.

"Yes," Dr. Jalloh answered. "Bod groups require dis training so dey can learn how to resolve deir differences drew more peaceful means."

"Is there an even split among our students?" Sammi asked. We were expecting twenty-four students.

"Yes. I was trying to avoid a power imbalance when I selected dee students for dis training," Dr. Jalloh confirmed.

"That should help," Cory agreed.

I eyed Dr. Jalloh uncertainly. I couldn't imagine university students throwing chairs at one another. Nor could I erase those vandalized hostels from my mind. "These groups have been fighting for power and control on your campus. Everywhere they look they are reminded of the violence they have suffered at the hands of the other group. We cannot expect an open dialogue from students who are afraid to enter a classroom. We need to conduct this training on neutral ground."

Rafael rejoined the group. "I just spoke with Emmanuel.

There is a conference room available at the hotel. We can use the hotel shuttle to transport students from the university if that would help."

"That's perfect!" Shae exclaimed.

"We're staying at the Radisson Blu Mammy Yoko Hotel. Are your students familiar with Mammy Yoko's efforts to bring peace to the Lpaa Mende region?" I inquired curiously.

"Yes," Dr. Jalloh answered. "My students will view dis as a great honor. Dey will conduct demselves respectfully while inside dee Blu Mammy Yoko hotel."

Cory smiled, visibly relieved. "We will send the hotel shuttle tomorrow morning at eight o'clock. We'll provide lunch and return them by five o'clock."

"I regret our university is in such poor condition," Dr. Jalloh fretted. He shook the wrinkles out of his jacket before tugging it back on.

"Maybe we can inspire the students to make some improvements," Sammi offered brightly.

"You are welcome to join us at the hotel anytime your schedule allows," Shae added.

He smiled. "I will stop by tomorrow."

Momka and his cousin, Amad, were standing outside their vehicles when we returned to the parking lot.

Rafael helped me into Momka's SUV. "I'm pleased you moved the training to the hotel." He joined me in the third row.

"Me too," Jase agreed. He joined Kadyn in the back seat.

Everyone else was riding with Amad, so Momka eased out of the parking lot.

I threaded my fingers with Rafael's. "I'm afraid we'll be working through dinner. We weren't aware of the animosity between these students or the violent conflict threatening this university. We need to help these students work through their differences so they can build peace in their community."

"How are you going to do that?" Kadyn asked.

My brow furrowed. "I'm not entirely sure. We have to build some understanding of the theories and the strategies we'll be applying first. We need to model a conflict and a mediation. Something... huge. A conflict even more appalling than the one they're currently immersed in. Something that will really grab their attention. They need an 'a-ha' moment that will force them to connect the dots before we mediate their conflict."

Jase peered into the back seat. "Why do you have to resolve their conflict?"

"These students will serve as role models, trainers, and mediators for their peers. They'll lose credibility if they can't resolve their own conflict." My eyes snagged on the decrepit buildings outside my window. Freetown was a crowded and chaotic city full of contradictions. Despite a highly developed city center, there was a staggering amount of poverty. The street children and the shantytowns broke my heart. The homes in this section of town were lean-tos comprised of thin corrugated metal or plywood walls with no windows or doors.

There were three major slums in Freetown. We were driving by one of them but remained on the outskirts. Momka warned they would throw rocks at our SUV and try to rob us if we ventured any closer. As frightening as that was, I felt it important to bear witness to this poverty so I could better understand the challenges people in Sierra Leone faced.

I handed Momka my passport when the police stopped our vehicle at the immigration checkpoint. There were over a million people living in Freetown. Most were refugees displaced during their civil war. They'd spent their entire lives immersed in violence and poverty. No wonder their average life expectancy was only 45 years old.

"Are you okay?" Rafael whispered.

"Yes. Just thinking." After seeing the university and the shantytown, I felt guilty about our luxurious accommodations. How would our students perceive those accommodations? Would they think we were above spending time at their university?

Momka parked next to a cluster of palm trees when he pulled in front of the hotel. "Will you require my services dis evening?"

"No, thank you," I replied. "We'll be working here at the hotel for the rest of the night."

"You will eat dinner?" he persisted.

"Yes," Rafael answered, "but we'll be eating here at the hotel."

"You should try dee ground nut stew. My cousin is dee chef here dis evening, and ground nut stew is his specialty," Momka announced proudly.

I smiled. I was beginning to think Momka was related to everybody. He must have come from a very large family. "Thanks, Momka, for taking such good care of us."

He beamed at me.

We met the rest of our group inside the hotel. "I'm going to pay for the conference room and the food for our training," Cory informed us. "Let's eat in the restaurant by the pool so we can discuss our agenda and strategize about the training."

"We'll grab a table," Kadyn offered. Sammi and Brogan remained with Cory. The rest of us joined Kadyn.

Emmanuel intercepted us when we crossed the lobby. "You have decided to hold your training here?"

"Yes." Rafael slipped him a tip while shaking his hand. "Thank you for securing the conference room."

A wide, toothy smile brightened his face. "Dis is why I am here." His eyes met Kadyn's. "I have learned dee meaning behind your name."

A single eyebrow rose on Kadyn's face.

"Kadyn means fighter," Emmanuel revealed.

I sucked in a breath. "Kadyn! That's so true. You served in the military, you protect our borders, and you fought to save me!"

Emmanuel looked relieved. He seemed pleased Kadyn was fighting for honorable things. "I have also learned dee meaning behind your name, Jase, but I would like to know dee relationship between you two." His chin rose toward Rafael.

"Rafael hired me to protect Kristine," Jase answered carefully.

"So, dee Archangel Rafael assigned a healer to Kristine, dee woman who follows Christ. I am not surprised." Emmanuel's eyes softened when they met mine. "God has sent two healers and a fighter. You are protected on all sides."

Every time Emmanuel revealed something about our names, something inside of me slid into place. "What about Shae?" She was standing next to Kadyn with her mouth agape.

"I do not know dis name, Shae," Emmanuel apologized, "but I will learn dis for you. You are a peacekeeper too?"

Shae nodded. "Yes. Kristine and I work for the same NGO."

He offered her his hand. "I am Emmanuel, the concierge

for dis hotel."

"It's a pleasure to meet you," Shae murmured sweetly.

"I will look for you tomorrow." Emmanuel bowed before walking away.

"How fascinating," Shae mused.

We continued on into the restaurant. "Can you accommodate a party of nine on the deck?" Kadyn asked the hostess.

She counted out nine menus. "Yes. We can pull two tables togeder if you would like."

The deck offered a stunning view of the beach and the outdoor pool. Rafael and Jase helped our waiter pull two tables together before we ordered our drinks. Sammi, Cory, and Brogan joined us a few minutes later.

We ordered quickly so we could focus on the training. Rafael, Kadyn, and I took Momka's advice and ordered the ground nut stew. Sammi and Shae ordered the potato leaf stew. Cory ordered okra stew, and the rest of the guys ordered a creole dish named *Krin Krin*. We added a couple orders of cassava bread and plantain chips to share before our waitress walked away.

Cory waited for the small talk to die down. "We're going to have to mediate their conflict," he finally announced.

The waitress returned with our drinks. We were trying the palm wine and Star Beer she recommended. Each of us had sparkling water. Kadyn was drinking Sprite, no ice.

"I agree. They won't have any credibility as mediators or trainers if they are embroiled in a violent conflict." Sammi grimaced after tasting the wine.

"We can't squeeze this in without taking something off the agenda." Shae sighed. "I think we should remove secret societies and tribal initiations from the agenda."

I shoved the palm wine aside. The milky drink was far too bitter for me. "I think we should proceed as planned tomorrow morning. Our students should have a good understanding of the theories and the strategies we're applying before we mediate their conflict."

"Agreed," my teammates quickly replied.

"We should change the fishbowl exercise," I opined. The fishbowl exercise was scheduled to take place after the initial instruction, before the students started practicing in simulations. During the fishbowl exercise we formed a small circle inside the student circle so our students could observe us applying the various strategies and techniques.

"So, you don't want to mediate the mining conflict during the fishbowl exercise?" Cory surmised.

I took a breath and slowly released it. "No. I think we should mediate a conflict far more appalling than that. We need to choose a conflict that will prove heart wrenching for them. They need an 'a-ha' moment that will force them to connect the dots between the conflict we are mediating and the conflict they are currently immersed in. The conflict we choose should motivate them to resolve their own conflict."

The waitress delivered the entrees, bread, and plantains.

Sammi reached for the bread. "What do you have in mind?"

I glanced apologetically at Cory, Kadyn, Jase, and Shae. "I want to draw on the darkest time in American history, so they know we aren't judging their country. I want them to understand we've been there, that our country has overcome a similar conflict, and they can do the same."

"Go on," Cory murmured cautiously.

"I want to mediate the segregation of public schools," I confessed.

Sammi leaned forward. "You want to mediate Brown versus the Board of Education?"

I nodded, then cringed when everyone fell silent.

"That could work," Shae mused. "Race, like ethnicity, is tied to identity. Since their political groups are formed on the basis of ethnicity, they are fighting over which ethnic group governs their school, and they're discriminating against one another on the basis of ethnicity with their unwritten rules about who is entitled to walk into the classroom first."

Deep in thought, Cory rubbed his jaw. "Someone on our team would have to argue that blacks should not be allowed to attend white schools, that they should not be treated equally. If our students value their education, they'll be outraged that someone would suggest such a thing. Maybe, if they look beyond their own conflict, at what happened in our country, they'll realize they are on the fast track to making that same mistake. Essentially, this is the same argument their political groups are making… One ethnic group is fit to govern their school while the others are not. That same ethnic group must receive special treatment, such as entering the classroom first, or the nonconformists will be met with violence. What a crock."

Sammi stifled a giggle. "How could they not connect the dots when they refer to their political groups as the Blacks and the Whites?"

"It's risky," I admitted, "and it's going to require some acting on our part. If we really want to get their attention, then Sammi or I will have to say some pretty hateful things… things that are contrary to our beliefs."

Cory nodded. "It's not like Shae or I could argue those points. It has to be someone who is white."

"If this situation were playing out in real life, we'd assign co-mediators whose race or ethnicity mirrored the conflicting parties. We will need a black and a white mediator as well as a black and white student if we're going to model this appropriately," Shae stated. "Think about the advice you would give our students if they were going to mediate the conflict between their two political groups. You'd recommend they co-mediate with a member from each group."

"You're right," Cory agreed.

"I think that's a terrible plan," Rafael interjected. "If Kristine behaves like a racist and acts convincingly enough to drive this point home, those students might think she hates black people. That could make her a target while she's here. The same holds true for Sammi if she argues against equal education for black people."

"We'll make sure the students understand this was an act when we debrief." I knew Rafael was right, but I also knew this conflict would resonate with our students better than any other conflict we could possibly dream up.

"What if Brogan and I act as the white students who are fighting for segregation and Kadyn and Jase act as the black students who are fighting for desegregation? That way, all four of you can mediate the conflict," Aidan suggested.

"I'm game," Jase stated.

"Me too," Kadyn agreed.

"We can't ask you to do that," Cory objected.

"You're not asking, we're offering," Brogan insisted. "I would just ask that you provide the same debrief afterwards, so the students understand this is an act... that neither of us would advocate for such a hateful thing."

Sammi and Cory exchanged worried looks.

Shae bit into a plantain chip. "This wouldn't be the first

country we had to flee when things got ugly."

Kadyn laughed.

Rafael groaned.

"Okay, Sammi and I will write a one page briefing. We'll distribute the briefing to the students so they understand the history behind the conflict. I'd like you two," Cory pointed to Shae and me, "to coach these guys." He gestured toward Brogan, Aidan, Kadyn, and Jase.

"You should include all of the really ugly stuff... the civil war, the KKK, and the church burnings," I replied. "Those students should be horrified before the fishbowl exercise even begins.

Cory nodded his agreement. "We'll proceed with our instruction on theories and strategies tomorrow morning. After we break for lunch, we'll distribute the briefing and begin the fishbowl exercise. If all goes well, we'll mediate their conflict on Tuesday. We'll hold off on the simulations covering vigilante violence and the excessive use of force by law enforcement until we're done mediating their conflict."

"When we mediate their conflict, we should encourage them to mediate from the table," Shae advised. "Each student should bear some responsibility for mediating that conflict. That experience will help them mediate that very same conflict among their peers."

"I couldn't agree more." Suddenly famished, I dug into the ground nut stew. The stew tasted like peanut butter, but there were chunks of tomato, diced chicken, and spices that added a fair amount of heat.

We reflected on the day's events while we ate. Sammi and Cory went to work in the business center shortly after dinner. The rest of us commandeered chairs on the opposite side of the pool so the other hotel guests wouldn't overhear us practicing the fishbowl exercise.

Rafael and I lingered by the pool long after our friends had retired. A few random couples remained on the deck, enjoying the balmy night.

"I love how passionately you fight to right the wrongs in this world," Rafael whispered admiringly. He was sprawled out on a lounge chair, absently caressing my arm while I snuggled against his chest.

"You're the same way." Our entire circle of friends seemed to be hardwired that way.

He drew me to my feet as he stood. "Dance with me."

I eyed the other patrons nervously. "The other guests…"

He tucked my hand against his chest as he began to sway. "… will see two people who are deeply in love sharing a romantic moment."

I relaxed into his arms. I felt exhausted, but I was far too nervous about the training to sleep. "I'm worried about tomorrow."

"Don't be," Rafael whispered. "God's going to work a miracle, just you wait and see."

* * * * *

The tension eased from my shoulders. I loved our hotel room. The glazed porcelain tiles looked like hard wood floors. A large contemporary mural hung above the bed against a dark gray wall. The bed linens were soft and luxurious, the mattress so comfortable I was secretly plotting to take it home with me.

"Well?" Rafael demanded.

"I don't know." I couldn't think. The man was sitting on my bottom massaging my back while I was lying half naked in bed.

His hands dropped to my sides. "Maybe this isn't the best time for a massage."

"No! I... I need a massage." Every muscle in my body ached from that fishbowl exercise. Brogan, Aidan, Kadyn, and Jase took their roles very seriously. They didn't allow Cory or me any slack when we mediated their conflict. Thankfully, Sammi and Shae had joined the conflicting parties so they could demonstrate how to mediate from the table. They shared their parties' positions, but they proved more willing to compromise as the moderates on each side.

Rafael's fingers poured into my shoulders like liquid gold. "Then tell me how you're feeling about today."

"I feel cautiously optimistic. They understood the theories and the strategies we discussed. The fishbowl exercise was a little intense. I thought we might lose some of our students when Kadyn threw that chair." He was so convincing, they'd forgotten it was an act.

"That was your defining moment," Rafael claimed. "I could see the light bulbs clicking on with the vast majority of students. Some looked embarrassed and ashamed."

"I hope that will inspire them to seek change." My eyes slid closed. Rafael's thumbs were coaxing the stress from my lower back. "This massage feels heavenly. Please don't stop."

Rafael chuckled. "What's your plan for tomorrow?"

"We're going to tear down enemy images, establish common ground, and build trust... although not necessarily in that order."

He kneaded my arms. "How do you achieve that?"

I melted into the pillow. "We're going to identify all the interests, values, and needs they have in common. We'll have them share what they respect and admire about one another.

Then, we're going to blindfold them, stand them on a chair, and have them fall back in one another's arms."

His hands stalled. "You cannot be serious."

"As a heart attack." I smiled against the pillow. "We can't mediate their conflict until we change their perspectives on one another. Trust me, the mediation will prove far more effective if we improve their perceptions."

"What's the end goal?" Rafael wondered.

"We're going to ask them to establish some strategies for reducing violence and improving their school," I answered.

He loosened another knot in my shoulder. "What about their political ideologies?"

"Their political ideologies should have no bearing on the quality of their education or the security of their school. If they want to establish a student government, then we'll encourage a power sharing arrangement. If either party feels the need to prove their superiority, then they'll be encouraged to do so through good deeds, not through violence or intimidation."

Rafael laughed. "God, I love the way you think."

I rolled over so I could face him. "I love the way your hands feel on my body. Kiss me."

"Don't tempt me," he warned. "You don't know how enticing it is to have a brilliant, scantily clad peacekeeper pinned beneath me."

I bit back a smile. "There's nothing wrong with kissing. Kissing is perfectly acceptable as long as it doesn't lead to other things." I now knew how Eve felt when she offered Adam the apple.

Rafael linked his fingers in mine before pressing my hands into the pillow. "Then I shall kiss you senseless." He trailed warm, wet kisses along my collar bone, my shoulders, neck, and jaw before delving deep inside my mouth. Within seconds, I was lost in the most intimate kiss I'd ever known.

* * * * *

I popped the lid off the Expo marker. "Do you want to be part of the problem or part of the solution?"

"The solution!" the students exclaimed. I'd posed this question so many times, it had become our new mantra.

My hand hovered over the Post-it easel. "Then I want each of you to identify three things that you *personally* can do to improve your school."

Their hands shot into the air.

Shae called on the students while I recorded their suggestions.

"I can organize a fund raiser dat will enable us to restore dee hostels."

"I can clean up litter."

"I know how to paint."

"I can solicit donations from local businesses."

"I can encourage oder students to help in our university newsletter."

"I can post someding on Facebook."

"I want to start a peer mediation program."

"What about a peer mentoring program?"

"We can do bod!"

I ripped sheet after sheet off the easel. Cory and Sammi posted them at eye level on every wall in the room. Once the ideas were on the table we established committees and strategies for recruiting other students. Our brainstorming session ended the day on such a positive note, the students didn't want to leave.

"We will firm up our plans and establish a timeline for accomplishing your goals in the morning," Cory assured them. "Then, we're going to strengthen your mediation skills. Wear comfortable clothes tomorrow!"

We exchanged glances when the students filed out of the room.

"I can't believe how well that went," Shae whispered.

"Me either," Sammi confessed.

"They were on fire," Cory agreed. "Not a single one of those students wanted to maintain the status quo. They want change. Better yet, they want to *be* that change." His eyes met mine. "Great mantra by the way."

"Thanks." I smiled, thoroughly pleased with how the mediation had gone.

Dr. Jalloh rose from his chair in the back of the room. He'd been silently observing the process with Kadyn, Rafael, and Jase. "Do you have any idea what you have done?"

My teammates and I froze.

His eyes glimmered with unshed tears. "I have never seen my students dis excited. You have inspired a movement, a movement dat could change everyding for our university."

"A great deal of work remains to be done," Cory warned. "Your students are energized now, but they'll become discouraged when challenges arise. Can you identify areas where the faculty, the administration, and the alumni can help?"

Dr. Jalloh nodded. "Yes. I will solicit deir help tonight."

"We'd like to hold a small awards ceremony, acknowledging our students' efforts on Friday. Would it be possible to hold this awards ceremony at the school?" I inquired.

He fished the cell phone from his pocket. "I will see if

dee amphideater is free. May I invite dee media?"

"Not if it puts our students at risk," Sammi replied. "The APC and the SLPP have been frequenting the campus, fueling enemy images, and inciting violence. I'm concerned that our students will face some backlash when these political groups discover they are collaborating with one another." The political groups the students had formed on campus were linked to these larger political groups. Most of our students bore scars from lacerations and cigarette burns as a result of their initiation into these groups. A defection or questions surrounding their loyalty could compromise their ability to secure jobs once they graduate from school.

Dr. Jalloh frowned. "Dis could be a problem eider way. I will consult wid dee provost on dis. I do not wish to put dee students at risk."

"We would love for you to join us tomorrow," Shae said. "Perhaps you can advise the students on how the faculty and the alumni can help."

Dr. Jalloh nodded. He shook our hands and said goodbye.

Rafael, Kadyn, and Jase joined us when Dr. Jalloh walked away.

I gave Rafael a hug. "I'm starving. Are you guys up for an early dinner?"

"Absolutely," Jase answered.

"I could eat," Kadyn agreed.

Rafael tucked me beneath his arm. "Momka recommended a restaurant a few blocks from here. Should we give that a try?"

"Sounds good." Shae reached for her satchel.

"I'll carry that." Kadyn eased the satchel out of her hand and anchored it over his shoulder.

Sammi linked arms with Cory as we filed out the door. "Are we driving or walking?"

"Driving," Jase answered decidedly. He called our drivers while Rafael texted Brogan and Aidan.

Emmanuel waved us over when we entered the lobby. "I have learned dee meaning of Shae's name. Shae means courteous."

Shae's cheeks turned the prettiest shade of pink.

"That fits her well," I assured Emmanuel.

Within minutes we were being seated at Tessa's. Tessa's was owned by Momka's Aunt Theresa. Her son, Ivan, served as her co-chef. Since this was a family owned restaurant, and Momka and Amad were obviously family, they joined us.

I ordered the *Chicken Shawarma,* which was served on pita bread with a fresh cucumber and tomato relish and tahini sauce. Shae ordered grilled chicken with *Jollof Rice* and plantains. Everyone else ordered seafood.

We'd barely placed our orders when Momka and Amad pulled a bunch of board games from a storage closet in the back of the restaurant. They deposited Sorry, Monopoly, Connect Four, and Scrabble on top of our table. "Tonight is game night," Momka announced.

"Dibs on Scrabble!" Shae and I exclaimed.

Kadyn reached for the box. "Rafael, would you like to join us?"

He smiled. "Sure. Why not?"

Sammi sifted through the remaining boxes. "Momka, would you and Amad like to play Sorry with Cory and me?"

"Yes," Amad answered.

"Certainly," Momka agreed.

Brogan eyed Aidan and Jase questioningly.

Jase grabbed the Monopoly box. "I get to be the car."

"As long as I'm the banker," Aidan countered.

Brogan's expression grew pained.

The waiter distributed three baskets of rice bread between the board games.

Sammi shuffled cards while the guys set up their pawns. "Do you want to go to the market tomorrow?"

Shae handed me the bag after counting out her tiles. "I'd like to pick up some souvenirs."

"Me too. Are the markets still open after four o'clock?" I asked Momka.

He nodded. "Yes, dee market is open until six o'clock."

Cory sampled the bread. "When do you want to go to the orphanage?"

"Thursday after the training or Saturday morning appear to be our only options," I noted with a frown. We were flying back to Portugal on Saturday and returning to Virginia on Sunday.

"I'll call the orphanage tomorrow morning to ask which time works best for them," Rafael offered.

I rearranged my tiles while silently scoring my options. "Will you ask how many children they are caring for? I want to make sure we have enough candy for the children at the orphanage before we distribute candy at the market."

Rafael nodded. He was too busy scrutinizing his tiles to respond.

Our food arrived a few minutes later. We settled in to enjoy the traditional Sierra Leonean cuisine and a little friendly competition.

Momka's aunt and his cousin, Ivan, stopped by our table to chat for a little while. They surprised us with Benny cakes for dessert. The atmosphere was so relaxing and fun we vowed to return the very next day.

* * * * *

"Kri?" Shae mewled. We were being swarmed by children in tattered clothes.

"I told you this was a bad idea." Jase was trying to establish some sort of perimeter around me that would keep the street children an arm's distance away. Kadyn was guarding Shae in much the same way.

Rafael chuckled. "They're fine. The candy's almost gone." He snapped another picture with his cell phone.

The children crammed the Starburst, Skittles, and Tootsie Pops inside their mouths. They were thoroughly confused by the Sour Patch Kids, but that confusion morphed into toothy smiles, wide eyes, and squeals of delight. Some of the children followed us through the market but most wandered away once they realized our bags were empty.

The King Jimmy Market was a lively place. Brightly colored umbrellas and corrugated metal shaded the merchants' tables. Still, poverty was reflected in the merchants' faces, in the street children's wary gazes, and in the skeletal frames of the dogs nosing the litter that lined the muddy passageways.

Momka and Amad were serving as our honorary tour guides. Amad led us through a crumbling brick building where additional merchants were selling their wares. "Dee Portuguese built dis market in dee early nineteen hundreds. Dere have been no renovations by dee government since dat time."

Momka diverted us to a nearby tunnel. "King Jimmy Market was not always such a pleasant place. Dis market was once dee center of dee slave trade. Dousands of people were forced into dis tunnel in heavy leg irons and handcuffs."

Rafael and Jase edged closer to me when we entered the gloomy tunnel. Kadyn drew closer to Shae. Brogan and Aidan remained with Sammi and Cory, who were trailing behind us.

Tears pricked my eyes. Centuries later, I could still feel the fear and anguish of the people who were torn from their families and herded like cattle through this cramped space. My heart remained heavy despite the sunlight that greeted us on the other side.

Amad stopped in front of a stone wall overlooking the ocean. "Dee slaves were secured to dis wall so dey could not escape. Dey were forced to stand here for hours even in dee rainy season."

Iron rings remained embedded in the wall. I lifted one of the heavy metal rings. My mind filled with images of people struggling to break free. My shoulders sagged as I began to cry.

Rafael gathered my face in his hands. "We cannot change the past, but we can work to make this world a better place." He brushed my tears away with his thumbs.

We walked in silence down the stone stairs that led to the dock. Narrow weathered boats lined the heavily littered shore. "Dee slaves were led down dese stairs to dee jetty where dey were loaded onto boats to dee Americas," Momka noted solemnly.

We huddled against the harsh reality. There was no denying what had transpired here. Ghostly images of men, women, and children being whipped and caned while forced aboard those boats still haunted this dock. I was both saddened and dismayed by the role our country had played.

Quietly, we followed Momka and Amad back into the market. We purchased dozens of necklaces and bracelets.

Some were strung with polished seashells, others with wooden beads. We purchased spices, vibrant fabrics, reed baskets, and hand carved wooden masks. Momka and Amad encouraged us to haggle on the prices. Not a single one of us could bear the thought. While their shackles were not visible, these people were still enslaved. Poverty was an ugly master, and man was still to blame.

* * * * *

Brogan and Aidan led the training Thursday morning. They taught our students how to read non-verbal communication, assess the conflict environment, and de-escalate conflicts. Rafael, Kadyn, and Jase taught them how to reduce risk and improve personal security. We ran our students through another conflict mapping and simulation so they could practice these new found skills.

I loved seeing how our team meshed. Each of us was working toward improving human security, but in different ways. Like a complex puzzle, we accomplished far greater things than one might anticipate when studying a single piece.

We stopped by Tessa's before driving to the orphanage. Momka's aunt had overheard us discussing the Saint George Orphanage when we returned for dinner Wednesday night. She promised to have enough Benny cakes prepared for all the children if we stopped by before visiting the orphanage. A sugary treat made with sesame seeds and orange rind, Benny cakes tasted more like a sweet, crisp biscuit than a traditional cake.

The orphanage was located on the outskirts of town. Momka and Amad helped us unload the books Rafael had purchased. Unbeknownst to me, he'd been sending Brogan and Aidan out on shopping excursions to purchase books from local bookstores when they weren't participating in the training. They'd acquired nearly two hundred books appropriate for a variety of age groups.

I kissed Rafael on the cheek before grabbing a box. "Thank you for buying the books."

His box appeared weightless when he shrugged. "After seeing how much the children at the Casa Pia Orphanage enjoyed their books, how could I not?"

"I love that you purchased the books from local bookstores," Sammi remarked. "I'm sure that made the bookstore owners very happy, and it helps the local economy."

A woman appeared at the door. She was wearing a long loose-fitting dress. Light blue circles of varying sizes were interspersed throughout the bright blue material. Her hair was hidden beneath a scarf made from the very same fabric. "Welcome. Mr. Garcia?"

Rafael shifted his box so he could shake her hand. "Please, call me Rafael."

"I am Miss Lucee, dee administrator for dee Saint George Foundation Orphanage. Please come in." She held the door while we stepped inside.

Sammi, Shae, and I were wearing the same scarves we used to cover our hair at the market. Momka's aunt made a few minor adjustments when we arrived at the restaurant so they didn't look half bad even though the three of us were wearing blouses and slacks.

Rafael introduced everyone before explaining the boxes. "We brought candy from the United States, books we purchased in Freetown, and Benny cakes from Tessa's Restaurant. The owner, Theresa, is Momka's aunt. She made the Benny cakes herself."

Momka's chest puffed out proudly. "I am sure you will find dey are dee best Benny cakes in town."

Miss Lucee looked pleased. "I would like to wait on dee treats until after dee children have eaten supper. Dee children just finished deir studies. Dey have some time before supper if you would like to distribute dee books."

"Would you mind if the children wrote their names inside the books?" I asked. "We brought enough for everyone. We'll encourage them to share, but we thought it would be nice if each child could keep a book for himself."

She weighed the question carefully. "Yes. Dat would be fine. Do you require pens?"

I smiled gratefully before shaking my head. "We brought pens."

She escorted us to their recreation center. "We currently have one hundred and seventy-five children staying wid us. Dee ages vary from five to fifteen years of age. We do not care for infants here, only school age children. Most are former street children. We feed and clode dem, provide medical care and an education so dey can gain employment and qualify for university when dey are older."

"Thank you for allowing us to meet your children," Shae said respectfully. "We've been working with a lovely group of students from Fourah Bay College. I wonder if they might be interested in mentoring some of your older children."

My eyes widened. "Shae, that's brilliant. They can start their very own Big Brothers Big Sisters program in Freetown! We should give them the contact information for that organization tomorrow."

Cory chuckled. "There you go again, planting seeds."

I grinned. We were, in fact, planting seeds.

The children eyed us warily. They wore clean clothes and solemn faces. These children had not been coddled in any way. Life had hardened them at far too early an age.

The children gave Miss Lucee their undivided attention when she entered the room. "Dese are dee special guests I was telling you about. Dey have brought you gifts. Please treat dem wid dee same respect dat you show me."

Miss Lucee organized the children into seven separate lines, with twenty five children standing in each line. The children's books were boxed separately from the young adult novels, which made things easy. Momka and Amad helped us distribute the books.

We sat and read with the younger children after the books were distributed. The older children seemed a bit more leery of us.

We grew animated after a while. There was a bit of one-upmanship involved when we realized our goofy antics and exaggerated voices were reeling the older children in. They were all in by the time we decided to act out the Three Little Pigs. We reinvented the fable, recruiting some of the children to play additional wolves and pigs until the story took on a life of its own. The children and the staff were laughing by the time our play drew to an end.

* * * * *

Friday was the final day for our training. Sadly, I couldn't remove my head from the toilet long enough to attend the awards ceremony.

Rafael pressed a cool washcloth to my face. "Do you think this is food poisoning?"

"Maybe." I was loathe to blame Momka's Aunt Theresa.

We'd eaten at her restaurant after visiting the orphanage. We enjoyed her place so much, we'd deemed it our home away from home. We'd eaten there three nights in a row.

"You haven't had any ice or tap water?" Rafael prodded.

"No," I answered weakly. I was very careful about drinking bottled water.

"Can you get Cholera from food?" Rafael wondered aloud. He was researching the Cholera outbreak on his phone.

"I haven't eaten any fresh fruit or vegetables. Besides no one else in our group is sick, and we've been eating pretty much the same thing."

He looked unconvinced. "Maybe you picked up a virus at the orphanage."

"In less than twenty four hours?" I shook my head. "It has to be the tiger prawns I ate last night."

He stretched out his legs and pulled me into his arms. "You shared your prawns with me, and I'm fine. I think we should fly out tonight. If this continues on into tomorrow, then you're going to require some medical attention. Lisbon is a far better option than Freetown."

"I don't want to cut the trip short for Kadyn and Jase," I protested.

"We're ready to leave now," Jase announced from just outside the door. "Is she decent?"

I gaped at Rafael.

"She's dressed," he answered. "I gave him a room key in case of an emergency."

My eyes widened. "I didn't even hear him slide the card through the door."

He smoothed my unruly hair back into place. "How could you? You were vomiting."

352

Jase's six foot three frame filled the bathroom doorway. "I have the Emetrol."

I closed my eyes as another wave of nausea taunted me. "What's Emetrol?"

"Anti-nausea medicine." Jase broke the seal on the box and handed the bottle to Rafael. "I'm sorry that took so long. This proved difficult to find."

Rafael filled the cap. "You're both packed?" He handed me the cap.

Jase nodded. "We packed as soon as we heard she was sick. Brogan and Aidan will stay with Sammi and Cory. They're flying back to Virginia tomorrow. Shae wants to fly back with us. She's worried about Kristine."

I drank the capful of medicine and leaned against Rafael's chest. Chills wracked my body while it threatened to reject the medicine. I ran through a mental list of all the things I'd eaten.

Rafael sent a text before scooping me into his arms. "I want you in bed while I pack."

Jase grabbed the wastebasket. "No one else is sick. What do you think this is?"

"Food poisoning would be my guess. Either way, I don't want Kristine seeking medical care here. With the Cholera outbreak, the hospitals aren't safe. I want her back in Lisbon." Rafael glanced at his phone. "The pilot and the flight attendant are ready to leave. Captain Anderson is filing the flight plan now."

Alarms sounded in my head. "There was fresh cucumber and tomato on the *Chicken Shawarma* I ate Wednesday night."

Jase's eyes widened. "You can get Cholera from raw vegetables if they aren't washed properly."

Rafael gritted his teeth as I began to heave.

* * * * *

"Sorry, love, time to buckle up." Rafael bundled me inside the duvet before lifting me from the bed.

My stomach roiled over the sudden movement.

Rafael pressed a bottle of water into my hand. "You're dehydrated. Please, baby, try to drink something." He snapped my seatbelt into place.

"Sorry, guys." I offered Kadyn, Jase, and Shae a half smile before twisting the lid and taking a sip. My stomach objected to the water and the sudden descent.

Rafael rubbed my back while I heaved into a small bag. My stomach was completely empty, so the bag wasn't even necessary.

"How long does food poisoning last?" I'd been vomiting for nineteen hours.

"One, maybe two, days," Kadyn answered.

"Maybe it's the flu." Shae's knee bounced while she chewed her bottom lip.

Rafael felt my forehead, my cheek, and the back of my neck. "She feels clammy."

My stomach lurched when the plane lost altitude.

"My apologies," Captain Anderson stated over the intercom. "We're in for a bumpy ride until we pass through these rain clouds."

Jase's fists clenched against his armrests. "I think you should go straight to the hospital."

I grasped Rafael's arm. "I don't want to go to the hospital. Please? Just let me sleep in your bed tonight. If I'm not better by tomorrow morning, I'll go. I... I just don't want anyone sticking me with needles right now."

He eyed me uncertainly until I burst into tears. "Kristine? Oh, God, please don't cry. I... I won't take you to the hospital tonight."

I breathed a small sigh of relief until we hit turbulence again. My fingers locked around his arm. I was so busy praying for a safe landing, I forgot all about the nausea.

* * * * *

I pulled the handle down on the toilet. I stared at the mini cyclone of water with disgust. All that effort to drink a glass of water wasted. There was no avoiding the hospital now. I pushed off the toilet and swayed.

Rafael caught me. My feet flew out from under me when he lifted me in his arms. "The hospital it is then."

"I'm still in my pajamas," I croaked. I'd ruined my voice hours ago.

"They see naked and half-naked people at the hospital all the time." He yanked a blanket from the bed and wrapped it around me.

"Not me," I whined. "I don't want to be naked in front of a bunch of strangers. I don't care how many degrees they've earned. I don't want my bottom hanging out in one of those raggedy hospital gowns. Don't let them take my panties away, and don't make me wear that godawful gown."

Shae rose from the couch. "You're taking her to the hospital?"

"Finally," Jase growled.

"I'm going with you." Shae grabbed her purse.

Rafael shook his head. "You should stay here unless you want to be quarantined."

"Quarantined?" My head lolled against Rafael's shoulder.

"We've been exposed to all the same people and places. If this is Cholera or Ebola, they may quarantine us," Rafael explained.

"Ebola?" Shae squeaked.

"There's been an Ebola outbreak in Liberia. I don't know that the virus has spread to Sierra Leone, but the hospital may take extra precautions since the two countries border one another." Jase tugged a leather jacket over his shoulders.

"You're going?" Kadyn stood uncertainly.

"Of course." Jase scowled. "I'm her bodyguard. I go where she goes."

"He's my healer," I giggled.

In three long strides, Rafael collected his jacket, cell phone, keys, and a large plastic bowl. He opened the door. "We'll let you know as soon as we learn anything."

"Stop spinning," I whispered.

His eyes cut sharply toward mine. "I'm not moving."

"Hide under the table," I pleaded.

His eyes widened.

"Earthquake," I whimpered.

My body fell limp before he made it to the elevator.

* * * * *

Death. I was pretty certain this was death.

"Sierra Leone," Rafael said.

Sierra Leone? I thought we left Sierra Leone. I held very still and pretended like I was dead.

Murmuring and hushed voices sounded all around.

I strained to hear.

"Mumble… mumble… Cholera."

I swallowed hard. My throat was parched.

Beeping. God, I hated that sound.

"Ebola," someone groaned.

"Ouch!" I swatted at the person who lifted my eyelid. The imbecile burned a hole through my retina with his pen.

"We're going to have to draw blood," the masked man said.

"Well, you're not getting it from my eye." I curled into a tight little ball after scooting to the other side of the bed.

"We should take additional precautions," his sidekick suggested. "Would you prefer to be quarantined with her or in a separate room?"

I started heaving again.

"We'd prefer to be together." Rafael pulled me to his chest as he slid next to me in the bed. "Can't you give her something for the nausea?"

"I'd like to know what we're dealing with," the man hedged.

Jase stood to his full height. "She's completely dehydrated. Order IV fluids."

I frowned. Something about this experience felt familiar.

Sleep claimed me before I could pinpoint what it was.

* * * * *

Rafael's hand brushed soothingly against my forehead. "How are you feeling?"

"Better," I acknowledged tiredly. "How long have I been out?"

He scooted closer, until our noses were touching. "Six hours. They've been running IV fluids and anti-nausea medicine. Do you feel nauseous?"

I stopped to think about it. "No, not really."

"The Zofran must be working," Jase noted with some relief.

Rafael's arms tightened around me. "The infectious disease doctor was here a few hours ago. The rapid test for Cholera came back negative. He doesn't believe this is Ebola since you aren't vomiting any blood. They're still running the bloodwork so they can be certain."

A doctor stepped through the sliding glass door. He was gloved, gowned, and masked to the hilt. "Sorry about the ensemble. The droplet precaution is still in place until we receive the remaining bloodwork, which won't be until sometime tomorrow." He eyed Rafael and Jase. "How are you two feeling?"

Rafael climbed out of bed. "I feel fine."

"Me too," Jase answered.

He approached the bed. "I'm pleased to see you are awake, Ms. Stone. I'm Doctor Cordeiro, the infectious disease specialist for the Hospital da Luz. How are you feeling?"

"Better." I fidgeted with the blanket, which was tangled around my waist.

"May I speak freely about your test results?" Amusement danced in his eyes.

"Yes, of course," I replied.

"We have ruled out Malaria, Influenza A and B, and Cholera. We are still waiting on the lab results, but I don't believe you have Ebola." He glanced at the nurse, who was wheeling in a monitor and a keyboard draped in plastic.

My brow furrowed while I studied the machine.

"Given the sudden onset, the intensity, and the fever that accompanied your vomiting, I believe you contracted food poisoning, but there's a complicating factor that aggravated these symptoms. May I?" Doctor Cordeiro tucked the blanket around my hips after lifting the hospital gown a few inches. "I'll admit this is a bit outside my area of expertise."

I squeaked when he squirted cold jelly onto my abdomen. My heart was racing. I didn't know if he was about to reveal some nasty tapeworm or a....

Rafael edged closer.

Doctor Cordeiro flipped the monitor on before pressing the hand held device to my stomach.

My heart was pounding so fiercely the room started spinning.

Doctor Cordeiro smiled. "There's our little culprit."

Tears leaked from the corner of my eyes.

"Where?" Rafael squinted at the screen.

The doctor pointed at a bean shaped shadow flickering on the monitor.

Jase drew closer. "What is that?"

Doctor Cordeiro's smile widened. "That, my friend, is a ten week old baby with a very impressive heart beat."

Rafael gaped at me. "We're having a baby?"

"I... I didn't realize I was pregnant." Between work, school, trips to Portugal, and Maxim's pipeline, I'd lost track of time.

He swept me up into a massive hug. "I love you so much!"

"That explains the fatigue." Jase was still scrutinizing the screen.

Rafael turned around and gave him a hug. "We're pregnant!"

Jase laughed. "Well, technically, Kristine's the one who's pregnant, which I think is hilarious. Aren't you two abstaining from sex?"

"We've been abstaining for all of a week." His smile widened when he did the math. "We made a baby during that massive snow storm." He made that sound like an insurmountable task.

"Congratulations." Dr. Cordeiro chuckled.

"Can we see him again?" Rafael peered eagerly at the screen.

"Certainly." Dr. Cordeiro lubed my tummy. "Zofran is safe to take during pregnancy, so I'd like to continue that medication through tomorrow morning. The food poisoning should improve by then. Let's see how your body tolerates clear liquids and soda crackers this morning. We should be able to discharge you just as soon as the remaining blood work comes through. We still have to rule out Ebola." He tapped at the monitor so Rafael could see where the baby was hiding. "I want you to follow up with an OB doctor as soon as you're discharged from the hospital. You may still experience some nausea and vomiting over the next few weeks, but it shouldn't be as bad as what you've experienced the last two days."

Rafael stared at the screen. "When can we hear the baby's heartbeat?"

"If my estimates are correct, you should be able to hear the baby's heartbeat next week." Dr. Cordeiro wiped my tummy with a towel. "Do you have any questions or concerns?"

My fingers skimmed my sunken stomach. "Will the food poisoning affect the baby?"

He shook his head. "As long as you stay hydrated and the baby receives adequate nutrition, your baby should be fine."

"Should we avoid travel?" Rafael inquired worriedly.

Dr. Cordeiro looked thoughtful. "I would avoid West Africa, and I'd wait until you were fully recovered from this food poisoning before boarding another airplane. Aside from that, travel should be fine." He offered me an encouraging smile. "I'll stop by tomorrow."

There was a long stretch of silence while Rafael gazed into my eyes. Tears spilled onto my pillow when he dropped to his knees and prayed.

* * * * *

Rafael's hand tightened around mine. A look of sheer bliss settled over his face as a loud swooshing noise sounded through the Doppler. "That's our baby," he murmured in awe. "His heart is beating really fast. Is that normal?"

"One hundred and fifty-four beats per minute is perfectly normal for eleven weeks," Dr. Barreira assured him. She scribbled a few notes onto my chart. "Based on the baby's measurements from the ultrasound, the dates you were together in January, and your hormone levels, your due date is October eighth."

A smile spread like wildfire across Rafael's face.

She tore a slip of paper from her prescription pad. "I'd like you to start taking prenatal vitamins with extra iron. Avoid sushi, deli meats, undercooked meat, unpasteurized dairy products, sprouts, caffeine, and alcohol."

"She drank wine while we were in Obidos and sangria for my birthday," Rafael admitted worriedly.

Dr. Barreira bit her bottom lip while she tried not to laugh. "One or two glasses will not hurt your baby, but do try to avoid alcohol from this point forward."

My shoulders relaxed. Thankfully, those were the only

two incidences where I drank alcohol that I could recall.

"You'll need an OB doctor in the United States since you'll be living in both countries over the next few months. Where do you plan to have the baby?"

I glanced at Rafael questioningly.

"We should be back in Virginia by then," he assured me.

"Very well. I'm here if you need me. It's best to have a physician in both places just in case your little one makes an early appearance. We'll be able to determine the gender of your child in nine weeks, sometime around May 28th, if you'd like to make an appointment with my receptionist."

I pushed off the exam table. "Can we purchase a Doppler to use at home? I'd like to share the baby's heartbeat with Rafael while we're apart."

She tucked my chart under her arm. "Yes. My receptionist can help you with that as well."

"Thanks, Dr. Barreira." Rafael shook her hand.

We left the doctor's office with said Doppler in hand. I set the device on the floor inside the Porsche. "Can we eat at the Confeitaria Nacional?"

"Sure." Rafael buckled me in so gently, you would have thought he was securing a Ming vase.

We were seated inside the toasty warm bakery within a matter of minutes. I dove into the savory *croquette*. I was so thrilled about the baby, I didn't even miss the *bica*.

Rafael ignored his food for the most part. "How are you feeling about all this?"

"Ecstatic but scared." I took a sip of orange juice.

He dragged his chair next to mine. "You're worried about having another miscarriage."

Tears filled my eyes.

"Me too." His arm slid comfortingly around my back.

"When do you want to make the announcement? Do you want to wait until we're a little further along?" Aside from Jase, we hadn't told a single soul.

The tension eased from my shoulders. "I'd prefer to wait until after the wedding." I lost Genevieve at eleven weeks. Although that miscarriage was triggered by a traumatic event, I was afraid I might lose this baby too. Our wedding marked the midway point in the pregnancy. That seemed like a safe time to make an announcement.

Thin flakes drifted toward his plate when he bit into his ham and cheese croissant. "Will you be showing by then? We could pursue a civil ceremony…"

I shook my head. "No. The ceremony we've planned is perfect. I don't want to cancel those plans."

Rafael frowned. "Until we're married, you're considered a single mother. I really wish I'd considered that before. I just… I thought it would take us longer to become pregnant." He sighed. "I was so afraid the hospital would force me from your bedside, that they wouldn't honor my wishes. If I were your husband, they couldn't deny me the right to care for you and to advocate on your behalf."

His fears shredded my heart. "I can sign a durable health care power of attorney. That would give you all the same rights."

Rafael turned the thought in his head. He shoved his chair aside, eased onto his knee, and clasped my hands in his. "I want our wedding to be special, but I want to be married now. I want our family to be complete. I want to be your husband and this child's father in every possible way. Please, baby. Honor me with a civil ceremony now. We'll keep that ceremony secret and proceed with the formal wedding in May. We can do both. Lots of couples do both in Portugal."

Tears streamed down my face. "I didn't think it was possible to love you any more than I did two seconds ago, but I do. God help me, I love you more than is humanly possible. Yes, I'll marry you. I'll marry you any time and any place your heart desires."

He burrowed his head against my tummy while he hugged me. "Then stay another day so we can be married."

My hand slid lovingly through his tousled hair. I hadn't a clue how Rafael would arrange for a civil ceremony in a single day, but I didn't doubt that he could pull it off. The more pressing concern was how I'd walk away from him when it was all said and done.

* * * * *

Rafael had arranged for the jet to fly Kadyn and Shae back to Virginia when the hospital confirmed we weren't exposed to the Ebola virus. I was staying until my stomach settled. After the OB appointment on Thursday, I agreed to stay a little longer so Rafael and I could be married. Jase remained with me.

Eva helped me shop for a dress, matching heels, lingerie, boutonnieres, and two small bouquets while Rafael made the necessary arrangements. Eva and Benjamim were privy to our secret since they were serving as our witnesses. Thankfully, Chief D'Souza possessed the necessary credentials to preside over the ceremony.

I spent the night with Eva, so Rafael and I wouldn't see each other before the ceremony. There were certain traditions neither of us were willing to relinquish, despite the fact this was a civil ceremony. Eva and I spent the morning at the spa, where my entire body was massaged, my nails painted, and hair elaborately coiffed.

Eva wore a taupe dress with embroidered sleeves. I chose an ivory lace dress that fell below my knees. Subtle glittering strands of gold were woven into the Bardot bodice and the A-line skirt. Lace scallops framed my collarbone, shoulders, and legs. Ivory heels and a pearl barrette completed the ensemble.

Rafael chose a small, intimate courtyard tucked between white washed buildings dripping with wisteria for the ceremony. He was standing in front of the fountain with Benjamim and Chief D'Souza.

I asked Jase to escort me into the courtyard. He looked stunning and surprisingly at ease in a suit and tie. I wasn't sure if it was his knowledge of the baby or his refusal to leave my side during the Cholera scare, but something had shifted in our relationship. My hard headed, formerly Special Ops bodyguard became teary eyed when I pinned his boutonniere. Rafael, Benjamim, and Chief D'Souza already had theirs.

Jase and I remained hidden against the building when Eva entered the courtyard. Someone began strumming a Portuguese guitar.

My stomach fluttered nervously. I couldn't believe we were getting married. I forced myself to breathe before kissing Jase on the cheek. "Thanks for escorting me."

He folded me in his arms. "Thanks for making my friend so happy." We entered the courtyard arm in arm.

Rafael's breath caught. He took a step forward, but Chief D'Souza stayed him with a gentle touch on his arm. Rafael looked devastating in a black suit that showcased his broad shoulders, trim waist, and muscular legs. He wore an ivory shirt and an ivory and gold tie. I tried not to cry when I saw the love and adoration reflected in his eyes.

Chief D'Souza's wife, Mariana, a small contingent of officers, and their wives formed a small, private audience. Chief D'Souza's service pin with the Order of Christ Cross glinted in the sunlight.

Jase pressed a kiss to my cheek. He offered Chief D'Souza a polite nod before transferring my hand to Rafael's arm. He joined Benjamim when we faced Chief D'Souza.

"You look lovely," Chief D'Souza whispered while the guitarist finished his piece. He peered over our shoulders and cleared his throat while Rafael beamed at me. "I invite my brethren to bear witness and share in the celebration as I legally unite Rafael Tiago Garcia to his betrothed, Kristine Annabelle Stone."

The courtyard grew quiet.

Chief D'Souza continued. "I will conduct this ceremony in English, as requested by the bride and groom." He paused briefly. "Rafael and Kristine appeared before the Central Registry to complete the preliminary process of marriage on the 26th day of March. The registrar has confirmed that Rafael and Kristine intend to marry in this the *Santa Maria de Belém Parish* in the municipality of Lisbon on this 27th day of March. She has authenticated the necessary publications." Thankfully, we had the required documents on hand after presenting them to Father Ramires.

Rafael smiled when he caught me peeking up at him.

"The registrar has further declared that in accordance with our national laws, there is no impediment which would prevent this marriage. She has therefore authorized this marriage." Chief D'Souza read several articles from their civil code relevant to the contract of marriage, the equality of spouses, and the duties of respect, fidelity, cooperation, and assistance before the guitarist poured himself into a song.

My pulse quickened. The courtyard fell silent once again.

"You may face one another and join hands," Chief D'Souza whispered.

Eva held my bouquet.

Chief D'Souza smiled encouragingly. "Rafael Tiago Garcia, will you take Kristine Annabelle Stone to be your wife? Will you love her, comfort her, honor and cherish her through sickness and in health, forsaking all others, as long as you both shall live?"

Rafael's eyes captured and held mine. "I will." His voice rang strong and true.

My heart thundered in my ears.

Chief D'Souza's voice dimmed. "Kristine Annabelle Stone, will you take Rafael Tiago Garcia to be your husband? Will you love him, comfort him, honor and cherish him through sickness and in health, forsaking all others, as long as you both shall live?"

"I will," I answered breathlessly.

He nodded his approval. "May I have the bride's ring?"

Benjamim handed him the beautifully braided band.

Chief D'Souza pressed the ring to the Order of Christ Cross. He whispered a silent prayer before handing it to Rafael. "Rafael, as you place this ring on Kristine's finger, please repeat after me. 'With this ring, I thee wed.'"

Rafael eased the glittering band over my left ring finger. "With this ring, I thee wed."

"May I have the groom's ring?" Captain Anderson had retrieved Rafael's wedding band from Brady before flying to Portugal late last night.

Benjamim handed Chief D'Souza the ring.

Chief D'Souza pressed the platinum band to the Order of Christ Cross. He repeated his silent prayer before handing it to me. "Kristine, as you place this ring on Rafael's finger, please repeat after me. 'With this ring, I thee wed.'"

I slid the ring over the tip of his finger before gazing up at him. "With this ring, I thee wed."

His eyes glistened with unshed tears.

A single tear escaped my lashes. I grew dizzy with disbelief.

"Rafael Tiago Garcia and Kristine Annabelle Stone, through your vows and the exchange of rings you have declared your love and commitment to one another. It is with immeasurable pleasure that I pronounce you husband and wife. Rafael, you may kiss your beautiful bride."

Rafael captured my tear with his thumb as he grasped my cheek. My eyes closed while I savored the feel of his hand. Somewhere in the darkness our lips met in a feather soft kiss. We lingered there breathlessly until he coaxed me into a gentle kiss.

I whimpered softly. My hands traveled his shoulders… grasped the nape of his neck. Rafael groaned. He crushed me against his chest as he claimed what was rightfully his. I melted into his arms while the universe simply ceased to exist.

Eva was fanning herself by the time he ended the kiss.

Cheers erupted all around.

Chief D'Souza grinned. "We will now sign the marriage certificate. Benjamim and Eva will join us as witnesses." He retrieved a pen and the certificate from a pocket inside his suit jacket. The marriage certificate had been rolled into a tight scroll. My heart raced while we signed the document. I couldn't believe we were officially husband and wife.

Rafael pulled me in for another passionate kiss.

"You are allotted one kiss," Chief D'Souza ribbed. "I'd like to present Mr. and Mrs. Garcia!"

Cheers erupted once more.

Rafael kept a firm grip on my waist while everyone congratulated us. He proved unwilling to release me for anyone, Chief D'Souza included. We followed our guests into the restaurant next door. How Rafael had finagled an early dinner was beyond me. Early dinners were virtually unheard of in Portugal. Minutes whittled into hours while we dined on steamed clams, lobster, and steak. Rafael surprised me with a wedding cake before whisking me away.

I felt giddy, and I hadn't indulged in a single drop of wine.

Rafael eased his Porsche through a private gate when we arrived in Cascais. He'd secured some elaborate fortress for the night. He scooped me out of the car and strode toward the door.

"What are you doing?" I squealed.

He strode through the house like he knew where he was going. "I'm consummating our marriage."

I gaped at the glass wall overlooking the ocean. "I'm pretty sure we've already done that."

He stopped abruptly. "Will that hurt the baby?"

Laughter exploded from my lungs. "Your child is perfectly safe. I'm sure he'll enjoy the exercise."

Rafael grinned as he resumed walking. "Are you up for this?"

My heart beat a thunderous score. "I want you to make love to me until I no longer know where my body ends and yours begins."

His eyes heated as he lowered me onto the bed. I eased the jacket over his shoulders while he loosened his tie. He kicked his shoes and socks aside.

Rafael knelt on the bed. "How long has it been?" His

369

hand slid longingly up my leg. The ivory heels remained in place.

"I don't know," I admitted breathlessly. "Four, maybe five, weeks?" We hadn't made love since he was in Virginia, when he was helping me with the invitations.

His eyes widened when he discovered the old fashioned garter holding the silk stockings in place. I unbuttoned his shirt while his fingers dipped beneath the fragile strip of lace wedged between my legs. "I'm sorry," he whispered. With a sharp tug, he tore the thong.

I arched into his hand while his fingers danced between my legs. "I've never wanted you more than I do in this moment. Please, I need to feel you inside of me."

Rafael removed my dress while I forced the shirt down his arms. His trousers quickly followed. He was gloriously naked while I remained in my heels, silk stockings, ivory garter, and demi lace bra. He forced the bra beneath my breasts before circling the nipples with his tongue. "How have I failed to notice this?"

My breasts had doubled in size, a change I'd failed to notice until purchasing lingerie yesterday. I moaned wantonly while he thoroughly consumed each breast. Pleasure pulsed between my legs. My fingers clenched the duvet. "Rafael," I panted. I reached for his hips so I could position him between my legs.

Rafael lifted my knees until they were well above his waist. I writhed in the most exquisite pain while he thoroughly ravished my neck. His hands kneaded my breasts. "I'm sorry," he murmured before plunging deep inside my mouth. The world tilted when Rafael buried himself to the hilt.

We lost ourselves in another intoxicating kiss while he

waited for my body to adjust. Slowly, he began to thrust.

"Husband," I whispered.

"Wife," he replied. His eyes sought mine. "Mrs. Garcia." His eyes closed against the emotions that evoked. "You're finally mine." He buried his face in my neck as he began to cry.

I gently caressed his back. "I fear I was intended for you long before I was born."

He lifted his head.

I grasped his face in my hands. "I love you more than you could possibly know."

"We're a family now."

I nodded.

"I love you." He clasped my hands in his as he forced them above my head.

I arched against him. My desire had grown as unbearable as his.

Rafael pulled back and thrust. In long, demanding strokes he erased the boundaries between his body and mine. He drove us higher and higher, knit us tighter and tighter, until there was no him... no me... only us.

* * * * *

I sighed contentedly as I curled against Rafael's side. He'd flung the windows open at some point during the night. The waves eventually coaxed us to sleep. I'd lost count of the amount of orgasms he'd wrung from me.

My heart stalled. I didn't want to leave.

"What's wrong?" Grudgingly, Rafael opened his eyes.

I stretched deliciously sore limbs while untangling myself from his legs. "How am I supposed to pick up where I left off when so much has changed? I'm supposed to return to Virginia today, where no one will know we're pregnant and married except Brady and Jase."

Rafael linked his hand with mine. "Do you want to tell people?"

I forced myself to think. "I don't want to tell anyone about the baby until we're further along."

He nodded.

I ran my fingers along the whiskers that darkened his jaw. "But I want to scream the fact that we're married from the rooftops."

Rafael laughed. His hand dipped beneath the sheet so he could feel my belly which was ridiculously flat. "I feel the same way, but I don't want Maxim to know. I don't know how he'll react when he discovers we've been married. I'd prefer to be present when he does."

I admired the braided diamond band gracing my left hand. "I should return this to you before I leave, but I'll still picture it there."

His fingers skimmed my hip. "Do you mind if I wear my ring? I'll remove it when I travel to Virginia and when our friends arrive just before the wedding."

I grasped his hand so I could see how the ring looked on his finger. "No. I would prefer you wear my ring. Did you read the inscription?"

Rafael bolted upright. He removed the ring so he could read the inscription. "Broken together?"

I admired the beautiful script before sliding the ring back onto his finger. "I couldn't stop thinking of all the tragedies, the heartache, and pain that life has thrown our way. We ended up together, despite all the obstacles and frankly dismal odds. But what if God intended it that way? Man has been broken since the Garden of Eden, but we were never meant to be *broken apart*. We were meant to be *broken together* until He comes for us."

His lips brushed against my knuckles. "The inscription couldn't be more perfect." He tugged the sheets toward my hips so he could rest his head on my tummy. It was some time before he spoke again. "You're so thin, I'm having a difficult time picturing our baby in there."

I combed my fingers through his hair. "I'll look like a beached whale by the time October rolls around."

"I'll worship you even more when your belly is round. That's my child in there." His fingers curled possessively around my side. "I'm having a really hard time letting you go. I don't want to miss a second of this pregnancy, and I feel this gut wrenching need to keep you and the baby close."

My heart clenched. "I feel the same way, but I'm so close to graduating. I need to return to Virginia so I can finish my degree."

He linked our hands together once more. "I want you to earn your degree, but I don't want you to leave."

"I'll take good care of our baby while we're apart. We'll be together before you know it," I promised.

Rafael glanced at the clock before climbing up my body. He pushed just inside of me when our bodies aligned. "I have four hours to change your mind."

Chapter 8 – The Proof of Your Love

I pushed off the toilet. My reprieve ended as morning sickness reared its ugly head again.

"You can't go to work," Jase growled from the doorway.

I splashed water on my face. "I'm going to work. I've already missed a week, and I'm pretty much out of leave."

He watched me brush my teeth. "Why are you returning to work when you're leaving in seven weeks?"

"I'm not entirely sure I am leaving," I argued unreasonably.

Jase laughed.

I stomped downstairs.

"What's wrong?" Brady asked.

Jase folded his arms across his chest. "She's being hard headed again. We should tie her up in bed."

Brady's eyes widened.

"Morning sickness," I rebutted. "It won't be pretty if you tie me to the bed."

Jase growled. "The toilet then."

"It wouldn't be the first time," I grumbled. "Let's go."

Jase grabbed a bottled water, soda crackers, and a large plastic bowl. "Just in case."

Brady followed me into the garage. "How are you going to hide this from Shae?"

"My stomach will settle once there's food in there." I sincerely hoped the baby was listening.

They eyed me skeptically.

We climbed into the Jeep. "The baby is demanding food. He doesn't like waking up to an empty stomach," I recalled from my previous pregnancy.

Jase stopped by Starbucks so they could feed me a bacon, egg, and Gouda breakfast sandwich.

"This works," I purred happily.

I made it through the first day without giving the baby away. I called Rafael the second I got home so I could play the Doppler over the phone. Brady and Jase snuck into my bedroom when they heard the sound. They stood mesmerized while Rafael sang the baby a Portuguese lullaby.

The rest of the week progressed in much the same way. I crawled into bed thoroughly exhausted after my classes on Tuesday, Wednesday, and Thursday. Still, I played the Doppler every night so Rafael could hear the baby's heartbeat. Brady and Jase popped their heads inside the room more often than not. They nodded, reassured, each time they heard that steady swooshing sound. They doted on me like a couple of midwives and plied me with food.

Kadyn invited himself over for dinner Friday night. I thought he might reveal something juicy about Shae since she was behaving oddly at work.

"I got it!" Jase yelled when the doorbell rang.

I glanced at Brady, worriedly. "He doesn't know about the baby or the wedding."

"We're fully capable of keeping your secrets." He gave me a hug.

I wondered how many secrets the Templar kept.

Kadyn deposited three paper bags on top of the counter. "I hope you're in the mood for Chinese food."

Jase eyed me uncertainly.

"Chinese food sounds great." I gave Kadyn a hug. "Would you like a Sprite?"

He shot me a curious look. "Yes, please." He shook hands with Brady and Jase. "You're welcome to join us. There's plenty of food."

I set four Sprites on the counter while Brady retrieved the plates. We loaded our plates with steamed dumplings, Crab Rangoon, shrimp fried rice, General Tso's Chicken, and beef with broccoli before traipsing into the family room.

Kadyn set his plate on the coffee table. "Where's your laptop?"

I set my plate next to his. "In the office. Do you want me to get it?"

He started flipping through the channels on my television. "Please. There's something you should see."

I grabbed my laptop and plopped next to him on the couch.

Kadyn typed a URL into my browser before handing me the computer. "Check this out."

I read the headline aloud. "NATO ships enter the Black Sea." I read the first paragraph to myself before jumping to my feet. "Oh my God! NATO exercises. In the Black Sea! The defense shield is being installed!" Relief collided with fear. I burst into tears.

Jase beat Kadyn to my side. "Are you okay?" He eased me onto the couch.

Kadyn looked stunned. "What's going on?"

"Hormones," Brady muttered. He quickly realized his mistake. "You know, that time of the month. She's completely exhausted between work and school and… uh… *Aunt Flo*."

"Aunt Flo?" Jase mouthed.

Kadyn stilled. "You're pregnant."

My tears stopped as abruptly as they'd begun. "How could you possibly know that?"

He looked thoroughly embarrassed. "Well, I've been hugging you for three years now."

"I'm not even showing," I objected.

All three men eyed my chest.

I covered my breasts. "Stop that!" I glared at Brady. "Aunt Flo? Seriously? What kind of cover up is that?"

Kadyn tried not to laugh. "Does Rafael know?"

"Yes. We discovered I was pregnant when I was in the hospital. I don't want to tell anyone until I'm further along. I'm worried I might have another miscarriage." My voice grew panicked. "Kadyn, I'm serious. I don't want anyone else to know."

The smile slid from his face. "What about Shae?"

I shook my head. "You, Rafael, Brady, and Jase are the only ones who know. Although, Shae might figure it out if I start vomiting at work."

He sank next to me on the couch. "Why were you so upset about the military exercise?"

"I'm just worried. They're expanding the pipeline. Maxim needs to get the defense shield in place before Putin discovers that construction. As if that's not pressing enough, this is a very tight race. Maxim would like to take credit for these accomplishments so he can win the election, but he can't do that until the defense shield is in place. He's worried Putin will retaliate."

Jase looked up from his plate. "When's the election?"

I cringed. "April tenth, and Maxim and Yulia are still neck and neck."

"That's only seven days away," Brady stated.

"I know." I shoved my plate aside.

Kadyn glanced at my computer screen. "They've created a diversion. I bet they're moving munitions from Poland as we speak."

Jase stood. "When did Maxim first meet with Secretary Gates?" He strode into the kitchen, where he piled more food onto his plate.

Kadyn thought back. "January sixteenth."

Brady did the math. "That was two and a half months ago. Those launch pads may already be in place."

"What about Russia's satellites?" I persisted. Kadyn warned me that type of activity could be detected by satellite.

Jase shrugged. "We're not above tampering with satellite feeds when the situation warrants."

I found that oddly reassuring. "Would this situation warrant such a thing?"

"We're trying to prevent World War III," Kadyn answered evenly. "When did Maxim receive funding for the pipeline?"

"USAID issued the check on March thirteenth." My knee bounced nervously.

"Three weeks ago," Brady murmured.

"Maxim is determined to move quickly. They don't have far to go and the terrain is relatively flat," I added.

Kadyn bit into a spring roll. "You know... he just might pull this off."

I wondered how it was possible to want and dread the same thing. "I'm going to hang out at the Ukrainian Embassy on Election Day with Oni, Konstantin, and Shae. Would you like to join me?"

"What time?" Kadyn reached for his Sprite.

"Voting ends at two o'clock eastern time. They should have a preliminary count by five or six o'clock."

Kadyn glanced at the calendar on his phone. "Sure. I can join you." He frowned at my plate. "I don't know much about growing babies, but aren't you supposed to eat?"

"If you don't eat, I'm shoving a feeding tube up your nose," Jase growled.

I couldn't resist the eye roll. "Great. Now I have *three* midwives plying me with food."

"I'm drawing the line at delivering the baby," Brady warned. "Hey, where's the heartbeat machine?"

Kadyn raised a single eyebrow.

"The Doppler is upstairs." I cracked open my chopsticks.

Brady rose from his chair. "Do you want to hear the baby's heartbeat?"

"Sure," Kadyn agreed.

Brady bolted up the stairs. "Hey! Can I look for the baby this time?" Thus far, I'd been the only one rubbing the Doppler over my tummy. Apparently, that was about to change.

Jase's chopsticks stopped short of his mouth.

"Don't worry, I'll make sure you get a turn." Secretly, I loved how invested they were in this pregnancy.

* * * * *

I popped my head inside Shae's office. "Maxim just called."

Shae smacked her head on the desk. She flopped onto her chair as she tossed a paperclip onto the desk. "Stupid paperclip."

I bit my lip, trying not to laugh. "They've been working day and night on the pipeline. Maxim said they're about halfway done." I sank onto the chair across from her desk. "The mobile launch pads and the missiles are in place. Their missileers have been trained. They're still building the more permanent launch pads, but he feels they have enough coverage to insulate against an attack while they complete the remaining work."

Shae shook her head in disbelief. "How did he manage to accomplish all that?"

"I think his relationship with Prime Minister Azarov and his appointment to the Ministry of Foreign Affairs helps. They've moved quickly because they must. Failure to do so could compromise their national security. There's not a lot of transparency there anyway. You know how it is."

Shae unraveled the paperclip. "Ukraine doesn't have an EPA or special interest groups getting in the way. They have a huge unemployment problem, so I'm sure plenty of people were begging to work on that pipeline regardless of the hours or the demands."

I nodded. "What does Konstantin think about all this?"

"He's a mess," she confessed. "He's worried Putin will retaliate when he discovers what they're doing. He's still amassing troops along the eastern border. Everyone's afraid Russia will invade if the election doesn't go the right way."

"Right way," I scoffed. "In other words, Putin is threatening to invade unless the Ukrainian people vote a pro-

Russian candidate into office."

"Putin has planted people inside Ukraine who are delivering that very message." Shae huffed out a breath.

My heart sank. "Well then, things are about to turn very ugly."

Her brow furrowed.

I rubbed my forehead. Sadly, that failed to drive my fears away. "Maxim was hoping to avoid this, but he hasn't been able to gain a respectable lead in the polls. He's going to announce these accomplishments today. Their security forces are on high alert in case Putin retaliates. Several international organizations have arrived to observe the election. He's hoping that will help keep Putin in check, at least until after the election."

Shae dropped the mangled paperclip.

* * * * *

"I think you should go into hiding," Rafael argued forcefully.

I rolled my eyes at the phone. "I'm not going into hiding. I'm staying here so I can finish my coursework. Graduation is only a month away."

Silence.

I pulled a pair of yoga pants out of the drawer and tugged them on. "Rafael?"

"Are Brady and Jase in the room?"

I glanced toward my bedroom door. "No." Thank God. I was half naked after all.

"Go get them and put me on speaker phone," he growled.

The hair on the back of my neck rose. "Okay. I just… I

need to finish changing." I wiggled into a loose fitting shirt before scurrying downstairs.

Brady and Jase were huddled inside the kitchen. They stopped talking when I walked into the room.

"Rafael is on the phone." I switched over to speaker phone.

"Jase," Rafael gritted. "You're aware of Maxim's announcement?"

His eyes slid toward mine. "Yes. The story has yet to break in the United States, but it's been all over the news in Ukraine. We're monitoring Russia's media outlets. Putin hasn't responded... yet."

"I want the links to every news story you've seen. You do realize what this means?"

Brady edged closer to me. "Yes. We've recruited additional men to guard the perimeter. Ethan is gathering Intel, and he's instituted a number of other countermeasures to safeguard her at work and school."

My eyes narrowed. "What are you talking about?"

Rafael blew out a breath. "Is she sitting down?"

Brady helped me onto one of the high back stools. "She is now."

He softened his tone. "Kristine, that pipeline will cost the Russian government billions in lost revenue. Putin will be livid. If he cannot openly retaliate against Ukraine, he will order his regime to hunt, torture, and kill those who aided and abetted in this project. He will pursue anyone deemed precious to Maxim with a vengeance, so he can force him to abandon that pipeline. Putin is former KGB. Surely you understand what that means."

I gripped the granite countertop. "The SVR will be looking for me."

Jase's hand raked through his hair. "I tried to warn you... this makes you an even bigger target."

I was dangerously close to vomiting.

"I don't know how discreet Maxim was when he visited Kristine. You said he had several men walking the perimeter when he was at the townhouse, blocking the entrance to the coffee shop, and patrolling USAID. Still, if he was being followed..." Rafael trailed off ominously.

Brady set a glass of water on the counter in front of me. "How do you want to proceed?"

"I want Kristine to see if she can finish her coursework remotely. I want her to request a leave of absence from Seeds for Peace. I don't want her going anywhere near the Ukrainian Embassy on Election Day. I don't want her eating any food the three of you haven't prepared yourselves, I don't want her crossing any streets, and I want you out of the townhouse by five o'clock tomorrow."

Tears streamed down my cheeks. Tragically, it seemed, my efforts to free the Ukrainian people from Russian aggression would cost my freedom in the end.

* * * * *

I drew the thick fleece blanket over my knees. Installation of the missile defense shield aired as breaking news on all the major news stations in the United States. Thankfully, there was no mention of Kadyn or me, only Maxim and Secretary Gates. Given that news release and Putin's thinly veiled threats against Ukraine and the United States, Ukraine's presidential election was receiving some air time as well.

My eyes remained glued to the television. The current

news feed depicted the USS Porter. The U.S. Navy destroyer was patrolling the Black Sea alongside NATO forces.

Brady sat up and took notice. "The USS Porter launched Tomahawk Land Attack Missiles during the Shock and Awe Campaign in Iraq."

Jase looked up from his laptop. "We've increased our force structure in Europe. They're calling it Operation Atlantic Resolve." He read part of the news story aloud. "We've positioned hundreds of Abrams tanks, Bradley fighting vehicles, a convoy of Stryker combat vehicles, and Paladin self-propelled howitzers near the Russian border."

Kadyn whistled. "That's impressive." He handed me a slice of ZBQ Chicken Pizza. Jase had deemed the pizza safe because Kadyn watched while it was being made.

Brady loaded up his plate.

Jase had negotiated Rafael down from his list of demands, so we were in the townhouse for the time being. Kadyn joined us instead of going to the embassy. "How long do you think it will take them to tally the votes?"

My phone beeped with an incoming text. "It's Shae. The exit polls are in."

I dropped the phone when it began to wail. I glared at Brady and Jase. They'd recently started messing with my ringtone. "A crying baby? Really?" I picked up the phone.

Kadyn and Jase laughed while Brady snickered. "You should get used to that sound."

I shot to my feet when I saw the name reflected on the screen. "Maxim, are you okay?"

"*Da, milaya kotyonok.* I am more than okay. We have won the election!"

Kadyn grabbed me when I swayed.

I sank back onto the couch. "You're… you're… you're

the President of Ukraine?"

A deep, hearty laugh rolled through the phone. I couldn't recall the last time I heard Maxim laugh so freely. "The inauguration is in two weeks. You will attend?"

My heart stalled.

Maxim's voice softened. "I want you to hold my father's Bible when I'm sworn into office."

My vision blurred while I battled the demons that provoked.

* * * * *

Dr. Sandstrom twirled a pen between his fingers while he pondered my predicament. "You are one of the most courageous women I know. Why change now?"

My hand flitted to my stomach.

His eyes softened. "Ah, well that is understandable. Still, what example would that set for your child?"

I frowned.

"You cannot abandon those you care for and everything you've worked so hard to achieve so you can go into hiding. You are not the sort of person who could live peacefully with that decision. The fear, frustration, and anger would forever change you," he warned.

I wondered how he knew me so well. "Rafael is concerned that my participation in the swearing in ceremony would alert Putin to my involvement with Maxim."

He set the pen on his desk. "The SVR exploited your relationship with Maxim once before. They held you captive until the Prime Minister and the President of Ukraine signed the treaty allowing the Russian naval fleet to remain in Sevastopol."

I took a deep breath and blew it out.

"You're already on his radar," he argued with some regret. "Admittedly, the inauguration would place you in the spotlight once again, but Maxim's position as president could offer a layer of insulation that didn't exist before. Your friend will have a lot more resources at his disposal; security forces, Intel, and the missile defense shield."

I chewed my bottom lip. Dr. Sandstrom was making all the same arguments I'd made to Rafael.

He leaned back in his chair. "If I were you, I'd go and support my friend. I wouldn't linger any longer than I had to, but I would go. Kristine, this is a huge accomplishment. This could change everything for Ukraine. You played a role in this. You deserve to be there, to stand beside your friend at the inauguration, and to share in the celebration. Don't allow the SVR to rob you of this."

Tears pooled in my eyes. "I want to go. I really do…"

"Then go," he insisted.

Butterflies attacked my stomach. "What about my studies?"

"If you flew to Ukraine on the twenty-third and returned on the twenty-seventh like Maxim suggested, you'd only miss one day of class."

"Can I finish my remaining coursework remotely?" I was still on the fence about requesting this, but I promised Rafael I would ask.

"I'd prefer to have you in class. Besides, I loathe the idea of you going into hiding." He started humming "This Little Light of Mine."

I cracked a smile.

His eyes sparkled. "Have you selected a topic for your final paper?"

"Yes." I breathed a small sigh of relief. "I'm mapping the Russia/Ukraine conflict so I can develop strategies for resolving their conflict."

He smiled unabashedly. "You should share those strategies with the President of Ukraine."

* * * * *

"Please, Rafael? I'll only be there for three days." I wasn't counting the two additional days of travel required to and from Kyiv since those days involved ten hours of flight time and a two hour layover in Germany or France.

"I?" he bristled. "This will be a 'we' not an 'I' if it happens, and I'm not so sure this should happen."

"'We' as in 'me and my security team' or 'we' as in 'you might be willing to join me?'" I inquired hesitantly.

"Kristine, do you honestly think I'd allow you to go to Ukraine without me?"

I chose to ignore the word "allow." "Maxim said I could bring my own security team, and he promised a staggering amount of security to reinforce their efforts to keep me safe. He invited us to stay with him at the presidential residence, which is heavily guarded. I have no interest in venturing off by myself, so there will be very little opportunity for the SVR to intercept me."

"By intercept do you mean torture, kill, or kidnap?" he queried mildly.

"All of the above," I conceded with forced nonchalance.

"I can't believe you're even considering this," he grumbled. "If we do this... and that's still a very big if... we're going to do this my way. I'll be handling your security, not Maxim. You will not walk or sit or stand anywhere I haven't approved. You won't touch a single speck of food or drink a single drop of fluid until I've tested it first. Do you understand?"

"Yes," I conceded grudgingly.

"Good. Now let me speak with my son," he demanded just as gruffly.

"How do you know it's a boy?" I challenged with a lighthearted laugh.

"I just do. Now please lift up your shirt, set the phone to speaker, and place it on your tummy so I can speak with my child."

"Stop being so bossy," I taunted.

"Wife," he growled. "I'd like to speak with my child."

"You are," I retorted. "The phone is already on my belly."

He huffed out a breath. "Son, you should know how poorly your mother is behaving. An elbow to the belly would be good right about now. Can you make her sick again, so she can't travel to Ukraine? I'd much prefer she hang out in bed and read those books I sent. Is she still reading to you every day?"

I folded my hands behind my head and smiled. I loved hearing Rafael dote on our child.

* * * * *

"Surprise!" Cenia, Marie, Oni, Sammi, Shae, and Gabi yelled.

I froze. "I'm pretty sure my birthday is in June."

Cenia laughed. "This isn't a birthday party. This is your bridal shower."

I grinned at my friends. "Thank you. That's very sweet."

Cenia patted Jase on the arm. "Kadyn and Roger are watching baseball in the theater room downstairs. Why don't you and Brady join them?"

Jase ducked his head toward hers conspiratorially. "Maybe you can talk her out of going to Ukraine."

The smile slid from her face. "You've been holding out on me again."

"Why would you go to Ukraine?" Gabi protested.

Shae's arm slid protectively around me. "Maxim was elected president. We're attending his inauguration."

"You're going too?" Cenia sputtered. "Wait. I need a drink. Does anyone else want a mango martini? I'm pretty sure I'll handle this better if I drink a couple of martinis."

Marie laughed. "If you have an extra shaker, I'll help you mix the drinks."

"Can you make mine virgin?" I inquired hesitantly.

Every woman in the room stopped talking.

I crossed my fingers behind my back. "I have a ton of homework I have to get through tonight. I can't afford to dumb down my brain any more than it already is."

Cenia's eyes narrowed. "Dumb doesn't even begin to capture how insane that decision is. I cannot believe you're going to Ukraine."

"Would you like to come with me?" I teased. "You could be part of my security team."

She gaped at me. "How did you get Rafael to sign off on this?"

I bit my bottom lip. "I plied him with sex?"

Oni giggled.

Shae laughed. "Men. They'll agree to anything when you ply them with sex."

* * * * *

Rafael met us in Germany. Thankfully, my vomiting had subsided by the time he boarded the jet, or he would have ordered us back to Virginia. The Zofran helped, although I was questioning whether the baby was to blame. Most of my friends presumed it was nerves. They knew I was terrified despite the brave front. They were my saving grace. They kept me sufficiently engaged, which helped keep my anxieties at bay.

I gazed at my husband's handsome face... his soft brown eyes, tousled hair, and the five o'clock shadow that made him so damn irresistible. I wasn't sure why, but I drew comfort from the fact that we were married. Our marital status wouldn't deter the SVR, but it would deter Maxim should that prove necessary. I belonged to Rafael in every way imaginable. That knowledge changed me somehow.

I nodded off while Rafael strategized with Jase. He was sitting beside me, absently caressing my leg. I woke with a start when he stopped.

He kissed me before whispering in my ear. "I'm not going anywhere." His hand grazed my tummy.

I trailed my fingers over the stubble shadowing his jaw. "Good. Thank you for being here."

A melodic "ding" sounded over the intercom. "*Dobryy den'.* This is your pilot, Captain Anderson. Heavy cloud cover awaits us in Kyiv. It's a chilly forty-six degrees. The local time is four-thirty p.m. We'll be landing in thirty minutes."

Ethan eased two suitcases from an overhead bin. Shae gasped when he unzipped them. "There should be enough ankle holsters, shoulder harnesses, guns, and ammunition for everyone," Ethan announced.

Rafael removed his jacket before joining him. "I asked Ethan to pack earpieces and smartwatches imbedded with Bluetooth microphones so we can communicate discreetly." He quietly considered Shae and me. "I wasn't sure whether you would want one."

Shae took a step forward, then backed away. "I don't think so."

I shook my head. "If I heard about all the people you suspect, I'd end up a complete mess."

"You will remain with one of us at all times then." Rafael looked pointedly at Shae. "That includes you, my friend. I don't care if that rubs Konstantin the wrong way. I don't know him well enough to trust him with your life."

Shae's bottom lip quivered.

Kadyn rose from his chair. "I'll watch over Shae."

"Me too," Marie agreed.

"We all will," Cenia assured her.

I still couldn't believe they'd insisted on joining us. I should have known. This circle of friends had proven time and again they'd lay down their lives for me.

Rafael and Ethan slid guns inside their holsters and harnesses before tucking an additional gun against the small of their backs. Brogan, Aidan, Brady, and Jase did the same. I suddenly realized why they were wearing suits. They were using the suit jackets to hide their weapons.

Cenia, Roger, Phil, Marie, and Kadyn strapped their weapons into place before inserting their ear pieces. While they tested their communication devices, I wondered what Maxim would think of our eleven person security team.

Cenia pulled three tactical folding knives from her backpack. She tucked one into her pants at the small of her back before pressing another into Shae's hand. "I know you're not comfortable packing a gun, but you should carry something." She handed the third knife to me. "Tuck this beneath your bra if you're wearing a dress. Aim for the femoral, the jugular, or between the second and third ribs." She pointed to each location, tickling me when she said "ribs."

"We've been cleared to land at the Kyiv International Airport," Kari announced. "Please make sure your seatbelts are fastened, seat backs are in the upright position, and all those sweet looking guns are stowed." She started cracking up. "I'll be strapping on a couple of those bad boys myself."

Everyone laughed. I'd grown to adore Kari. She always knew what we needed most, whether it was privacy, a warm cup of tea, a strong cup of coffee, or a joke to lighten the moment.

I shoved the knife inside my bra, which wasn't easy considering the cut of my dress. I was wearing a black sheath dress, the pearls that belonged to Rafael's mother, and pointy half d'Orsay heels from Sergio Rossi. Eva purchased the black and white snakeskin heels for me during one of her shopping sprees. I couldn't bear to part with them so I'd taken them back to Virginia with me.

Rafael nodded his approval when he saw what I was doing. He helped me into a black elegantly hooded raincoat that swirled around my ankles like Little Red Riding Hood's cape. This too was Eva's doing. The woman had impeccable taste in clothes.

We fastened our seatbelts. "Thank God we're landing in Kyiv and not Sevastopol." I couldn't bear to see the tarmac where Michael had been shot.

Rafael peered at the landscape barreling toward us. "Kyiv is difficult enough."

My knees bounced. The plane grew eerily silent when the wheels touched down. I popped another Zofran. I was on the verge of throwing up.

Rafael handed me his bottled water.

Captain Anderson rolled past the main terminal. He parked near a hangar at the far end of the airfield.

Rafael stood. "Wait here." He looked at Kadyn. "Sit on her if you see any muscles twitching."

Kadyn unfastened his seatbelt so he could stand next to me.

Ethan and Brady joined Rafael at the front of the aircraft. Rafael scrolled through some messages on his cell phone before speaking into his smartwatch. They strode off the plane as soon as the ground crew positioned the stairs. Jase stood just inside the door so he could monitor the tarmac while keeping an eye on me.

Kadyn squeezed my shoulder. "Breathe," he reminded me.

How could I with all those men standing on the tarmac? Although, these men differed from the ones who haunted my dreams. Very few were dressed in black. Most were wearing military uniforms or suits. Maxim seemed utterly relaxed in his three piece suit. He leaned casually against a black SUV while speaking with Konstantin.

Rafael crossed the tarmac, flanked by Ethan and Brady.

Roger peered out the window. "I bet you a hundred bucks Rafael punches him."

A smile tugged at Kadyn's lips. "I don't think he will. There are too many men wielding guns who could misconstrue what's going on."

"Maybe that's why the aircraft is still running," Phil mused thoughtfully.

"I'd punch him for kissing my fiancé," Roger boasted.

Cenia patted his shoulder. "Sure you would, honey. You'd punch the president of a foreign country while he was surrounded by armed forces who were chomping at the bit to kill somebody."

"I would." He winked at me.

Everyone laughed.

I stood and gave him a hug. "Thank you for making me laugh."

"Ready?" Jase asked.

I took a deep breath and blew it out. I didn't respond because the answer was "no." Brogan and Aidan stepped out in front of me. I followed them down the stairs. Jase and our remaining friends trailed close behind.

Shae and I walked arm in arm once we hit the tarmac. Jase walked alongside me, Kadyn alongside Shae. Brogan and Aidan stepped aside when we joined Maxim and Rafael.

Konstantin kissed Shae on the lips. "Thank you for coming."

She nodded politely.

Maxim kissed my cheek before I could process her lukewarm response. "You honor me with your presence."

I gave him a hug. "Thank you for inviting us."

Amusement danced in his eyes. "Your security detail is larger than mine."

I eyed the security forces standing stiffly along the tarmac. "I think you miscounted."

Maxim laughed. "Most of these men have been ordered to protect you and your aircraft, and this doesn't include the security team that arrived yesterday."

I glanced at Rafael questioningly.

"I arranged for a security detail out of Portugal. They're

positioned between the airport, Maxim's residence, and Mariyinsky Palace."

"How many?" I inquired breathlessly.

"Twenty-eight intelligence and security officers," Maxim answered.

My eyes widened. "Can you accommodate that many people?"

Maxim chuckled. "If this ensures your safety, then I am happy to have them." He shook Kadyn's hand. "Thank you for coming, Kadyn. Your assistance has proven invaluable."

Kadyn nodded. Once.

I introduced Maxim to my remaining friends.

He reached for my elbow after shaking their hands. "You will ride with me. I can accommodate two more people in my SUV. I've secured additional SUVs for the remaining individuals."

"Jase and I will join you," Rafael assured me.

"Brogan and I will ride with Shae," Kadyn announced decidedly.

Konstantin's eyes narrowed, but Kadyn's tone brokered no room for argument.

We piled into the long line of SUVs. All the vehicles looked the same; black paint, heavily tinted windows, and no defining features such as presidential emblems or flags. Rafael, Jase, and I joined Maxim in the third vehicle. Maxim's bodyguards sat in the front. I joined Maxim in the second row. Rafael and Jase sat in the back.

"I've arranged for a small, intimate dinner to welcome you and your friends at eight o'clock this evening. That should allow you some time to rest. The swearing in ceremony will take place on the floor of the Ukrainian Parliament at three o'clock tomorrow. I plan to sign the

Ukraine-European Union Association Agreement before the inaugural ball. The ball is being held at Mariyinsky Palace, which adjoins the Ukrainian Parliament," Maxim advised us.

"I understand Mariyinsky Palace is merely a ceremonial residence. Did you acquire the former president's home?" Jase asked.

"Yes, but I plan to dismantle that opulent resort, auction the items, and return the funds to the Ukrainian people." His eyes sought mine. "Each president is allowed to select his own private residence. I've chosen a modest home that can still accommodate guests. The grounds are extensive, which helps ensure privacy. The layout is very secure. I promise, you will be safe there."

"How has public sentiment been since the election?" Rafael queried.

"My countrymen are pleased about the pipeline. They are hopeful this will strengthen our economy. They are worried that Putin may retaliate, but the missile defense shield helps alleviate some of their concerns. The Ukrainian people recognize this defense shield is meant to protect all of Europe. They feel honored the United States would trust us to protect the EU. This has become a source of national pride, the fact that you would count us among your allies."

Tears welled in my eyes. "Maxim, I am so happy for you."

He grasped my hand. "I want you to know how much I appreciate your efforts to help my country. You owed us nothing… less than nothing when one considers what the SVR did to you… but still you helped us. I will never forget what you have done for me and my country." He kissed my hand before releasing it.

My chin quivered. Maxim's words evoked a confusing

array of emotions, which threatened to release a floodgate of tears.

Our convoy turned onto a narrow lane interspersed with budding trees. We stopped briefly at a gatehouse. Our driver spoke with the guards before following the other vehicles through the tall wrought iron gate.

"The sleeping quarters inside the guest house are being used by your security detail and mine." Maxim nodded toward a large stone house.

A sprawling lawn and a small pond separated the guest house from the Tudor style mansion looming before us. Several guards were patrolling the grounds.

"It's beautiful," I breathed.

Maxim smiled, obviously pleased. "There are ten bedrooms, five in each wing, which should be enough to accommodate your friends."

"Thank you for having us." I still couldn't believe we were staying at the presidential residence. Several phone calls had transpired between Rafael and Maxim before Rafael agreed Maxim's residence was the safest location for us.

Our SUV stopped in front of a massive garage. Maxim helped me step out of the vehicle since Rafael and Jase were sitting behind us. Rafael linked his fingers in mine when he joined us.

Maxim took it all in stride. Within minutes, he was ushering us inside. While the house was quite large, it was far from opulent. I found the stone walls, the deep mahogany wood, and the masculine undertones soothing. The warm hues reflected in the brown leather furniture, the artwork, and rugs were consistent with his previous home. They fit him perfectly.

"I'll take your coats," the butler offered in flawless

English.

Rafael freed me from my coat before removing his own.

A low growl rumbled through Jase's chest when he caught Maxim eying my dress.

Maxim shot Jase a disapproving look. "Kristine looks stunning. A man would have to be dead not to appreciate that."

Kadyn helped Shae out of her coat.

"Where's Konstantin?" I asked.

Shae shrugged.

Maxim reached for my arm. "I'd like to show you the house before escorting you to your rooms." A modest sitting room sat to the left of the foyer. This room held brown leather chairs and a mahogany bar I recognized from his previous home. Maxim's office was across the foyer, directly opposite the sitting room. His office opened into a good-sized library.

Maxim stopped in front of the formal dining room, which was clearly designed to entertain large groups. "Dinner will be served here this evening. You will be my first guests." A restaurant sized kitchen separated the formal dining room from a smaller, more intimate dining room. A powder room and a family room were secreted near the back of the house. The French doors inside the family room led out onto a massive stone terrace with a stunning view of Kyiv.

"What an amazing view," Cenia stated admiringly.

The terrace extended beyond a second set of French doors which opened into a formal living room on the opposite side of the house. A second powder room separated the living room from an unassuming door, the library, and Maxim's office.

Maxim opened the unassuming door and started down

the stairs. "You are welcome to use the sauna, gym, and lap pool. The central command center is located here." He pointed toward two solid doors near the bottom of the stairs. There are several escape routes... tunnels that lead to various locations on the property where vehicles are hidden in case of an emergency. My security staff will lead you to those should the need arise."

Our luggage was sitting at the top of the stairs by the time we reached the second floor. Maxim led us to the far end of the left wing.

I touched the intricately carved door sealing the room on the end. "This is the same door you had in your other house."

Maxim's eyes softened. "I'd like you and Rafael to stay here." He opened the door to the right of his room.

"I think we should sleep in the other wing," Rafael stated flatly.

"*You* are welcome to stay in the other wing, but Kristine will remain in the room next to me. You are not the only man who is concerned for her safety," Maxim replied dismissively. He briefly considered Jase. "You can sleep in the room directly across from Kristine. I'd prefer Shae stay in this wing as well. The rest is flexible."

Jase patted Kadyn on the back. "You can bunk with me."

Maxim brought my hand to his lips. "I'll ask the chef to serve dinner at nine o'clock so you can get some rest."

"Thank you." I edged closer to Rafael.

Rafael kissed my forehead. "I'm going to speak with the security staff. Jase will sit with you until I can join you."

I was too tired to object. I changed into a camisole and sleep shorts in the adjoining bathroom before easing between the crisp, cool sheets.

Jase settled into the armchair next to the window. "Try to get some rest."

"Thank you for being here." I yawned and promptly fell asleep.

Rafael was sleeping beside me by the time I woke. He stirred when I reached over to retrieve my cell phone from the nightstand. "What time is it?"

"Eight o'clock," I answered. "You can go back to sleep. I'm going to shower before dinner."

He pulled me close. His body warmed mine. "Can I join you?"

His sleep-roughened voice left me longing for more amorous activities. "Sure."

"I'd like to speak with my son first." He lifted my camisole so he could kiss my tummy. "I've missed you. How are you doing? Is your mommy taking good care of you?"

I giggled softly. "I'm eating well and drinking lots of water if that's what you're asking."

He rubbed his bristly cheek against my stomach. "I've missed this and you. How many more days must we endure this separation?"

"Three more weeks," I answered. "We're nearly there."

He picked me up and carried me to the shower. "I would prefer we were never parted again."

I nodded. "Is this going to work? Maxim's place, I mean. Would you prefer we stay in a hotel?"

Rafael turned the jets on. He removed his clothes and mine while we waited for the water to warm. "No. Maxim's right. This place is a virtual fortress, and he has it locked down tight. We're safer here than we'd be at any other location in Ukraine. It's just... Maxim's affections toward you can be trying at times."

I pulled him into the shower. "Maxim's affections are irrelevant. I'm married to you, and I'm carrying your child." I grabbed the soap and worked a lather into my hands so I could wash his shoulders and chest.

The tension eased from his shoulders. I knelt in front of him so I could wash his legs. His eyes darkened when I reached between his legs. "Kristine," he pleaded hoarsely.

I pulled him deep inside my mouth. Around and around my tongue swirled while I clenched his hardened shaft. His fingers curled against the wall. I knew he needed this. He needed to know I desired him above all others, especially in this place where Maxim wielded so much power.

I yelped when Rafael lifted me by my armpits and pinned me against the cold tile. I wrapped my legs around his hips. "I want you… only you," I whispered.

His lips collided with mine. He pressed just inside of me. "I need you. I need every part of you." He lavished me with his tongue. My neck, my breasts, my mouth… he was everywhere at once.

Rafael thrust, pulled back, and thrust again.

I held fast as the water pelted us. "Don't stop."

His finger slid to that unthinkable place. My breath caught when he claimed this part of me. He'd never… no one had ever… claimed this part of me. My vision blurred as pleasure pulsed between my legs.

He stole my objection with a kiss. His tongue thrust, his finger thrust, everything thrust at once. *Pure ecstasy* pebbled my breasts. Rafael plundered every crevice while I clung to him. We spun higher, wound tighter, until my head fell back against the wall. Rafael suckled my breasts, forcing me over the edge. We exploded violently… pulsed relentlessly… as one.

My toes gradually touched the ground.

Rafael washed my hair while our breathing slowed. "Thank you."

I offered him a wry smile. "That should make dinner a bit more bearable."

He laughed. "I should think so. If not, I'll request a 'do over.'"

I lathered his hair. "I'd like a 'do over' either way, immediately following dessert."

He pressed the entire length of his body against mine. "Maybe we should skip dessert."

I trembled with anticipation.

We rinsed, toweled, and dressed quickly. "I don't know what to do about these," I complained when I stepped out of the bathroom.

Rafael's eyes widened. We'd dressed separately, so this was his first glimpse of my dress. "I have a few ideas," he murmured, then shook his head. "You can't wear that dress."

I blew out an exasperated breath. I hadn't a clue what one wore to dinner inside a presidential residence. After conferring briefly, the girls and I had decided Maxim's celebratory dinner required an evening dress. We'd packed multiple dresses to cover our bases, but this was the only other evening dress I'd packed besides the one I'd chosen for the ball. "This dress wouldn't look so bad if these weren't spilling out." I tried smooshing my breasts.

"That just makes it worse," Rafael choked.

The midnight blue gown was elegant enough, but it was cut low in the front. My breasts, which appeared to have grown yet another cup size, were spilling out. The built in bra was forcing a generous amount of cleavage. I glared at Rafael accusingly. "Your son did this to me."

Rafael laughed. His thumbs tickled my nipples into hard peaks while his tongue traced the cleavage. "Remind me to thank him later."

"That's not even remotely helpful." I rubbed my nipples back into submission while I backed away.

Rafael tugged me back against his chest. "Maxim's eyes will be all over you either way. Now, let's get this dinner out of the way so I can unwrap my son's gifts." A wicked smile played on his lips.

"You're terrible," I teased him. Still, my body hummed with anticipation.

Rafael knocked on Jase's door. A pained expression claimed Jase's face when he saw my dress. Kadyn just laughed. We collected Cenia, Roger, and Shae before meeting the rest of our friends downstairs.

The smile slid from my face when I realized everyone had a drink in his hand. This was Simferopol all over again. There were sure to be toasts, and I knew Maxim would notice if I wasn't drinking. He'd take offense unless I offered a viable explanation.

Maxim met us at the base of the stairs. "You look exquisite, *kotyonok*. Please, won't you join me?" He whisked me right out from under Rafael's arm with nary a thought about how Rafael might respond.

I shot Rafael an apologetic look. "I... I'm not up for drinking alcohol this evening. I'm afraid my stomach hasn't recovered from the flight."

Maxim forced his eyes from my bodice. "Will cranberry juice and Sprite suffice?"

"Yes," I nodded. "That sounds perfect."

Maxim requested the drink from a nearby waiter. Several waiters were milling about with appetizers and drinks. He led me into the formal living room. "Prime Minister Azarov and his wife are here. They are anxious to see you."

My fingers clenched Maxim's arm. My heart was pounding. Hard. Prime Minister Azarov had offered me a job in the Ministry of Foreign Affairs after meeting me at a charity event last year. Maxim and I had joined the Prime Minister and his wife for the symphony, shortly before the SVR abducted me. The SVR had used me in the worst possible way, forcing the former president and the Prime Minister to sign a treaty allowing Russia's Black Sea Fleet to remain in Sevastopol in order to secure my release.

Maxim's eyes softened when he saw how scared I was. He pulled me close while gently caressing my back. "Mykola and Lyudmyla have been worried for you. They have been praying for you for months. Mykola wishes to thank you for all that you have done, and they both want to ensure you are truly okay."

I blinked back tears.

Maxim released me when the waiter arrived with my drink. He leveled Rafael with a single glance before testing the drink himself. He handed me the glass.

"Kristine!" Lyudmyla exclaimed. She kissed both cheeks before pulling me into a warm embrace. "Your courage and strength humble me. I am so sorry…"

Prime Minister Azarov promptly cut her off. "*Milaya moya*, I am certain Ms. Stone would prefer to discuss more pleasant things." He wiped his wife's lipstick away before gently kissing my cheek. "Thank you for helping us secure the pipeline and the defense shield." He waved dismissively toward the rest of the guests. "And they thought it was your beauty that inspired me to offer you that job. We showed them, didn't we?" He winked.

"Mykola, who is this exquisite creature you hold in your arms?" a distinguished looking gentleman with glasses demanded.

Prime Minister Azarov laughed. "This is the woman who encouraged Maxim to steal your job so he could secure the presidency." His eyes sparkled with mischief. "Ms. Stone, I don't believe you two have met. This is Ukraine's Minister of Foreign Affairs, Leonid Kozhara."

I sucked in a breath. "Minister Kozhara, I'm so sorry. I didn't mean…" I glanced at Maxim worriedly. "Well, maybe I did mean…" My cheeks heated as words failed me.

Maxim's laughter warmed the room. He tucked me protectively under his arm. "Do not worry, *kotyonok*. Leonid agrees that was a brilliant move. I doubt Secretary Gates or USAID would have negotiated with me if I hadn't been representing the Ukrainian government in some formal capacity."

Understanding dawned in Minister Kozhara's eyes. "Ms. Stone, I should have recognized you, but alas those photographs did not do you justice. You are the young woman who stole my country's heart in that media storm last year." He gently kissed my hand. "As well you should have. We owe you a debt of gratitude."

Tears threatened once more. "I… I just hope it helps. I've been so worried about how Russia might respond."

"The defense shield will limit Putin's options," Prime Minister Azarov assured me.

I caught sight of Kadyn. "Please, allow me to introduce you to my friend, Kadyn. He's the one who convinced Secretary Gates to meet with Maxim."

I broke away from Maxim so I could retrieve him. I linked my arm in Kadyn's while I steered him toward the group. "Kadyn, I'd like you to meet Prime Minister Azarov, his wife, Lyudmyla, and Ukraine's Minister of Foreign Affairs, Leonid Kozhara. This is my friend, Kadyn Rand. He's the director of new technologies for U.S. Customs and Border Protection."

The men shook hands. A lengthy conversation ensued about Ukraine's eastern border. I tried my best to follow the conversation, but I was worried about neglecting Rafael. He should be standing beside me, as my fiancé, not blending into the woodwork like my security detail.

Lev intercepted me on our way into the dining room. He planted a quick kiss on my cheek. "Kristine, thank you... for everything. We are so pleased you are here. Should you require a cup of coffee..." He grinned boyishly.

I smiled my first genuine smile of the evening. "Thank you, Lev. It's good to see you again. Congratulations, and thank you for helping Maxim secure the presidency. I understand that was no small feat."

He blushed, unaccustomed to compliments.

My eyes narrowed when I saw Konstantin talking to Shae. I stepped forward, intending to join them, but Maxim angled me toward the head of the table.

"I would like you to remain by my side." He offered me the chair to his right.

Prime Minister Azarov and his wife claimed the chairs to Maxim's left. Minister Kozhara and the Chairman of the Verkhovna Rada, Ukraine's parliament, sat next to them. Two Supreme Court justices and three women I had yet to meet joined them. Lev, Konstantin, and Shae rounded out that side of the table. Kadyn sat at the end, opposite Maxim, so he could remain close to Shae. Rafael claimed the seat next to me. The rest of our friends filled the remaining seats.

I leaned over and whispered in Maxim's ear. "Since when does twenty-five people comprise a small, intimate dinner?"

He blanketed my hand with his. "I would have preferred a candlelit dinner for two, but you invited all of these guests." He waved toward my side of the table. "The least I could do was offer them someone to talk to."

He kissed my hand before standing to address our guests. "We have many things to celebrate this evening, the least of which is a presidency. We celebrate a more secure Ukraine... a more secure Europe as well. Soon, everyone in this country will sleep more soundly. Soon, every Ukrainian will have food in his belly. And this is only the beginning. The future holds great things for our country, for the EU, and the United States. We will protect and care for one another as allies should. We will work together to right the wrongs in this world... as comrades and as friends. Thank you, each and every one of you, for joining me in this endeavor."

Everyone raised his glass. A number of other toasts ensued while the first course was being served. The dinner began with *borshch*, the same savory soup Oni had prepared for us. This was quickly followed by *varenyky* and *banosh* with *brynza*. I waited patiently for Rafael to sample each dish before digging into my food. Having lost my previous two meals on the jet, I was beyond ravenous.

Maxim was thrilled. "You are enjoying the food."

I smiled, mildly embarrassed by my voracious appetite. "Oni cooked some of these same dishes for us in Virginia. They're so good."

He looked pleased. "How is Oni?"

I reached for my cranberry juice. "She's doing well. We invited her to come, but she was afraid she might never leave if she saw her family. She wants to finish her studies before she returns, and she's immersed in final papers right now."

"As are you, I presume."

I nodded. "I only have one paper remaining... a paper about Ukraine."

"Really?" His interest piqued.

"I'm developing strategies to resolve the conflict between Russia and Ukraine," I explained.

He grinned. "You will share that analysis with me when you are done?"

I laughed. "If you're looking for something to read that will lull you to sleep, then sure."

His eyes burned bright. "Still, you seek to help my country. Kristine, I will read everything you write... multiple times." He kissed my cheek. "I will leave you to entertain your friends while I engage our remaining guests. Please return to me before you retire. In my dreams, you always return. I shall endeavor to keep it that way."

An unspoken thought passed between us. If there had been one less twist in the road, I could have easily fallen in love with this man. Maxim sensed this, but he was far too honorable a man to force my hand. I gently squeezed his hand. "I could use some fresh air. Would you mind if I ventured out onto the terrace?"

His eyes met Rafael's. "Please ensure her safety while we're apart." He rose politely when we stood, as did the remaining men.

Rafael retrieved my coat from the butler before escorting me outside. With the city lights, the view from the terrace was stunning at night. Rafael hugged me from behind. His hands slid inside my coat so he could rub my belly. "Are you okay?"

I leaned back so I could rest my head against his chest. "Yes. I just needed some time alone with you. I know we're here to support Maxim, and he has an image to uphold, but I feel like I'm neglecting you in the process."

Rafael nuzzled my neck. "I can picture you with him, you know. You actually seem very well suited for one another."

I sighed softly. "I think that is the illusion he is striving for." I turned to face Rafael. "Maxim may need me, but I need you."

He looked unconvinced.

I cradled his face in my hand. "Think about it. Every time I veered down the wrong road, God created a roadblock. Countless events in my life have driven me closer to you. You, Rafael, are the man God intended for me. I can feel his hand in this. Can you?"

"Yes," he admitted, "as if he'd forged you from my soul."

* * * * *

My fingers caressed Maxim's Bible. The brown leather bound book was worn and charred around the edges just like the wooden cross he wore around his neck. I wondered what horrific event these objects had survived and whether that same incident had claimed Maxim's family. Maxim had revealed that the KGB killed his entire family, but he never explained how. I was beginning to suspect arson.

I looked up at the monitor while adjusting the earpiece that translated the proceedings into English. The Speaker of the Parliament was welcoming their more distinguished guests by name. Several foreign ambassadors and presidents from other countries were in attendance, including the United States. Kadyn was sitting next to Secretary Gates. While

Rafael and Jase were permitted to remain with me, the rest of our friends had been escorted into the balcony.

Rafael, Jase, and I were observing the inauguration from a hidden chamber adjoining the parliament. Architecturally, the exterior of the Verkhovna Rada looked like the United States Supreme Court. There were a few distinguishing features. Yellow and blue Ukrainian flags surrounded this building, and they had quite literally rolled out the red carpet for Maxim. The inside of the Verkhovna Rada was fashioned a lot like our House of Representatives. I found these similarities comforting, given my time on the Hill.

"How are you holding up?" Rafael inquired worriedly.

"Good," I lied. My knee was bouncing wildly. "I still can't believe Maxim invited us to dinner last night. He could have invited the Secretary General of NATO, Secretary Gates, and the President of the United States. Why would he invite us? He should be rubbing elbows with them now."

Rafael shook his head. "Maxim is not the sort of man to forget the people who helped him. You believed in him, and you and Kadyn helped him when no one else would."

Jase felt my forehead. "Do you still feel like throwing up?"

"No. The Zofran helped." I stilled my trembling hand against the gold and cream embroidered suit I'd so carefully selected for this event. "I wish I'd known Maxim was breaking with tradition."

Jase froze. "How so?"

I took a deep breath and slowly released it. Maxim and I had met privately for breakfast so he could brief me on the inauguration and explain my role. "Historically, the President of Ukraine has sworn his oath alone. This will be the first time anyone has held the Ukrainian Constitution and the

Peresopnytsia Gospels for the president." I glanced at the Bible. "He's also adding his father's Bible to the stack. No president has ever done that before."

"It will be interesting to see how the parliament views those changes," Rafael mused.

"Not to mention the citizens of Ukraine. Those changes are very symbolic. Maxim's honoring God, country, and family as he swears this oath. By including Kristine in the ceremony, he's publically acknowledging his alliance with the United States." Jase looked at me. "This is dangerous. Maxim is thumbing his nose at the frothing bear next door while inviting Lady Liberty into his parliament."

I hugged Maxim's bible while tucking my head between my knees. "Now I'm going to throw up."

"You can't. The Chairman of the Constitutional Court of Ukraine just stood. They're ready for you," Rafael warned.

"Holy crap." I nearly dropped the Bible. "I can't believe I just said that. I'm holding his father's Bible!"

Rafael laughed. "Maybe we should pray."

As if in slow motion, the door to the parliament opened. Maxim looked stressed, but he smiled the moment our eyes met. "Are you ready?"

"We'll be praying," Rafael encouraged softly.

"Me too," I whispered, although my prayers would be silently spoken.

I clutched Maxim's Bible to my chest before accepting his arm. Together, we stepped onto the parliament floor. "I'm so proud of you, Maxim. I've known it since the moment you came crashing through that door. You are a good man. You've devoted your entire life to strengthening civil liberties, to reducing poverty, and to protecting your people. This title simply acknowledges what you've been doing all along."

His pace slowed as we neared the podium. Maxim's eyes remained on me, despite the immense crowd surrounding us. "Regardless of what the future holds for us, you will always be my first lady, Kristine. I could not love you more than I do in this moment."

Tears slipped through my lashes. Frankly, I was relieved. With my vision blurred, I couldn't see all the intimidating men standing before me. I handed Maxim his father's Bible so the chairman could arrange the books in the proper order. I remained standing to Maxim's right.

The chairman handed me the Peresopnytsia Gospels, a Slavic manuscript dating back to the sixteenth century. This was the first known translation of the four gospels of the New Testament into the Old Ukrainian language. Every Ukrainian President sworn into office had taken his oath on these gospels.

Maxim's fingers trailed longingly over the manuscript. I couldn't blame him for wanting to touch it. Very few people were allowed to touch the Peresopnytsia Gospels.

The chairman set the Ukrainian Constitution on top of the Peresopnytsia Gospels. The two inch thick legal sized document was bound inside a burgundy leather cover with gold embellishments. My eyes widened when I felt the weight of the constitution on top of the Peresopnytsia Gospels. When combined, the two books were pushing thirty pounds.

Maxim smoothed his hand over the constitution before setting his father's Bible on top of the document. He kissed the charred cross hanging around his neck and placed his right hand on top of the books. He rested his hand in a way that ensured he was touching all three books at once.

Please, God, give him the courage and strength to see this through.

Maxim's voice rang strong and true. "I, Maxim Markov,

elected by the will of the people as the President of Ukraine, assuming this high office, do solemnly swear allegiance to Ukraine."

Guide him as he governs this country. Help him serve selflessly.

"I pledge with all my undertakings to protect the sovereignty and independence of Ukraine…"

Protect him, protect his people and their country.

"…to provide for the good of the Motherland and the welfare of the Ukrainian people, to protect the rights and freedoms of citizens…"

Free them from the evils of this earth; from poverty, corruption, violence, and fear.

"…to abide by the Constitution of Ukraine and the laws of Ukraine, to exercise my duties in the interests of all compatriots, and to enhance the prestige of Ukraine in the world."

Command every thought, word, and deed so that Maxim's actions reflect your will. When they do, we will rejoice in your name; for the kingdom, the power, and the glory are yours and yours alone. Amen.

Maxim signed the oath of office and handed it to the Chairman of the Constitutional Court before rescuing the heavy books from my trembling arms. I offered a subtle nod and an encouraging smile before backing toward the mahogany wall where Rafael and Jase were waiting for me.

Maxim stepped forward so he could receive the official symbols of presidential power. Trumpets sounded as men in uniform strode down both aisles. They were carrying an assortment of objects atop burgundy pillows. The first officer to Maxim's left presented him with a thin booklet.

Maxim held the passport sized ID for everyone to see. Applause thundered throughout the parliament as he accepted the Presidential ID.

The chairman lifted a necklace from the pillow to Maxim's right. He placed the necklace around Maxim's neck. My earpiece indicated this was a badge, but it looked more like twenty or thirty metals woven together in a heavy gold, red, and blue enamel necklace.

The chairman handed him the Great Seal of the President of Ukraine. Maxim held it up for everyone to see. The applause was deafening.

Next came the Presidential Mace. Again, Maxim held it so everyone could see.

"What is a Presidential Mace?" Jase asked.

"A ceremonial staff," Rafael answered.

I couldn't fathom what a ceremonial staff might be used for.

The applause died down when Maxim stepped behind the podium. We stood completely spellbound while he gave his inaugural speech. Maxim listed the economic and security problems plaguing his country before unveiling his strategies for resolving them. He made an impassioned plea to the parliament, encouraging them to join in his fight against poverty, elitism, corruption, and human rights violations.

When Maxim announced his intention to sign the trade agreement with the European Union, he received a standing ovation. I wasn't surprised. President Yanukovych's failure to sign that trade agreement, and his decision to strengthen ties with Russia instead, had fueled an uprising that drove him out of office. Maxim's plans to strengthen ties with the EU, the United States, and NATO led to another standing ovation.

The applause grew thunderous when he mentioned Russia. "I will not tolerate Russia's meddling in Ukraine's governance, their incursions over our eastern border, or the annexation of Crimea. The insidious threat posed by the SVR ends now. Ukraine is a sovereign nation, and we demand to be treated as such. Any trade agreements with Russia will be mutually beneficial, or I will refuse to sign them. Putin will not dictate our future. We, the people of Ukraine, determine our own future."

Maxim's rich baritone voice rang out as he sang their national anthem a cappella. A choir standing opposite him in the balcony gradually joined him. They were wearing Ukraine's traditional clothing. In a crescendo, the parliament, and nearly every person in attendance, layered their voices over Maxim's.

A single tear slid down my cheek. Maxim's inauguration was the most remarkable event I'd ever seen. Here too, God's hand was evident. I was certain I'd never regret bearing witness to this monumental event.

* * * * *

I sank into the chair next to Shae. "How are you holding up?"

Her shoulders lifted in a delicate shrug. "I'm okay."

"You look beautiful." Her evening gown looked like a starlit waterfall. "How are things going with Konstantin?"

"I'm not sure," she answered honestly. "He's so tight lipped, we hardly speak anymore."

I studied her sullen expression. "Is he planning to move back to Ukraine?"

"I think he'd like to, but Maxim asked him to remain at the embassy for now." She eyed Brady and Jase, who were conversing a few feet away. "Where's Rafael?"

"He's in the foyer, speaking with the security detail out of Portugal." Tons of people were milling about Mariyinsky

Palace in anticipation of Maxim's arrival for the inaugural ball. Security was proving a logistical nightmare given the chaos surrounding us.

Shae's eyes morphed into two giant saucers.

"Kristine," Kadyn called from directly behind me.

The look on Shae's face was enough to make me bolt from my chair and turn around. I grasped the top of my chair. "Ma... Ma... Mr. President."

President Obama reached for my hand. "Ms. Stone, I've learned some wonderful things about you."

"About me?" My eyes shot to Kadyn while I shook his hand.

President Obama chuckled softly. "Senator Rockefeller mentioned your interest in funding the Odessa-Brody Pipeline in a Senate Democratic Caucus meeting in January. Mark Sondell shared his impressions of you when I met with the IMF back in February, and USAID called me about your request last month. When you set your mind to something, you don't mess around."

I fidgeted nervously. I wasn't sure how to respond.

His eyes warmed. "I admire your initiative and your determination to improve human security in Ukraine and in the EU. Secretary Gates is thrilled we've found a home for the missile defense shield."

"That was Kadyn's idea," I insisted.

"I've already thanked Mr. Rand. I asked him to introduce me to you, so I could thank you too. I truly appreciate everything you've done, Ms. Stone. Senator Rockefeller told me you were targeted and harmed by the SVR when you were here on a peacebuilding trip in June. I understand these efforts may come at a high cost for you, so I'll tell you the same thing I told Mr. Rand. If you are threatened, I want to hear about it. Do you understand?" He placed his business card in my trembling hand.

My vision blurred. "Yes, sir."

He patted me on the back. "You are truly courageous, Ms. Stone. I'm pleased to have finally met you."

Kadyn introduced President Obama to Shae, Brady, and Jase. I forced myself to remain standing until he was lured away.

"Did we...?" Shae sank into the chair next to me.

I shook my head. "How did we get to this... *this place*... where our actions have such grave consequences... where we dine and dance with presidents?"

"I haven't a clue," she whispered.

I rose from my chair. "I need water and some fresh air."

"I'll grab some Perrier," Brady offered.

Shae's eyes narrowed. "You're drinking water?"

I glanced at Jase. His hands rose as he backed away.

Shae rose from her chair. "You didn't drink alcohol at your bridal shower or last night."

"Don't say it," I pleaded. "Please, Shae. We're not telling anyone until I'm further along."

Her eyes glistened with tears. "I thought you were mad at me. You've been acting so weird the past few months. You hide out in your office, you barely speak to anyone, and you don't invite me over anymore. I thought you were mad at me."

"I'm not mad at you. How could I be mad at you? You're one of the sweetest people I know." I pulled her into my arms. "Rafael has been living in Portugal. He's working a high priority case for the Portuguese Police. He didn't want anyone to know. He was worried about how Maxim might respond."

Shae looked thoroughly confused. "But you and Rafael are still together…"

I nodded. "Very much so. This is a temporary assignment. We plan to live in Virginia, although we may have to bounce between both countries for a while."

"And the baby?" she whispered.

"We'd like to wait until after the wedding to make that announcement. I'm only fifteen and a half weeks along. I lost my first baby. I just… We want to wait until we're further along."

Shae offered a solemn nod. "I won't tell a single soul. I promise."

My eyes sparked with mischief as the tension eased from my arms. "Want to hear another secret?"

A radiant smile lit her face. She leaned closer.

"Rafael and I were married in a civil ceremony in Lisbon last month. He insisted on being married when he discovered I was pregnant." I laughed at the shocked expression on her face. "Don't worry. We're still proceeding with the formal ceremony next month."

"Oh, Kri! That's wonderful news." She squeezed the air from my lungs.

I chuckled softly. "One tiny secret remains."

She glanced at me uncertainly.

"There's an insanely handsome man who has fallen hopelessly in love with you. He's here, in this very room. I'm certain he'll ask you to dance, but it's not Konstantin."

Warm fingers slid lovingly down my arms. "You are wearing my colors."

I trembled when Maxim's voice rolled over me. I was wearing a royal blue evening gown with gold beads stitched in a regal design that framed my shoulders, chest, and waist. The gold beads dipped below my hips before spiraling across my lower back. Slowly, I turned around. "So you own gold and blue now?"

Maxim laughed. "That precise shade of blue and gold are the only two colors that appear on my country's flag. Of course I own them." He pulled me close. "Do you deny you chose this dress for me?"

"No," I answered breathlessly. I didn't dare move. Maxim was clearly aroused. Any move I might make would only arouse him more.

"Let's dance," he whispered silkily.

I tried not to panic. Jase was being restrained, as was Brady. Rafael was nowhere to be found. "But they haven't served dinner yet."

"They can dine while we dance." He issued a single command in Russian to the men standing behind him.

"Maxim," I objected.

His fingers clenched my hip as he steered me toward the dance floor. "You would defy a presidential order?"

My heart stalled.

Maxim pulled me close when he stepped onto the dance floor. As if on cue, the orchestra began. "You belong with me, *kotyonok*, for the next thirty minutes at least." He grasped my hand while cradling my back. He peered deep into my eyes as he began to dance.

My breath caught. This wasn't the same waltz I'd danced with Kadyn. This was an International Waltz, which was slower and far more intimate than the American Waltz. I straightened my spine and held my chin high when I realized that millions of people were watching us. The event was being televised.

Maxim sighed. "Rafael is safe. He has been detained by

an elusive security problem. That is all. Please, *kotyonok*, relax and enjoy the dance."

My eyes narrowed. "Was this elusive security problem fabricated?"

He smiled. "Perhaps."

I tried not to laugh at his audacity. I took a deep breath and slowly released it. The tension eased from my shoulders and back.

His mood grew pensive. "Do you know there are conspiracy theories surrounding you?"

My brow furrowed.

"You disappeared so abruptly. This sparked a great deal of speculation. Information about your capture and the SVR's violent acts eventually reached the media. Most have speculated that I hid you someplace safe after rescuing you. Others have claimed my love for you is so great that I have imprisoned you inside my home and refuse to share you with the outside world. Some claim I've been hiding you and our unborn child."

My jaw fell slack.

"I have often wished that one were true." Maxim released a long drawn out breath. "Your appearance at the inauguration today dispelled any belief that you may be carrying my child... which makes it all the more ironic that you are in fact with child."

My feet stalled.

Maxim pulled me closer so I could follow his lead without thinking. "You didn't think I would notice? Your breasts are fuller, your skin radiant. Kristine, there is only one thing that could make you more desirable."

The room blurred. Our entwined bodies continued to move in small, intimate circles. I gripped Maxim's hand a little tighter. "Please," I whispered. I couldn't bear to hear it.

"If you were carrying my child." His eyes brazenly caressed my face, my neck, and breasts. "Throughout my life, there has only been one thing I desired for myself."

My eyes filled with tears.

"You, Kristine. You are the only thing I have ever desired for myself, but I fear this world has conspired against me."

His eyes captured and held mine. "I would not wish this for you, but if anything should ever happen to Rafael... I would welcome you and your child with open arms."

Tears spilled down my cheeks.

"I will wait for you, Kristine. I may be frail and gray before you are free to marry me, but I will wait... as long as it takes."

Chapter 9 – The One

I tucked my feet against the bench, hugged my knees to my chest, and gazed at the Potomac River. Soft pink cherry blossoms softened the edges along the shore. I took a deep breath, savoring the rich, earthy scent of freshly cut grass. Slowly, I unraveled my thoughts.

Rafael had spent the last two weeks in Portugal while hunting pedophiles. Sadly, there seemed to be a never ending stream of sick individuals who preyed on helpless children. He was flying to Virginia now. My final paper was submitted last week. Course grades were released yesterday. I was graduating summa cum laude, as was Shae. I couldn't believe we were finally graduating.

My thoughts spiraled back to the inaugural ball. Maxim was the only man I danced with that night. I was too wrecked to dance with anyone else. I toyed with my food while failing to maintain any sort of conversation with my friends. Rafael offered to take me back to Maxim's place, but I wanted to see Kadyn and Shae dance. We left shortly after that. I didn't reveal what Maxim had said. I hated keeping that from him, but I was certain no good could come from Rafael knowing about that promise.

I was still deeply in love with Rafael, but for reasons I could not comprehend, I still mourned what could have been with Maxim. After lamenting that fact for weeks, I decided there are some things we are not meant to understand. The stars never fully align the way any one person wants them to. They shift over time, often in unpredictable ways, so I was done speculating about what the future might hold for me... or for anyone else. I was leaving that up to God, for now. I was fairly certain it would play out the way he intended either way. That idea was somewhat liberating.

My thoughts drifted closer to home. Shae suspected Kadyn was the person I'd been alluding to at the inaugural ball. While I refused to confirm or deny her suspicions, I was pleased she seemed receptive to the idea. She had yet to end her relationship with Konstantin, but she was seeing less of him. Kadyn was spending more time at my place. He liked hanging out with Brady and Jase, and he enjoyed listening to the baby's heartbeat even more than Brady.

I was eighteen weeks pregnant, well beyond the first trimester, but the baby was still wreaking havoc on my stomach. I felt nauseous more often than not. This inspired the men to cook, but they weren't just plying me with food. They were competing for the most enticing dish.

My hand slid lovingly over my stomach while I unraveled my legs. The tiniest baby bump had finally formed. I couldn't wait to show Rafael.

"That is the most beautiful thing I've ever seen," he cooed.

My heart stalled as I spun around. "You're here? Already?"

His laughter warmed me from the inside out. "I couldn't wait to see you, so we left last night." His hand claimed my tummy as he slid onto the bench. "I can't believe he's finally making an appearance."

I scooted closer. "I may have to buy Spanx to wear under my wedding dress so he doesn't show."

Rafael frowned. "Spank? I don't want you spanking my child."

I stared at him for a couple of heartbeats. When I realized he was serious, I laughed until I cried. "I'm not spanking your child. Spanx are a type of undergarment. They'll pull my stomach in so he doesn't show."

He shook his head. "I don't want you squishing him. Besides, I've waited months for this little guy to show. He'll be hidden by the bouquet if he's visible at all."

I burrowed beneath his arm. "What names are you contemplating these days?"

He looked thoughtful. "I can't seem to move beyond Michael, Antonio, Leandro, and Gabriel."

I looked up, surprised. "Antonio?"

He smiled, sadly. "My father's name was Antonio."

"I know a website where we can research the meaning behind their names." I pulled the website up on my phone and typed in the first name. "Michael means gift from God." I typed his father's name. "Antonio means worthy of praise." I typed Chief D'Souza's name. "Leandro means lion… and Gabriel means God is my strength."

"I think we should wait to see what he looks like. He may inspire his own name." He stood and reached for my hand.

"That's true." We walked toward the house.

Rafael drew me close. "Have you felt him move?"

"I can feel little flutters, like champagne bubbles, but I haven't felt him kick yet. Are you looking forward to the sonogram?" Our appointment was scheduled for May thirtieth.

He stopped, abruptly. "I need to get the house ready."

I stood between him and the house. "What do you mean 'ready?' Ready how?"

"I want to knock out a few walls so we can merge our townhouses into a single home. We need space for our little ones to run around."

My eyes narrowed. "Currently, we're only expecting one… and he won't be running any time soon. Can't this wait until we return from Lisbon?"

He shook his head. "I don't want you or the baby breathing in all that construction dust. Renovations should begin the minute we fly back to Portugal. I want that work completed by the time we return."

I gaped at him. "We're flying out in three days. There's no way you can arrange that massive of undertaking in three days."

He smiled that panty dropping smile of his. "Would you care to wager a bet?"

I eyed him warily as we began walking again. "What kind of bet?"

"If I don't have a construction team, a list of renovations, and a set of blueprints drafted before we leave, I'll reveal where we're going for our honeymoon."

My foot stalled on the top step. "I thought your schedule wasn't going to allow for a honeymoon."

"Chief D'Souza granted me five days of leave so I can take you on a proper honeymoon. That gives us eight days from our wedding day when you count the weekends."

I turned around and blocked the door. "You should tell me now."

His eyes lit with amusement. "Or else?"

I folded my arms across my chest. "I won't let you inside the house."

He choked back a laugh. "Surely, you know better than that."

I shook my head defiantly.

This time Rafael really laughed. He picked me up and tossed me over his shoulder with very little effort. "Are Brady and Jase inside?"

"How should I know?" They were sitting on the steps before Rafael arrived.

Rafael pushed the door open. "Brady? Jase!"

They bolted from the family room but stopped short when they saw me dangling from Rafael's shoulder.

"I'm taking my wife upstairs so we can have wild, passionate sex. Do either of you have a problem with that?"

Brady chuckled. "Have at it."

Jase groaned. "I'm out of here."

My head fell against Rafael's back. "I can't believe you just said that."

Rafael strode upstairs. "You're my wife, this is our house, we'll have sex when and where we want." He spent the next three hours proving just that.

* * * * *

Dean Bartoli's voice rolled through the auditorium. "Shae Ann Garlington, summa cum laude." He shook her hand and handed her the degree while the school photographer snapped their picture.

427

Cheers erupted from our classmates, colleagues, family, and friends.

"Way to go, Shae!" Kadyn shouted.

She grinned as she crossed the stage.

That put a smile on my face. I fiddled with my honor cords while the eighteen classmates who separated us walked across the stage. Finally, the only things separating me from my degree were three solid stairs and half a stage.

The dean's voice rang out again. "Kristine Annabelle Stone, summa cum laude."

My stomach fluttered as cheers erupted. I gaped at the billowy black robe. *Did the baby know my name?* I walked across the stage in a daze. I snapped out of it when the dean handed me the tightly wound scroll and shook my hand. He patted me on the back.

Dr. Sandstrom rose from his chair behind the dean so he could give me a hug. "Congratulations."

"Thank you," I whispered. "Promise me, we'll remain friends. That you'll keep in touch."

He nodded, his eyes softening before he returned to his seat.

I walked toward the stairs, where Rafael was beaming up at me.

He handed me a dozen long stemmed roses, scooped me up, and twirled me in his arms. "I'm so proud of you, baby. You did it!" He planted a quick kiss on my lips before I scampered off to my seat.

I watched Rafael walk back to his seat. He was sitting next to my cousin, Lexie. I still couldn't believe he'd sent the jet to Montana to retrieve my family so they could see me graduate. He'd deemed them an early graduation present when they arrived late last night.

Shae leaned over her seat so she could give me a hug. We cheered for our remaining classmates. Finally, the last student crossed the stage.

Dean Bartoli's chin rose. "Degree recipients, please stand." He waited for the auditorium to quiet. Then… "I confer upon each of you that degree for which you stand, the Master of Science in Conflict Analysis and Resolution, with all the rights and privileges thereunto appertaining. You may move your tassels. Congratulations, graduates!"

Tears of joy, relief, and gratitude fell during the applause. We followed our dean and faculty into the foyer, where we exchanged tearful hugs and promised to keep in touch. We remained together until our families claimed us.

Shae and her family joined us for dinner. We met at Mokomandy, a hugely popular restaurant in Sterling, Virginia. Mokomandy served an eclectic mix of Korean and Creole food on small plates, like tapas. Rafael had commandeered the entire restaurant, which had recently won numerous awards.

I gave him a quick kiss on the cheek before dropping onto the chair next to my mom. I squeezed her hand beneath the table. "I still can't believe you're here."

"Neither can I," she admitted. Like me, she was soaking in the small, contemporary restaurant… the wood tables, the cushy white chairs, and the canvas wrapped photographs displaying artfully presented dishes. A bright red wall framed a large stainless steel kitchen that glistened behind pass through windows at the far end of the restaurant. A long, narrow bar sat empty behind us.

Lexie snagged the chair across from me. "Thank you for sending the jet. I can't believe it has a built in chess set and a bed!"

"How am I supposed to fly on a commercial airplane after that?" Nate asked.

Everyone laughed.

A waiter stopped by to collect our drink orders.

Dad peered down the table at Rafael. "Is that the same aircraft you're sending for the wedding?"

My family waited with baited breath.

Rafael smiled. "Yes, sir. We'll send the jet back for you on Wednesday."

Kari and Brent were going to be busy over the next few days. They were flying my family back to Montana tomorrow, picking Rafael and me up on Sunday to fly us to Portugal, returning to Montana so they could retrieve my family on Wednesday, stopping in Virginia to pick up our friends, and then flying into Portugal Thursday morning.

The waiter returned with our drinks.

Cenia ducked out of his way as he began distributing the drinks. "Is Dan coming?"

Happily, I claimed my cranberry Sprite. I'd been addicted to the tart concoction ever since Maxim introduced me to it. "Yes. Dan and Kimme will be joining my family."

"I can fly to Montana to accompany Dan if he needs help getting through this," Kadyn offered.

I had briefed my entire family on Dan's PTSD so they'd be prepared if his anxieties flared. "Kimme thinks he'll be okay since he's not flying on a commercial aircraft. He's met my Dad, Lexie, and Nate so he should be comfortable with everyone. He has sleeping pills and a bed if he needs them."

Kadyn nodded. "Let me know if that changes."

"I'd like to propose a toast to Kristine and Shae." Rafael stood and raised his glass. "You two are the most phenomenal women I know. You have overcome more challenges in the past two years than most people face in a lifetime. You juggled full time studies against full time jobs that required international travel. Still, you graduated summa cum laude. What you have accomplished is nothing short of remarkable. Your determination to continue on with your studies and your careers in peacebuilding despite the horrors you faced in Ukraine is truly humbling. What you intend to do with your degrees is even more humbling. It is truly an honor to know you."

"Hear! Hear!" Shae's father shouted. Our friends and family tapped their glasses.

"I love you," Rafael whispered.

I gazed at him adoringly. "I love you too."

* * * * *

Rafael eyed my bouncing knee. "Are you okay?"

I pawed at my seatbelt. "This is taking forever. Why haven't we leveled off?"

His brow furrowed. "Do you need to use the restroom?"

I was still trying to figure out how a baby the size of a green pepper could squeeze the life out of my bladder. "No," I grumbled irritably. "I don't have to pee."

He continued studying me. "Are you worried about the wedding?"

"What? No, of course not." I forced my knee to stop.

He looked stumped. "Then why are you so anxious to get out of your seat?"

The intercom dinged. "We've reached thirty-six thousand feet, which is our cruising altitude..."

"Finally!" I ripped the seatbelt off.

Rafael stood.

I grabbed his arm and dragged him to the bedroom. "I *need* sex."

"Last night wasn't enough?" He choked back a laugh.

I tugged my shirt off. "I don't know why, but I need sex really, *really* bad." My shoes, socks, jeans, and undergarments fell to the floor.

His eyes heated while amusement danced on his lips. "Well, I'm happy to help you with that."

I watched him undress. "This is your son's doing. You do know that?" I pushed him onto the bed.

Rafael grinned when I climbed on top of him. "That's one thoughtful kid."

I groaned when he latched onto my breast. "I need you inside of me. Now."

He suckled my breasts while I positioned him. Suddenly, he grabbed my hips and thrust.

Pleasure licked my core. "Don't move," I pleaded.

He stopped breathing.

"I just... I'm on the verge of... Oh, God!" Spasms wracked my body.

Rafael laughed while he gently caressed my back. "That was easy."

"I'm not done," I whimpered.

He stared at me in disbelief.

My eyes narrowed. "Well you shouldn't have laughed. I felt that, and... Ugh!" I grunted when Rafael rolled me beneath him.

He forced my hands over my head and thrust. "How's this?"

My eyes glazed over. "Better."

"How about this?" He thrust even harder.

I moaned more than spoke my response.

He buried himself to the hilt.

"More," I pleaded. There was something terribly wrong with me. My skin literally crawled with need.

His hands squeezed my breasts. He pinched both nipples while he thrust. I braced my hands against the headboard. My ankles slipped. My hips rose.

Rafael pinned my knees to my shoulders and thrust... hard and fast... then deep and slow. Every time I neared release, he switched it up. I grew mindless with lust.

Finally, Rafael lost it. He pounded *relentlessly*.

My hands fisted in his hair as I dragged his lips toward mine.

He drove inside of me with unconscionable force. Once... twice... three times.

The room sheeted white. My back arched as the most intense orgasm I'd ever known tore through me. Rafael groaned as he pulsed inside of me. I writhed beneath him, savoring the heat.

"More?" he inquired warily.

My nipples hardened against his chest. I pulled his hips close until he was buried deeper than he'd ever been before. "Lots, lots more."

* * * * *

I tucked the towel around my chest and rose from the thickly padded bed. The heated stone massage was heavenly. I loved that the Penha Longa Spa offered massages outside next to their botanical garden, a contrast pool, and a private waterfall. I dipped my toes into the Jacuzzi before perching on the tile. I'd read somewhere that pregnant women weren't supposed to submerge their bellies in Jacuzzis, so my legs would have to suffice for now.

I took a deep breath, savoring the soft, soapy scent of the botanical gardens and the salty tang of the ocean. Birds chirped happily while I basked in the sun. This place was so peaceful, I could linger here for days.

I couldn't believe how calm I felt. We were getting married in less than twenty-four hours. My friends and family were settled into the hotel. Every wedding guest was here... well, everyone except Maxim. He was busy running a country, so I wasn't expecting him to show.

I felt a flutter in my tummy. I leaned back and caressed my stomach. Babies did weird things to your body, and they demanded everything in the extreme. I wasn't just nauseous, I was *insanely* nauseous. I wasn't just hungry, I was *ravenously* hungry. I didn't just have to pee... I had to pee *now*.

And the sex, *holy cow*, the sex. Now wasn't that the best kept secret among the pregnant crowd? Every nerve ending in my body felt so much more sensitive. Blood was pounding in places I never even new existed. I didn't just need sex, I was pretty certain I'd die without it. Now I knew why men liked their women barefoot and pregnant, and why women truly loved being pregnant. All those extra hormones turned them into sex addicts.

We had spent nearly the entire flight in bed having sex. I slept while Rafael worked the next day. When he arrived home, I greeted him at the door naked. We enjoyed another night of marathon sex. Tuesday and Wednesday played out the exact same way. Our friends and family arrived Thursday, and now here we were at the Penha Longa Resort, just hours away from our rehearsal dinner. Since we were planning to sleep separately tonight, I was left questioning whether I could survive two and a half days without sex.

"A penny for your thoughts." Shae dipped her toe in the Jacuzzi and sat down beside me.

I chuckled, too embarrassed to respond.

"Are you worried about the wedding?" she inquired curiously.

I shook my head. "Not at all. I feel calm and oddly content."

She wiggled her toes in the water. "I thought weddings were supposed to be stressful."

I shrugged. "Maybe it's because we're already married."

She gazed out over the garden.

"So, no Konstantin?"

She shook her head.

I tried not to smile. "Is Kadyn your plus one then?"

She humored me with a sidelong glance. "I think maybe he is."

I studied my friend. "How do you feel about him?"

She peered down at the water. "Conflicted. I don't really have the best instincts when it comes to men."

"Are you physically attracted to him?" I couldn't imagine anyone answering "no" to the question.

She sighed softly. "Yes, but I don't want to do anything that could compromise our friendship."

I turned that thought in my head. "Kadyn isn't an all or nothing kind of guy. Things didn't work out between us, and we're still really good friends."

She quietly considered me. "Why didn't it work out between you?"

I took a deep breath and blew it out. "Honestly? After everything that happened with Michael, I didn't feel I deserved him. When I returned from Paris, he made it very clear we could only be friends. I worked hard to perceive him

435

as such. I tried to view him differently when he admitted he still had feelings for me, but that switch proved permanently disabled for me. Rafael came along and swept me off my feet, and... well, you know the rest. I'm deeply in love with Rafael. For me, there is no one else."

She eyed me worriedly. "Do you have any regrets? Any regrets at all?"

My eyebrows rose. "About Kadyn?"

She nodded.

I shook my head. "Not at all. Kadyn taught me what true love really is. I was such a mess when I met him. He built my confidence and my trust, and he showed me how to love selflessly. I am so grateful for Kadyn. He will forever remain one my most cherished friends."

She gazed out over the garden again.

I nudged her shoulder with mine. "You can trust him with your heart. I promise. He will never hurt you, and he won't abandon you if it doesn't work out."

A single tear slid down her cheek.

I pulled her against me. "You deserve to be happy, Shae. I don't know what kind of crap these other men have been feeding you, but you're beautiful, you're intelligent, and kind. You should be with someone who appreciates that, someone who's willing to make you a priority, someone who treats you like gold."

She sniffled softly.

I leaned forward so I could peer into her eyes. "There's no sense worrying about it. This will be out of your hands once Kadyn sees you in that bridesmaid dress."

Shae laughed.

I stood and pulled her to her feet. "Let's track down the rest of the girls so we can get our nails done."

* * * * *

Rafael turned heads as we crossed the lobby. He was
wearing a black dress suit and a crisp white shirt without a tie.
The tailored suit accentuated his lethal frame, while his
tousled hair lent a decidedly playful air. Throw in the five
o'clock shadow and the look was utterly beguiling. I was
wearing an elegant jumpsuit with a white twist-style halter
top, a thin gold belt, and black flowy pants. Glittering gold
and black Jimmy Choo heels and a gold cuff bracelet
completed the ensemble.

Rafael opened the door leading out onto the deck. "How
do you feel?"

"Like a wet noodle. The heated stone massage was
wonderful." I paused to admire the view. Lush mountains,
pink clouds, and a lavender sky framed the teal green pool.

He led me around the softly lit pool. The salty air felt
balmy, maybe even a little cool. "Did you sleep?"

We weren't expecting much sleep between the rehearsal
dinner and the wedding, so everyone slept this afternoon. I
bunked with Shae since my sex crazed hormones couldn't be
trusted to sleep in the same room with Rafael. "For three
hours. Did you get any sleep?"

"A little." He stopped at the outdoor bar, where he
ordered a glass of *Vinho Verde* and a cranberry Sprite. "Are
you hungry?"

"Ravenous," I assured him. Our friends were socializing
along the outskirts of the linen clad tables, just a few feet
away. I waved at my parents, but they too were ensnared by
the view.

"Let's get started then." Rafael nabbed a fork off one of

the tables. He tapped it against his glass as we neared our friends.

Everyone quieted.

He quietly considered our guests. "Thank you for joining us. Your willingness to climb out of bed at four-thirty in the morning so we can be married at sunrise speaks volumes about your love for us. On the off chance there's still confusion about that, we are being married at five-thirty in the morning not five-thirty at night."

There was a smattering of laughter.

Rafael smiled as he raised his glass. "This is just one of many ways you've shown your love for us, and *that* is why you're here. Each of you has had a hand in how Kristine and I view friendship, family, and love. You helped shape this relationship. Thank you for guiding us down this path, for building our relationship, for standing beside us in good times and bad. Tomorrow we consecrate our love. But tonight? We celebrate *your* love. Tonight, we rejoice in you."

We tapped glasses and drank to Rafael's toast.

Through misty eyes I gazed at my family and friends. I whispered a silent prayer thanking God for each and every one of them.

* * * * *

Lexie extracted me from Rafael at eleven o'clock. She insisted it was bad luck for him to see me the day of the wedding. We dreamed and reminisced while sprawled on her bed. Jase settled into a chair on the other side of the room. He refused to leave my side.

I must have fallen asleep because Jase was suddenly shaking me. "You're going to be late for your appointment."

He shuddered when he caught sight of my hair. "The sooner we get down there the better."

"Quit picking on my cousin." Lexie flung a pillow at him.

Jase dodged the pillow before holding up his fingers in the sign of a cross. "She's not the only one who needs help." He laughed when she ran to the mirror.

We took the fastest showers on record, brushed our teeth, and slathered deodorant on before following him onto the elevator, across the lobby, and into the spa.

My feet stalled when we entered the spa. "Dan, what are you doing here?"

A slow, lazy smile slid across his rugged face. "I'm here to guard you and your ladies in waiting."

Kimme giggled.

Shae popped open a Diet Coke.

Cenia and Marie walked through the door. "I can't believe we're getting our hair and makeup done at two o'clock in the morning."

Jase shook his head. "I can't believe I'm hanging out in a spa."

Dan snickered. "I plan on shooting the nail polish off that far wall."

The receptionist blanched.

I briefly considered confiscating their guns. "Whatever you do, don't let Rafael come in here. I don't want him to see me before the wedding. Don't shoot him, just… extract him from the room."

Dan tipped an imaginary hat. "Roger that, pretty lady. No one gets past me."

"Good." I followed the receptionist and my friends into the salon.

Marie sank onto the far chair. "Any idea where Rafael's taking you for your honeymoon?"

I climbed into my stylist's chair. "No." Rafael had, in fact, secured a construction team, a list of renovations, and a set of blueprints before we left Virginia, so I hadn't a clue where he was taking me.

Kimme eased onto the chair next to me. "Maybe you'll stay here. This place is so dreamy."

I laughed. "Honey, you ain't seen noth'n yet." I couldn't wait for my friends to see Monserrate Palace glowing against the night sky and the gardens at sunrise. I grew giddy just thinking about it.

The receptionist delivered lemon water, herbal tea, and pastries on small silver trays while the stylists worked on our makeup and hair. They kept our makeup soft and natural while going all out on our hair.

My pale blond hair was piled atop my head in large, loose curls that were woven into an elaborate design. A pearl head piece was tucked along the left side. Soft tendrils framed my face in the most romantic way. While their upsweeps, braids, and curls varied, my friends looked equally stunning.

We gathered our garment bags and climbed into the sleek black limousine at precisely four o'clock. We rolled into the parking lot at Monserrate Palace twenty minutes later. My heart stalled when I saw Rafael's limousine.

"How are you going to ensure you don't see one another?" Cenia inquired worriedly.

Jase looked up from his cell phone "Kristine and Rafael are getting ready at opposite ends of the palace. I've already confirmed Rafael and the rest of the guys are in their room." He eyed Dan. "Would you mind watching over the girls while I change into my tux?"

Dan's chest swelled. "I would consider it an honor."

Jase typed his number into Dan's cell phone. "Kadyn will join you shortly." He offered me his hand as he stepped from the car. "You know where you're going?"

"We're getting ready in the piano room at the far end of the palace. There's a gravel trail in front of the palace steps that branches off to either side. We're taking the trail to the right. Rafael and the guys are in a room just off the main entrance on the left." I pointed toward the main trail. We couldn't see much beyond the parking lot. This area was heavily treed, and it was still dark.

"They've lined the trail with luminaries," Cenia exclaimed.

"That's so romantic," Marie breathed.

We gathered our things. Jase led the way. Dan positioned himself on the end so we were sandwiched between the two men while walking the trail.

Lexie sucked in a breath when the trail opened up. "My God, that is a real honest to goodness palace."

We stood dumbfounded by the view. Most of the palace glowed a soft shade of gold, but all three domes blazed crimson against the starlit sky. My heart sang while tears welled in my eyes.

Dan nudged us toward the palace. White chairs were set in a semi-circle around the fountain. A white aisle runner glowed in the moonlight.

I handed Jase the envelope and gift I'd tucked inside my purse. "Can you give this to Rafael?" I'd purchased a Qlocktwo watch that displayed the time in words across a square face fashioned like a word find game for the groom's gift.

He nodded. "I'll see you soon."

Dan took the lead when I veered to the right. This trail wasn't lit by luminaries, but the palace lent just enough light.

A groundskeeper met us at the base of the stairs. "Ms. Stone, the room is ready for you."

"*Obrigada*," I replied.

More stunned glances and gasps ensued when we entered the palace.

Lexie tentatively touched the wall. "How could anyone possibly carve this fine of detail into an entire wall?" In varying ornate patterns, birds, flowers, and leaves had been carved into each and every wall. They'd been painted in deep burgundy, ivory, and gold tones.

"Look at the ceiling," Cenia murmured. The rose marble columns that lined the hallway were topped with fine filigree arches that rivaled the intricate walls. The lights hidden behind the columns offered a fine dusting of gold along the ceiling and floor.

I walked toward the gold and ivory piano room at the far end of the hall. "We've reserved the palace through noon so you can explore all you want." The piano room was my favorite room in the palace. Tall, arched windows framed the circular room beneath an ivory and gold filigree dome shaped ceiling. The same intricate pattern that graced the ceiling filled the top portion of each window. The wood inserts were so finely carved it appeared as if lace valances were hung against the windows. Tall marble columns sat between each window supporting additional filigree arches painted in gold. More than anything, I wanted to lie on the floor and admire that room for a solid twenty four hours, just so I could see how the sun and the moonlight played through all the windows.

"This is the most romantic room I've ever seen," Shae noted reverently. "I may never leave."

"Me either," Marie agreed.

I glanced at my cell phone. "Father Ramires will be here in twenty minutes. I don't know how long he's staying, so you might want to get dressed."

My friends took turns ducking behind the privacy screens that were set out for us. One by one they appeared in the deep purple gowns.

Lexie gave me a hug. "I love this dress."

"Me too." Kimme spun in front of the full length mirror. "I feel like a princess."

I gave her a hug. "I'm so glad you're here. I have a small gift for each of you." I handed my friends the lavender gift bags containing the amethyst necklaces and earrings I'd purchased for them.

"Thank you, Kri." Shae hugged me.

Marie offered me another hug. "I know you don't want us to see you in your wedding dress, but can we at least help you get the other garments in order?"

"Sure," I agreed.

Lexie pressed a small velvet box into my hand. "Here are the pearl tear drop earrings you requested." They were the same earrings she wore on her wedding day.

"Is that your something borrowed?" Kimme inquired curiously.

I popped the lid open so I could admire the earrings. "Yes. The pearl necklace I'm wearing belonged to Rafael's mother, so that's my something old. The pearl headpiece is my something new. The pearl earrings are borrowed, and…" I wiggled my toes, "this Tiffany blue polish is my something blue."

"Oh my God! I love these shoes!" Cenia held up the jeweled Chanel sandals for everyone to see.

Lexie frowned. "What's that on the bottom?"

Cenia turned the shoe over, gasped, and then grabbed the other shoe. "Rafael wrote you a note." She giggled before handing me the shoes.

"These stay on tonight," was scrawled across the bottom of the right shoe. "Mrs. Garcia," was written across the left.

My cheeks heated. "That man…"

My friends laughed as Marie finished the sentence. "… is crazy in love with you."

A light tap sounded against the door. "Kristine?"

"Father Ramires," I breathed.

Cenia gave me a hug. "We're going to explore this wing while you meet with him. We'll move outside at five-fifteen but remain hidden until we hear Pachelbel's 'Canon in D.'"

Lexie stopped short of the door. "If we're walking ahead of you, who is walking the trail with you?"

I frowned. "I hadn't really thought about that. Dan and Kadyn should be in their seats by then. The trail is only a short distance…"

She threw her hands on her hips. "With your luck, the Russian mafia or the SVR will kidnap you right out from under Rafael's nose. I'll walk with you until we round that corner behind all the chairs."

I chewed my bottom lip.

Her eyebrows rose. "Are you suggesting that I can't protect you as well as Kadyn or Dan? I earned a double black belt, I still spar, and I can still kick…"

I cupped my hand over her mouth. "Father Ramires is standing right outside that door."

She licked my hand.

I jerked my hand away. "Ewww. What did you do that for?"

Her shoulders lifted in a delicate shrug. "You were messing up my makeup."

I just shook my head. "Fine. You can come back and help me dress, and you can walk me down the trail but not the aisle. Happy?"

"Yep." She grinned.

I opened the door for Father Ramires. "Hi, Father, thank you for coming."

He clasped my freshly licked hand in his. "You look lovely, Kristine. How are you feeling?"

I waited for the girls to leave. "Good. Elated, really."

His eyes warmed. "May I?" He extended his hand toward my tummy. Rafael told Father Ramires about the civil ceremony and the baby shortly after I returned to Virginia. Any embarrassment he may have felt was outweighed by his desire to have Father Ramires praying for our unborn child.

I nodded.

He pressed gently against my womb. "God, we pray your blessings for this unborn child, for your protection, and a healthy birth. Lord, who has blessed Kristine Annabelle Garcia with the joys of motherhood, grant her comfort in all anxiety and help her lead her child in the ways of salvation. Lord, who has chosen Rafael Tiago Garcia to know the pride of fatherhood, grant him courage in this new responsibility and render him an example of justice and truth. Amen."

"Amen," I repeated softly.

He promptly removed his hand. "Have you been fasting?"

I nodded. I purposely avoided the pastries and the tea at the spa so I could take communion during the wedding.

He eyed me thoughtfully. "I heard you stopped by the church to make your confessions on Thursday."

"Yes, Father." We made our confessions shortly before our friends arrived.

He smiled. "Is there anything burdening your heart that I should be aware of?"

I shook my head. "I feel peace for the first time in a very long time. I'm very excited to begin this next chapter in my life."

"Splendid. Then we'll proceed with the ceremony as planned." He glanced at his watch. "Most of the guests have arrived. Can you be ready by five-thirty?"

I walked him to the door. "I just need to step into my dress."

"Very well then. I'll see you in fifteen minutes." His white robe billowed against the door when he stepped into the hall.

Lexie squeezed through the door. "Jase stopped by to check on you, but he's with Rafael now. Dan and Kadyn just left so they could join the other guests. That makes me your bodyguard."

My phone pinged. I glanced at the screen. "Charlie sent one of his inspirational texts."

She unzipped the garment bag. "I'm surprised he's not here."

I helped her ease the dress from the bag. "Charlie's in-laws were in a car crash over the weekend. They've been discharged from the hospital, but they still need help getting around."

She nodded, sadly. "I'll add them to my prayers." Charlie started sending Lexie inspirational messages when she had her kidney transplant. He was still texting her three years later, even though they'd never met in person. "What does Charlie have to say?"

446

I scrolled through the message. "Be assured of your Father's blessing, his presence, his favor, and his surrounding grace. Who you are and everything you have is the result of his favor. He is your sun and shield, and his honor validates you. Your Father smiles on you with his compassion and his full blessing as you seek him. He has written this day of your life in his book. Be blessed in the name of the one who rejoices today in doing you good. My thoughts and prayers are with you. Love, Charlie."

"He is a kind man." She rolled her eyes at my dress before removing it from the hanger. "This is a wardrobe malfunction just waiting to happen."

I ducked behind the privacy screen so I could undress. The only undergarment I needed was a thong, since the dress had a built in bra. I wasn't planning to wear stockings because I was wearing sandals, and I wanted my nail polish to show.

Lexie helped me step into the dress, but she stopped just short of my stomach. Her eyes flew to mine.

I laughed at the astonished look on her face. "Surprise!"

The dress fell to the floor as Lexie rose. "You're pregnant?"

"Nineteen and a half weeks," I confirmed.

She flung her arms around me. "Kri! I'm so happy for you!" Abruptly, she held me at arm's length. "Are you okay? Is the baby okay? I mean, everything is going to be okay, right?"

I laughed. "The baby is fine. We just want to wait on the announcement until I'm a little further along."

Her eyes darkened. "I'm going to kick that man's ass. He should have married you the second he learned you were pregnant."

"He did," I assured her. "We were married in a civil

ceremony shortly after we discovered I was pregnant."

Her arms folded across her chest. "Why am I just now hearing this?"

I bent down to retrieve my dress. "We've only been married a few weeks. I know I should have told you, but it's been a little crazy between Maxim's election, graduation, and the wedding."

She turned me around so she could untangle the pearls draped across my back. "I don't care how busy you are. That would have required a five minute phone call."

"Yeah, right." I fastened the sandals before stepping out from behind the privacy screen. I stood in front of the mirror. "Do you think this is too revealing?"

She eyed me critically. "I can barely see your tummy, and that's just because I'm looking for it. Honestly, I doubt anyone will notice. They'll be too busy gaping at that neckline and the back of your dress."

I laughed. "That's the part I was worried about."

Her eyebrows shot up. "Oh! In that case, I think you're fine. The dress is a little steamy, but it's also very romantic. You look stunning, Kri."

Cenia rapped on the door. "We just received the ten minute warning, so we're going to head down the trail. Your bouquets are on the table right outside the door."

"Thanks!" I gave Lexie another hug. "Shall we?"

She linked her arm in mine. "Absolutely."

My breath caught when I saw my bouquet. Carefully, I brought the breathtaking display of white calla lilies, deep purple roses, lavender, and white wisteria to my nose. "This smells heavenly."

"Mmmm," Lexie agreed. Her eyes were barely visible above her bouquet.

"When did I start enjoying flowers?" I wondered aloud.

Lexie peeked through the main door while I gathered my train. "All clear."

Our heels clicked against the stone terrace and the short flight of stairs leading into the gardens. Thankfully, the trail was hidden behind bushes and trees. Although we couldn't see anything beyond the trail, we could hear the string quartet playing Bach's "Jesu, Joy of Man's Desiring." The rest of my bridesmaids would be waiting at the fork in the trail until they began playing Pachelbel's "Canon in D." That was their cue to walk down the aisle.

I glanced up at the sky. The clouds glowed deep purple and orange in the early morning dawn, but the landscape was still dark. I could make out the shapes of bushes and trees, but the flowers would remain hidden until the sun crept over the hillside. The lush forest surrounding the palace grounds smelled fresh and earthy. A few rambunctious birds chirped over the music.

The deep, rich tones of the cello wafted through the trees. A violin followed, then another, and finally the viola. Pachelbel's "Canon in D" evoked so much longing, I stopped walking. "It's time." Suddenly, it didn't matter that Rafael and I were already married. My heart raced, and my nerves scattered.

"I love you, Cuz." Lexie maneuvered her way around my bouquet so she could give me a hug. She hurried around the bend, so she could watch the other girls walk down the aisle. She reappeared a few seconds later. "Two down, three to go. Will you be okay, standing here alone?"

I inched closer until a large shrub was the only thing blocking me from view. "I'll be fine. Rafael has men patrolling the palace grounds."

She nodded her approval before joining the other women.

I took a deep breath and blew it out. Still, my heart raced. *Why was I so nervous?* "We're already married," I scolded myself. That didn't help.

I peered around the bush. A light smattering of fresh lavender and deep purple rose petals dusted the runner beneath Lexie's feet. While soft, the palace lights illuminated the terrace where everyone was sitting. My eyes widened when I saw all the people. Rafael, Father Ramires, our groomsmen, and bridesmaids stood waiting for me. *How could this fairytale wedding belong to me?*

I shrank back behind the bush. *Why did I insist on walking alone?* This wasn't a small courtyard filled with strangers. This was nearly everyone I knew and a bunch of people from the police force. Within seconds, they would be watching me walk down that aisle. They would be listening while I spoke my vows and declared my love for Rafael.

The baby kicked right where my hand rested with the bouquet. I dropped the train. Ever so slowly, a smile replaced the stunned look on my face. That was an honest to goodness kick… the first kick I'd ever felt. I couldn't wait to share the news with Rafael. "Okay, little guy, walk me down the aisle."

I took a deep breath before straightening my train. I pressed my hands against my stomach behind my bouquet. Slowly, but surely, I stepped into the clearing. My feet stalled when everyone stood, so I took another deep breath and fixed my eyes on Rafael. The music carried me the rest of the way.

With a tender smile, Rafael offered me his hand. He bowed slightly as he brought my fingers to his lips. "You have stolen my heart all over again."

I cupped his face in my hand. "As you have stolen mine."

Father Ramires waited for the string quartet to finish playing Pachelbel's "Canon in D." "Dearly beloved, we have gathered here today to witness and celebrate the joining of Rafael Tiago Garcia and Kristine Annabelle Stone in marriage." His warm brown eyes sought ours. "I ask you to state your intentions for the sacrament of holy matrimony."

Rafael spoke first. "I, Rafael Tiago Garcia, come here freely and without reservation to join Kristine Annabelle Stone in holy matrimony. I promise to love, honor, and cherish her all the days of my life."

Father Ramires smiled.

I took a deep breath before reciting the lines we'd been asked to memorize. "I, Kristine Annabelle Stone, come here freely and without reservation to join Rafael Tiago Garcia in holy matrimony. I promise to love, honor, and cherish him all the days of my life."

"Will you accept children as gifts from God and raise them according to the laws of his church?"

Rafael and I grinned at one another. "I will."

He nodded his approval. "Let us pray."

Rafael and I knelt on the padded kneeler.

Father Ramires rested a hand on each of our shoulders. "Heavenly Father, Rafael and Kristine have declared their intentions to enter into holy matrimony. Their lives reflect your love in countless ways, from the love you rain down on them, from the family and friends who surround them, through the love and compassion they've shown others, and the love that has long been reflected in their relationship. On this glorious morning, I lift them up unto you, so that you may strengthen their love for one another, for you, and for others. Allow your love to shine through them today and always. I pray this in the name of the Father, and the Son, and the Holy Spirit; who live and reign as one God forever and ever."

"Amen," we replied.

Rafael offered me his hand as we stood.

Father Ramires reached for his Bible. "Our meetings over the past few months have shed some light on the hardships you have faced, your character, your faith, and your relationship. After some reflection and prayerful consideration, I have chosen three scripture readings that should prove especially meaningful to you." He opened his Bible. "First, from the Old Testament, Ecclesiastes 4:9-12: 'Two are better than one, because they have a good reward for their toil. For if they fall, one will lift up the other; but woe to one who is alone and falls and does not have another to help. Again, if two lie together, they keep warm; but how can one keep warm alone? And though one might prevail against another, two will withstand one. A threefold cord is not quickly broken.' This is the word of the Lord."

"Thanks be to God," we replied. Our guests offered the same, customary response.

Father Ramires sought another page in his Bible. "And now a reading from the New Testament, **Colossians 3:12-14:** 'As God's chosen ones, holy and beloved, clothe yourselves with compassion, kindness, humility, meekness, and patience. Bear with one another and, if anyone has a complaint against another, forgive each other; just as the Lord has forgiven you, so you also must forgive. Above all, clothe yourselves with love, which binds everything together in perfect harmony.' This is the word of the Lord."

"Thanks be to God," we replied once more.

Purple clouds gave way to orange as the sun peeked behind the palace.

Father Ramires sought one final bookmark. "The Holy Gospel reading from John 15:12-17: 'This is my commandment, that you love one another as I have loved you. No one has greater love than this, to lay down one's life for one's friends. You are my friends if you do what I command you. I do not call you servants any longer, because the servant does not know what the master is doing; but I have called you friends because I have made known to you everything that I have heard from my Father. You did not choose me, but I chose you. And I appointed you to go and bear fruit, fruit that will last, so that the Father will give you whatever you ask him in my name. I am giving you these commands so that you may love one another.' This is the Gospel of the Lord."

"Praise to you, Lord Jesus Christ," rang through the garden.

Father Ramires set his Bible on the small table to his left. "Through the sacrament of marriage you become a conduit for God's love. His love flows through you, strengthening your union, your family and friends, the communities where you reside, and all the other lives you touch. And so, this marriage is not just about you. You have been called to serve others. This is a responsibility you regularly embrace, but it can feel overwhelming at times. There will be times when you question whether you have anything left to give. The good news is this... like all sacraments, this sacrament brings grace. God's grace will strengthen your ability to give and receive love. By reserving a place for him in your relationship you will strengthen your ability to love and care for one another and for others." He smiled. "Rafael and Kristine, you have declared your intention to enter into holy matrimony. Please face your beloved and join hands while you declare your consent."

I handed Lexie my bouquet so I could place my chilly fingers in Rafael's warm hands. My heart stalled the moment our eyes met. I fell into his eyes and saw Rafael for the very first time… the devastatingly handsome man, the archangel with healing powers, the gallant knight, the passionate lover, and the doting husband who was on the cusp of becoming a father. In that moment, I fell hopelessly and irrevocably in love with him. So powerful were the feelings that evoked that I nearly collapsed.

A well-muscled arm locked around my back. Rafael dragged me to his chest. His right hand still clenched my left. "I, Rafael Tiago Garcia, take you, Kristine Annabelle Stone, to be my wife, to have and to hold from this day forward, for better or for worse, for richer, for poorer, in sickness and in health, to love and to cherish through life and in death."

His heart thundered against my chest. Our breath mingled, our lips mere inches apart, as he awaited my response. I stared, thoroughly transfixed by the passion burning in his eyes. Breathlessly, I offered the same solemn vow. "I, Kristine Annabelle Stone, take you, Rafael Tiago Garcia, to be my husband, to have and to hold from this day forward, for better or for worse, for richer, for poorer, in sickness and in health to love and to cherish through life and in death."

He lowered his lips to mine. The garden glistened in the early morning light while our souls entwined.

"You have declared your consent before God and these witnesses. What God has joined, let no man separate," Father Ramires announced loudly.

Rafael froze just before our lips met. My cheeks flushed red. I'd forgotten Father Ramires was there, not to mention our guests.

"May I have the rings?" Father Ramires continued.

Benjamim held our wedding bands in the palm of his hand.

Father Ramires made the sign of the cross over the rings. "May the Lord bless these rings, which are offered as a token of your love and fidelity." He handed Rafael my wedding band.

Rafael placed the ring on my finger. "I offer this ring as a sign of my love and faithfulness in the name of the Father, the Son, and the Holy Spirit."

Father Ramires handed me Rafael's wedding band.

I slid it over Rafael's finger. "I offer this ring as a sign of my love and faithfulness in the name of the Father, the Son, and the Holy Spirit."

Chief D'Souza handed Father Ramires a black velvet bag. I hadn't a clue what the bag contained or why it was being included in the ceremony.

Father Ramires made the sign of the cross over the bag. "May the Lord bless these coins, which symbolize Rafael's desire to share all that he has with his beloved." He handed Rafael the bag.

Rafael placed the soft velvet bag in the palm of my hand. "On the day that my parents were married, my father offered these coins to my mother while he vowed to share everything he had with her. I offer you these same coins while I repeat that promise. My love, I offer you every possession I have, and I promise to provide and care for you always."

My throat clogged with tears. "Thank you," I finally whispered.

"Please kneel," Father Ramires encouraged.

I passed the coins to Lexie.

Rafael clasped my hand as we kneeled. Father Ramires offered the Eucharistic prayer. We sang "Holy, holy, holy," before joining him in the Lord's Prayer. Tears crept through my lashes when he prayed over us. Warmth flooded me as Rafael and I shared our first communion together. God cemented his place in our relationship as we accepted the body and blood of Christ.

Father Ramires offered one final blessing while he made the sign of the cross. "May the Lord bless your marriage with good health, happiness, and love. May he surround you with family and friends who will share your joys and support you through the trials to come. May he fill your home with children, with family, and friends. May he strengthen your faith in him and your commitment to one another. May he guide you on the paths of righteousness and protect you as you serve others. May he strengthen you, comfort you, and bring you peace."

"Amen," we replied.

Father Ramires helped me from the kneeler before turning us around. "I present to you... Mr. and Mrs. Rafael Garcia!"

Cheers erupted when Rafael swept me into his arms. He grinned as he held me suspended a few inches above him. Slowly, he allowed me to slide down his chest until our lips met. My arms locked around his neck as he lowered me to his chest.

Rafael's lips slanted over mine. His tongue sought mine in a provocative kiss that felt far more carnal than it should have. Desire sparked across every nerve ending, but the baby chose that precise moment to deliver a hefty kick.

Rafael's eyes widened as he broke the kiss. "Was that..."

I laughed. "Undeniably, yes."

His eyes lit with joy as he swung me around again.

Our friends and family clapped while he clasped my hand and led me down the aisle.

Father Ramires encouraged our guests to walk down to the pond so they could enjoy pastries and drinks while we took pictures with the wedding party.

Rafael had other plans. Instead of taking the trail that circled back toward the palace, he swept my legs out from under me and carried me down a different trail. Benjamim and Lexie must have diverted everyone else toward the palace because no one followed us.

Rafael stumbled inside an abandoned stable. Grudgingly, he released me. "I want to feel the baby again."

I tried not to laugh. "Your child kicks when he wants to, not when you command it."

He dropped to his knees. His hands splayed over my stomach. "Please kick."

I held my breath while we waited for the baby to respond.

He didn't.

Rafael eyed my sandals as he lifted my dress. "God, I love those shoes... and this dress was nearly the death of me. I had to recite soccer plays while you walked down the aisle, and when I felt those pearls against your back..." A low growl percolated in his chest.

I stood spellbound while he lifted the dress.

He nuzzled my tummy.

My hands fisted in his hair. I leaned back against the wall. My nipples hardened as my body responded to his heated breath. "Rafael."

His eyes darkened as he gazed up at me.

My eyes slid closed. "I need..."

"Here?" His fingers clenched my thong as he awaited my response.

"Here," I pleaded. "Now."

His tongue teased my core while the thong fell to the floor. Over and over he stroked until my body began to tense. He pulled my leg over his shoulder, clamped down, and sucked. Hard.

"Rafael!" I screamed. My body convulsed as the orgasm tore through me. He pinned me to the wall as he continued the assault. A second climax ripped through me.

Rafael stood. I trembled, still basking in the pleasure pulsing through me. His eyes heated. His lips demanded mine. "Kristine," he groaned. He lifted me and thrust.

My arms and legs locked around his massive frame. Rafael's hands protected my back while he drove inside of me. Again and again he thrust until our bodies spiraled out of control. There was nothing gentle about this lovemaking. This was raw, unadulterated sex fueled by lust.

"Rafael," I cried. I couldn't believe he was about to wring a third orgasm from me in less than fifteen minutes' time.

He thrust forcefully... stilled... then flooded me with heat.

I disintegrated in his arms.

His eyes sought mine while our breathing slowed.

We both gasped when the baby flipped in what quite obviously was not a kick. This was a full body roll.

"How soon can we leave the reception?" Rafael growled.

I winced. "Three, maybe four, hours?"

He offered me a pained expression.

We pulled our clothes back into place, then strolled back to the palace hand in hand. I felt sated and blissfully content.

The wedding party was looking for us inside the palace. Benjamim winked while Lexie smirked. I ducked inside the piano room so I could freshen up. We spent a half hour with the photographer before seeking out our guests.

I stopped to admire the gardens on our way to the reception. Birds of Paradise perched in front of the palace. Wisteria crept over stone ledges to kiss the mossy green walls along the stone steps leading to the pond. Bright pink flowers bloomed in the Rhododendron trees while lush ferns, violets, and primrose framed the endless expanse of lawn. Beyond that, a lush green forest blanketed the surrounding hilltops.

Our caterer was working inside a large white tent next to the pond. A handful of waiters were carrying platters of fish, ham, and prime rib to the banquet tables, while others distributed drinks and offered breakfast pastries. An unfathomable amount of food crowded six long banquet tables. The chef appeared to be serving breakfast, lunch, and dinner all at once.

Tables and chairs dressed in stark white linens sat alongside the sparkling pond. Two black swans drifted curiously toward our guests, presumably looking for bread. A jazz vocalist and her band were performing next to the parquet floor, although no one was dancing... yet.

The jazz vocalist announced our arrival mid-song. "Please join me in congratulating Mr. and Mrs. Garcia!"

Cheers echoed all around us.

Rafael tucked me beneath his arm while we crossed the dance floor. The jazz vocalist handed him the microphone. "Thank you for being here today. Our chef has prepared an exquisite meal. Hopefully, this makes up for the fact that we dragged you out of bed at such an ungodly hour."

Everyone chuckled.

A waiter delivered two champagne flutes, which he carried on top of a silver tray. Rafael's glass was filled with champagne. Mine was filled with orange juice. Our guests were already holding flutes filled with champagne or mimosa, although some were sipping *bica*.

"I'd like to feed my bride. I promise we'll circulate as soon as we've had an opportunity to eat. The caterer is serving brunch buffet style so please grab your plates and join us. In the meantime, I'd like to propose a toast to this stunning woman standing beside me."

His eyes sought mine. "Thank you for leading me away from the cold and vengeful path I was on. You have gifted me with so much… faith, hope, friendship, laughter, passion, love, a new family, supportive friends, and more reasons for living than I can possibly cite. I no longer feel the need to avenge my parents' death. I know now that I can honor their lives, their love for one another, for Michael, and me; by embracing life, by loving you, and cherishing all the good things in my life. I'm still determined to make this world a safer place, but I've come to realize that I am more capable of achieving that goal with you standing by my side. To you, Kristine… my angel, my lover, and friend." Rafael entwined his arm with mine while we drank to his toast.

We loaded our plates with traditional Portuguese and American dishes before claiming our seats at the head table. Rafael asked our attendants to walk through the buffet with us, so they too were settling in with their plates.

Kimme dropped into the chair directly across from me. "This place is unbelievable. The palace is exquisite, but the gardens… the gardens are truly breathtaking. I swear my heart stopped when the sun crept over the horizon. I feel like we've stumbled into an enchanted garden. I mean... how is this even real?"

I smiled, secretly thrilled. "The gardens extend well beyond the palace. You should walk the grounds after we eat."

Kadyn pulled a chair out for Shae. "I'm surprised Maxim didn't show."

"Me too." Jase scoured the surrounding forest.

I registered his absence with disappointment and relief. "I'm sure he has more pressing matters to tend to."

Cenia looked up from her plate. "Where are you going for your honeymoon?"

"That's a surprise," Rafael answered smugly.

"Italy?" Kimme guessed.

"Fiji!" Shae exclaimed.

"Belize?" Ethan ventured.

"Spain," Marie added.

Rafael laughed.

"We should place bets," Cenia suggested. "The winner gets to be the newlyweds' first dinner guest when they get back."

"Count me in," Kadyn replied, "but I want to choose the dish."

"Clam linguine?" I guessed.

"What else?" He grinned.

"When are you planning to return?" Lexie inquired worriedly. I could tell she was thinking about the baby.

I glanced at Rafael.

"We hope to wrap up the investigation by the end of June," Chief D'Souza confirmed. "We still have a few preliminary hearings to get through, and we need Rafael to testify against any defendants who go to trial."

"Why can't you live here?" Eva pouted.

"We'll be dividing our time between both countries," I assured her.

Marie set her fork down. "What about work?"

I took a deep breath and blew it out. "Seeds for Peace has agreed to hire me on a consulting basis, as my schedule allows. I plan to volunteer at the Casa Pia Orphanage or find another NGO to work for while in Portugal."

"I manage finances for an NGO with a humanitarian arm. I can help you secure a job there," Benjamim offered.

Rafael brought my hand to his lips. "I think you would really enjoy working for them." By "them" he meant the Templar.

I nodded, although intimidated by the idea. "I'll e-mail my curriculum vitae to Benjamim when we return."

Rafael eyed my empty plate. "Shall we cut the wedding cake?"

"Sure." I pressed a kiss to his cheek when he helped me to my feet.

We visited with our remaining guests before seeking out the cake table. I had caught a glimpse of the cake earlier, but this was my first opportunity to see it up close. Deep purple roses sat atop the four tier cake. A variety of purple flowers were scattered along the remaining tiers. The bright white icing was decorated in alternating patterns. The bottom and third tier were carved in a flawless diamond pattern, while the second and top tier boasted an intricate filigree design that mirrored the filigree carvings above the arches and windows inside the palace.

"It's beautiful," I whispered.

Rafael tensed.

Confused, I followed his gaze. My heart stalled. I reached for the hand painted *matryoshka* dolls. The nesting dolls were painted with painstaking precision... a blond bride with blue eyes, fair skin, and soft pink cheeks... and a dark haired groom with brown eyes and caramel colored skin. The bride looked angelic, but the groom had a fierce look on his face.

"Maxim," I breathed.

Rafael scoured the gardens. "How? Surely, someone would have seen him. Could someone else have delivered these for him?"

My thumb grazed the groom's face. "I don't know. Konstantin and Oni aren't here. I suppose he could have given these to the pastry chef or the caterer. If Maxim were here, he would have stayed and spoken with us."

Rafael drew me close. "He may have felt uncomfortable."

"Maybe," I murmured.

For some reason, that thought weighed heavy on my heart.

* * * * *

I pushed up from Rafael's chest. "Greece? Did Kari just say Greece?"

Rafael smiled without opening his eyes. "Yes. I've rented a villa on Santorini Island."

I opened both of his eyes with my thumbs. "Santorini... as in the Greek Island with white washed houses; an active volcano; a crater filled with water; and beaches filled with red, black, and white lava pebbles?" I had just read about this island in one of the travel magazines at the spa!

Rafael chuckled. "That sounds about right."

"Yes!" I dove for the suitcase Rafael had stashed inside the closet. "That's awesome. No. That's more than awesome. That's perfect. I've always wanted to visit Greece."

Rafael kissed my neck when he joined me. "You should pick a sun dress or shorts. It's very warm here." Thankfully, he had encouraged me to buy a swimsuit and a couple of summer dresses for our honeymoon. Eva helped me shop for loose fitting clothes since I wasn't quite ready for maternity wear.

Another "ding" sounded over the intercom. "*Kalispera.* This is your pilot, Captain Anderson. A brilliant blue Aegean Sea and a balmy seventy-four degrees await us in Santorini. The local time is six-ten p.m. We'll be landing in thirty minutes."

I pulled a light blue halter dress from the suitcase. The empire waist was comfortable and helped hide my tummy.

Rafael tugged on a loose-fitting pair of faded blue jeans before pulling a white t-shirt over his head.

My jaw dropped. "You look really sexy." I'd never seen him in such light colors before. The tousled hair and the mischievous spark in his eyes didn't help. We hadn't had sex since our tryst in the stables. We were both so exhausted when we boarded the jet that we went straight to bed and slept, a fact I was now regretting.

"That dress matches your eyes perfectly." He traced the deep V between my breasts. His fingers dipped beneath the material as he began kissing my neck. "The villa is less than eight miles from the airport."

"Thank God," I breathed. My body was already pinging with need.

Rafael kissed my jaw, my chin, and lips before releasing me. He zipped the suitcase and set it back inside the closet.

I stepped inside the bathroom to brush my teeth. I freed my hair from the bobby pins and finger combed the curls before joining Rafael in the main cabin.

Kari handed me a bottled water. "Please fasten your seatbelt. We'll be landing shortly."

The wheels touched down twenty minutes later. I remained glued to the window. "How can the water be so blue? And all those white washed buildings... Oh my God. It's so beautiful."

Rafael laughed. "We could jump in the water and touch the buildings if only you were willing to step off the plane."

A silver Mercedes convertible sat idling in front of the airport. A man with a clipboard was leaning against the car. Rafael signed the documents attached to the clipboard. The man examined Rafael's driver's license before handing him an envelope. He waved politely, then sauntered away.

Rafael set our luggage in the back seat while I climbed into the car. He slid behind the wheel, pulled a piece of paper from the envelope, and typed an address into the GPS. "Ready?"

I was too busy gawking at everything to reply.

"Mrs. Garcia," he murmured silkily.

"Yes?" My cheeks heated when my nipples pebbled beneath the dress.

"I really like this dress." His fingers dipped beneath the hem.

My legs clenched. "How long does it take to drive eight miles in Santorini?"

"Twenty minutes according to the GPS." His hand lingered on my thigh when he pulled away from the curb.

I cursed all those needy little hormones wreaking havoc on my girlie parts. "I'll never make it that long."

"Michaela Residence is not far." Rafael chuckled. "While there are houses nearby, the villa is positioned on the hillside in a way that ensures privacy. You can sunbathe naked if you like."

I wondered whether I was capable of such a thing.

"The villa has a spectacular view of Akrotiri, the volcano, and the Aegean Sea," Rafael continued. "I've arranged for a personal chef to visit the villa once a day. He's already prepared our evening meal and stocked the refrigerator with items for breakfast and lunch tomorrow. He should be gone by the time we arrive."

My stomach growled at the thought of food. "That sounds wonderful."

"I'm a little worried about the volcano," Rafael admitted. "Santorini experienced a few small earthquakes recently. The volcano hasn't erupted since 1950, but there is some concern it could become active again."

"I would have preferred to remain oblivious about that." I pulled my wind whipped hair away from my face and tied it into a knot at the base of my neck.

"We'll leave if they experience any tremors this week," Rafael assured me. He shifted into a lower gear before turning onto a steep, narrow road.

"How?" I wondered aloud. Brent and Kari were flying back to Portugal so they could take our friends and family back to the United States. We weren't expecting them to return until the end of the week.

Rafael turned right. The Mercedes hugged the hillside. "I've located a helicopter and a pilot who can fly us to Athens if need be."

I breathed a small sigh of relief. "I swear, you think of everything."

He flashed a quick smile before studying the GPS.

All thoughts of earthquakes and volcanoes disappeared when he pulled alongside the white washed villa that would serve as our home for the next eight days. The house was sandwiched between a scenic lookout and another white washed house, but a white privacy fence framed the courtyard on either side.

Rafael retrieved our luggage before opening my door. "Mrs. Garcia." He bowed while offering me his hand.

"Mr. Garcia." I placed my hand in his, infinitely more enamored with the man holding my hand than the villa behind him.

We walked toward the house hand in hand. Rafael unlocked the door and set the luggage inside before whisking my legs out from under me. "Technically, this isn't our home, but I'm still carrying you over the threshold."

I kissed him affectionately while wrapping my arms around his neck. My eyes widened when I saw the stark white walls, the white washed open beam ceiling, white couches with thick white throw pillows, and filmy white curtains tied in knots against the windows and the sliding glass doors. Massive white lanterns held thick white candles on either side of the sliding glass doors. The blond wood coffee table and beige floor tile offered the only hint of color, aside from the artwork. "I've never seen so much white in my entire life."

Rafael stopped in front of the sliding glass doors. The courtyard held a pool and a pergola, which sat between the pool and a stone wall. Filmy white curtains were tied at all four corners against stone columns. Three white couches and a white coffee table sat beneath the pergola. The sapphire blue Aegean Sea sparkled beneath the evening sun. "Let's eat outside." Slowly, he allowed my feet to touch the tile.

"Dinner smells delicious." I followed him past a large dining room table. Blond wood formed the tabletop, but the legs were painted with white milk paint like the chairs. A large chandelier with white lanterns and clear crystals hung above the table. A white framed mirror and a massive bouquet of flowers adorned a matching buffet. The dining room was three parts dreamy, seven parts shabby chic.

A large galley style kitchen opened into a second, more casual dining room. White washed cupboards, sandy brown countertops, and modern appliances defined the kitchen. Rafael reached for the oven mitts.

I read the slip of paper sitting next to the wine. "Dinner: corn flour bread; a variety of olives; fresh tomato, onion, and herb salad; grilled *Barbounia*; fried potatoes; and *Loukoumades* for dessert. For breakfast tomorrow morning: croissants, ham, salami, cheese, fresh melon, yogurt, and honey. For lunch tomorrow: *Horiatiki Salata*, hearty wheat bread, and tahini. *Kalí óreksi*, Chef Loukas."

Rafael pulled a platter from the oven. He set it on top of the stove. The platter was loaded with small red fish and seasoned potatoes. "The oven is still warm, so we'll leave dessert in there for now." He retrieved the bread.

I peeked inside the oven. "I assume the *Barbounia* is fish, but what kind of dessert is *Loukoumades*?"

"You have always been a dessert first kind of girl," he teased. "*Loukomades* are doughnuts served with cinnamon and honey."

"Ah. So that's why the honey is sitting on the counter." I retrieved two bottled waters, the olives, and tomato salad from the refrigerator. "This fresh tomato salad looks really good." I wasn't sure about the fish. I was creeped out by the fact their heads and eyes were still intact.

Rafael grabbed the plates, silverware, and cloth napkins from the counter.

I followed him through the living room and out into the courtyard so we could eat beneath the pergola. "Look! The sun is starting to set." The white washed buildings of Santorini were bathed in orange and pink, but the Aegean Sea remained a soft blue color, which contrasted nicely against the orange and pink sky.

He set the dishes on the coffee table. "That view is breathtaking."

I placed the olives and drinks beside the plates so I could wrap my arms around him. "Thank you for choosing this place."

Rafael released the knot from my hair. He lifted my chin and pressed his lips to mine. He took his time, savoring me like a fine wine. With kiss swollen lips and dreamy eyes we gazed at one another, husband and wife.

"I love you so much it hurts." Tears pricked at my eyes.

"I know," he whispered. "I'm afraid my heart will stop beating if you wander too far."

We fell into a timeless embrace. The pain in my chest eased when I felt his heart beat against mine. Eventually, we retrieved the remaining food. A soft breeze tugged at the bound curtains. The curtains were so romantic, I released them.

Rafael lit the candles on the coffee table while I dished food onto our plates. "I cannot imagine a more peaceful place."

"This view reminds me of Saint-Tropez." I sighed contentedly.

He sampled the olives while pondering the sea. "We should visit Saint-Tropez before we return to the United

States."

"I agree." A small moan played on my lips when I tried the cherry tomatoes. "You have to taste the tomato salad. I swear, these are the best tomatoes I've ever eaten." I speared a tomato and offered him my fork.

He chewed, thoughtfully. "You're right. That's the best tomato I've ever eaten."

I popped another one inside my mouth. The deep red tomatoes tasted earthy and sweet. "Would you like some wine?"

"I'd rather wait and share the wine with you." He piled a few more tomatoes onto his plate.

I nabbed an olive. "Are we taking wine back to Portugal with us?"

Rafael nodded. "We'll take the wine the chef selects for us and purchase a few more bottles before returning to Portugal. That way, we can experience Santorini's wines together, after the baby is born."

I nestled closer. "That sounds wonderful."

Quietly, we enjoyed the main course. The fish was buttery and sweet, although neither of us could bring himself to eat the head or the tail. By the time we finished eating the warm cinnamon and honey laced doughnuts, the moon and the stars had replaced the sun.

The breeze tugged at the filmy white curtains until they hid the sea. Still, the moon shone through the pergola, casting striped shadows across our bodies.

Rafael pulled me onto his lap. His fingers clenched my hips when I straddled his waist. We both groaned when the telltale bulge in his jeans pressed between my legs. "Wife," he growled.

His possessive tone shot through my very core. Desire

pooled deep and low while goose bumps pricked my skin. "Husband," I answered in an equally possessive tone.

His eyes heated when I moved my hips. The muscles in his shoulders bunched while he removed his shirt. "I need to feel your skin."

My fingers caressed his abdomen and chest before tangling in his hair. My fists clenched. "Kiss me," I demanded. My lips slanted over his.

Rafael licked the cinnamon from my lips before diving deep inside my mouth. He stroked and teased my tongue while I basked in his seduction. My eyes slid closed. He trailed wet, erotic kisses along my jaw... behind my ear... down my neck.

Something warm and sticky spilled between my breasts. My eyes flew open. "Honey?" My nipples hardened even more.

Rafael lapped at the sugary sweet nectar while forcing the dress over my head. He drizzled honey over my breasts.

My back arched against his warm tongue while I shivered beneath his cool breath. Still, I needed more.

I freed him from his zipper.

He tore my thong.

With a honey infused kiss, he thrust. We both stilled. I could feel him throbbing inside of me, already nearing release. He deepened the kiss. One hand teased my breast. The other held my hip. Slowly, he rocked.

My entire body clenched. I anchored myself against the back of the couch. Rafael lifted my hips and thrust... once... twice... three times. He swelled, stretching and demanding more with every thrust. Our bodies rose and fell until we crested like the Aegean Sea.

My fingernails lanced his back when I began to climax.

With a growl, he spilled inside of me. My body quivered, relishing the heat.

The sheer white curtains shifted erratically in the breeze.

* * * * *

Rafael's hands bracketed my tummy. The chef was due to arrive any minute, but he showed no interest in getting dressed. We'd spent the entire day sleeping, eating, and making love. Rafael was determined to prove his theory that the baby enjoyed our lovemaking. Why? Because the baby kicked, elbowed, or rolled every time we stopped. I suspected the baby liked being jostled about and would react the same way if I were jogging and suddenly stopped. I made no attempt to prove my theory because sex was infinitely more fun than jogging.

Rafael laughed. "Did you feel that? He did it again!"

"I did." Feeling a baby move inside your tummy was one of the most amazing experiences in the world. I placed my hands on top of his. "Let's take a bath."

Rafael lifted his head. He garnered my attention every time he moved because he was the only dark object in the room. The giant four poster bed was surrounded by soft white curtains. The bed linens were white. The throw pillows were white... the walls were white... the furniture was white... the lamps, the candles... everything was white. The only other splashes of color were the clear blue sky and the azure blue sea peeking through the window.

The window was open so we could hear the waves. The beach was only two blocks away. The sheer white curtains framing the window were dancing in the breeze.

"The bath?" I repeated.

Rafael tore his eyes from my breasts. "You stay here and relax. I'll fill the bathtub." He pushed off the bed and strode into the bathroom.

I smiled. Rafael had been doting on me all day. He served breakfast and lunch before spoiling me with a long, luxurious massage.

I wrapped a sheet around me, lured by the only remaining color in the room. I was surprised there wasn't a screen or a protective rail around the window. My head rested against the tall white frame while I surveyed the landscape below.

A fat little house sparrow was perched on top of the pergola to the left of the window. He carried a small twig inside his mouth. He ducked beneath the pergola, stashed the twig inside a nest, and flitted off.

I thought about the little brown sparrow I'd seen in Ukraine, the one with the broken wing. I'd questioned whether he would survive. I wondered if he'd thought the same of me.

The baby elbowed me.

I rubbed my tummy. "Missing your daddy already?"

Rafael's broad chest warmed my back. He wrapped his arms around me and rubbed my belly affectionately. "Of course he does."

I leaned into him, savoring the heat. "You're nesting."

He chuckled softly. "Why do you say that?"

"The renovations," I answered.

He rested his chin on my shoulder. "What do you want to do about the baby's room?" He'd been toying with the idea of converting his bedroom into a nursery and a playroom. All we had to do was knock out part of the wall separating our bedrooms, extend the hallway, and insert new walls and

bedroom doors along the newly formed hallway. The
bedrooms would be a little smaller because part of the space
would be used for the hallway. Not that it mattered. Our
bedrooms were huge. A five foot strip wasn't going to make a
whole lot of difference.

"I think we should proceed with the structural changes,
but I don't want to decorate or furnish that room until after
the baby is born." I couldn't bear to see the same devastated
look on Rafael's face that I'd seen on Michael's face when he
walked by that empty nursery.

Rafael twined his fingers with mine before pulling me
away from the window. "Where will the baby sleep while
we're decorating his room?"

"In a bassinette near our bed." I dropped the sheet on
the bed on our way to the bathroom.

Rafael helped me up the stairs leading into the large
garden style tub. The stairs, the tub, and the adjoining shower
flaunted a swirling blue faux paint finish that mimicked the
ocean. Recessed lighting and thick white candles lined the
edge of the privacy wall. A large white seashell sat in the
corner, next to a white basket filled with toiletries and face
cloths.

I groaned when I sank into the steamy water. "This feels
heavenly."

Rafael stepped in behind me. "Can we swap my bed for
yours?"

"Sure." I knew how he loved that bed. "I can't believe
we're going to have a six bedroom house." Rafael was using
one of his bedrooms as a weight room. Still, that left us with
three guestrooms.

"They poured our new steps and installed the front door
today. We have one main entrance now. Our old doors were

replaced with windows, which were installed yesterday." The contractor was texting updates.

"So there's one large foyer and two staircases leading to the top floor," I recounted.

"The stairs have been modified so they curve and meet at the top." Rafael poured body wash into his hand. Slowly he lathered my arms, chest, and back.

"I'm glad we don't have to make any changes to the other bedrooms." I was still trying to envision the new layout for the ground floor. According to the blue prints, we were keeping both offices on opposite ends of the foyer. We had two formal living rooms and two family rooms between us. Rafael was planning to turn the formal living room on his side of the house into a billiards room. His family room was being converted into a theater room with three elevated rows of black leather recliners. We were keeping both kitchens. Rafael felt the theater needed a kitchen. But we were knocking out the wall between our dining rooms so we could entertain more guests.

Rafael poured more soap into his hand. "We're going to need those bedrooms. Brady and Jase may never leave after they see the theater and game room."

I laughed. "Brady asked me to call and play the Doppler over the phone when we return to Portugal. Those two are as enamored with this little guy as you are. Kadyn too."

His hands slid lovingly toward my tummy. "Maybe I should buy the townhome next to mine."

* * * * *

"Do you want to enroll in a childbirth class in Lisbon or Alexandria?" I studied Rafael in a sidelong glance. We were walking back to the villa after exploring Akrotiri Town.

Rafael slowed. "There's a class?"

I laughed at the stunned expression on his face.

"What do they teach in this class?" he inquired worriedly.

We stopped walking. "They review pain medications and other strategies for coping with labor and delivery."

He sucked in a breath. "You're going to be in pain... like real, excruciating pain."

I forced a soothing tone, although his reaction left me feeling panicked. "Women have babies all the time. I'm sure I'll be fine." Secretly, I was questioning whether it would hurt more than having a stun gun shoved inside my vagina. I doubted I could ask that question in class.

He began pacing. "I can't bear to see you cry. I nearly lost it when you had food poisoning. I might kill someone if I see you in pain."

I stepped in front of him. "I'm stronger than you know. Besides, who are you going to kill? We chose this, remember?"

He growled his retort.

I wrapped my arm around him when we resumed walking.

Rafael pulled me close. "I want to be in the delivery room. I promise I won't kill anyone. I just... I want to help."

"I'd like your face to be the first face our child sees," I agreed.

We both sensed the moment the sun kissed the sea. The surrounding buildings glowed orange and pink. We stopped to admire the view.

Rafael fit my back to his chest while wrapping his arms around me. "Are we really doing this?"

I cradled my tummy, which had grown substantially over

the past week. "Yes, my valiant knight. I believe we are."

$$* * * * *$$

I folded my arms over the edge of the infinity pool and gazed at the sea. The sea and the sky were on fire. The land? The deepest, darkest coal bobbing in molten lava. I may as well have been peering inside a volcano.

A soft sigh escaped my lips. Our honeymoon was nearing an end. I wanted to burn this image on the back of my eyelids so I'd never forget this exquisite island.

Soft, warm lips nibbled my neck.

I spun around. "How do you swim without making a sound?"

Rafael grasped the edge of the pool, boxing me in his arms. "You'll never guess what the chef is preparing for us."

"*Tomato-kefides?*" I suggested hopefully. *Tomato-kefides* were deep fried tomato fritters mixed with onion, herbs, and butter. They looked like a red hushpuppy, but they tasted a million times better. Of all the Greek food I'd sampled thus far, *tomato-kefides* were my favorite, although the pan fried feta was a close second.

A smirk played on his lips. "No. He's grilling an entire bushel of oysters."

My eyes widened. "Aren't oysters an aphrodisiac?"

"Yes." He kissed the sweet spot behind my ear. "I don't believe we'll be sleeping tonight."

My toes curled against the bottom of the pool.

"We haven't made love in this pool," Rafael murmured. He tugged my bikini off. His heated gaze pinned me in place while he pulled my legs around his waist. His thickened shaft slid between my legs.

My breath caught when I realized he was already naked. I balked at the thought. We weren't hidden behind curtains. The sun was setting, but there were lights illuminating the pool. "What if the chef..."

"He's grilling on the other side of the house. We're at the far end of the pool, and all our unmentionables are hidden from view. Besides, I'm pretty sure he knows we're having sex." He lifted me a little higher.

"So much for being hidden," I groaned. My hands tangled in his hair while he suckled my breasts.

He pulled me down and thrust. Hard.

"Rafael!" I cried. Without warning, he buried himself to the hilt.

"Kristine," he gritted. He pulled back and drove inside of me again.

My heart beat wildly against my chest. Rafael wasn't asking. He was demanding my consent.

His teeth raked my breasts. He sucked hard, then flicked my nipples with his tongue. They hardened like pebbles inside his sinful mouth. His hands tightened around my hips. He captured my lips. We fell into a frenzied kiss.

Rafael was unyielding. He thrust until I surrendered *everything*. I no longer cared who witnessed our love making. I needed each thrust more than my heartbeat.

We were panting... thrusting... straining... until... *ecstasy*. We both screamed. Molten lava filled me while the sun licked the sea.

Chapter 10 – Photograph

Dr. Barreira squished warm gel on my tummy. "How are you feeling?"

"Good. Great, actually. Is it normal for pregnant women to turn into sex addicts?"

She burst out laughing. "A high sex drive during pregnancy is quite normal. There's a lot of extra hormones and blood coursing through your body." She swirled the hand held device through the slick gel, spreading it around the bulge in my tummy. Silently, she studied our child.

Dr. Barreira pressed a couple of keys on the ultrasound machine. Two little x's appeared on the screen. "The baby is twenty-six centimeters long, which is perfect for twenty-one weeks." She shifted her angle, and the shadow morphed into a baby.

Rafael's eyes widened. "That's him. That's our baby! Look, Kristine, he's sucking his thumb."

Dr. Barreira looked thoroughly amused. "What makes you think you're having a boy?"

Rafael shot her a look suggesting that was the most ridiculous question she could possibly ask.

With a chuckle, she moved the device. "Would you like me to confirm or deny your suspicion?"

"Yes," we answered breathlessly.

She tilted her head and frowned. "The umbilical cord is in the way. Let's try another angle. Can you roll onto your left side?"

Rafael hovered over me anxiously. The paper on the exam table crinkled while I rolled onto my side.

This time she smiled. "Looks like you're right."

A smug look settled over Rafael's face. "I knew we were having a boy."

Dr. Barreira grinned. "Congratulations." She typed "It's a boy!" onto the screen before printing two pictures. She handed each of us a copy.

A nurse stepped inside the room. She handed Dr. Barreira a slip of paper.

Dr. Barreira glanced at the paper before sifting through my chart. "Your blood work came back normal. I don't see any signs of birth defects or genetic disorders. There's some extra protein in your urine and your blood pressure is at the high end of the normal range. I'd like to see you in two weeks so I can check those levels again."

Rafael tensed. "Is there a problem?"

She wiped the gel from my tummy so I could sit up. "A certain amount of protein is normal. This is a little more than I'd like to see at this stage in the pregnancy. If her blood pressure and protein levels remain where they are, we'll be fine. I just prefer to err on the side of caution."

Rafael released his breath. "Thank you, Dr. Barreira." He helped me from the table.

We made the appointment and stepped outside. Rafael scooped me up and swung me around. "We're having a boy."

I grinned. "I heard."

His smile widened. "He was sucking his thumb."

"I saw." Laughter bubbled up from my lungs.

His eyes softened. "Can we tell everyone now?"

Slowly, I nodded. "Yes. I think we should. Maybe I can convert this picture into a formal announcement."

We began walking toward the car. "I have to head back to work. Do you want to hang out at the station for a little while? You can scan the picture and use my computer to make the announcement."

Since Brady and Jase were in Virginia, I had three options: remain inside the flat, spend time with Eva, or go to the station. "I'll hang at the station for a little while, but I want to see if Eva is free so we can shop for maternity clothes."

He smoothed the loose-fitting dress over my tummy. "Don't buy any loose-fitting clothes. Buy clothes that will hug your tummy so I can see my baby."

My heart sang. I loved how enamored he was with my new body.

* * * * *

My eyes raked over Rafael's handsome face, his broad shoulders, trim waist, and well-muscled legs. I was certain I'd never tire of looking at this man. How such a lethal physique could wring so much pleasure from my body was truly a mystery, but he had three times thus far today.

He squeezed my hand with a gentleness that belied his strength. "Hungry?"

"Always," I teased.

He pulled me close, obviously pleased.

I wondered whether it was possible to be too happy. The last two weeks had been nothing short of perfect. While I missed my friends in Virginia, I didn't miss school or work. Every ounce of tension had disappeared from my body. These days I felt only four things... overwhelming joy, desire, pleasure, and contentment. "So, Restaurante Eleven?"

"The chef is phenomenal." Rafael's hand settled against the small of my back as we neared the deep red building with the massive *eleven* scrawled across the front.

Benjamim, Eva, Chief D'Souza, and Mariana were waiting inside. "*Feliz aniversário, meu amiga!*" Eva exclaimed. She kissed me on both cheeks before handing me a gift bag. Benjamim, Mariana, and Chief D'Souza did the same.

My cheeks heated. "Thank you."

The hostess led us across the hardwood floor and out onto the terrace which overlooked the city and the Tagus River. The sky glowed pink and blue, promising yet another spectacular sunset.

Rafael pulled a thickly padded chair out for me. "I've ordered the eight course tasting menu with wine pairings, although Kristine and I will be sampling their non-alcoholic wines."

I kissed his cheek. "Thank you."

His hand sought my tummy beneath the linen clad table.

Benjamim snapped a picture and texted it to me.

Eva eyed us adoringly. "Are you still playing the Doppler for Brady and Jase?"

Rafael chuckled. "Every day."

A soft smile played on my lips. While Rafael no longer needed that assurance, since he could feel the baby move,

Brady and Jase were demanding regular updates. Playing the Doppler had become a part of our daily routine, along with weekly updates for Kadyn, Shae, Cenia, Marie, Lexie, Kimme, and my mom. I was relieved everyone knew about the baby, but keeping them informed was a full time job.

Two waiters stopped by with duck *foie-gras* and our wine.

Rafael reached for his glass. "To my beautiful wife, who twines me around her finger a little more each day. *Feliz aniversário, meu amor*." His hand clasped my neck while he fit his lips to mine. He teased and tempted me with the kiss before tapping my glass and sampling the wine.

I marveled at the crisp cherry and oak undertones in the non-alcoholic wine. "This is wonderful."

Rafael smiled. "My gift is waiting for you at home. I was afraid if I gave it to you before dinner, you'd refuse to leave the flat."

My curiosity spiked. "What is it?"

His smile widened. "A surprise. Suffice it to say, I've assigned a bodyguard while I'm at work to help you manage this gift."

I frowned. "Why?"

"Because you'll be venturing outside the flat a lot more often while I'm at work," he answered evasively.

"Oh! Maybe it's a car," Mariana exclaimed.

Rafael shook his head. "It's not a car."

Eva's eyes widened. "A motorcycle?"

Rafael's eyes danced with amusement. "My pregnant wife *will not* be driving a motorcycle."

I wracked my brain all through the *foie-gras*, the lobster ravioli soup, the scallops with caviar, the oysters, the fish, and the duck. Still, I couldn't fathom what it was. The tangerine *crème brûlée* and the *mignardises* the chef served for desert were too decadent to think of anything else. I splurged for a change and savored a cup of *bica*.

The baby was thrilled. He started doing back flips.

Eva paled when Rafael pressed her hand to my tummy. "Does that hurt?"

I smiled. "Not at all."

"Thank God," she breathed.

Rafael eyed Benjamim. "I assume congratulations are in order?"

My eyes flew to Eva's. "You're pregnant?"

"Fifteen weeks," she confirmed with some relief. "Our baby is due in December."

Tears flooded my eyes. "Oh, Eva! That's the best birthday present ever. We get to be pregnant together. Our children will be friends!" Everyone rose from the table to give her a hug.

Rafael pulled our chairs together. Each couple snuggled closer when we returned to our seats.

"How did you know?" I asked Rafael.

"The amount of relief in her voice when you assured her the baby's kicking didn't hurt," he answered with a chuckle.

Mariana and Chief D'Souza's children were grown and attending college. They shared some of their experiences and offered advice while we discussed our pregnancies and dreamed about our children.

I'd forgotten about Rafael's present until he eased the Porsche into the garage. By then, it was pushing midnight.

"You still haven't figured out what it is?" Rafael ribbed. We stepped inside the elevator.

"I can't imagine what sort of present would require me to leave the house." My eyes widened with understanding. "A job... with the Templar?"

He shook his head. "We can pursue that after the baby is born. For now, I'd like you to focus on your happiness and health, the baby, and maybe one other thing…"

The elevator dinged.

I waited anxiously while Rafael swiped his card.

My mouth fell open when I saw Jase sitting in an awkward position on the dining room floor. There was an explosion of fur. A puppy leapt over him, cocked his head, and barked.

"A Shih Tzu?" I cried. "You got me a Shih Tzu?" The room spun as my past caught up with me. A sharp pain tore through my chest.

Rafael caught me. Slowly, he eased me onto the floor.

Jase and the brindle puppy eyed me worriedly.

"Cade," I groaned. "How did you know?"

Rafael smoothed my hair while cradling me in his arms. "I saw you walk him. You carried on such long conversations with that dog, it made me laugh. When Michael told me he died…" He shook his head sadly. "I know how much you loved that dog."

I bit back a sob. Cade had seen me through so much.

"I wanted to give you a puppy for your birthday last year, but you were leaving for Ukraine. I've struggled to find the right time ever since. If it's too soon…"

I sifted through time. "It's been two years."

"I thought he could keep you company while I'm at work. I read a blog that listed all the benefits to getting a puppy when you're pregnant. A young dog tolerates a baby's tugging and pulling better than an older dog. He'll view the baby as a member of our pack. They'll help keep each other entertained." He grinned at the puppy. "Besides, I could use some practice."

I grasped his hand. "You don't need any practice. You do just fine taking care of me."

"A puppy is more demanding and unpredictable, although you do get into a lot of trouble," he teased.

I eyed the little ball of fur uncertainly. "Will he have to be quarantined when we travel between Portugal and the United States?"

Rafael shook his head. "He has to have all his shots and a letter from the veterinarian confirming he's in good health before we fly to the United States, but he won't have to be quarantined. He'll have a pet passport so he can fly with us. He can join us in Saint-Tropez."

My eyes shifted to Jase. "Hey."

A smile played on his face. "Hey."

My chin lifted. "Are you here to watch over me again?"

"When I heard Rafael was considering someone from Portugal..." his voice trailed off.

"Jase forbid it," Rafael revealed with some amusement.

"I'm relieved it's you." Brady and Jase were like family. I didn't want anyone else watching over me.

"Would you like to meet the newest member of our pack?" Rafael asked. He shifted me in his arms.

The puppy crouched down, wagged his entire bottom, and tore off in the other direction. He had a difficult time gaining traction on the hard wood floor.

We burst out laughing.

The puppy tried to stop, but he ended up skidding across the floor.

Jase laughed even harder. "He's been doing that all night."

I looked at Rafael. "Do you have any dog treats?"

He stood. "These are the ones the breeder

recommended."

I followed him into the kitchen.

Rafael retrieved a bag with soft strips of meat and a box of dog biscuits from the top of the refrigerator.

I opened the bag and sniffed the soft jerky treat. "This should work." I kissed Rafael before joining Jase on the floor. "Does this puppy have a name?"

He shook his head. "Not yet."

Rafael leaned against the breakfast bar. "I thought you might want to do the honors."

I studied the puppy, who was boldly sniffing the air. A black button nose and shiny black eyes were the only features visible beyond the explosion of fur. A small tuft of white fur jutted from his forehead and chest. The rest of his coat was streaked in gold, brown, and black. "He's adorable."

Jase eyed the mound of fur. "Any names come to mind?"

The puppy locked in on the treat. Slowly, he inched forward.

I held the treat in the palm of my hand while trying to avoid eye contact. "Bica?"

Rafael shook his head.

The puppy inched a little closer.

"Blaze?"

Jase wrinkled up his nose.

"Gunner?"

Jase chuckled.

Rafael shook his head again.

The puppy stopped and stretched his neck as far as it would go.

"Bear?"

Rafael smiled. "That one I like."

The puppy snatched the treat, stretched out on his tummy, and began to chew.

I stroked his silky soft fur. "Bosco?"

The puppy's ears perked up.

"Bosco," Rafael repeated.

The puppy stood and trotted over to him.

"Bosco," Jase agreed.

He glanced at us.

I smiled. "Bosco it is then."

* * * * *

"I swear that dog is trying to kill you," Jase grumbled.

"He's not. He just doesn't know which way to walk." I stepped out of the tangled mess, shortened the lead, and locked the retractable leash. Jase and I resumed walking. "Did you get a chance to see the house before you left?"

Jase nodded. "They're putting the finishing touches on the theater room now. The theater lighting is really cool."

I pulled Bosco a little closer so he wouldn't trip the other pedestrians. "What about the front of the house?"

"You'd never know there were two separate entrances," Jase assured me. "Did you know he knocked out the wall separating the two garages, so you can access all the cars from either side of your house?"

I shook my head. "He adds something new every week."

Jase's arm rose protectively before we crossed the street. "The dining room looks great. I like the tables you picked out." We'd ordered two square counter height tables in espresso.

Bosco clambered over the curb.

I laughed when he began prancing in front of us. "I hope

sixteen chairs are enough."

Jase walked to a nearby tree. "You've still got the table in your sunroom if it's not."

We stopped and waited for Bosco to pee. I wondered how his paws were fairing on the tiny mosaic tiles. "Do you think they'll finish by the time we return next month?"

Jase nodded. "I heard the investigation is drawing to an end."

"Thank God. I hope they got everyone." We started walking back toward the flat. A five pound puppy with four inch legs didn't have to walk far.

Jase slowed. "Do you mind if we stop at the bakery?"

We waited for a couple of cars to pass before crossing the street. "I don't mind, as long as you order two extra *croquettes* and *natas* for me."

"I think you should order the food while I sit outside with Bosco. I don't want you waiting outside by yourself," Jase stated apologetically.

I handed him the leash. "What would you like?"

He grinned. "*Croquettes* and *natas,* only twice as many as you."

I knelt down and mussed the hair on Bosco's head. "Would you like some *bica?*"

Jase helped me up before pulling a metal chair out with his foot. "*Bica* sounds great."

I rubbed my tummy, recalling how active the baby was after the *bica* last night. I would have enjoyed a repeat performance but thought it best I order juice.

I stepped inside the warm, fragrant bakery. I ordered a mix of lamb and veal *croquettes* and a dozen *natas* so we could share some with the doorman and Rafael when he returned home from work. I almost forgot the *bica* and the orange juice. *Pregnancy brain,* I thought.

The man handed me a small cookie. *"Para o seu cachorro."* He pointed out the window.

I turned toward the window. "For my dog?"

He smiled. *"Sim.* For your little puppy."

"Obrigada," I replied with a smile.

He set the drinks and pastry bags on the counter. *"Você é bem-vindo."*

I gathered the bags and drinks and joined Jase outside. "I don't know if this is a dog treat or a real cookie, but the gentleman who waited on me wanted Bosco to have it."

Jase pulled a chair out for me. "Would you like me to taste it?"

My jaw dropped. "You would do that?"

Jase shrugged. "If it came from this bakery, how bad could it be? Besides, I've eaten far worse things."

I sniffed the biscuit before handing it to Bosco. "Why don't we let Bosco be the judge?"

Bosco gobbled it up.

I twisted the lid off my orange juice.

Jase sipped his *bica.* "You seem so happy and relaxed here. Are you sure you want to go back?"

I glanced at him in surprise. "I think I could be happy anywhere, as long as I'm with Rafael. I'm relaxed because school is behind me. Maxim has been elected, I'm not working, and I'm getting plenty of sleep."

He looked thoughtful. "Do you miss work?"

"A little," I admitted, "but it seems pointless to return when I have to ask for maternity leave in a few months."

Jase dropped a Euro on the table after finishing his *bica.* "You and Rafael have been through a lot. Still, you're two of the kindest people I know. You deserve to be happy, and you deserve some time off from work."

"Thanks, Jase." Bosco was nodding off. I eased onto the sidewalk, snapped a photograph, and scooped him up. His paws rested on my tummy while I cradled him against my chest.

Bosco was quite the surprise, but I couldn't deny he felt right.

* * * * *

"Should I be worried that you're fondling my pregnant wife?" Rafael planted his feet against the floor. The door closed behind him.

I ignored his gruff tone and waved him over. "Come here!"

Jase held Bosco over my tummy.

Rafael sat on the other side of me.

"Watch," I whispered.

Jase balanced Bosco on my belly. He slowly removed his hands.

Bosco bounced as the baby attempted to kick him off.

Rafael laughed a deep, hearty laugh.

I grinned.

He lifted Bosco from my tummy and kissed the top of his head. "Poor dog. Is our baby picking on you?"

"He doesn't like anyone touching her belly," Jase insisted. "You try."

Rafael passed Bosco to Jase before resting his hand on my tummy.

The baby kicked hard enough to move Rafael's hand.

His eyes widened. "That's a really strong kick."

"I know." My hand joined his.

Jase retrieved Bosco's leash. "I'm taking Bosco for a thirty minute walk so the two of you can do whatever it is that married people do when they haven't seen each other all day."

Rafael raised a single eyebrow.

I stood and pulled him toward the bedroom. "Thanks, Jase. I owe you one."

* * * * *

I smoothed the coral sundress over my basketball sized belly before handing Rafael my cell phone. "Will you take a picture of my tummy?"

He set my phone on the counter. "Only if I can take it with my phone."

I bit my bottom lip. "Will you text the picture to Brady?"

A frown marred his handsome face. "Why?"

"He's feeling left out because Jase gets to feel the baby kick. He wants a belly shot so he can see how big the baby is."

Rafael set his phone on the counter. "Those two need to stop ogling my pregnant wife, find nice girls to marry, and knock them up."

I tried not to laugh. "Kadyn wants a picture too."

Rafael groaned.

"They're not looking at me," I reasoned. "They just want to see my belly."

He pulled my back to his chest so he could cradle my tummy in his arms.

My eyes slid closed. I loved the feel of his body wrapped so protectively around mine. "The more invested they are in this pregnancy, the more likely they are to babysit for us when the baby is born."

Soft, full lips caressed my neck. "That could prove useful." Rafael slid the strap over my shoulder so he could release my breast. He kissed my shoulder while lowering the other strap. Warm, strong hands kneaded my breasts, tugging both nipples into stiff peaks that threatened to send me to my knees.

"How long will Jase be gone?" I panted. I shifted my bottom against his erection, anxious to relieve the tension between my legs.

Rafael forced my chin back as he sought my lips. He tugged at my panties until they slid down my legs. "The virtual shooting range should keep him busy for a while." His hand followed my spine as he forced my chest against the table.

I gasped when the cool wood pressed against my swollen breasts.

With a well-muscled thigh, he forced my legs a little wider. His t-shirt and sweats made a soft swooshing sound as they tumbled to the floor.

I gripped the other side of the table.

His fingers dipped between my legs as he lifted the dress. "You're so ready."

I whimpered when I felt the soft, velvety tip of his erection slide into place. Heat licked my skin everywhere our bodies touched. I squirmed against him.

Rafael reached for my hips.

I sucked in a breath.

With an ominous growl, he thrust.

The room sheeted white.

Rafael allowed no time to adjust. I clung to the table as he slammed inside of me. Over and over he thrust...

demanding… possessing… owning every part of me. There was something primal and raw fueling this… *need.*

My breasts scraped against the cold table. Fire licked between my legs. Our bodies wound tighter and tighter, then spiraled into something unrecognizable. I prayed it would never end, even as I yearned for my release.

Rafael grabbed my hips, slammed inside of me, and cried, *"Kristine!"*

I disintegrated when he pulsed inside of me.

* * * * *

Dr. Barriera studied the slip of paper. She looked… crestfallen.

Rafael gripped my fingers so hard they hurt. "What's wrong?"

She held one finger up while she reached for the blood pressure cuff. "I want to check her vitals again." She wrapped the cuff around my arm, positioned the stethoscope in her ears, and pumped. The seconds ticked by while she listened. She eyed the gauge.

"Breathe," Rafael whispered.

Fear slinked through the room.

Dr. Barreira removed the stethoscope from her ears. "Kristine's blood pressure is well outside the normal range. She has too much protein in her urine." She pressed her fingers into my shins. "The swelling in her legs suggests her kidneys are not functioning properly. I'm afraid she has preeclampsia."

"Which is?" Rafael smoothed his fingers over my leg as if trying to erase what Dr. Barriera had seen.

She set my chart aside. "Preeclampsia is a pregnancy

complication characterized by high blood pressure, fluid retention, and protein in the urine. It's worrisome for a number of reasons. Preeclampsia can reduce blood flow to the placenta, which means less oxygen and nutrients for the baby. It can cause seizures and damage Kristine's organs. It can also cause a placental abruption which can prove life threatening for Kristine and the baby."

Rafael stumbled back. He looked like he'd just been hit by a grenade. "No. That can't be right. Run the tests again."

"I've run them... multiple times." She looked at me. "That's why I asked to see you twice this week."

"I knew my blood pressure was elevated, but I didn't realize it could cause all those problems," I admitted shakily.

She stepped a little closer. "Are you experiencing any headaches?"

"A few. Nothing too disabling," I added hastily.

"Vomiting... pain in your right side?"

I shook my head. "No vomiting or pain."

"Is there a cure, a treatment, or a medication she can take?" Rafael sat next to me on the exam table. He folded me in his arms.

"The only cure for preeclampsia is delivery." Dr. Barriera eyed me worriedly.

My heart stalled. "No! It's too soon. The baby will die."

The color drained from Rafael's face. "Can a baby survive at twenty-three weeks?"

"There's a ten to twenty percent chance your baby could survive delivery. Your baby only weighs five hundred grams." She looked at me. "Approximately one pound."

One pound? One. Pound. I shook my head. Forcefully. "I won't. I refuse."

"You're putting your own life at risk if you continue with

this pregnancy," she warned.

My heart raced. Blood thundered in my ears. "I don't care. I'd rather die than end this pregnancy."

Rafael sucked in a breath. "This cannot be happening."

"Please," I begged. "I'll do anything you ask."

She tore her eyes from mine. "I'd like to measure the baby again." She tapped a few keys on the ultrasound machine.

Rafael adjusted the pillow while I eased onto my back. His hands shook as he pushed my shirt out of the way.

Dr. Barreira squirted gel on my tummy. She studied the baby from a variety of angles, took some measurements, and printed a couple more pictures. "We can try to get you to twenty-six weeks. There's an eighty percent chance your baby will survive if he's delivered at twenty-six weeks."

The vise around my heart eased a fraction of an inch.

She wiped the gel from my tummy. "I'm going to order two steroid injections to help accelerate the baby's lung development. They hurt like hell, but they're worth it. I want you to limit your salt intake and drink lots of water. The water will help flush toxins from your body. I'm also going to prescribe a blood pressure medication." She looked at Rafael. "Purchase a blood pressure cuff when you pick up the prescription. I want her blood pressure taken four times a day. Text me the results." She scribbled her phone number on a prescription pad.

Rafael stared at the prescription.

Dr. Barriera's expression turned fierce. "You are to remain on complete bed rest. No physical exertion or stress. We'll give this a week. If that doesn't work, then I'm going to admit you. I want to see you in two days so we can check your urine and blood again. If you want to have the baby in the United States, you might want to think about returning within the next few days. This will not be a full term pregnancy. You won't make it more than a few weeks."

I reached for Rafael.

She gently cleared her throat. "I want you to continue having sex."

Rafael crushed me to his chest. "But you said…"

She took another deep breath. "I know. No physical exertion. However, preeclampsia is an immune response. There's a protein in the sperm, HLA-G, that can help regulate and suppress Kristine's immune response to the fetus. Her body is treating the fetus like foreign tissue. HLA-G can help suppress this response and reduce the risk for complications. You just… You need to approach this in a way that minimizes stress and physical exertion for her."

Rafael nodded. Once.

I swiped a rogue tear from my cheek. "I don't understand. We've been having sex. Lots of sex. Shouldn't that be suppressing my immune system now?"

"We lived apart the first five months of this pregnancy," Rafael reminded me. "We'd come together for a few days, then separate for weeks."

Our decision to live separately so I could finish my degree threatened our child's life? I sighed dejectedly.

"I'm sorry," Dr. Barriera whispered. She stepped quietly from the room.

A wounded sound escaped Rafael's chest when I collapsed in a pool of tears.

* * * * *

Bosco tumbled off the pillow. He shook his head before

attempting to climb it again.

Rafael leaned against the doorframe. "How are you feeling?"

"Bored," I confessed.

In three long strides, he joined me on the bed. "The contractor is still working on the renovations."

I cupped the side of his face. He looked so tired, it made my heart ache. "Any idea when he'll be done?"

Rafael helped Bosco up onto the pillow. He kicked his shoes off so he could stretch out beside me. "A week tops."

I curled against his chest. "So we'll remain another week?"

Bosco walked a couple of tight circles before settling in to sleep.

Rafael's fingers sifted through my hair. "I think the children's hospitals in DC and Virginia are better equipped to manage a high risk pregnancy and a premature baby, but I don't want you breathing paint fumes or drywall dust. I'm afraid we're going to have to wait a few more days."

I hugged him a little tighter. "What about Saint-Tropez?"

He rubbed my back. "Saint-Tropez can wait."

My eyes slid closed as the tension eased from my shoulders. "Can you fly back to Virginia with me?"

"Yes." His relief was evident. "I have to return for a preliminary hearing, but that shouldn't last more than a few days."

I studied his face. "How many people have you arrested so far?"

"Nine." He propped himself up with his elbow after easing me onto my back.

I tried to smooth the worry lines from his face. "Have you captured everyone?"

"We've arrested everyone we have sufficient evidence against. Hopefully, those arrests will deter the rest." He grasped my hand. "This conversation is getting off track. We need to discuss the preeclampsia."

"Why? I'm on bedrest. I'm drinking lots of water. I'm taking the medication Dr. Barriera prescribed..."

"And you're not getting any better," he interjected.

"I'm not getting any worse," I countered.

"We need a plan," he persisted. "What happens if you have a seizure? What if your body shuts down and I'm forced to choose between you and the baby?"

"Then you choose the baby." I tried to distance myself from him.

Rafael captured me with his leg, then eased on top of me, effectively pinning me beneath him. "Kristine, you're asking me to sign your death certificate. There's still a chance the baby could survive if you deliver early. If your organs start shutting down... there's no recovering from that. And if your body shuts down, the baby's life would be threatened either way."

"You could put me on life support." I struggled to break away.

Rafael grasped my face. He forced me to look at him. "I'm your husband. I'm supposed to take care of you. It's my job to keep you safe and to protect you from harm. I've been trying... for years. You can't ask me to stop now."

I grasped his hands, which remained on either side of my face. "You have to protect our child."

Storm clouds rolled through his eyes. "And if I choose to save you instead? Will you forgive me if I grant permission for an emergency C-section?"

"I don't know," I whispered.

Rafael's forehead fell against mine. "Please don't ask me to sacrifice your life for his."

Chapter 11 – Like I'm Gonna Lose You

I gaped at the dining room. Aside from our garages being linked, this was the first real change I'd seen since setting foot inside my house. We'd entered through the garage. My kitchen, family room, and sun room all looked the same, but the dining room was huge and clearly built to entertain.

My formal living room was gone. That space had been transformed into a massive foyer with double mahogany doors. I could see Rafael's office and the new billiard room from the dining room. The black, white, and gray color scheme Rafael used to have was gone. Warm, neutral tones offered continuity throughout the main floor. The elegantly curved staircases on either side of the foyer were breathtaking. The design was so perfect, I couldn't even picture what my staircase looked like before the renovations.

Rafael nodded his approval. "Let's check out the theater room."

Bosco squirmed. He was eager to explore his new home. I set him on the floor. We crossed through the dining room into what used to be Rafael's family room.

Rafael ushered me through the double wood doors. A large movie screen hung on the wall to my right. Deep burgundy curtains framed the screen on either side. Three elevated rows of black leather recliners sat to my left. Thin strips of lights lit the carpeted stairs leading to the recliners. The tray ceiling glowed along the edges, and little pinpricks of light shown like stars throughout the rest of the ceiling.

"How fun," I whispered. The theater felt so authentic, it demanded a whisper. I wondered whether I'd ever bother with a public theater again.

Rafael sank into one of the chairs. "I can't wait to hear the speaker system. Maybe we should watch a movie tonight."

"Sounds good," I agreed. "I want to see the upstairs."

Rafael and I peeked inside the billiard room before walking upstairs. "I know Brady is anxious to see you. I was thinking of ordering pizza and inviting him over for dinner."

We turned around when Bosco barked. I laughed. He was trying to follow us, but he couldn't pull his hind legs over the first step.

Rafael jogged back down the stairs and scooped him up.

I waited at the top of the stairs. "I'd like to see Kadyn, Shae, Cenia, and the rest of the gang. Can we invite them too?"

He set Bosco on the floor. "As long as you rest and let me do all the work." He led me into what used to be his bedroom.

"Rafael," I gasped. White walls, white linens, white furniture, and white filmy curtains sent me reeling back to Santorini. Large canvas wrapped photographs of the Aegean Sea offered brilliant pops of blue against the stark white room.

He folded me in his arms. "I know you're scared, and you want to wait on the nursery. I thought this would make a beautiful room regardless of how we use this space."

I burrowed into his chest. "It's perfect." The only thing we had to do was replace the bed with a crib, but I wasn't willing to risk that... yet.

He led me to our bedroom. "I'll send a text inviting everyone over for dinner and a movie. You rest. I'll walk Bosco. We'll join you just as soon as we can."

I nodded gratefully, undressed, and crawled into bed. I felt tired and a little depressed. I could see everything I'd ever dreamed my life would be, but it was still dangling just outside my reach.

Rafael brushed my hair aside so he could plant a kiss on my cheek. "Sleep, my love. I'll stand guard."

He was worried I might have a seizure. Each of us whispered his own prayer when my eyes slid closed.

* * * * *

"Rafael said I could sleep over." Shae set her bag and her Scrabble game by the stairs. "This place looks amazing. It's like it was always meant to be this way."

I gave her a hug. "Would you like the grand tour?"

Rafael pulled her from my arms. "I'll give her the tour. You're supposed to be lying down."

I rolled my eyes. "You were in the theater room. Someone had to answer the door."

Shae gaped at my tummy. She gave a little yelp when Bosco bolted into the foyer.

I laughed. "That's Bosco."

"Oh my God. He's so adorable!" Shae knelt on the floor. Bosco tried to escape, but she caught him, ruffled his fur, and rolled him on the floor. "Look at all that fur. I could just eat him up."

The doorbell rang.

Rafael strode toward the door. "Kadyn. Good to see you." They clasped hands and patted one another on the back.

Kadyn set his duffle bag on the floor. His eyes widened when he saw my tummy. "Wow. That's impressive." He hugged me gently before joining Shae on the floor. "So, this is Bosco."

I looked up when Rafael opened the door. Brady and Jase stepped inside. Each of them carried a suitcase.

Brady set his bag by the door. "May I?"

I gave him a hug. "Of course."

Brady dropped to his knees so he could hold my belly in his hands. He grinned when the baby kicked. "That's awesome."

Shae frowned. "I want to feel."

"Me too," Kadyn interjected.

Rafael growled. "Can we move into the family room so Kristine can sit down?"

Jase set his suitcase down. "She should put her feet up."

Kadyn's eyes narrowed. "Kri? What's going on?"

I swallowed nervously. "I'd rather wait until everyone arrives. I don't want to have to explain twice."

The doorbell rang again.

Shae paled. "Is there something wrong?"

Rafael greeted Cenia and Roger. Bosco bounded toward them.

Jase steered me toward the family room before I could

give them a hug. "She's not supposed to be on her feet. She's supposed to be on bed rest."

Kadyn noticed the dining room. "Two tables?"

I chuckled. "Rafael likes having you guys around."

"And you don't?" He joined me on the couch. "May I?"

Jase and I exchanged smiles. "Sure."

Kadyn smoothed his hand over my belly.

Shae sat on the other side of me. Her hand joined Kadyn's.

The baby rolled.

Kadyn smiled.

"That's a baby," Shae breathed.

Cenia dropped a kiss on my cheek. "I've missed you. You look great, Kri."

Kadyn moved next to Shae so Cenia and Roger could join us.

Rafael led Phil, Marie, Ethan, and Dakota into the family room. "We're just waiting on Brogan and Aidan now."

He turned on his heel when the doorbell rang again. "Scratch that. Everyone's here."

Cenia eyed my tummy uncertainly. "How do you feel?"

I grasped her hand and pressed it to my belly. "I feel tired, anxious, excited, content, and terrified."

"All at the same time?" Roger marveled.

I nodded. "All at the same time."

His hand joined Cenia's. Their eyes met. "I can't wait to see you like this."

She blushed.

"Are you?" I gasped.

She smiled. "We're due in January."

"Our circle of friends is growing again." Tears welled in my eyes.

Cenia gave me a hug.

Brogan and Aidan joined us. They held twelve boxes of ZPizza in their arms.

Cenia and Roger rose. Congratulations sounded all around.

Brogan and Aidan set the pizza on the counter.

Brady and Jase served the drinks.

Rafael joined me on the couch. "I'd like to catch everyone up to speed before we eat."

Our friends gathered around.

He grasped my hand. "Kristine has preeclampsia, a pregnancy complication that has placed her and the baby's life at risk. Our OB doctor in Lisbon has encouraged us to deliver the baby."

"But you're only six months along," Cenia objected.

Rafael forced an even tone. "Kristine wants to delay the delivery a few more weeks, so we can increase the baby's chance of survival."

"What kind of odds are you working against?" Phil demanded.

"The baby has a forty percent chance of survival at twenty-four weeks," Rafael answered. "Kristine's blood pressure keeps inching up despite the blood pressure medication Dr. Barriera prescribed. Each day she remains pregnant increases her risk of seizures and multiple organ failure. She could die if she remains pregnant much longer."

Shae shook her head. "No. That can't be."

Kadyn pulled her close when she burst into tears.

"We're meeting with Dr. Meinig first thing Monday morning," Rafael revealed. "We're hoping he'll allow her to remain on bed rest here at home, but he may insist on admitting her. They can monitor her more closely at the hospital. Kristine wants to delay delivery for two more weeks. The baby's chance of survival increases to eighty percent at twenty six weeks."

Our friends stared at us.

"I'm sorry," I whispered.

"We wanted you to be prepared," Rafael added. "Just in case."

"In case Kristine or the baby dies?" Aidan's hands clenched while he tried to rein in his frustration.

Rafael nodded. He kissed my hand and drew me closer.

Kadyn retrieved a box of tissue for Shae. "Do your parents know?"

I lifted my head from Rafael's chest. "Yes. They're flying in tomorrow. They won't leave until after the baby is born."

Cenia squared her shoulders. "What can we do to help?"

Rafael sighed. "I have to return to Lisbon after the doctor's appointment so I can testify at a preliminary hearing in that pedophile case. Kristine's parents will be here, but they don't know their way around. Brady and Jase will be staying here indefinitely. I don't want Kristine left alone in case she has a seizure."

"We can cook meals," Marie offered. Dakota agreed.

"I can run any errands you might need," Ethan offered.

"We haven't thrown a baby shower." Cenia frowned. "We need to shop for the baby."

My heart clenched.

"We're going to hold off on that for now," Rafael stated. "Once the baby is born and everyone is stable, we may take you up on that offer. I have a feeling he will be in the NICU for a while. He only weighs a pound right now."

Dakota gasped. "That's so tiny."

He pressed his hand to my tummy. "Prayers, moral

support, and some company while Kristine is on bed rest. That's what we need more than anything."

"You know we've got this," Brogan stated. "You won't face this alone." He knelt before me. "Kristine, I'll do anything… anything you need."

Tears streamed down my face.

Kadyn cleared his throat. "I think we should pray." Our friends clasped hands while forming a tight circle that included us. "Please, Lord, hold Rafael, Kri, and their unborn child in your loving arms. Protect them, guide them, and keep them safe from harm. Strengthen their faith and understanding. Ease their fears and doubts. Allow them to feel your presence. Grant us a miracle. Allow Kri to carry this baby to term and bless us with a healthy baby. In Jesus's name we pray. Amen."

Rafael and I stumbled blindly into their arms.

* * * * *

My head popped up when I heard the garage door opening below the house.

"Stay put," Jase growled. He set a steaming mug of peppermint tea on the end table next to the couch.

My heart beat anxiously while I waited for my parents to appear. We'd already broken the news to them, but I was worried about how my mom would respond once she saw me. I was praying my father wouldn't cry.

"Where's my baby girl?" Dad bellowed.

Bosco's head popped up. He was curled next to me on the couch.

I rubbed his ears. "It's okay. They're supposed to be here."

Brady rose from the couch.

My parents hugged me long and hard.

Bosco sought cover in Jase's arms.

I squeezed my father's hand. "How was your flight?"

"Good." He smiled. "I really like your flight attendant and the pilot Rafael hired."

Mom pulled Bosco from Jase's arms. "He's even cuter in person. How's he adjusting to his new home?"

The tension eased from my shoulders. "Good. He has yet to clear the stairs, though."

Rafael set their luggage in the foyer. "Brady and Jase will be watching over Kristine while I'm away."

"It's good to see you again." Dad shook their hands.

Mom set Bosco on the floor so she could give them a hug. "Are you still worried about the SVR?"

Rafael shoved his hands in his pockets. "They may target her in an effort to manipulate Maxim, given her role in his inauguration."

Dad nodded solemnly. "Thank you for keeping her safe."

Mom studied me. "You're looking a little puffy, honey. Are you feeling okay?"

"I'm tired, which is ridiculous since I'm resting all the time." I'd been battling a headache for three days now, but I wasn't about to admit that in front of Rafael.

"We're going to see the OB doctor tomorrow," Rafael informed them. "You're welcome to join us."

"If you don't mind," Mom replied.

Rafael nodded. "Would you like me to show you around the house before I start dinner?"

"Sure," Dad agreed. "I want to see the theater room Kristine's been raving about."

Mom followed them into the dining room. "I'd like to help with dinner."

I eased back onto the pillows.

Brady dropped next to me on the couch. "Are you feeling okay?"

"Not really," I admitted.

Jase grabbed the blood pressure cuff. He shoved the stethoscope in his ears and wrapped the cuff around my arm. He pumped air into the cuff and studied the gauge. "One-fifty-eight over ninety-five. We'll check it again in fifteen minutes. If it rises above one-sixty..."

"I know," I groaned. "You have to take me to the hospital."

Brady pulled my feet onto his lap. His fingers kneaded the soles of my feet. "Why don't you try to get some sleep? That may help lower it a bit."

Jase turned the lights down in the family room. "I'll move the ingredients for the Chicken Marsala over to the kitchen across from the theater room so the noise doesn't wake you when he starts cooking."

"Thanks, Jase." I whispered another prayer before tumbling into sleep.

* * * * *

"Kristine?"

I opened one eye and promptly slammed it shut. "Can you turn the lights down? It's a little bright."

"Remind me to purchase black out blinds," Rafael murmured softly.

"I'll order them while you're in Lisbon," Jase answered from the doorway.

Rafael smoothed his hand over my hair. "Do you want to take a shower before we head to the doctor?"

"No. My head hurts too much to shower." I grimaced when he sat me up.

Rafael and Jase exchanged glances. "I want you to drink some water." Rafael raised a glass to my lips.

I drank half the glass. "My stomach feels sick."

Jase's long legs ate the distance between us. "I think we should head to the doctor's office."

Rafael set the glass on the nightstand. "I agree. Will you let her parents know we're leaving early while I help her dress? We'll meet you downstairs in fifteen minutes."

Jase strode from the room.

Rafael eyed me worriedly. "Do you need to use the bathroom?"

I nodded.

He helped me from the bed. "I'll find something comfortable for you to wear while you wash up and brush your teeth."

I swayed when he released me.

"Kristine!" Rafael panicked. "What's going on?"

I rested my head against his chest. "My head hurts. I feel dizzy. I think... I'm going to be sick."

He scooped me in his arms. "Screw the bathroom. We're heading to Dr. Meinig's office."

"Rafael!" I cried. "Please. I'm going to throw up."

He carried me into the bathroom and held my hair while I heaved into the toilet. "How long have you had this headache?"

"This is the fourth day," I groaned miserably.

His jaw clenched. "Why did you keep this from me?"

I sank against his chest. "I didn't want you to worry."

He grasped my chin so I was forced to look at him. "If you're going to keep secrets, then I'm going to ask the doctor to admit you so we can monitor you more closely."

"I'm sorry." My eyes slid closed. The bathroom was even brighter than the bedroom.

He set me on the vanity, washed my face, and brushed my teeth. I felt so miserable, I began to cry. He grabbed the trash bin before carrying me downstairs.

My parents were pacing anxiously at the bottom of the stairs. "Is she okay?" Dad asked a little too loud.

"No," Rafael answered. "We need to leave now."

"Jase went to retrieve the Lincoln Navigator. He should be idling outside the garage." Brady scooped Bosco into his arms. "I'll walk Bosco. Let me know if Dr. Meinig sends you to the hospital. I'll meet you there if he does."

Rafael nodded.

Within seconds, I was tucked inside the vehicle next to my mom.

"Did you take her blood pressure?" Jase asked.

Rafael shook his head.

Jase stepped on the gas.

"Your father ran a bunch of red lights when I was in labor with you," Mom revealed in an effort to distract me. "Imagine how crazy these two will be."

Dad pretended to shudder. "Those poor nurses."

"Those nurses will be just fine as long as they make Kristine their top priority," Jase growled.

"See?" Mom patted my knee.

I reached for her hand while I curled into my seat. "I'm so glad you're here."

The receptionist's eyes widened when Rafael carried me into the office. I saw Dr. Meinig twice before graduation.

Brady and Jase had joined me for those appointments since Rafael was in Lisbon. "Ms. Stone?"

"Mrs. Garcia," Rafael growled. "If Dr. Meinig isn't available, I'm taking her to the hospital."

She jumped up and led us to an exam room. "He'll be in shortly."

Mom followed us into the room. Dad hung back in the lobby with Jase.

Rafael turned the light off before setting me on the exam table.

"How's your head?" Mom asked.

I groaned my response.

Dr. Meinig stepped inside the room. "Mrs. Garcia?"

"Hi, Dr. Meinig. I'm sorry we barged in early. I'm not feeling very well, and my husband is… worried." I wanted to say "crazy," but I figured the joke would be lost on Rafael.

Dr. Meinig shook Rafael's hand. "Mr. Garcia. Have you wrapped up your investigation in Lisbon?"

"Yes, but I have to return for a preliminary hearing, which is being held over the next few days. This is Kristine's mother, Anne Stone. She'll be taking care of Kristine while I'm gone."

"Mrs. Stone." Dr. Meinig shook her hand before shifting his attention to me. "What's going on?"

"Our OB doctor in Lisbon diagnosed me with preeclampsia ten days ago," I explained miserably. "The blood pressure medication she prescribed doesn't appear to be working. I've been fighting a headache for four days, and I started vomiting this morning."

Rafael handed Dr. Meinig the medical file Dr. Barriera had copied for us. "Kristine's blood pressure was one-fifty-eight over ninety-five last night. I didn't get a chance to check it this morning. As you can see, she's still in her pajamas."

Dr. Meinig flipped through the chart before reaching for the blood pressure cuff. "Dr. Barriera encouraged you to deliver the baby?"

I nodded. "I want to wait until twenty six weeks."

He checked my blood pressure. "One-sixty-two over ninety eight." He checked my pulse, then peered into my eyes. "Let's see how the baby is doing."

Rafael eased me back against the table. He lifted my camisole.

Dr. Meinig squirted gel on my tummy.

Mom inched closer.

Dr. Meinig pressed the Doppler against my belly. The baby's heartbeat galloped through the room.

Rafael looked relieved.

"His heartbeat is a little fast, but that's common at this stage of development. Let's take a closer look." Dr. Meinig retrieved the ultrasound machine from another room. He squished a little more gel on my tummy before spreading it around with the hand held device.

Mom grasped my hand.

Dr. Meinig studied the baby. He clicked a few keys on the ultrasound machine. "Your child is measuring eleven and a half inches and weighs a little over a pound." He wiped my tummy with a towel before digging his fingers into my shins. "Your kidneys are struggling. I need a urine sample so I can check your protein levels."

"I'll help her to the bathroom," Mom offered.

Rafael helped me off the exam table before releasing me to my mother.

She wrapped her arm around me. "How's your head?"

I stretched my arm out, afraid I might fall. "Awful. This

has got to be the worst migraine I've ever had."

We shuffled into the bathroom. Mom wrote my name on a plastic cup. "I'm going to see if the nurse has some soda crackers and Tylenol. Don't try to stand until I return." She closed the door behind her.

My eyes slid closed. I was so thankful I didn't have to pee in front of Rafael. I set my urine sample on the counter.

The door creaked open. "It's me." She held four packages of soda crackers, a bag of ice, a bottled water, and two white tablets in her hand. "We're going to kick this headache." She helped me up and stood so that her leg touched mine while I washed my hands. We dropped the sample by the lab on our way back to the exam room.

Rafael and Dr. Meinig were talking in hushed tones when we stepped inside the room.

Mom tucked me into the chair closest to the door, twisted the lid off the water bottle, and handed me a cracker.

Dr. Meinig rolled the stool directly in front of me and dropped onto the seat. "You need to deliver this baby."

I tried to force the soda cracker around the lump in my throat.

"The baby is okay, but you're not." He looked up when the nurse entered the room.

She handed him a slip of paper.

He glanced at the lab results. "I want a CBC and a Comprehensive Metabolic Panel STAT."

She hurried from the room.

Dr. Meinig braced his hands against the arm rests on my chair. "Your kidneys aren't functioning properly. The baby's head is near your cervix. If you deliver now we can induce labor and deliver naturally. If you wait, odds are high we'll have to do an emergency C-section."

"He's only a pound," I whispered fearfully.

His eyes held mine. "I've delivered a baby this size before. She spent some time in the NICU, but she survived."

"One more week," I pleaded. "Please."

The nurse returned. She was carrying a caddy filled with needles and vials.

Dr. Meinig rolled out of the way. He added a couple of notes to my chart while she drew my blood.

Rafael knelt in front of me. "Please, Kristine. It's time."

Tears welled in my eyes. "A few more days. *Please*. Let's try to get to twenty-five weeks. The baby has a fifty to seventy percent chance of survival at twenty-five weeks." I'd done my research. I knew every statistic.

Dr. Meinig set my chart on the exam table. "You will remain here until I see the results of your kidney and liver panel. We should have those results within the hour." He strode out of the room.

Mom shoved another cracker at me. "You need to eat so you can take the Tylenol. I'm going to catch your father and Jase up to speed." She handed Rafael the water, crackers, and tablets before leaving the room.

Rafael's eyes met mine. "Eat so you can lie down."

I forced two more soda crackers down my throat before downing the water and Tylenol. "Rafael…"

He shook his head. A somber expression marred his handsome face. "I can't lose you, Kristine. After everything we've been through… *I refuse*. I will not stand by and watch you die. Please. Have faith. Our child will survive."

Tears splashed against my hands. I wasn't sure whether they were his or mine. "I can do this, Rafael. Just a few more days. We'll be twenty-five weeks along on Friday."

"You should lie down." He grabbed the bag of ice my

mother left on the counter and helped me onto the exam table. He tucked the ice against the base of my skull before draping a towel over my eyes. "Please, baby, try to relax. Just... *breathe.*"

A chair scraped across the floor as he settled in next to me. He curled one arm around my tummy and one around the top of my head. "Rest," he whispered softly.

I tried to focus on my breathing. Large blobs of light pulsed behind my eyes.

Rafael whispered a lengthy prayer.

A warm blanket settled over me... or maybe it was peace. Eventually, I drifted off to sleep.

Hushed voices woke me. My wrist struck Rafael's face when I reached for the towel covering my eyes.

Mom squeezed my hand encouragingly. "How do you feel?"

"Tired," I replied.

Dr. Meinig stepped closer. "I'm going to change your blood pressure medication. I'm also going to prescribe Prednisone, which should temper your immune response."

Rafael helped me sit up.

Jase handed me a warm cup from Starbucks. "Dr. Meinig approved this."

I gaped at Dr. Meinig. "You prescribed coffee?"

He shrugged. "One cup of coffee won't hurt the baby, and the caffeine will ease your migraine."

My eyes narrowed. "Is this supposed to soften the blow? Are you going to force me to go to the hospital?"

He exchanged some unspoken communication with Rafael. "You may return home for now, but I want to see you tomorrow. This new blood pressure medication and the Prednisone should help buy us a few more days."

I exhaled softly.

Dr. Meinig frowned. "If your blood pressure rises above one hundred and seventy, if the headache persists, if the vomiting resumes, if you experience any bleeding, difficulty breathing, or feel pain in your right side; we are admitting you so we can deliver this child."

He locked eyes with my parents. "Preeclampsia can lead to multiple organ failure, stroke, seizures, permanent brain damage, and coma. I want her monitored twenty-four seven."

My father paled.

He looked pointedly at me. "I want you to promise me that you'll be completely honest about how you're feeling. No more hiding symptoms."

I nodded guiltily.

"Begin these medications immediately. I'll see you in the morning." He glanced at Rafael. "Make sure they have my cell phone number." He nodded toward my parents.

Rafael gathered me in his arms.

I pushed against his chest. "I want to walk."

He shot me a look that would have leveled the Empire State Building.

My lips slammed shut.

* * * * *

"Stubborn has two 'b's'," I objected.

Jase grinned. "I know. I couldn't resist."

Shae rolled her eyes. "People in glass houses…"

Kadyn laughed.

I removed Jase's tiles from the board. "Like any of us have room to talk." We were sprawled out on my bed playing Scrabble while my parents walked Bosco.

My phone chimed with an incoming text. "Rafael." I read the message, dialed his number, and put him on speaker phone. "Hi, baby."

"How are you feeling?"

Jase and I exchanged smiles. "Good."

"How's your blood pressure?"

"One-forty-nine over eighty-nine," Jase replied.

"At least it's heading in the right direction." His relief was evident.

"Dr. Meinig said the Prednisone and the new blood pressure medication are working. I see him again on Thursday, but I get to stay home indefinitely."

"You sound perky," Rafael noted suspiciously.

Shae laughed. "That's the Prednisone talking."

"What are you guys doing?" he inquired curiously.

"We're playing Scrabble," Kadyn answered.

"She's supposed to be in bed," Rafael grumbled.

I bit my bottom lip. "I am in bed."

Silence.

"You're playing Scrabble in bed?"

I giggled. "Yes."

"All four of you are lying in my bed?"

"Hurry home," I said.

"Kristine," he growled.

Everyone burst out laughing.

"You should expect a spanking when I return home."

That conjured up a whole lot of images it shouldn't have. "You wouldn't."

"I promise you. I will," he replied evenly.

Shae started fanning herself with the Scrabble rule book.

A wicked smile tugged at my lips.

My friends waited with baited breath.

"Husband," I replied, "I look forward to seeing you on Friday."

* * * * *

Cenia marched into the kitchen with a casserole dish. "I made lasagna."

Jase's stomach growled.

I helped Bosco climb onto the couch. "Sounds good. Will you be joining us?"

"Yes. Roger's parking the car." Cenia set the lasagna on the counter. She gave my parents a hug. "It's good to see you again." She scooped Bosco up before sitting next to me on the couch. "How are you feeling?"

"Good." I smiled. "How are you feeling?"

"Nauseous and tired," she admitted.

I updated my parents. "Cenia's due in January."

Dad grinned while Mom gave her another hug. "Congratulations!"

Bosco barked again.

"I got it!" Brady shouted.

Roger sauntered in with a grocery bag. "Salad, dessert, and wine for those of us who aren't pregnant."

Dad clasped his hand. "I understand congratulations are in order."

Roger set the bag on the counter. "Thanks. Are you sure you don't want to move here? We're going to need babysitters." He kissed me on the cheek. "What did the doctor have to say?"

"He's pleased with how I'm responding to the blood pressure medication. He's tapering me off the Prednisone now. I have another appointment on Wednesday so he can see how my body responds."

"You're still pretty swollen," Cenia noted. She joined Roger in the kitchen.

"That's the Prednisone," I explained. "My kidneys are improving."

My parents set the table.

Cenia tossed the salad. "Is Rafael still flying in tomorrow?"

"He flies in late tomorrow night." I sighed. "The judge scheduled another hearing for next week, so Rafael has to return Sunday night."

Mom shook her head. "That poor man. He must be losing his mind."

I threw Bosco's squeaky toy. "Our timing sucks, as usual."

Roger pulled the cork from the wine bottle. "Does he have to testify at trial?"

"Yes, but those trials won't begin for a few months. Most of the defendants will seek a plea agreement. They don't expect very many defendants to go to trial."

Jase helped me from the couch. "You and the baby should be strong enough to travel by then."

We joined my parents at the table. "I really want to go back for Christmas. Eva is expecting her first child in December. I'd like to be there for that."

"You have to return before January twenty-fourth," Cenia warned. She slid a piece of lasagna onto my plate. Strings of cheese stretched between the spatula and my plate.

"I'll be back long before then," I assured her.

"Maybe we should join them in Lisbon for Christmas," Dad murmured.

Mom scooped salad onto my plate. "I'm not missing my

grandchild's first Christmas."

I grinned, thoroughly excited by the idea. "You're going to love Lisbon at Christmas."

* * * * *

A growl sounded low in Bosco's throat.

My eyes flew open.

Brady glanced at his cell phone. "Rafael's home." He pushed off the chair and walked downstairs.

I sat up. My heart raced for reasons I couldn't explain.

Bosco whined.

Rafael and Brady's voices echoed through the foyer.

I set Bosco on the floor.

Bosco trotted out into the hallway. He peeked through the balcony, sat back on his haunches, and wagged his tail.

Brady scooped him up as soon as he reached the top step. "Come on, little guy, you're sleeping with me tonight."

I swallowed nervously.

The seconds ticked by.

I touched my toe to the floor, tiptoed into the hallway, and peered over the balcony.

Rafael cleared his throat. "Looking for something?"

I yelped as I spun around.

Rafael stood, with his arms folded, at the top of the other staircase. "Where are you supposed to be?"

I took a few steps back.

In three long strides, he obliterated the distance between us. "Anxious for that spanking?"

"You wouldn't dare," I whispered.

His eyes darkened.

I felt for the doorway. "My parents are sleeping in the

other room."

He stepped forward, forcing me inside the bedroom. "Then you should keep your voice down."

"Rafael, I..." My eyes widened when he shut the door. I risked another step back.

He tugged the black cotton t-shirt over his head. "How's your blood pressure?"

My eyes snagged on his chest. "Good."

His smile widened. "Good." He tugged at his belt.

I shook my head while backing away.

Rafael lunged.

My head spun from the speed at which he secured me. I tried to get away.

He popped me on the bottom.

I was so surprised he'd followed through on the threat, I didn't know what to say.

In one fluid motion, he pinned me against the bed. "That's for sneaking out of bed." He tugged the camisole over my head.

I knew he was playing. Still, I struggled to get away.

He rolled me over and popped me on the bottom again. "That's for inviting other men into *my* bed."

"Rafael," I objected. That one smarted a little bit.

His eyes heated. He tugged my sleep shorts off and popped me on the bottom again. "That's for being stubborn."

I tried crawling out from beneath him.

He tugged my panties down and swatted my bare bottom. "That's for keeping secrets from me."

A switch flipped as pleasure pulsed between my legs. "You can't punish me for that. You keep secrets too."

Rafael rolled me over. He eyed my breasts while pinning

my wrists above my head. "I don't keep secrets."

A single eyebrow arched against my forehead. "The Templar don't keep secrets?"

He frowned. "The secrecy required for criminal investigations and for the protection of others doesn't count."

"Obidos... Santorini... Bosco?" I persisted.

He smiled that panty dropping smile of his. "Those weren't secrets. They were surprises."

"My headache was a surprise."

His eyes widened. He swatted me on the bottom again.

My hands clenched. "Ow! Why did you do that?"

"Because I can." He pulled me onto my knees before popping me on the bottom again. "That's for scaring the crap out of me." He grasped my shoulder and thrust without warning.

"Rafael," I gasped.

He caressed my back, pulled back, and thrust again. "That's for being everything I ever needed."

My heart stalled. There was something in his tone.

"Kristine," Rafael pleaded.

Suddenly, everything changed.

I choked back a sob as understanding dawned.

Rafael wasn't playing. With all the risk and uncertainty surrounding this pregnancy, Rafael was seeking control. He was afraid of losing the baby, scared I might die, worried he might not be there, and frustrated that we were still being torn apart.

My heart ached. I wanted to offer some assurance, comfort him in some small way. I couldn't offer any guarantees with this pregnancy. The only thing I could offer him was me.

Rafael pulled me against his chest. His bristly cheek tickled my neck while his chest warmed my back. He remained anchored deep within me. The soothing scents of cedar and cloves enfolded us. His arms tightened until I could no longer discern where his body ended and mine began. He held me captive... suspended... possessed.

A soft moan escaped my lips.

I heard every promise he'd ever whispered.

Rafael kissed my shoulder... behind my ear... across my neck.

My eyes closed. I ran my fingers through his hair while his hands grasped my breasts. My body arched against his.

Time stood still.

I savored... *everything.*

How his breath felt against my ear.

How his strength surrounded me.

How his palms felt against my swollen breasts.

How, with a single pinch, his fingers beckoned the most exquisite pleasure.

How he stoked my need; stretched and filled every part of me.

Slowly, Rafael began to move.

I relinquished all control.

His hands moved in concert with every stroke.

I stewed in my desire... basked in his need... luxuriated in the pleasure he wrung from me. Still, I sought one last thing. I curled my hand behind his neck, urging him forward until our lips met in a deep, drugging kiss.

I prayed it would never end.

* * * * *

"I hate this," I whispered. My arms tightened around Rafael's neck.

His rock hard abs pressed against an equally hard baby. "Me too."

My eyes sought his. "Are you coming back on Wednesday or Thursday?"

"Wednesday night." He sighed. "Please. I'm just asking for three days. Three days to get through this hearing. Promise me you will remain healthy. Listen to Dr. Meinig. Stay out of trouble while I'm gone."

"I'll try." I rolled onto my tiptoes so I could kiss his pouty lips.

He backed me toward the couch. Thankfully, everyone had cleared out so we could say our goodbyes. "Speaking of trouble. Have you heard from Maxim?"

My eyes lit with excitement. "Yes. The pipeline is up and running."

"Congratulations," he stated admiringly. "Did you ask him about the wedding?"

I frowned. "I swear this pregnancy brain is getting the best of me. After hearing about the pipeline, I totally forgot."

We sat on the couch. Rafael's hand slid across my tummy, then froze. "What's that?"

I grasped my belly. "I'm not sure."

We watched my tummy bounce every three seconds or so.

"Are you having contractions?" he inquired worriedly.

I shook my head. "I don't think so. I don't feel any cramping or pain."

Mom paled when she saw us. "Is something wrong?"

I waved her over. "Come feel this."

She sat next to me on the couch. Warily, she placed her

hand on my belly. After three little bounces, she smiled. "The baby has hiccups."

Rafael's eyes widened. "How is that even possible?"

I laughed. "You know, we really should buy a pregnancy book."

My mother looked stunned. "Kristine! You're twenty five weeks along and you still don't have a book?"

"The last three months have been a little crazy," I argued weakly.

She stood. "Your father and I will remedy that first thing tomorrow morning."

* * * * *

Brady dropped onto the couch. He leaned back and stretched his legs. "What are you working on?"

My grip tightened around the pen. "Letters for Rafael and the baby."

Jase set his coffee cup on the counter. "Why are you writing letters?"

I bit my bottom lip, reluctant to respond.

Brady studied me a bit more closely.

Jase plucked one of the letters from the end table. Quietly, he read the first few lines. "You don't think you're going to make it."

I gathered the stack of letters, including the one from Jase's hand. "I'm just erring on the side of caution."

He eased next to me on the couch. "How long are you planning to delay the delivery? Truthfully?"

My arms curled around the baby. "As long as I can."

"Dr. Meinig is planning to deliver the baby on Friday. Rafael believes you're delivering his child then. When were you planning to tell them?" Jase demanded.

The baby elbowed me.

I stared at my tummy. "I was hoping Dr. Meinig would delay the delivery if I was feeling better."

"Are you?" Brady leaned forward while bracing his elbows against his knees.

I frowned. My thoughts had drifted toward the baby. "Am I what?"

"Feeling better," Jase nearly growled.

I took a deep breath and blew it out. "I've been feeling a little off, but I think that's because Dr. Meinig tapered me off the Prednisone."

"Your blood pressure is creeping up again. Do you have a headache?" Brady persisted.

I shook my head.

Jase's eyes pierced mine. "Then what's off?"

"I feel edgy and tired, which could be the Prednisone. I feel anxious about the pregnancy, like there's another shoe about to drop. I also feel depressed, but that's because Rafael is gone."

They exchanged glances.

"I was going to ask Dr. Meinig about delaying another week when I see him on Wednesday." I tucked the letters inside my padfolio. "Why would we deliver the baby early when I'm feeling okay?"

"You know that could change on a dime," Jase replied. "That Prednisone was meant to buy you a little time. You can't take it indefinitely."

Brady scooted a little closer. "Is there anything we can do to help you cope with your anxieties?"

"You could watch Phantom of the Opera with me," I suggested hopefully.

Jase frowned. "I thought Oni was coming over to watch that with you."

"She asked for a rain check." Oni flew back to Ukraine over summer break so she could spend time with her family. She returned late last night, but she was exhausted from the flight.

"Why Phantom?" Brady grumbled. "Wouldn't you rather see Clash of the Titans or Iron Man Two?"

I eyed the two men. "Have you guys ever seen Phantom?"

They shook their heads.

I smiled as I pushed off the couch. "Good. Who's popping the popcorn?"

* * * * *

"How's Bosco?"

"Good." I set my laptop on the nightstand. "He climbed the stairs for the first time last night. He's still too scared to walk down, though."

"Is he still chewing on stuff?"

"Oh, yeah. He chewed Jase's Keens yesterday. I ordered him another pair. I also ordered a bench for the foyer that has storage under the seat so people can hide their shoes in there."

Rafael laughed. "Poor Jase. That's the third pair of shoes he's lost to that dog."

I grinned. "He must have the best smelling feet in the house."

"Or the worst," Rafael mused.

I pulled Bosco closer so I could rub his ears. "How's Eva feeling?"

"Nauseous and tired," Rafael answered. "Benjamim is taking good care of her, though."

I sank against the pillows. "I wish I could be there with you."

"Me too. How are you feeling?"

"A little headachy, but nothing like the other day. I see Dr. Meinig tomorrow, so we'll see what he has to say."

"What time is the appointment?" Rafael asked.

I gave Brady a thumbs up when he peeked in to check on me. "Three o'clock."

"I was hoping to participate by phone, but I'll be flying over the Atlantic Ocean by then."

I curled around Bosco. "What time will you be home?"

"The hearing ends at five, which is noon your time. Barring any traffic or airport delays, I should be home by nine o'clock."

My eyes slid closed. "This is it, right?"

Rafael sighed. "Chief D'Souza spoke with the judge. He won't schedule any more hearings until after the baby is born."

I yawned as sleep tried to claim me. "Will you bring *natas*?"

"Of course." I could hear the smile in his voice.

"Will you bring some for Jase too? He's as addicted to those things as I am. Actually, if you could bring two or three dozen. My parents like them too."

Rafael chuckled. "Your wish is my command."

* * * * *

Bosco licked my face.

Gently, I pushed him away.

He nudged my chin with his nose. He whimpered, then pawed at my hand.

"Sorry," I groaned. I lowered him onto the floor. "Go find Jase. He'll walk you."

Bosco sat and quirked his head. He whimpered again.

I pulled Rafael's pillow against my ear.

Bosco trotted toward the door. He parked his bottom on the floor and groaned.

I closed my eyes and prayed. "Please, God, make him stop."

Bosco ran back to the bed and barked.

"No," I groaned.

He ran to the door, whimpered, and barked again.

"Hey, Bosco. Do you need to go outside?" Brady leaned over to pick him up.

Bosco jumped through Brady's arms. He bolted toward the bed. This time he tried to jump up.

Brady tried picking him up again. "Hey, little guy. Your mommy is trying to sleep."

Bosco leapt over Brady's hand, ran a circle around him and lunged for the bed. He barked, then barked again.

"Make him stop," I choked on a sob.

Brady froze.

Bosco growled and tugged at the duvet.

"What's going on?" Jase demanded.

"I don't know," Brady answered. "I thought he needed to go outside, but he keeps running back to Kristine."

Jase pulled the pillow from my head. "Are you okay?"

"No." Tears streamed down my face.

"Get the blood pressure cuff." His voice was low and lethal enough to raise the hair on the back of my neck.

Brady ran downstairs.

Jase softened his tone as he knelt beside me. "What's wrong?"

"My head hurts so bad, I can't sit up. Please, Jase, make it stop."

Brady ran into the room with the blood pressure cuff. He was breathing hard.

Jase sat next to me on the bed. He wrapped the cuff around my arm, shoved the stethoscope in his ears, and pumped. His eyes widened. He released the air and pumped again. "Get the SUV."

"What is it?" Brady eyed me anxiously.

"One-eighty-two over one-eleven," Jase gritted through clenched teeth.

"Oh, crap." Brady ran from the room.

"I'm going to pick you up. I'm sorry if this hurts." Jase tucked the duvet around me and lifted me from the bed.

Mom met us at the bottom of the stairs. "Krissy?"

"Mom, I..."

Bosco barked from the top of the stairs.

"I'll get him," Dad said. "You guys go. I'll walk Bosco and catch a cab or you can send Brady back for me."

The Lincoln Navigator was idling outside. Brady jumped out and opened the back door. "Gentle. Watch her head," he warned.

Jase leveled him with a look. Carefully, he set me inside, fastened the seatbelt, and lowered the seat back as far as it would go.

Mom climbed in on the other side. "How long has your head been hurting?" She tucked a bag of frozen peas beneath my head.

"A few hours," I answered miserably. "I thought I could sleep it off."

Jase climbed into the front passenger seat. "Did you call Dr. Meinig?"

Brady nodded. "He's going to meet us at Fairfax Hospital. He's calling ahead to alert the Emergency Room. They'll admit her through the ER." He pulled away from the garage.

My heart sank. "I don't want to go to the hospital."

Mom squeezed my arm. "Honey, you've done all that you can. You're two days shy of twenty-six weeks. The baby has close to an eighty percent chance of survival. You've taken the steroid shots. He's going to be okay."

"Please," I begged. "We haven't even settled on a name. We... we need to wait for Rafael."

Brady ignored the stop sign. "What time is it, in Lisbon?"

"A quarter after two," Jase gritted.

Brady accelerated well beyond the speed limit. "Rafael is still in court. Text him. If he's done testifying, he may be able to leave early."

Jase's thumbs flew over his phone. "He'll go insane. He's facing a seven and a half hour flight."

"I know," Brady acknowledged grimly.

Jase looked at my mom. "What happens if Kristine is unable to make decisions? Will the hospital allow you to make decisions for her?"

She frowned. "I'm not sure."

I grasped her hand. "I want the baby baptized right away. Please, Mom, just to be safe."

"Have you chosen godparents?" Worry lines carved her face.

"We were going to ask Kadyn and Shae." I choked on a sob. "Tell Rafael I'm sorry. If anything happens to the baby... tell him I understand."

Jase eyed me worriedly. "Understand what?"

"If he wants to leave me. Please, make sure Rafael gets the letters. They're in the office on the desk."

"Rafael will never leave you." That low, lethal tone was back.

Brady ran the light. He merged onto I-395.

I shook my head. I dared to believe that once, but I knew better now. Nothing destroys a relationship more quickly than losing a child. "My chest hurts."

"Her breathing is shallow, like she's not getting enough air." My mom sounded stressed.

"Try to focus on your breathing... deep, calming breaths," Jase encouraged.

"Shit!" Brady yelled. "Rush hour should be over by now."

"Turn your hazard lights on and take the shoulder. I'll dial 911." Jase's phone rang. "It's Rafael."

My head swam when I tried to sit up. "What is that awful smell?" I could smell something burning. The smell reminded me of the smoldering vehicle outside San Fernando, Mexico. "I think I'm going to be sick."

"*Kristine!*" Rafael's voice was pure anguish.

How I longed to pull him through the Bluetooth.

A low hum pulsed through my bones before the world fell dark.

* * * * *

"Kristine?"

"Rafael?"

"No, Mrs. Garcia, it's Dr. Meinig. How are you feeling?"

I sifted through sluggish thoughts. "Dizzy and tired." My hand flew to my stomach as understanding dawned. Panic seized my heart. "Is the baby okay?"

"The baby is fine. We have you hooked up to a fetal monitor." He turned the volume up so the baby's heartbeat entwined with mine.

I breathed a small sigh of relief while tears crept from my eyes. "What happened?"

"You suffered a grand mal seizure on the way to the hospital. We're treating you with magnesium sulfate and Zofran to help with the nausea. We're waiting for a delivery room to open up so we can deliver your baby."

The room spun when I tried to sit up. "Are you sure the baby's okay? Is he in danger if we wait?"

He glanced at the monitor. "No. The baby is fine. It's you I'm worried about."

I reached for his hand and missed. I blinked. Twice. I still couldn't see straight. "If he's okay, can we wait until Rafael arrives?"

Mom sat next to me on the bed. "Rafael is still seven hours away."

The vise on my heart tightened. "Please," I begged. "Don't make me face this without him."

She pulled me into her arms. "Shhh. Krissy, you need to stay calm." She plucked a few tissues from the tissue box and gently dabbed my face.

Dr. Meinig turned toward the monitor when an alarm sounded. "Please, you need to lie down." He helped me roll onto my left side. "If you lie on your left side, we can increase blood flow to the baby." He looked at my mom. "What time is Mr. Garcia due to arrive?"

She glanced at her watch. "He should be here by six

o'clock."

He took a deep breath and blew it out.

Mom tucked a pillow inside my arms. "Rafael left as soon as he heard, honey. Thank God he was done testifying."

Dr. Meinig adjusted the fetal monitor belt. "I can't make any promises, but I'll try to delay a few more hours. We'll see how your body responds to the magnesium sulfate." He turned the volume down on the monitors, studied them briefly, and jotted a few notes in my chart. "I'll check back in a half hour. I have another patient who is in labor right now. You're not allowed out of bed. The magnesium sulfate compromises your vision and stability. Please use the call button if you need anything. No food or water for the rest of the day."

I tried to relax. "Thank you, Dr. Meinig."

Mom rose from the bed. "Do you mind if I invite your father, Brady, and Jase in? I'm sure they're worried sick."

"No. That's fine." I was too tired to maintain any sort of conversation, but I knew I'd find their presence comforting.

Dad strode in first. "How are you feeling?"

"Just ducky." My head hurt but no longer to the extreme where I'd welcome death.

"I can tell," he joked. "What kind of fashion statement is this?" He mussed my hair.

I tried to smooth the tangled mess. "I fried it during the seizure."

Dad laughed. He dropped a kiss on my cheek before claiming the chair next to the bed.

Mom pulled a comb from the tub of supplies lying on the nightstand next to the bed. She started working through the knots. "Wow. I can't even remember the last time I combed your hair."

Jase squeezed my foot. "I'm demanding hazard pay. I thought I was going to have a heart attack. Brady came this close to rolling the car on the exit ramp." He held two fingers up about an inch apart.

"They dispatched an ambulance and a police escort, but I beat them to the hospital. I hate the beltway," Brady grumbled.

I reached for his hand.

He gave me a hug instead. "I'm glad you're okay."

Jase sank onto the padded bench beneath the window. "Kadyn and Shae are on their way."

I bit back a smile. "I hope she brings her Scrabble game."

Jase chuckled. The tension eased from his face.

"Rest," Mom whispered.

My eyes closed, gratefully. "I wish Rafael was here."

"Me too," she admitted softly.

Chapter 12 – Love Will Set You Free

I frowned before my eyes flew open. "I think my water broke."

Mom rushed to my side. She lifted the blanket and stumbled back. "Get the nurse."

Jase bolted from the room. "Emergency! Room six-twenty-nine!" Footsteps pounded down the hall.

"Oh, God," I cried. Blood soaked the sheet beneath me.

Kadyn hit the call button just as the machines began to alarm. He too ran from the room. "We need a nurse!"

Mom grasped my hand. She placed her other hand on my stomach. "Please, Lord, lay your healing hands on my child. Protect my daughter and her baby. Keep them safe from harm. Guide their doctors and nurses…"

A cramp tore through me. I doubled over in pain. "The priest, Mom. Please, I want the baby baptized right away."

"I'll find the priest." Shae hurried from the room.

Four nurses rushed in with Kadyn. One grabbed the fetal monitor strip while another peered beneath the blanket. "We have to deliver the baby. Now."

My heart ground to a complete stop. "Where's Dr. Meinig?"

"Page the anesthesiologist and the OR. We need B positive blood sent STAT," the nurse ordered.

The nurse next to her plowed into Jase before fleeing the room.

My parents kissed me. "We'll be praying the whole time, honey. We'll be right here waiting for you and the baby."

One nurse grabbed the IV and piled the monitors on the bed while the other two pulled the rails up, released the brakes, and wheeled me toward the door. "Mrs. Garcia, we need to perform an emergency C-section. You'll have to go under general anesthesia. I need your consent for a blood transfusion. There are risks…"

My ears began to ring. "Yes. I'll accept the risks. Where's Dr. Meinig? Someone needs to call Dr. Meinig and my husband." My entire body began to shake.

Jase appeared. "Rafael is here. He just texted me from downstairs."

"I want to see him," I pleaded. "Please, I need to apologize. I need to say goodbye."

"Your husband can't be inside the operating room, not when you're going under general anesthesia." Everyone squeezed inside the elevator.

"What floor are we heading to?" Jase demanded.

"Two," the nurse answered. "Sir, this is a staff only elevator."

Jase shot off a quick text. "I'm Kristine's bodyguard. I go where she goes."

"You won't be allowed inside the operating room," she warned.

The alarms grew louder.

"She's tachycardic. She's going into shock."

The elevator dinged. The doors slid open.

My stomach cramped again.

"Mrs. Garcia? I'm Father McHugh. I'm here to baptize your baby. May I administer the Sacrament of Anointing of the Sick?"

"Yes." My chin quivered.

He pulled a small vial from his pocket. "Do you wish to make a confession?"

Everything blurred as the bed picked up speed. "It has been three weeks since my last confession." I tried to list my sins. My thoughts were so muddied, I couldn't identify a single one. "I've been on bed rest. I don't believe I have any sins to confess."

He spread oil on my forehead with his thumb while making the sign of the cross. "Through this holy anointing, may our Lord Jesus Christ in love and mercy help you with the grace of the Holy Spirit." He did the same with my hands. "May the Lord Jesus Christ who frees you from sin save you and raise you up."

Frankincense and Myrrh tickled my nose. With a deep, shuddering breath, my eyes slid closed.

Jase squeezed my hand. We swerved around the corner at a nauseating rate of speed.

My eyes flew open.

"Room three!" someone shouted.

"I'm here!" Dr. Meinig yelled. He was breathing hard by the time he reached us. "Kristine, we can do this. I promise, we'll take good care of you and your baby."

Tears dampened my cheeks. "Is the baby okay?"

He glanced at the monitors. "His heartbeat is erratic, as is yours. I'm afraid you've both lost a great deal of blood. He may have lost oxygen as a result. We need to deliver him now."

I shivered. "I'm so cold. Why am I so cold?"

Jase kissed my forehead. "I'll be standing right outside the door."

"Kristine!"

The bed slowed.

The doors to the operating room pressed inward.

Rafael lunged for me. "I love you. I will always love you. No matter what."

"I love you too," I sobbed. "I'm so sorry. I never meant to hurt the baby."

He reached for Jase as the doors slid closed.

"Knock her out!" Dr. Meinig yelled. "Now!"

"I'm working as fast as I can," a disembodied voice answered.

They transferred me to the operating table. Paper crinkled all around me.

My teeth chattered. The table shook right along with me.

Something cold splashed against my stomach.

I flinched. My stomach cramped again.

Someone held my shoulders and legs in place.

Alarms sounded again.

Dr. Meinig's eyes appeared between a cap and a mask. He held a scalpel in his hand. "Hurry," he snarled.

"Please, just take the baby. I don't care how much it hurts!" I prayed for the scalpel to pierce my skin.

Someone smoothed a hand over my head. "We're praying for you," she whispered.

"Okay, brave girl, count back from one-hundred."

I forced the numbers through clenched teeth. "One-hundred, ninety-nine…"

Darkness welcomed me once again.

* * * * *

"Mon coeur."

My eyes flew open. I shook my head, then shook it again. White whispered all around me. "Am I in Greece?"

Michael laughed.

Tears pooled along my lashes. I never thought I'd hear that sound again. I sat up expecting pain. There was none. "Michael?" I whispered.

He smiled when our eyes finally met.

My heart skipped a couple of beats.

He stepped a little closer. *"Tu m'as manqué."*

"I've missed you too." I stared at the little girl in his arms. I knew with every fiber of my being that this was the child I'd lost. Relief and an overwhelming sense of joy washed over me. I'd always pictured them together, but now I knew. Michael and Genevieve were truly together.

"Are you happy?" He sounded more curious than anything.

I tore my eyes from Genevieve. "Sometimes. Mostly, I'm scared."

"Don't be." He touched my hand. Peace settled over me like a warm blanket on a chilly night. "I want you to be happy."

"Are we dead?" The thought wasn't as alarming as I thought it would be.

He shook his head. "Love never dies."

"I poured your ashes in the ocean," I whispered.

"An act of love," Michael replied.

A tear slid silently down my cheek. "You died trying to save me."

"Also an act of love." His thumb traced the cross on my hand before he stole the tear from my cheek. "How many lives have you saved?"

"I'm not sure." Jean and Kadyn were the only two people who came to mind.

He smiled. "There are more than you could possibly count, although most are unaware of that fact."

I eyed him curiously. Michael didn't have the same effect he used to have on me. There was no passion... no physical attraction... only love. Although, I was hesitant to say "only," because that love felt all-encompassing.

He tucked a strand of hair behind my ear. "You need to go back. He's not finished with you yet."

I nodded. While there was a part of me that longed to remain with Michael and Genevieve, I was okay with that. I caressed my daughter's cheek. Her smile was truly glorious.

Michael kissed my forehead. "Take care of my brother... and our girl."

I stared at him, thoroughly confused. "Our girl?" How could I care for Genevieve when she was here with him?

Michael laughed. "God has a wonderful sense of humor."

* * * * *

A cool hand pressed against my cheek. "Mrs. Garcia, can you open your eyes?"

Lead weights held them firmly in place. I shook my head, then groaned. Pain ricocheted through my entire body.

A light pierced my eyes. "Ow! What is it with you people and those obnoxious lights?"

A woman chuckled. "She's awake all right."

"My name is Mary. I'm a nurse at Fairfax Hospital. Do you remember why you're here?"

I bolted upright. Pain ripped through my lower abdomen. I sucked in air.

Strong hands captured my shoulders and eased me down again. "Easy. You don't want to pull your stitches."

My hand flew to my stomach. "My baby. Oh, God! The baby." I began to sob.

The monitor alarmed.

"Mrs. Garcia, you need to calm down. Breathe with me. In... Out... Good. Deeper this time. In... Out... That's better." Mary smoothed my hair back so it no longer covered my eyes. "Your baby is in the NICU. She's a fighter just like you."

"She?" I managed through strangled tears.

"Your husband had the same reaction." Mary chuckled.

I grasped her hand. "Rafael. Is he with her?"

"Yes. He asked me to call the NICU as soon as you came to. He'll meet you back in your room."

I shook my head. "I don't want him to leave the baby."

She eyed the monitor again. "Your husband needs to know his wife is okay. I'm going to call down to the NICU, then we'll wheel you to your room."

My eyes slid closed while I breathed through the pain. A million unanswered questions remained.

Mary hesitated. "On a scale of one to ten, how would you rate your pain?"

I forced my eyes open again. "Nine. Ten when I move."

"The Fentanyl must have worn off. Dr. Meinig ordered

Morphine. I'll get that started for you." She tugged the curtain aside, then walked away.

I tried to organize my thoughts.

Mary breezed back in. "I'm going to add the Morphine to your IV. You're going to feel some pressure on your neck that will creep over your head and settle over you like a heavy blanket. Don't worry. That's perfectly normal."

My wrist hit the railing on the bed. "I don't want Morphine. I want to see the baby, and I can't think straight when I'm on pain medication."

The pity that flashed in her eyes was quickly hidden away. "You'll be on magnesium sulfate for the next two days. You won't be allowed out of bed as long as you're on that medication. I'm sorry, but you won't be able to see your daughter until you're off that medication."

My heart beat frantically. "I won't see my baby for two days? What... what if she doesn't make it?" I hadn't a clue what kind of shape she was in. The monitor alarmed when I started crying again.

"I'm sorry, Mrs. Garcia. The magnesium sulfate is not optional. Your blood pressure is too high. You're still at risk for seizures. Pain drives your blood pressure even higher. So, I'm going to add the Morphine." She pushed the syringe into the IV. "There. Let's see if that doesn't help."

I shook my head. I couldn't risk pain medication. I needed a clear head. I needed to see my baby before... before... "Ugh." The pressure on my neck was *unbelievable*. I shivered when the Morphine crept over my head. My body filled with cement. "That feels awful."

"Just give it a minute." Mary smiled when my shoulders relaxed. She watched the monitor while the cuff on my arm puffed up again. "That should do the trick. Are you ready to see your husband?"

"No." I didn't want him to leave the baby. *How could they keep me from my baby?* I closed my eyes so I wouldn't have to deal with Mary.

My eyes flew open when a man wearing green scrubs began moving the bed. I squeezed them shut again. I was already dizzy enough.

Two metal doors popped open.

"Krissy!" Mom cried. She walked hurriedly alongside the bed. "How are you feeling?"

"Tired... dizzy... and sore. How long have I been out?"

My father jogged up beside her. "A little over two hours. Rafael's with the baby now."

I shook my head. "My nurse called the NICU. He's meeting us in my room." I closed my eyes against all the moving objects. "Will you sit with her while he's with me? She shouldn't be alone."

"Her parents are the only ones allowed inside the NICU right now," Mom answered regretfully.

The bed rolled to a stop. My escort pushed the button for the elevator. He glanced at my parents. "You can join us." He backed the bed onto the elevator.

I tried wrangling my thoughts while focusing on my mom. "Was she baptized?"

"Yes. Father McHugh baptized her shortly after she was taken to the NICU. The NICU nurses allowed Kadyn and Shae to join Rafael and the priest for the baptism."

The elevator doors slid open. The bed bounced when the wheels hit the gap between the elevator and the floor. My pilot made a sharp right. He pushed a button for another set of doors before pushing me down a long hallway.

My teeth started chattering.

My parents walked alongside me.

"Did you get to see her?" I couldn't recall if I'd asked that question. I felt thoroughly disoriented between the Morphine, the cold hallway, and the jostling.

"Just briefly, when they wheeled her Isolette out of the operating room." Mom reached for my hand. "Honey, she's so tiny."

Tears welled in my eyes. "Did Rafael name her?" Surely, a name was required for baptism.

She released my hand when the bed swung around another corner. "Rafael should be the one to tell you."

"Kristine!" Rafael shouted hoarsely. The bed stopped abruptly when he flung his body over the railing. He scooped me up into a gentle hug. "Kristine, I was so afraid I'd lost you. I thought… I thought…" He scattered tear stained kisses all over my face before shuddering. "I'm so glad you're okay."

"How's the baby?" My heart beat anxiously.

"She was having some difficulty breathing, so they put her on a ventilator. Her heartbeat is strong. Her kidneys and liver were impacted by the blood loss, so the gastroenterologist and the nephrologist will be monitoring her labs over the next few days."

The bed started rolling again. "How much does she weigh?"

"One and a half pounds. She's no bigger than my hand." Rafael pulled out his phone and showed me a picture. You could barely see the baby beneath all the patches, wires, and the ventilator. The tiniest diaper imaginable was folded around her bottom. A thin layer of hair darkened her head.

I started crying again.

My pilot slowed before backing into a room. A young

nurse with chestnut hair followed us. "Mrs. Garcia, my name is Jenny. I'll be taking care of you this evening. How are you feeling?"

"Sluggish," I replied accusingly.

She eyed the monitor. "That's the Morphine. Are you in any pain?"

"No." I shivered. "I'm just... cold."

She ran a temporal thermometer across my forehead, strapped a cuff around my arm, and checked the swelling in my legs. "I'll grab a couple of blankets from the warmer. I'd like you to get some rest. Visiting hours are over, but I'll give you a half hour with your family. I understand you were just wheeled out of recovery. Your husband can remain throughout the night. Everyone else is welcome to return at eight o'clock tomorrow morning."

Rafael warmed my hands between his. "I have to divide my time between Kristine and the NICU. There are some security concerns, which I can explain. My wife has bodyguards. They're on their way back from the cafeteria now."

"Her bodyguards can stay." She paused just inside the doorway. "I'll be right back. I'm going to get the blankets."

Rafael lowered the railing on the bed.

My heart clenched. "You shouldn't leave the baby for too long. I don't want her to feel alone."

He sat, carefully. "They kick everyone out during the nurse shift change. I can't return for another thirty minutes." He grabbed a couple of tissues and gently dabbed my cheeks.

Mom chewed her bottom lip. "Have you eaten?"

Brady and Jase strode into the room. Kadyn, Shae, Cenia, and Roger walked in behind them. The nurse returned with the blankets.

Jase handed Rafael a brown paper bag. "I brought sandwiches… ham, turkey, and roast beef." He leaned over and kissed my forehead. "How's our little mama?"

"Tired." The blankets were so warm. Everything grew hazy. "Does our baby have a name?"

"Gabriella Michaela Garcia," Rafael answered.

I smiled. Rafael had chosen the feminine versions of Gabriel and Michael, two of the four names we'd been considering for our son. "So that's why Michael referred to her as *our* girl."

* * * * *

The bed dipped. A well-muscled arm slid cautiously between my abdomen and chest. Rafael tucked my back against his chest. "Another nurse shift change," he explained tiredly.

"How's Gabriella?" I whispered. Jase was sleeping on the fold out chair next to us.

"She's still on the ventilator. They drew blood a few minutes ago, so we'll know more about how her liver and kidneys are faring when those lab results are in." He pulled me a little closer.

I fought the urge to cry. I argued with my physicians and nurses over the magnesium sulfate when they rounded this morning. They refused to discontinue the medication so I could go to the NICU. Rafael's regular updates and pictures were the only things keeping me sane. "What time is it?"

"Seven-thirty. The NICU nurse asked whether you plan to pump. They'll store the milk for us. We have to feed Gabriella through a feeding tube for a few weeks at least."

The thought that I'd be feeding my child through

industrial pumps and tubes rather than nursing and holding her in my arms made my heart ache even more. "The lactation nurse is supposed to stop by today. I'll see if I can rent a pump."

He stifled a yawn. "She looks so fragile, I'm afraid to touch her."

"I wish we could hold her." My body felt like an empty husk.

Rafael smoothed the hair from my face. "How do you feel?"

"Tired and sore," I answered honestly. "Every time I fall asleep the nurse comes in and wakes me up. The lab technician was here an hour ago, drawing blood. The doctors rounded shortly after that."

He slid the phone from his pocket. "I'll text a quick update and ask everyone to hold off on visiting until noon so you can get some sleep."

Jase's hand carved a trail through his closely cropped hair. He rose from the chair. "You both need sleep. I'm going to head downstairs for a bite to eat. I'll ask the nurses to give you a couple of hours. I'll stand guard outside the door if I have to." He tugged his boots on and strode from the room.

"Sleep," Rafael repeated wistfully. He finished the text, sank onto the pillow, and linked his hand with mine.

"I can't believe we have a little girl," I whispered.

"Dr. Barriera must have mistaken the umbilical cord for something else." He chuckled. "Do you think our daughter will be as stubborn as you?"

A smile tugged at my lips. "I hope so."

He pressed a kiss to my cheek. "Me too, love. Me too."

* * * * *

The nurse bolted from the room.

Mom froze just inside the doorway. "What's wrong?"

I wiped the tears from my cheeks. "Jase nearly strangled my nurse."

Dad eyed him warily. "Why?"

"Your daughter was in excruciating pain. The nurse was pushing on her incision, trying to force blood from her uterus. She didn't offer any pain medication before the procedure, which is completely unacceptable." Jase folded his arms across his chest.

Dad cracked a smile. "Sounds like you set her straight."

Jase nodded.

Brady walked in and gave me a kiss. "Hey, pretty lady. What's the latest on our baby?" He set a cheerful display of yellow and orange roses on the nightstand next to the bed.

"She's off the ventilator. She's on a CPAP now." I showed him the picture Rafael texted from the NICU. "Her liver and kidney function are declining. The neonatologist said those organs could still recover. It just takes time." I was trying my best to remain optimistic and to focus on the positive.

Dad sank onto the bench beneath the window. "When do you get to see her?"

Pain ripped through my lower abdomen when I tried sitting up. Moisture dotted my forehead while I gritted my response. "Tomorrow, as long as my blood pressure continues to improve."

Mom adjusted my pillows. "Any idea when the rest of us can see her?"

"Tomorrow. Possibly. Only two people are allowed inside the NICU at one time. Every visitor must be accompanied by a parent so Rafael will have to take you back one at a time."

Jase refilled my water.

"I can stay with Kristine tonight if you'd like to go back to the house to get some rest," Brady offered.

"I'm not leaving," Jase growled.

I reached for his hand. "I want you to get some rest. You're one of the few things keeping me sane, Jase."

His eyes softened. "I'm not leaving you."

I squeezed his hand. "Why don't you take a few hours to shower, change, and rest while everyone is here? You can come back and spend the night if you'd like."

"I'll stay here until you return," Brady promised.

Jase conceded with an abrupt nod. "Text me if you need anything." He kissed my tear stained cheek.

Cenia and Roger greeted Jase when he strode from the room. Roger handed me a gigantic teddy bear. "This is for you, not the baby."

"Thanks." I gave each of them a hug.

"How's Gabri?" Cenia asked.

A smile tugged at my lips. "Looks like Jase won the bet."

"What bet?" Roger joined my father on the bench.

I sent Jase a quick text. "He bet you'd shorten Gabriella's name in less than a day. I gave you guys a week."

Cenia laughed. "What did you bet?"

"ZPizza." I glanced at the response from Jase. "Looks like I'm buying dinner tonight."

Kadyn and Shae stepped into the room. "Mind if we join you?"

* * * * *

Rafael eased the wheelchair onto the elevator. "Are you ready to meet your daughter?"

"Yes." My heart fluttered anxiously.

He pressed the button for the second floor. The doors slid closed. "You shouldn't stay for too long. We don't know how your blood pressure will respond now that you're off the magnesium sulfate."

"Yes, Mom." I rolled my eyes at him.

He planted his hands on the arm rests. "I'm going to ask the NICU nurse to take your blood pressure thirty minutes in. If your blood pressure is too high, I'm wheeling you right back to your room."

"Fine." I pouted. The shower had proven downright exhausting. My stitches hurt so bad I couldn't step into my panties or sweats. Thank God my mother had arrived in time to help me dress. I was annoyed by all the limitations. I belonged with Gabriella, but my body wasn't cooperating.

We scrubbed up and checked into the NICU. The doors clicked open. Rafael stopped at a tall metal shelf. He tugged a gown over my arms before donning one himself. He pushed the wheelchair past the first room.

My eyes widened when I saw all the Isolettes. "How many babies are there?"

"Eighty-nine, but they're spread across four rooms. Gabriella is in NICU room two." He stopped in front of the nurse's station.

My jaw fell slack. The fact that I didn't know which infant was mine completely shredded my heart.

A young but confident looking woman looked up from her clipboard. "Good morning, Mrs. Garcia. I'm Faddwa, Gabriella's nurse. Would you like to help me change her diaper?"

My eyes teared. "I'd love to."

Rafael eased the wheel chair next to Gabriella's Isolette. "Our little miracle."

I choked down a sob. "She's so small." I couldn't believe this tiny baby was the same child who'd been kicking and rolling inside of me for the past few months. She felt so much bigger than she looked.

Faddwa opened the other side of the Isolette. She repositioned Gabriella so she was lying on her back. "No more CPAP. Your daughter's breathing so well, she just needs the nasal cannula."

Rafael opened the two circular doors on our side of the Isolette. "She's determined and strong, just like her mommy." Gently, he cupped the top of her head.

Faddwa covered Gabriella's eyes with a foam eye mask before handing me the baby wipes and a diaper that was smaller than the palm of my hand. She pointed to one of many tangled wires surrounding our child. "This is the arterial line, the only line you really need to avoid."

My eyes raked over the monitor, the electrodes, the tape, the wires, the clamp on her belly button, and the feeding tube in Gabriella's nose. Fear spiked through me. "Is she okay?"

"Don't let Gabriella's size fool you. She's doing better than a lot of our full term babies," Faddwa assured me.

My hand shook while I removed Gabriella's diaper. I cleaned her bottom with the wipe before taping the new diaper into place. "No wonder you're afraid to touch her."

Rafael tickled the palm of her hand with his pinky finger. Gabriella grasped his finger.

Faddwa latched the doors on her side of the Isolette. "Has your breastmilk come in yet?"

I handed her the small plastic container I'd nearly

forgotten. "Yes. I'm afraid there isn't much."

She gladly accepted the container. "Two ounces is more than enough. I'll load some into a syringe so you can feed your daughter."

I rested my forehead against the Isolette. Relief evaded me. Fear permeated my thoughts, but mostly I felt robbed. I also felt like a complete failure as a mom. This wasn't the life I envisioned for my child. I'd dreamed of soft blankets; soothing music; a safe, pain free world; and long hours nestled inside my arms.

Rafael pulled me into his arms as I began to sob.

* * * *

Brady wheeled me onto the elevator. He pressed the button for the ground floor.

I frowned. "Where are we going?"

"Outside," he answered determinedly.

A sharp, jagged pain ripped through my abdomen when I turned too quickly to look at him. "But I haven't been discharged yet."

He shrugged. "We're just going out for some fresh air."

I tried not to panic. Leaving the hospital felt wrong. I couldn't leave Gabriella behind. "Rafael's expecting us in the NICU."

Brady wheeled me off the elevator. "Jase has a surprise for you."

I grimaced when I turned too quickly again. I gaped at him. "A surprise? What kind of surprise?"

He patted my shoulder. "Patience, my friend."

The doors slid open. I gulped in surprisingly crisp air. A tiny bit of tension eased from my shoulders. "I can't believe it's so cool outside." July was hot and humid most of the time.

"The temperature broke with the storm last night." Brady wheeled me down the sidewalk to our right.

My eyes widened. "Bosco!"

Bosco's ears perked up. He sprinted toward me.

Jase had to jog to keep up. He scooped him up and set him on my lap. "I thought this little guy might put a smile on your face."

I lifted him so I could bury my face in his fur. "Bosco. How's my sweet boy?"

Gleefully, he licked my chin.

"He cries for you day and night." Brady rubbed Bosco's ear. "He's still my hero, though."

I eyed him questioningly.

Jase rested his hand on my shoulder. "How much do you remember about the morning we brought you to the hospital?"

"Bits and pieces. Nothing concrete," I answered honestly.

Brady knelt beside me. "You were sleeping. Bosco started barking, but he wouldn't let me take him for a walk. He kept circling back to your bed until we checked on you. It's like he knew you were about to have a seizure and was trying to save you."

I pressed a tearful kiss to his head. "Thanks, Bosco." My chin rose. I looked at Brady and Jase. "I want to thank you too. You've sacrificed your personal lives so you can watch over me and keep me safe. I know you're supposed to be my bodyguards, but you're not. You're so much more than that. You're family, *my family*, now."

Rafael caressed the top of my head. "Well said, my love.

I couldn't agree more."

Brady smiled. "You know, we may never move out."

Jase clasped Rafael's hand. "You got my text."

Rafael nodded. "Thanks for bringing Bosco. I've missed this little fur ball." He mussed the hair on Bosco's head. "Would either of you like to meet Gabriella? They're allowing extended family to visit her in the NICU now."

Brady shot to his feet. "Are you serious?"

Rafael winked at me. "Do you think Brady and Jase could pass as my brothers?"

I grinned. "Absolutely." Jase's blue eyes might inspire some debate, but I doubted the NICU nurses would look beyond their lethal frames and swoon worthy faces.

"I'll sit with Kristine and Bosco while you visit Gabriella. I'll go in with Kristine when you're done," Jase offered.

Brady hugged him. "Thanks, Jase. I'll drive Bosco home while you visit Gabriella. Dinner's on me tonight, little brother."

"I'm bigger than you are," Jase grumbled.

"That may be true, but I'm three months older than you." Brady chuckled.

Rafael looked at me. "Maybe I should put an offer on the townhouse next door."

* * * * *

Shae looked up from her Kindle. "Hey, Kri. It's good to see you on your feet."

"Easy." Rafael kept his arm wrapped securely around me.

I shuffled toward my family and friends, who were camped out in the NICU waiting room. Again. "They finally discharged me."

Shae stood and gave me a hug. "Free but not free," she noted keenly.

Slowly, I lowered myself onto the chair next to her. "I'm not leaving here without my baby."

"She could be here for months," Dad warned me. "You need sleep."

Rafael sank onto the chair next to me. "I've been trying to convince her to go home and get a good night's sleep. I can stay with Gabriella through the night and sleep tomorrow while Kristine sits with her."

"We can divide our time as well, so neither of you are sitting here alone," Shae offered.

Rafael shook his head. "Parents and spouses are the only ones allowed inside the hospital after eight o'clock at night."

Kadyn looked thoughtful. "The hospital allowed Kristine's bodyguards to stay the night. Maybe you should assign a bodyguard to Gabri."

"They won't consent to a bodyguard when she's in a locked unit. Besides the NICU staff think Brady and Jase are my brothers," Rafael answered.

I brightened. A little. "I could do the same for you."

Kadyn eyed me uncertainly.

"I'll claim you're my brother so you can go back and see her," I explained excitedly.

Kadyn barked out a laugh. "How many pain meds are you on?"

I reached across Shae so I could swat his arm. "I'm not taking any pain medication. I hate the way those drugs make me feel."

Mom folded her arms across her chest. "You don't doubt her ability to pull it off, do you?"

Kadyn shook his head. "No, ma'am. Your daughter accomplishes everything she sets her mind to."

She stood. "The nurse shift change is over. Come on. I'll vouch for you."

Kadyn helped me to my feet. "Now I know where you get that fierce determination from."

Dad chuckled. "Now if that isn't the pot calling the kettle black."

Mom looked pointedly at Shae. "Come on, Shae. You're the closest thing Krissy's ever had to a sister. You may as well be adopted too."

* * * * *

After a great deal of negotiation, Rafael and I forged a manageable routine. I spent my days with Gabriella while he spent the nights. We ate breakfast and dinner together during the nurse shift changes. We overlapped our visits by an hour or two so we could snag a few precious hours together. Rafael slept during the day. I slept at night, curled around Bosco. Between our friends and my parents, I was never alone. Still, our lives hung suspended at the hospital.

* * * * *

The charge nurse intercepted us on the way to Gabriella's Isolette. "Thank you for the generous gift."

My eyes slid toward the brand new rocking chairs scattered between the Isolettes. "Gift?"

She smiled. "An employee from the furniture store revealed your name."

I sighed. "That was supposed to be an anonymous

donation." The NICU had eighty-nine babies, ninety-five when operating at full capacity, but they only had two rocking chairs in the entire unit. I wasn't the only woman recovering from a C-section who was forced to stand if she wanted to see her baby. An hour or two would have been manageable, but for those of us spending the entire day and most of the night by our child's side, it was exhausting and painful. "Our friends helped pay for the rocking chairs. The donation was a group effort."

Her eyes softened. "Please thank them for me."

Rafael pulled one of the rocking chairs next to Gabriella's Isolette. "Have you received Gabriella's lab results yet?"

"The neonatologist will be rounding shortly. He wants to speak with you about those results." She wandered off to speak with another family.

My heart stalled. "Is it just me or was she dodging that question?"

"She was avoiding the question," Rafael gritted. Today marked Gabriella's one week anniversary in the NICU. Her liver and kidney function were still declining, which is why we were riding her labs. Her life and ours hinged on those lab results.

I opened the door to Gabriella's Isolette so I could rest my hand on her chest. I cringed at the bandages on her tiny little heels. Her skin was so thin. Surely, it would rip when they removed the bandages? I cupped her head, and my heart sank. She looked puffy. Her eyes and her skin were tinged yellow. There was no denying something was wrong.

"Mr. and Mrs. Garcia, I don't believe we've met. I'm Dr. Graham." The young, lanky physician shoved black rimmed glasses up the bridge of his nose.

Rafael shook his hand. "I understand you have some news for us?"

He backed away while noting Rafael's intimidating frame. "Perhaps we should speak somewhere more private. I'll see if the nephrologist and the gastroenterologist can join us."

Rafael frowned. "I'd like to know what's going on."

He glanced briefly at his clipboard. "Your daughter's creatinine is one point eight and her BUN is thirty-eight. She's retaining fluid which could compromise her lungs and heart. We're at a bit of a crossroads to be honest. We can attempt dialysis. We'd have to perform surgery to place the dialysis catheter. Or…" He swallowed nervously.

"Or what?" Rafael growled.

Dr. Graham stepped behind Gabriella's Isolette. Clearly, he wasn't thinking straight because he'd boxed himself in between two Isolettes. "Well, her bilirubin is extremely elevated. While some jaundice is to be expected, her bilirubin is nearing the point where it can lead to brain damage. We still have options, phototherapy and a blood exchange transfusion, but there are no guarantees with those interventions. Your daughter could still end up with brain damage and multiple organ failure. Before we subject her to surgery, you might want to consider taking her home on hospice."

"*No,*" was so tangled around my heart it came out sounding strangled.

Rafael looked at me. "Hospice? What is hospice?"

"Hospice is taking her home to die." I stared at Dr. Graham accusingly.

Rafael's jaw clenched. "I want to speak with the nephrologist and the gastroenterologist. Now." The tension rolling off his body raised the hair on my arms.

The neonatologist bolted from the room.

Within minutes we were seated inside a private counseling room. I insisted my parents; Father McHugh; Faddwa, our favorite NICU nurse; Brady; Jase; Kadyn; and Shae join us. I wanted them to hear the prognosis and our treatment options first hand. I didn't want to repeat any of this. Ever.

Dr. Graham began by summarizing his concerns. I tried not to hear my mother and Shae crying when he encouraged us toward hospice. He made his case a bit more vehemently than before. There was an awkward silence after he spoke.

Rafael looked at the nephrologist. "At what point do you recommend dialysis?"

She leaned forward in her chair. "We recommend dialysis when the creatinine hits two point zero for infants. We need a day or two to secure a surgeon and an operating room and a few days after the dialysis catheter is placed to begin peritoneal dialysis. So dialysis would not begin until four or five days after that decision is made."

Rafael shifted his attention to the gastroenterologist. "We started phototherapy three days ago. Do you typically see improvement in the bilirubin within that amount of time?"

"Not necessarily." She shifted uncomfortably. "Gabriella has only been exposed to conventional phototherapy. I'd like to see how she responds to intensive phototherapy before drawing any conclusions about her liver."

Rafael and I exchanged glances. "You don't recommend transfusion?"

She shook her head. "No. That's an option of last resort, and I don't think we're quite there yet."

I slowly released the breath I was holding. "Do you share

Dr. Graham's concerns about brain damage?"

Her cheeks heated. "No. I think we can turn the bilirubin around before it reaches that point. She's keeping her food down; her muscle tone and startle reflex are fine. I'm not seeing any evidence of Kernicterus." Her eyes slid toward the neonatologist. "You should request a neurology consult if you're concerned about brain damage."

He nodded.

The gastroenterologist looked at me. "Livers are very resilient organs. They can take a huge hit and recover, but they are slow to recover. Intensive phototherapy is very effective. Even if that doesn't work, your daughter still has options. She just needs time."

Hope, I thought. *She's offering us hope.* My throat clogged with tears.

Rafael sandwiched my ice cold hands between his. "Dr. Graham, do you have any children of your own?"

"No," he grumbled.

Rafael looked at the nephrologist. "Do you?"

She smiled. "Two girls."

"What would you do if this was your daughter?" he asked.

The room fell silent.

She took a deep breath and blew it out. "I'd start dialysis."

Rafael turned to the gastroenterologist. "And you?"

Her eyes grew fierce. "My son is six months old. I'd demand every possible intervention. I'd fight to save his life."

Rafael pulled me close. "Then we fight. We'd like to start intensive phototherapy as soon as possible. We won't pursue dialysis unless her creatinine hits two point zero."

We remained seated while the physicians cleared out.

Father McHugh encouraged us to join hands as we began to pray.

* * * * *

Rafael dropped onto one knee. His lips met mine in a surprisingly passionate kiss when he crawled onto the blanket. "You look beautiful this morning."

I stared at him, stunned. I'd been so focused on Gabriella, I'd forgotten what it felt like to be… us.

He reached for the thermos of coffee. "Thanks for bringing breakfast."

I'd purchased nearly every pastry La Madeleine had to offer, packed a thermos of coffee, two mugs, our picnic blanket, and Bosco so we could eat outside. The cafeteria was wearing on me. The whole hospital was, really. "How's Gabriella? Any news on her labs?"

Rafael handed me a mug of coffee. "Her bilirubin dropped, but the creatinine inched up. She's at one point nine now."

I wondered how it was possible to feel both fear and relief at the exact same time. I blew the steam off the coffee before taking a tentative sip. "I'm glad her liver is doing better."

Rafael bit into a ham and cheese croissant. "The neurologist will be evaluating her today. Do you want me to stay?" He handed Bosco a piece of ham.

Bosco swallowed the morsel whole. He sat perfectly still while waiting for another piece.

I chuckled softly. Bosco was watching Rafael so intently. "You should go home and get some sleep. Brady's bringing my parents by. I'll make sure one of them is with me when the neurologist arrives."

"The neonatologist wants to schedule the surgery to place the dialysis catheter," he revealed tiredly.

My heart began to ache. "I want to hold her before she goes through surgery. I want Gabriella to know she's loved. She deserves something good, something comforting and kind, before enduring any more painful experiences."

He handed Bosco another piece of ham. "Faddwa is working today. She would be the most likely to consent. Will you text me if she approves? I'll come back to the hospital so I can hold her too."

I picked at a chocolate filled croissant. "Of course. We should be together for that."

We watched a yellow medevac helicopter land on top of the hospital. Rafael sipped his coffee, thoughtfully. "I've been meaning to ask you..."

My eyes met his.

He continued cautiously. "You mentioned something about Michael when you were wheeled out of recovery. Do you remember?"

"I remember." I stared at the palm of my hands. I could still feel the crosses the priest had drawn.

"Why were you talking about Michael?" he whispered.

I shook my head. "I don't know how to explain this when I can barely comprehend it myself."

"Try," he encouraged softly.

"You'll never believe me." I sighed.

He lifted my chin so I was forced to look at him. "I promise you, I will."

My heart clenched. "I saw Michael and Genevieve when I was in surgery."

Rafael paled.

I took a deep breath and slowly released it. "I asked him if we were dead. He said, 'Love never dies.'"

Rafael swallowed. Hard.

I picked at a blade of grass. "Michael said I had to go back, that God wasn't finished with me yet. He said not to be scared. He wanted me to be happy. He said, 'Take care of my brother and our girl.' I was confused because I thought he was talking about Genevieve. But now I know. He was talking about Gabriella."

My eyes widened when I saw Rafael was crying. I crawled onto his lap.

He clung to me while he rocked. "I believe you," he whispered again and again.

* * * * *

I rested my head on Rafael's lap, hoping to catch a nap. The nurse shift change was nearing an end. I was planning to stay the night since Gabriella was scheduled for surgery first thing in the morning. In less than twelve hours, some stranger would be cutting into our child. I kept having to remind myself that this was a life-saving intervention. Operating on a child who weighed less than two pounds felt so wrong. I closed my eyes with a ragged sigh.

"Kristine?"

"Maxim?" I bolted upright. My stitches pulled. My face sheeted white.

Maxim fell to his knees. "Oni told me what happened. I came as quickly as I could."

I stared, dumbfounded, before bursting into tears.

Maxim pulled me into his arms. He whispered soothingly in Russian while I cried.

I brushed my tears aside with a deep, shuddering breath. "I'm sorry. I got your suit wet."

He shook his head. "It is only a suit."

A smile teased my lips. "I can't believe you came."

"I wish you would have called me. I did not like hearing this news from Oni." He looked at Rafael. "Is it true she nearly died?"

Rafael nodded. "Her heart stopped, but it began beating on its own a few seconds later."

I stilled. "I thought you said Gabriella's heart was strong?"

Rafael glanced at me in surprise. "Gabriella's heart is strong. It was your heart that stopped."

My jaw dropped.

He frowned. "You don't remember?"

"How could she possibly remember? She was on Morphine and magnesium sulfate when Dr. Meinig told her." Jase set a large paper bag on the coffee table. He was treating us to dinner tonight.

Rafael's voice gentled. "Your heart stopped beating shortly after they began the C-section. You were in shock from the blood loss. That's why you received the blood transfusion."

"I received a blood transfusion?" You would think I'd remember this conversation. "Did they have to use a defibrillator?"

Rafael shook his head. "Your heart resumed beating on its own."

"You should have called me." Maxim glowered at Rafael.

"How did Oni know?" I reclaimed the chair next to Rafael.

"Shae told her." Maxim eased onto the chair next to me.

"How's your daughter?"

When I couldn't answer, Rafael answered for me. "Gabriella's kidneys are failing. She's scheduled for surgery first thing in the morning so they can place a dialysis catheter."

Maxim's jaw clenched.

I slid my hand in his. "Would you like to meet her?"

He stared at me, speechless.

"Do you mind?" I asked Rafael.

He patted my leg, reassuringly. "Maxim came all the way from Ukraine. He should meet her."

I led Maxim to the window where we were required to check in. "We'd like to see Gabriella Garcia."

The receptionist's eyes narrowed. "Another brother, Mrs. Garcia?"

I shook my head. "This is Maxim Markov. He's the President of Ukraine and a very dear friend of mine. He's flown a considerable distance and will only be here a short time."

Her jaw dropped. She promptly snapped it shut. "He has to scrub up, just like everyone else."

Maxim removed his suit jacket. He set it next to Rafael before joining me at the sink. He removed his cufflinks, rolled up his shirt sleeves, and followed my lead.

The doors clicked open. I stopped at the metal shelf. I handed Maxim a gown before pulling one over my arms.

He tugged the gown over his dress shirt while we walked to NICU room two. He stopped abruptly when he saw the Isolettes. "Kristine," he pleaded brokenly. He closed his eyes against the image.

"She's over here," I whispered soothingly. I knew how difficult it was to see all those babies fighting for their lives.

His eyes widened when we neared her Isolette. "She's no bigger than my hand."

I opened the little round door. Gabriella squirmed when I rested my hand on her chest. "Would you like to hold her hand?"

Maxim's eyes glistened with unshed tears. He moved to the other side of the Isolette, opened the door, and offered her his pinky finger. His breath caught when Gabriella grasped his finger.

He inventoried every patch, tube, bandage, and wire while I tried to wish the jaundice away. Thank God her liver was doing better.

Maxim's hand covered mine so Gabriella's chest rose and fell against both our hands. "Will you pray with me?"

"Yes." Every thought, every breath was a prayer these days. We joined hands over the top of the Isolette.

"Ancient of Days, Father Most High, this is yet another thing I cannot endure without you. Gabriella is your child. Guide her parents and physicians. Allow them to feel your presence. Heal Gabriella's kidneys; ease her pain and suffering. You alone can heal this child. You are our strength, our Savior, our hope. I pray this in the name of the Father, the Son, and the Holy Ghost."

Together we whispered, "Amen."

One of the night nurses approached the Isolette. "Faddwa told me you want to hold Gabriella before her surgery. She was worried the neonatologist would intervene earlier today. He's not working this evening, and things are much quieter now. Would you like to hold her?"

"Yes, please." I choked back tears.

Frustration rolled through Maxim's eyes. "They wouldn't allow you to hold your child?"

I shook my head. "This will be the first time."

Gently, he caressed Gabriella's head. "I'll retrieve Rafael. He should be here when you hold his child." He kissed me on the forehead. "I'm going to check into my hotel, but I'll return in the morning. What time is her surgery?"

"Seven o'clock." I cringed. "I don't know if the hospital will allow visitors at that hour."

Maxim's fists clenched. "Trust me. They will allow it."

I grabbed his arm as he turned to go. "About the wedding."

His eyes darkened.

I stepped back, warily. "Were you there?"

He frowned. "Of course I was there. Surely, you found the *matryoshka* dolls?"

My voice softened. "Why didn't you sit where I could see you, speak to us, or stay for the reception?"

He stepped closer. "As painful as that moment was, it was important for me to see. I wanted you to know I respect your decision, but I did not wish to ruin your day."

A tear stole silently down my cheek.

Maxim pulled me close. "I meant what I said in Ukraine. I will wait... as long as it takes." He stole my tear with his thumb, pressed a kiss to my cheek, and walked away.

* * * * *

I stared at the nurse in disbelief.

"Cancelled?" Rafael repeated. "Her surgery has been cancelled?"

She nodded. "The nephrologist cancelled the surgery when she saw Gabriella's lab results." The phlebotomist had drawn Gabriella's blood earlier this morning in advance of the surgery.

"What were the results?" I inquired breathlessly.

She flipped through a couple of pages on her clipboard. "Her creatinine dropped to one point six, and her BUN is at thirty-three. Her kidneys and liver are improving."

"Thank God." Rafael pulled me into his arms.

Gently, she patted my arm. "We'll remove her arterial line if those numbers continue to improve. Your friends will be allowed to see her, and you'll be able to hold her as often as you like once that line is removed."

I relinquished all the fear and all the tears that had accumulated over night.

Rafael held me while I cried. "The nurse shift change is about to begin. Let's grab some breakfast and call your parents." We walked out of the NICU arm in arm.

My eyes widened when I saw everyone sitting in the waiting room. My eyes slid toward Maxim. He looked smug. "You managed to get them all in before visiting hours?"

He nodded.

Rafael eyed our family and friends. "Gabriella's blood was drawn early this morning. Her liver and her kidneys are improving. She doesn't need surgery."

Their cheers echoed down the hall.

* * * * *

Time moves like molasses when you're living in fear. With faith and hope, time moves surprisingly fast. Our NICU days poured into weeks, then months. We celebrated every accomplishment... the day the arterial line was removed, the night the feeding tube was removed, the day the phototherapy was discontinued, and the day Gabriella graduated to the "feed and grow room."

Gabriella spent very little time in her Isolette once that arterial line was removed. Our friends proved anxious to cuddle with her. Our nurses wrestled her away a time or two, just so they could hold her. Cenia and Shae threw a baby shower at the hospital once Gabriella improved.

Our daughter was in the NICU for ten weeks. She weighed a whopping four pounds the day we drove her home. My parents surprised us by purchasing an elegant white crib, a blue rocker recliner, and a beautiful chest of drawers. Magically, our Santorini room was transformed into a whimsical nursery.

Gabriella thrived. She ate well, cooed, and giggled, all the while wrapping us around her little finger. My parents returned home. Lexie entered the fray and quickly won Gabriella's affections. Benjamim, Eva, Chief D'Souza, and Mariana spent a week with us. Brady, Jase, Kadyn, Oni, and Shae continued jockeying for our guest rooms.

I felt happy... blessed... content. So content, I was hesitant to climb out of bed. Rafael was wrapped around me, radiating heat and strength. The cedar and cloves from his cologne was coaxing me back to sleep. The house was still and dark. Still, Gabriella had conditioned me to wake every three hours. I didn't mind. This, too, was a blessing; the fact that I could nurse my child. Gabriella called to me without making a sound.

I eased out from beneath Rafael's arm, pressed a kiss against his prickly cheek, and slid from bed. Quietly, I tiptoed to Gabriella's room. Jase was sprawled out, dozing in the recliner next to her crib. She lay nestled against his chest. I thanked God for him before pressing a kiss to her head.

I admired my daughter's perky nose, her little bow lips,

tousled hair, and the long eyelashes that dusted her soft pink cheeks. I'd been praying every day... praying that life wouldn't break her the way it had broken me... but I knew, as surely as God was resting his hand on my shoulder and peering down at her too, that she'd never be broken and alone. She'd be *broken together* until the day he called her home.

A Note from the Author

Thank you for reading The Broken Series. I'll confess there is a part of me that doesn't want this story to end. I am considering a spin off series, but I'd like to hear from my fans on which characters they'd like to read more about before embarking on that endeavor. Also, I owe my youngest daughter a book and plan to tackle that first.

The first book I wrote was a children's book entitled Brave Just Like Me. I wrote Brave Just Like Me because I wanted to comfort and encourage medically fragile children who were facing a broad range of medical experiences. Like Gabriella in Broken Together, my oldest daughter suffered multiple organ failure at birth. Instead of taking her home on hospice, which we were encouraged to do, we chose to fight for her. She was on fourteen different medications, a respiration and heart monitor, and a feeding tube when we brought her home from the hospital. She began in-home dialysis shortly afterwards. She required several surgeries, including a kidney transplant just before the age of three. Words cannot convey how broken I felt during this period of my life. Still, my husband, our family, our amazing circle of friends (many of whom are mentioned in this book), and our Savior saw us through. Our daughter is doing remarkably well now, and we remain thankful for every second we have with her.

While The Broken Series is a fictional book series, there are little nuggets of truth woven into each novel. Many of you have already picked up on this. I'll admit, I got a little crazy in books two and three, especially with the back to back abductions. Still, you recognized that Kri was broken… that she was bound to make some poor choices… and you forgave her (and me). You held out hope (for both of us), and you encouraged us through to the very end. Thank you for that!

Each book in The Broken Series contains a special dedication, but I'd like to dedicate this series, in its entirety, to anyone who has ever been broken. There are a lot of painful experiences that may cause a person to feel broken; whether it's an abusive marriage, a failed relationship, a miscarriage, a life threatening medical condition, a stint in the NICU, the loss of a loved one, or PTSD. Like Maxim, I believe everyone is broken in some small way. If they aren't, they will be eventually. This is not a bad thing. It is through that brokenness that we find the courage and strength to do great things.

For those who are hurting, I'd like to offer some encouraging words. As insurmountable as it may seem, this moment is one snapshot in time. The frustration, the fear, the loss, and the pain you feel now will ease in time. There are brighter days ahead, and you will get there in time. Reach out to those around you… allow your friends, your family, and church community to help you through this process. Seek out others who are struggling with the same experience, so you can walk beside them. For we were never meant to be *broken apart*. We were meant to be *broken together*.

Love and hugs,

K.S. Ruff

Additional books by K.S. Ruff

the broken road

BOOK ONE IN THE BROKEN SERIES

Montana girl Kristine Stone was strong enough to break out of an abusive marriage, but is she strong enough for the road that lies ahead? For the first time in her life, Kristine finds she is able to control the direction her life takes. Haunted by her ex-husband and a newly acquired stalker, she decides to leave Montana to work in the US Senate. Kristine issues a moratorium on dating the moment she decides to move to DC. This does little to deter Kadyn Rand, the Air Force Captain, who threatens to tear down every wall she's ever built. Still, someone from her dark past refuses to be ignored, and Kristine finds herself in yet another fight for her life.

Air Force Captain Kadyn Rand is too stoic to be swept away by much of anything, but a vulnerable woman from Montana manages to do just that when she finds herself alone and in danger in DC. Kadyn tries to earn Kristine's love and her trust, but he soon learns it will take much more than that to save her from her past.

beautifully broken

BOOK TWO IN THE BROKEN SERIES

How many times can one woman be abducted? That's the question burning Kristine Stone when she finds herself staring down a dark and dangerous man from her past. When she refuses to leave with him, he forces her hand by threatening to kill the man she loves, along with thousands of others. Kristine fears his terrorist connections will enable him to make good on this threat, so she complies. She thinks she has it all figured out. If she takes the path of least resistance and does everything this man asks, he will eventually tire of her and let her go. Despite this well intentioned plan, Kristine discovers just how seductive this man can be. She is forced to choose between the love of two men and stands to lose everything in the end.

broken wings

BOOK THREE IN THE BROKEN SERIES

Just when she thinks she's gotten her life pieced back together, Kristine Stone wakes to a searing kiss from someone unexpected. This dark angel is determined to win her heart, and he refuses to play fair. This doesn't sit well with her former lover, Kadyn Rand, who yanks the rug out from under her when he confesses he wants to be more than just friends. She refuses to choose and gets roped into an impossible dating agreement, that she is quite certain will land her a one way ticket to hell. Amidst all this insanity, a new friend presents an exciting opportunity to work for an international organization devoted to peace-building. When Kristine joins her friend in Sevastopol to train university students in conflict resolution, she finds herself accused of being a spy by a security agency deeply entrenched in the former KGB. A chance run-in with the Russian Mafia proves beneficial as three men from her past are forced to work together in an effort to save her life.

in a broken dream

BOOK FOUR IN THE BROKEN SERIES

One long string of broken dreams… that's how Kristine Stone views her life. After a deadly altercation between the SVR and the Russian Mafia claims the life of someone she loves, Kri returns to Virginia feeling hopeless and lost. She discovers her best friend, Cenia, has become engaged. Cenia asks Kri to be her maid of honor. Kadyn is asked to serve as the best man, and the two former lovers are thrown together once more. Maxim makes an unexpected appearance, and Rafael is on a mission to win Kri's heart once and for all. A brief trip into Mexico threatens to derail everyone's plans when Cenia and Kri find themselves stuck in the middle of a gunfight between opposing drug cartels. Kri faces yet another abduction and is left questioning whether her life will ever be anything more than a broken dream.

82552906R00327

Made in the USA
Middletown, DE
03 August 2018